THE NIGHT
OF THE PANTHERS

Piergiorgio Pulixi

THE NIGHT
OF THE PANTHERS

*Translated from the Italian
by Carol Perkins*

Europa
editions

Europa Editions
214 West 29th Street
New York, N.Y. 10001
www.europaeditions.com
info@europaeditions.com

Translation by Carol Perkins
Original title: *La notte delle pantere*
Translation copyright © 2015 by Europa Editions

Library of Congress Cataloging in Publication Data is available
ISBN 978-1-60945-275-9

Pulixi, Piergiorgio
The Night of the Panthers

Book design by Emanuele Ragnisco
www.mekkanografici.com

Cover illustration by Luca Laurenti

Prepress by Grafica Punto Print – Rome

Printed in the USA

For Massimo,
incomparable teacher
and generous friend

THE NIGHT
OF THE PANTHERS

The Pack

Biagio Mazzeo: Chief Inspector, Narcotics division; head of the band of corrupt police officers;

Claudia Braga: Chief Inspector, Narcotics division; deputy head of the band of corrupt police officers;

Luca Zorzi: Inspector, Narcotics division;

Santo Spada: former bulldog of Narcotics; owner of the Bang Bang, killed by the 'Ndrangheta;

Giorgio Varga: Inspector, Narcotics division; Biagio Mazzeo's "shadow";

Zeno Marinoni: Sergeant, Narcotics division; "the bug man";

Oscar Fortunato: Chief Inspector, Traffic Police;

Vito Filomena: Inspector, Narcotics division;

Rino Vanzan, Franco Speranzon: veterans of the Narcotics division;

Carmine Torregrossa: Inspector, Crime Squad, old friend and former colleague of Biagio Mazzeo;

Mirko Giacchetti: ex-police officer, trusted by Biagio Mazzeo;

Cristiano, Ronny, Paolo, Manuel: other members of the pack.

The Police

Irene Piscitelli: Special Agent, National Crime Bureau;

Giovanna De Rosa: Police Commissioner;

Antonello Verri: Police Captain;

Valerio Bucciarelli: former supervisor and leader of the Narcotics division: deceased;

Nicola Santangelo: Deputy Commissioner and head of the Crime Squad;

Andrea Claudetti: Chief Inspector, Homicide division;

Carmen Brancato: Deputy Commissioner with responsibility for the Homicide division;

Ariana Manisci: Chief Inspector, Organized Crime division, of Albanian origin;

Roberto Messina: Crime Squad officer.

The Law

Augusta Barberi: a particularly ambitious prosecutor;
Leonardo Verdini: Deputy Warden; Biagio Mazzeo's man in the prison;
Niccolò Santini: criminal attorney, the pack's lawyer;
Corrado Tortora: Deputy Prosecutor.

The 'Ndrangheta

Domenico Pugliese: Calabrian crime boss;
Natale Pugliese: General Manager of the Lombardia, Domenico's son;
Gabriele Barranca: civil attorney in league with the 'Ndrangheta, Biagio Mazzeo's contact;
Mario Belcastro: leading figure in the Pugliese syndicate's financial and administrative structure.

The Others

Sonja Comaneci: Biagio Mazzeo's girlfriend: deceased;
Donna: old friend of Biagio Mazzeo and matriarch of the pack; Mazzeo believes she was involved in the death of Sonja, the woman he loved. Donna, who is in love with Biagio, knows many secrets concerning him;
Anna: the niece of Giorgio Varga, daughter of Omar, inspector killed by his brother;
Nicky: fourteen-year-old thief in love with Biagio;
Sergej Ivankov: powerful Chechen Mafioso, former leader of the Chechen separatist guerillas. He clashes with Mazzeo after one of the inspector's informers kills his brother, Goran, leading to a war with the Panthers;
Vatslava: right-hand and lover of Sergej, she also participated in the war against the Panthers, striking a brutal blow to Mazzeo, who punished her by allowing her to live but selling her to Albanian sex traffickers.

The Foreigners

Boran Paja: Albanian gang leader;
Adem Paja: Boran's uncle, boss of the Albanian Mafia.

Prologue

T he war had started. That was Irene Piscitelli's thought as soon as she saw the three corpses in the hangar. Rags in their mouths to stop them from screaming, and a bullet in the back of each man's neck. But there was something else that drew her attention: all three had had their hands cut off. From the amount of blood on the floor, it was clear they had been cut off while the victims were still alive. A fairly explicit message: stop stealing from us.

"Do you have any idea what happened?" Captain Antonello Verri asked this woman who looked more like a model than a police officer.

Of course she had an idea. Because in spite of her deceptive appearance—and her youth—Irene was a high-ranking officer in the National Crime Bureau. She had been sent specially from Rome to try to stop this war. Apparently, she had arrived too late.

"How many people know about this?" she asked, ignoring her colleague's question.

"Only a few. The officers who got the call, me, and that's it. I've held off calling Forensics, as you asked."

"Good. This a very delicate matter. I must ask you to order your men to forget all about this homicide and not talk about it with anyone. Especially not reporters. The National Crime Bureau will take over from here."

"But—"

"It's a matter of national security. If this gets out to the media, we're all in deep shit. Especially you and me."

Verri was about to reply when Irene's cell phone started ringing. He took advantage to go outside and tell his people to keep their mouths shut about the case and get ready to decamp.

"They've arrested Mazzeo," Irene said as soon as Verri came back into the hangar.

"What?" he said in shock.

"They've arrested your protégé Biagio Mazzeo. I advise you to go see what's happening."

After a few moments of surprise, Verri obeyed, leaving her alone. Irene didn't pay much attention to the scene of the crime. She didn't need to: she knew perfectly well who the victims were and who the executioners. On both sides, members of the Calabrian Mafia, the 'Ndrangheta. The murdered men, emissaries from the South. The killers, hitmen from the North. All men of honor who belonged to the same organization, but with different ideas about how the business should be divided up and who was in charge of whom. She had all that information because one of the men on the ground was her informer.

It was she who had persuaded him to come to the meeting, guaranteeing his safety. Now he was dead, and she felt the weight of it pressing on her heart.

You can't allow yourself to feel guilty now, she told herself.

Because the hardest part was still to come: bringing her superiors up to date. Admitting defeat. She dialed a number on her cell phone.

"Hello?" a man's voice replied.

"It's me. I got here too late. It's already started."

"How many?"

"Three. Their hands were cut off and taken away."

"Shit. Your man?"

"Gone."

"Damn! You have to stop them, Piscitelli. Now."

She raised an eyebrow. "There's one small problem, the man we chose . . . "

"Mazzeo."

"Precisely. He's just been arrested."

"Mazzeo?"

"He's at Headquarters right now, being questioned."

"Fuck! Think of something, but we need him. And we need him now. You have to stop them before it's too late."

It may already be too late, she thought.

"Bury everything and get Mazzeo out."

"It won't be eas—"

"Find a way and do it. They all say you're the best, don't they? Prove it."

Irene Piscitelli rang off and stood there staring down at the corpses for a few moments.

One of the officers she had brought with her from Rome called her over.

"A team's arriving," she said. "Get rid of the bodies and clean up. I have to rush to Headquarters."

"But—"

"When you've finished, burn everything."

She got in the unmarked BMW and told the driver she was in a hurry. She knew perfectly well that if they didn't move fast, they wouldn't be dealing with three corpses, but three hundred.

Biagio Mazzeo, she thought as the car sped out of the industrial zone. I really hope you're as good as they say you are.

On the Edge of the Abyss

> I should have been that I am,
> had the maidenliest star in the firmament
> twinkled on my bastardizing.
> —WILLIAM SHAKESPEARE, *King Lear*

Behind bars

T hings were more serious than he had imagined. They had been questioning him for hours, and they hadn't used kid gloves. Claudetti, the brute who'd arrested him, had roughed him up, not thinking twice about hitting a man in handcuffs. He said it was the least he could do to a cop who was not only on the take, but a murderer. *Murderer*: that word had been the refrain all through the interrogation. Along with *homicide*, the charge that Claudetti had come out with, determined to nail him. In his opinion, Biagio Mazzeo had killed his superior, the deputy commissioner who supervised Narcotics, because he was about to blow the lid on corruption in that very division, the division that Mazzeo led.

In spite of the third degree, he hadn't breathed a word. He had taken the blows in silence. Keeping his mouth shut was the best attitude to adopt. Especially since Claudetti was right: he really had killed his own chief. He had been forced to do so to save himself and his boys. And it wasn't just a question of safeguarding his badge, but of avoiding a long stay in prison. The deputy commissioner had found out too much about them. Biagio had had to shut him up forever. And he had done it the right way, turning the tables on him, making it seem as if he was the one on the take. But he had gone too far.

"Show your face, you lousy piece of shit," a voice snarled.

Biagio, lying on the cot in one of the holding cells in the basement of Headquarters, turned his head and saw two uniformed officers gripping the bars and staring through them at him. This procession had been going on for more than two hours now. They were all coming to see the highly decorated Narcotics inspector, the legend of the department, the man with the highest number of arrests and seizures, the scourge of dealers and felons. They were enjoying his downfall. They would grip the bars, throw their heads back, and spit into the cell, trying to reach him on his cot. In a cell that was ten feet by thirteen, that wasn't so hard to do. He got the feeling he was the main attraction in a fucking zoo.

"Hey, cop killer."

"Sleeping, Mazzeo? Want us to send in someone to keep you company? A nigger with a big dick suit you?"

"Go away. When I come out, which'll be very soon, I'll make you regret it." He turned his back on them.

"You know something, Mazzeo? I think you're looking at life."

"That's what I think too. But let's suppose it goes well for you and you get, I don't know, three years, in all that time who's going to fuck that little blonde of yours? What's her name. Sonja, right? I'll give her a good going over for you, what do you think?"

"And I'll give you a hand," the other man said. "We can do her on alternate days, right?"

This was too much.

Biagio placed his boots on the floor and stood up. All at once the cell seemed much smaller. "You have keys, don't you? Come in here and say that to my face. Come on."

The two exchanged wary glances. Biagio had a squad of twenty officers behind him, men as tough and corrupt as he was, men who'd follow him to hell and back if he only asked them. They were all on the second floor, being put through the mill. Claudetti was questioning them one by one, and he had told these two officers that he'd soon be arresting the other members of Narcotics. But for now they were all free. And if Biagio gave them these guys' names. . .

"Well?" he said, cracking his neck. "There are two of you and you have nightsticks, what are you afraid of? Are you scared I might tell my people to rough you up?" He laughed. "Naaah, I can do that myself. Come on, come inside."

"Murderer," they spat at him and left.

"Cowards."

He wiped the saliva from his leather jacket with a handkerchief and lay back down. The cot creaked beneath his two-hundred-plus pounds. He wondered why his lawyer was taking so long to get him out.

Sonja, he told himself. No, don't think about her. Best to forget her.

They came back at night. With reinforcements. There were five of them altogether. Their faces covered with ski masks. Their regulation nightsticks gripped tight in their hands.

Biagio stood up, took off his jacket, and shook his head, disgusted by their cowardice.

They attacked as one, hitting him on his arms and legs, forcing him to the floor.

"Cop killer!" one of them screamed between blows.

"Fucking criminal!" another yelled, pounding Biagio's back.

Drunk with rage, they hit him systematically, scientifically, avoiding his face.

One of the cops behind him dragged him violently to his feet, squeezing his neck with the nightstick. The others hit him on the abdomen, leaving him breathless.

"Do yourself a favor, Mazzeo. Hand in your resignation, or one of these days you'll be the one to end up dead," one of the men said, pressing the end of his nightstick to Biagio's cheek, while the other man kept choking him. "Got that?"

"Go fuck yourself," Biagio muttered.

The beating ended with a punch to the pit of his stomach that bent him double. The cop behind him released his pressure on the nightstick and let him go.

Biagio collapsed to the floor, trying hard to regain his breath, his face purple, the veins on his neck as thick as electric cables. "Cowards," he said, spitting blood.

That insult cost him a kick in the ribs.

"Dirty criminal," said the one who had choked him, aiming another blow at him with his nightstick. But Biagio leaped to his feet, grabbed the nightstick in mid-air, and kneed the man in the testicles. They had carefully avoided hitting him on the head. In possession now of the nightstick, he had no such qualms.

His first blow struck one of them full in the jaw. The man fell back against the wall, hit his head, and collapsed lifeless to the floor. But before Biagio could land another blow, the other three began beating him again, this time kicking him too to punish him for his act of rebellion.

"This was just the first warning," the leader of the group said. "Don't jerk us around, resign or we'll check you out ourselves. Forever."

Dragging away their unconscious companion, they left the cell.

Biagio lay on the floor for a few minutes more, quivering with pain. But what hurt him most was the thought of being stuck here while outside his world was falling apart.

He woke to find that he was lying on his cot. He couldn't remember how he had gotten there. His limbs were throbbing with pain. He had no idea what time it was. They had confiscated almost everything: cell phone, wristwatch, belt, shoelaces. He sat up on the cot and started massaging the parts where the pain was worst.

He heard footsteps. Even before seeing him, he knew it was Captain Antonello Verri, who had been covering him for years. Biagio wondered why on earth it had taken him so long.

"What the fuck happened to you?" Verri asked, seeing the bruises.

"You certainly took your time."

An officer opened the cell door and Verri came in. "Who was it?"

"What do you care?"

Verri sat down next to him, took out a cigarette, and lit it. "What the fuck have you been up to?"

"Bucciarelli was as corrupt as hell. I had to—"

"Don't give me that bullshit, Biagio. I'm not Claudetti."

If Jesus Christ in person had asked him the truth, Biagio would have told him the same lie. You don't tell anyone why you committed a murder. Especially the murder of a deputy commissioner.

"It's the truth, but you can believe whatever the fuck you like."

"Biagio, I'm the only person who can help you right now. Tell me the truth and maybe I can get you out of here."

"You *have* to, chief. You owe me that."

"I don't owe you a fucking thing. What happened with Bucciarelli?"

"I told you. I was bringing him in when he resisted arrest."

"Why the hell did you have to arrest him?"

"I told you."

Verri stood up angrily and walked out of the cell. "Have it your own way, Biagio. But this time I won't lift a finger for you if you don't tell me the truth. And you'd better talk soon, before your men go down too. Claudetti is putting them through the wringer right now, and he's bound to get something out of them, it's only a matter of time."

Before closing the cell door behind him, Verri turned to him.

"Get this name into your thick head: Irene Piscitelli. She's a bigwig from the National Crime Bureau who's been sent from Rome. She *is* Rome. She's young, she's a woman, but she's got balls. She's climbed the career ladder thanks to her brain, not her lovely legs. Just so we understand each other, she cut her teeth hunting terrorists, before being moved to organized crime. I'm sure she'll want to talk to you, and it's likely she'll also want to talk to some of your people, to figure out what's going on."

"What does Rome have to do with—"

"If she's here, it probably means she's been told to handle this business of Bucciarelli and the Narcotics division, now that we're all under the spotlight thanks to you. Let me give you a piece of advice: don't play around with her, don't piss her off, and don't disrespect her. She's dangerous. She's more intelligent and more powerful than you are, and she can send you to jail if she wants to without me or anyone else being able to do anything about it. I'll just tell you that she's the point of contact for all the Organized Crime divisions in the country, and that she answers directly to the Head of the National Police and the Minister in person. Have I made myself clear?"

"Yes, but why—"

"If there's anybody who can help you, it's her. Whatever she proposes, you agree to it."

Verri left without listening to another word. Biagio realized that he had never seen him so scared in the more than twenty years he'd known him. That meant he was really in trouble. He lay down to think. He was sure none of his men would talk. Claudetti could interrogate them for weeks without getting anything more out of them than a few *go to hell*s. What did worry him, though, was his men's families, because as long as they were in Headquarters, there was nobody to protect them. And a murdered deputy commissioner wasn't their only problem. They had a much bigger one. The 'Ndrangheta.

He knew they couldn't hold him for more than forty-eight hours, after which two things could happen: either the examining magistrate ratified the arrest, and in that case they would almost certainly keep him in custody for fear he could tamper with the evidence, or else they dropped the charges and released him.

An insistent ticking distracted him from these thoughts. The scent arrived before its owner, a young woman who stopped outside his cell. Choking back the pain in his limbs, Biagio stood up and approached the bars.

"Who the hell are you, sweetheart?" he said, looking the woman up and down. She was very tall and slim, with endless legs and a neck as supple as a panther's. Prominent cheekbones, an aristocratic nose, cat-like hazel eyes, and raven black hair gathered in an elegant bun.

She crossed her arms over her severe pantsuit. "My name is Irene Piscitelli, National Crime Bureau. I'm sure Verri has already told you about me." She smiled. "By the way, one thing I'd like to know, what does Verri call me: Rome?"

"What do you want?"

She responded with a curious look. "Did they beat you up before or after they arrested you?"

"I asked you what—"

"Are you losing your charm, Mazzeo? Are even your colleagues turning against you? If that was so, it'd be a pity."

"Here you are, signora," an officer said, bringing her a chair.

"Thank you."

Irene sat down outside Biagio's cell and took from her bag a small mirror and a lipstick which she began passing nonchalantly over her lips.

"I advise you to sit down."

"What the fuck—"

"The racket you heard earlier, do you remember? I had all the detainees taken upstairs, so that we could talk in peace without anyone listening to us."

It was true. Biagio had thought they were releasing them or transferring them. If the woman wasn't lying, then she really must be a bigwig.

"Someone's going to listen," he said. "The cells are full of bugs. I put a lot of them in personally."

She winked at him and took out what looked like a voice recorder, which she placed on the floor. She started it, and a little red light came on. "It's a frequency scrambler. It should screw up any bugs that are here."

"Well? What do you want?"

Irene shrugged and put the mirror and lipstick back in her bag. "To tell you a story. I just want to tell you a story."

"Then you won't mind if I go to bed," he said, collapsing onto the cot. "Stories make me sleepy."

"Once upon a time there was a boy. He came from a tough neighborhood, and had a very strict family. His father forced him to work for him, sending him to a construction site instead of to school."

"What did you say this story was called?"

"The Police screw Mazzeo over: Act One."

Biagio burst out laughing. "I like you. You have style, so I'm going to save you time. I'm not going to make any confession. I haven't killed anyone. I simply fired in self-defense. Now go to hell."

"Let me finish my story, I've been rehearsing it."

Biagio ignored her and turned on his side, hiding the grimaces of pain.

"Anyway, this boy grew into a young man who was, how should I put it, violent and impatient to live the good life. So he started stealing. Jewelry, cars, weapons. Until he met a police officer. Now in normal fairy stories, he would be a good police officer. Actually, he was a very bad police officer. This police officer protected the young man and persuaded him to become a police officer himself. And so the young man found himself wearing a uniform, only his character and his propensity for crime didn't change."

"This story's a bore."

"But he was good at one thing. He got the criminals off the streets like nobody else could. His methods weren't always very legal, but protected as he was by his mentor and by a group of colleagues he thought of as his friends, our hero managed to take control of a division, Narcotics, and then of the whole city, the Jungle, as they called it among themselves. The story might have ended there, but actually it's now that his downfall starts."

"Piscitelli, that's enough!"

She ignored him and carried on. "A wonderful opportunity presented itself: a major drugs seizure. 300 kilos of very pure cocaine from Serbia."

Biagio gave a start. "How the hell do you know about—"

"The three hundred kilos were supposed to arrive in the Jungle escorted by a somewhat particular group of police officers, who would act as guarantors for a transaction between the Serbs and a syndicate of Calabrians. Pay attention, because they're really the crux of the story. The 'Ndrangheta."

"What the hell—"

"And guess who was in charge of this group of police officers? But of course, our hero. Who wasn't content with acting as guarantor, but decided to kill the Serbs and the Calabrians and take the money and the drugs for himself, promising his men the dream life he thought they deserved, because even more than money there was something else this police officer really loved: his family. And that's what he did: he killed the Serbs and the Calabrians and, although the Calabrians hadn't brought the money, he stole the three hundred kilos of coke anyway, and claimed officially that he'd seized only a hundred."

Biagio had stopped breathing. Piscitelli knew everything about him and his squad. He was fucked.

"Even this could have been a great ending, don't you think? After all his difficulties, our hero defeats the bad guys, boasts to his chiefs about this major haul and keeps two hundred kilos of cocaine ready to sell for himself. But he's underestimated his enemies. One fine morning, the Calabrians decide to punish him by killing that old police officer who's been like a mentor to him. They shoot him down outside the pub he owns and warn our hero that the old man will be just the first. Either he gives them back their coke or they'll kill all the members of his squad, one after the other, and their families."

"How the hell do you know—"

"Wait, I've nearly finished. What I've told you so far could actually be the introduction to another good story, don't you think? A story of revenge: our hero has to avenge the death of his master and save his family, maybe at the same trying also to keep the cocaine and so guarantee a golden future for himself. Sure, it's more Hollywood than the Brothers Grimm, but it'd be a great story all the same, wouldn't it? A pity that something puts paid to our fairytale before it can even start. Our hero can't take his revenge because he's been arrested. He thought he was untouchable, but he was wrong. And now he has a whole lot of problems: there's a chance he might stay in prison forever because in his rise to power he's stepped on too many toes, and at the same time he can't protect his family, which is lost without him. It seems like an impossible situation to untangle, doesn't it?"

Biagio sat up on the cot and stared at the woman. It struck Irene that she had never seen such blue eyes before: they seemed almost fake.

"Well?" he asked, putting his hands together.

"There's a sudden apparition, a beautiful, intelligent, elegant fairy arrives waving a magic wand." She took out a gold badge indicating her status within the National Crime Bureau. "A wand that can perform the greatest magic tricks. The fairy could free the police officer, could help him to take his revenge and at the same time save his men. But . . . "

"There's always a but."

"Right. But our hero has to do something for her if he wants her to help him. Something he's sure not to like. He's torn, he doesn't know whether to trust her or not. The fairy could turn out to be a wicked witch who wants only to eliminate him once and for all. So, to make it clear to him that he can trust her, the beautiful fairy gives our hero an object."

She took something from her bag and threw it into the cell. Biagio grabbed it in mid-air and turned it over in his hands. It was a set of brass knuckles.

"An object to defend himself from the bad guys who'll be coming back that night to torment him. A little gesture to make it clear to him that he can trust her. In the hope that the night brings good counsel to our hero and that he'll be more willing to talk the next day."

With this, she stood up.

"You've forgotten to tell me what'll happen to our hero if he refuses the fairy's help," Biagio said, stuffing the brass knuckles into his jeans pocket.

"The fairy will show her dark side and put the whole of his family behind bars, making sure they grow old inside. And while they're there, who will protect their families from the vengeance of the Calabrians? But above all, with all the nasty things they've done, and all the enemies they've made for themselves in order to enforce the law, how long will they last in prison surrounded by people they put there themselves?"

"Enough of this bullshit," Biagio said, getting to his feet. "What do you want me to do?"

"What you've always done: clean up the mess. Think about how our fairytale might end. I'll see you tomorrow morning."

He watched her walk away, wondering who the hell she really was.

The ministry had put an apartment at her disposal, but in the current recession they told her she would have to share it with another officer. Irene hadn't the slightest intention of doing so—she hated the presence of strangers in her home—so she had decided to remain in her hotel even though her stay in the city was being prolonged.

She had been lying in the whirlpool bath for more than an hour. The water smelled of Eastern essential oils, and on the parquet floor stood a flute and a bottle of champagne she'd ordered from room service a few hours earlier along with a plate of oysters. She was thinking about Biagio Mazzeo and what she should do if next day he refused to cooperate.

A beep announcing a Skype call distracted her from her thoughts, forcing her to put an end to this idyll. She got out of the tub, quickly dried herself, and walked naked across the room with a towel tied around her head. She stopped by the computer. As usual, the caller's avatar showed no image. With *him* she communicated only aurally, without the aid of the webcam.

"Here I am," she replied, clicking the *receive* button.

"Shouldn't you have called me?" asked a male voice at the other end.

"I was very busy."

"I can imagine. Well? Did you meet him?"

"Yes."

"What impression did he make on you?"

"It depends on your point of view. In my opinion, he was on the edge, stressed out, drained, almost lost."

She was lying. She was more convinced than ever that using Biagio Mazzeo was a mistake, and she was hoping they would realize it too.

"Is that an objective observation or a personal impression of yours?"

She smiled, pleased that he couldn't see her. She loved their way of talking. "Both," she replied, taking a bottle of cream from the trolley. She put her foot up on a chair and started spreading the anti-ageing ointment on her leg, massaging it firmly. Her long legs were the strong point of her slender body and she took care of them obsessively with gymnastics and treatments of every kind.

"I don't need to remind you of the delicacy of this operation, do I?"

"No, you don't."

"What about the Bucciarelli matter?"

"We still have to tackle it," she replied, changing legs and starting to rub the other leg with her fingertips and then with her whole hands. "But I think I can handle it without too many complications. I have a plan."

"You always have a plan."

"That's why they all want me," she said with a smile.

"So can we say that the first approach was positive?"

"For the purposes of the operation?"

"What else? I'm not asking you for your opinion about his back-side."

"You could have said ass, I wouldn't have been offended."

"Are you by any chance trying to piss me off?" the Voice asked, colder now.

That's more like you, Irene thought.

"No. My first impression is that Mazzeo is an unsavory character. I'd say too much so. It's risky trusting someone like him. Once he's free, he could become unmanageable."

"He has a lot to lose, though. Right now, it's vital that you keep up the pressure on him. What he did is very serious, and he knows it. Just as it's clear that he knows the danger he's in, because those people don't use kid gloves. You must force him to agree."

"That's what I intend to do."

"I don't want to interfere with your plan, Piscitelli, but we're talking about stopping a Mafia war here. Mazzeo has to agree. Make it clear to him that you're not joking, that he has only one way to go. From the information you've given us we've seen that his weak point is his team. He'd get himself killed before he abandoned them. Use some of his men to get through to him. You have to persuade him."

She stared at the double bed. It was covered in files, photos, and reports on the Narcotics division and its members. For months, now she had been studying Mazzeo and his team, the *Mazzeo family*, as she had dubbed it.

"Did you hear me?"

"Yes," she replied, cleaning her hands with a handkerchief and picking up the file on Chief Inspector Claudia Braga, Biagio's right hand, identified by her as the weakest member of the team. "I'll do what you want."

"One last thing."

"I'm all ears."

"The next time you smear cream on yourself in the nude, I'd advise you to at least draw the curtains." With this, the Voice hung up.

Irene started for a moment and then smiled. She hadn't imagined they were so close.

She went to the window, which looked out on apartment blocks and hotels alive with lights. She removed the towel from her head and let it fall to the floor. Her damp hair slid down over her white skin. She took another step forward so that her breasts pressed against the glass and her nipples swelled in contact with the cold pane. She lifted the fingers of her right hand to her full lips and sucked them voluptuously. Then she let her damp fingers glide over her body, very slowly, until they reached her private parts, which she opened and began caressing.

A smile of contempt appeared on her face.

Jerk off over this, you sons of bitches, she thought, then turned and walked back to the bathroom with her head held high, like a queen.

That night, six of them came. This time they were in plain clothes, but their faces were still covered in black ski masks.

"Wake up, Mazzeo, it's time for your massage," the first of them said, entering the semi-dark cell convinced he was taking him by surprise.

A bad mistake. He was waiting for them.

The impact of the brass knuckles echoed in the cell like a whiplash. The man was flung backwards as if he had been shot.

For a moment Biagio emerged from the darkness, picked the officer's nightstick up from the floor, and winked at the others. Then he stepped back into the dark, cracking his neck and turning the stick. "Who's next?"

Nobody dared come forward.

"Christ, there are five of you. Do I scare you so much?"

"Give back the nightstick and we'll go."

Biagio held it up to them then put it down in the middle of the floor. He retreated until he had his back to the wall.

"Hands on the wall," they ordered.

He obeyed. As soon he heard them coming he spun around and struck one of them on the nose with the full destructive power of the brass knuckles. He followed through with a hook to the stomach and finished off with an uppercut to the chin that sent the man thudding into the wall. Two down.

He picked the nightstick up from the floor and the four men remaining took a step back.

Biagio shook his head and threw the nightstick at their feet. "Get out before I do you serious harm."

They seemed to be studying him. The bull-like neck, the broad chest, the veins sticking out on his powerful arms: he was like the human version of a nervous and aggressive pitbull. The sight of him inspired fear. The worst thing of all was those two cold eyes that seemed to shine with their own light even in the darkness.

"You—"

"Don't make me change my mind. Get the fuck out of here."

After a few moments' hesitation, they dragged out their two unconscious colleagues and left.

The detainees in the other cells applauded and whistled the retreat.

"That's enough," Biagio said in a loud voice, and the applause abruptly ceased.

Biagio removed the brass knuckles and hid them under the mattress. He lay down and thought again about what Irene Piscitelli had said. The bitch was trying to manipulate him, to force him to work for her. Things didn't work that way in his world. Usually he was the one to manipulate people, to use others.

This time, though, it doesn't seem to me you have a choice, boy, he said to himself, massaging his aching knuckles. He'd agree to what she proposed because he had to get out before the Calabrians struck again. And they would strike, he was sure of it, because he didn't have the slightest intention of giving them back their cocaine.

They called themselves a pack. Because they belonged to the same race: cops. They always moved around together, hunted together, they defended each other, and they didn't leave anyone behind. It was Biagio Mazzeo who had put them together. Like a father, he had welcomed and protected them, making it clear to them that with the work they were doing the only way to stay alive was to close ranks, become one big family, share everything. Other cops, those outside Narcotics, called them the Panthers, because they didn't mix with anybody else. Even though they wore the same badge, they were of a different mold. Biagio had formed them in his own image and likeness. He had taught them the laws of the street, the language of violence. He had made them rich and respected. He had given them a dream, the dream of taking over the city, the Jungle. And they had succeeded. But now the Jungle was in flames, and the pack was without a leader. The Panthers were no longer hunters, they had become the prey. And now, with Biagio behind bars, they didn't know what to do.

"We should never have stolen that coke," said the massive Oscar Fortunato, one of the oldest members of the group. "What the fuck were we thinking? Screwing with the 'Ndrangheta? We were dickheads."

The pack had gathered in the large basement of his villa. They had brought their families there to protect them from the vengeance of the Calabrians. Those bastards had already killed one of their number and threatened to carry on if the three hundred kilos wasn't handed back to them. The cops had chosen Oscar's house because it was the biggest. Right now it was best to stay together. And it was easier to defend one place than to split up and keep an eye on ten different places.

For their children, it was a game. A big adventure. The men walking around armed inside the house, the snacks of popcorn, the pizzas they shared while watching rented DVDs, staying up late having video game contests, sleeping in sleeping bags, the knowledge that they wouldn't be going to school for at least a week, Oscars's fantastic villa with its heated swimming pool in the big back garden where they could play for hours. A dream.

But for the cops it was the start of a nightmare. This was a house, not a fortress. And the people they were at war with didn't have many qualms about who they shot. As if that weren't enough, the Calabrians weren't their only problem: Claudetti, the cop who had arrested Biagio, was trying to put them behind bars too, and he was ready to play dirty just to succeed. None of them could afford to end up in jail right now.

"It's pointless getting upset now," said Claudia Braga, the only woman in the team, a tough cop chosen by Biagio as his right arm. "We screwed up, and that's it. Now we have to think about how to get out of this. And what do we do about our families?"

"I've spread the word," Oscar said, "and we have a dozen cops who'll take turns keeping an eye on the house, twenty-four seven. In here they'll be safe, but outside we can't guarantee anything."

"So they won't go out," said Giorgio Varga, the albino giant, the man closest to Mazzeo. "They'll stay here and they'll have to stay put until we find a solution to all this."

"Maybe we should give back the coke and end it like that," Oscar said.

"No," Giorgio retorted. "Until Biagio gets out we do nothing."

"He may not get out, Giorgio," Oscar replied.

"*He'll get out*, that's guaranteed," Claudia said. "I agree with Giorgio. Right now, the coke is the only thing we can bargain with. Even supposing we give it back, who's to guarantee they won't take their revenge all the same? We are cops after all, inconvenient witnesses. Once they get back the coke, we aren't worth anything to them anymore."

"What a fucking situation," Oscar sighed, passing his hands over his bald head.

At that moment, the door of the basement opened and Mirko Giacchetti, another member of the pack, cried, "Boys, it's best if you come up. Trouble in view."

"How do you mean?" Claudia asked, leaping to her feet.

"Cops. They want to talk with all of you."

"Fuck, Claudetti again?" Oscar said, exhausted after a day being interrogated in the offices of the Homicide division.

"No. A woman. I've never seen her before."

The Panthers exchanged worried looks.

"Who might you be?" Oscar asked the woman, who was accompanied by five uniformed officers. They had come outside to talk to her, without inviting her into the house: they didn't want their wives and children to be scared.

"I'm Irene Piscitelli, National Crime Bureau. Chief Inspector Braga?"

Claudia made her way through her colleagues to where Irene was standing. "That's me. What's going on?"

Irene smiled and took out a pair of handcuffs. "Your hands, please. You're under arrest."

Collateral damage

The officer opened the cell door and Irene Piscitelli came in, smiling. "Slept well?"

Biagio threw her the brass knuckles and she caught them in mid-air. They were encrusted with blood.

"I gather you used them," she said, raising an eyebrow. She put them in her bag, then cleaned her hands with a wipe.

"The forty-eight hours are up," Biagio said, sitting on the cot. "Why am I still here?"

His arms and pectorals were throbbing from all the press-ups he had done to kill time. Looking at him, Irene realized he had such intense animal magnetism that it was hardly surprising his men would follow him even into hell.

"Because the examining magistrate has ratified the arrest. Claudetti has requested another two days to collect more evidence, and has asked that you be kept in custody in the meantime to stop you from tampering with any of it."

Biagio shook his head. "Look, seeing as how you know all these things about me, I'm sure you also know that one of my men was killed. If you don't let me out, other people will be killed."

"I know. But why should I let you go? It certainly wasn't me who got you all in trouble. What do I gain?"

"My unconditional respect?"

She laughed. "You and I need to talk, but first there's someone here I'm sure you'll be pleased to see."

Biagio looked up, his sky-blue eyes alight with curiosity.

Irene leaned out of the cell and signaled to someone to step forward.

Biagio stood up and after a few seconds saw two officers escorting a handcuffed Claudia. He opened his eyes wide, incredulous. "What the fuck—"

"Take those off and bring her in," Irene ordered. "I imagine the two of you have a lot to say to each other. I'll leave you for five minutes."

One of the officers locked the cell door and walked off with Irene, leaving his colleague on guard outside the cell.

Claudia hugged Biagio and kissed him on the forehead.

"What the fuck happened, Cla?"

Biagio put the bugs in the cell out of use and made her tell him what had been going on. When she had finished, he pounded the wall furiously. "Shit! Tell me the charges again."

Claudia sat down on the cot. "Possession of drugs, abuse of authority, aiding and abetting, fraudulent misrepresentation, and corruption. It's all bullshit, Biagio. I swear to you I didn't have any drugs at my place, I've been framed. Who the fuck is this Piscitelli woman?"

"What did you tell her?" Biagio asked, ignoring the question.

"Nothing, obviously. She asked me about the team. She knows a heap of things. Old cases, people we've framed, Bucciarelli. I don't know how, but she knows a whole lot of things about us."

"But you—"

"I didn't say a word."

Biagio sat down next to her and put his arm around her. "You're good. Where are the others?"

"They're all at Oscar's. We took all the families there to protect them. Giorgio and Mirko have put together a dozen colleagues we can trust to keep an eye on the villa."

"Any news of the Calabrians?" he asked.

She shook her head. "How the fuck do we resolve all this?"

"I don't know. But I have to get out of here. Where's the cocaine?"

"It's still safe in the farmhouse. We left two guys on guard."

"Good. We mustn't come to any agreement with them for now. If we hand back the drugs, that'd be it for us. They'd kill us one by one as punishment. The cocaine is the one thing that's allowing us to stall."

"Yes, I know. Nobody has any intention of handing it back, not before consulting you, I'm sure of that."

"Good."

"Why did that bitch arrest me? What does she want from me?"

From you, nothing, Biagio thought. She's trying to force me to cooperate. And to do that she's ready to attack my associates.

"I have no idea. I only know that if you keep your mouth shut she won't be able to do a damn thing, believe me. Even if you end up behind bars, it'll only be for a few days, okay? We'll get you out, I swear it."

She nodded and lowered her eyes as if she was afraid of meeting his. "Biagio, there's something else I have to tell you. Sonja—"

"I know everything," he cut in.

"How can it be? She was recovering."

"The Calabrians. It must have been them. They killed her to get at me."

Thanks to his ambition, his woman too had gone. But that thought was banished from his mind. He knew that if he thought about her, it would all be over. The sense of guilt would tear him apart.

Claudia gave him a big hug. "I'm sorry, Biagio."

"Right now, we have to think about getting out of this mess. We have to think of the living, not the dead, okay? Because we *will* get out of this."

Two uniformed officers appeared and opened the cell door. "Come with us, Mazzeo. They want you upstairs."

Biagio stood up and squeezed Claudia's shoulder. "Whatever happens," he whispered, "whatever threats they make, you keep your mouth shut, sweetheart. Okay?"

Claudia nodded.

"I swear to you I'll sort this out. Trust me."

The two embraced for another few seconds, then Biagio let himself be handcuffed and the two police officers escorted him to the upper floors. The moment to make a deal had come.

The basement was filled with smoke. They were all chain-smoking. They hadn't slept a wink since Claudia's arrest. The tension had reduced them to a collective silence.

Giorgio Varga stared at his comrades. Without Biagio they were lost. He was the only person capable of keeping them united. Just one word from him would have been enough to raise their morale. But Biagio was behind bars. And now Claudia was keeping him company. They wandered up and down the basement, disorientated and nervous, wondering what would happen, or who would be next to be arrested. They had all been suspended while the internal investigation into the death of their superior was pending. The more time passed, the more they realized their backs were against the wall.

"We have to give back the coke," Oscar said suddenly, attracting all eyes to him. "It's the only thing we can do and you all know that."

"I already told you—"

"Yes, but they hadn't arrested Claudia then, Giorgio! Because tell me, what's the plan? Continue to hide here like mice? And for how long, tell me that? Until the Calabrians give up?"

"We have to wait until we hear Biagio," Giorgio insisted.

"Bullshit! We have to think of our families, make sure they're safe." Giorgio was about to retort when his cell phone started vibrating. An anonymous caller.

"Who is it?" asked Vito Filomena, one of the youngest in the group.

"I don't know. It's anonymous. Hello?"

"I'm losing my patience," said an unknown male voice. It didn't take Giorgio long to realize who it was. He put the call on loudspeaker and motioned to his partners to come closer.

"Who are you?"

"You know perfectly well who I am. Just as you know perfectly well that you and your men have something that belongs to us. Wasn't the old man enough to make you see that we want it back?"

"You shouldn't have killed him, we—"

"I don't want to hear any more bullshit. We aren't prepared to wait anymore. The next one will be the lady cop they arrested. As soon as she gets to prison, she's dead, got that? Dead. Give us back the cocaine immediately or as soon as she enters her cell she dies. And after her it'll be the turn of the others. Have I made myself clear?"

"Yes."

"If you want to save her, then give us back the cocaine. We'll call again in an hour to tell you where to hand it over."

With this, the man hung up. The Panthers exchanged forlorn glances.

"How do they know she's been arrested?" asked Zeno, one of the group.

"Those bastards are everywhere," Vito said, hysterically. "What the fuck do we do now?"

"There's only one thing we can do," Oscar replied, throwing his head back.

They took him to Commissioner Giovanna De Rosa's office. Antonello Verri and Irene Piscitelli were with her. They made him sit down and asked him to give his version of the death of Deputy Commissioner Bucciarelli. The meeting was unofficial, they reassured him: they simply wanted to get an idea of how to handle this unpleasant matter. Biagio did as they asked, and when he had finished his account he saw them shake their heads.

"I'll be quite frank with you, Biagio," Verri said. "Especially since the arrest of Inspector Braga, which throws further discredit on the police force, our prime interest is to prevent this tragedy being politicized, becoming a media event that will be uncomfortable for all us. Frankly we can't allow a news item like this to appear in the papers: a deputy commissioner shot dead by his own men during an attempted arrest for homicide and corruption, Jesus, it's something you see only in movies. Do you have any idea how damaging it would be to our image? Do you have the slightest idea of the repercussions this mess could have for the entire police force? Do you want to discredit us all in front of—"

"What's your proposal?" Biagio asked with a contemptuous little smile. "Because you *do* have a proposal, don't you?"

He had no desire to beat about the bush. He wanted to get this over with as soon as possible and get back to his men before they did anything stupid.

The three others exchanged glances. Irene Piscitelli nodded and Verri resumed speaking.

"This is our proposal: Bucciarelli was killed by friendly fire. That night, you and your men were there to arrest a fugitive, this person here . . . "—he passed Biagio the rap sheet of a Nigerian named Oyo Balewa—". . . just as your superior had ordered you to. You were there because you were carrying out an order. Bucciarelli was undercover, pretending to be a corrupt cop in order to get close to this scumbag, and had taken a room in that guesthouse to meet with him for an exchange of information or drugs, you decide. Once you entered, the situation got out of hand and Bucciarelli was hit. Balewa managed to run away and you preferred to give aid to your superior rather than follow the criminal. Period, case closed."

"So I'm the one who watches too many movies, am I?"

"Stop right there," Commissioner De Rosa cut in. "If we put it out like this, we all win: the widow will get her husband's pension, you'll come out of it clean, and the department's actions won't be called into question. We'll be mourning a hero, not a disloyal cop. You should know as well as I do, the hero card is the only one we can play in such cases."

"And our friend here?" Biagio asked, pointing to the photograph of the Nigerian.

"He died this morning in a shootout with the Traffic Police," Verri replied.

Biagio burst out laughing. "What a coincidence!"

"Well?" Verri insisted.

"This is all your idea, isn't it?" Mazzeo said, addressing Irene Piscitelli.

"Mazzeo," Verri said, "do it this way and you won't have to appear before the central disciplinary council, but only a simple disciplinary board chaired by Special Agent Piscitelli. It'll be just a matter of form. We all have an interest in closing this case as soon as possible."

"What about Claudetti?"

"You don't have to worry about him," the commissioner assured him. "We'll deal with him."

"But he's involved judges and—"

"I'll deal with him, don't worry," Irene cut in.

"The whole thing stinks, as far as I'm concerned. You could just be setting a trap for me. You're painting me into a corner, and when I have no way to turn you'll really screw me."

Irene smiled. "The agreement is non-negotiable, Mazzeo."

"And what will happen to me and my team?"

From their looks, he immediately realized this was the sore point.

"Narcotics will be disbanded," Commissioner De Rosa said.

"What!"

"Shut up and listen," Verri said.

"There are too many gray areas, too much suspicion hanging over the team, Mazzeo. Too many deaths, too many accusations of brutality. The other divisions hate you. And now Claudia's also been arrested. In view of the latest events, we have no choice but to send you a strong signal."

"How? By getting rid of us after all we've done for this fucking city? I have a friend who died on duty, have you forgotten that? I risk my ass every time I go out on the street, don't you understood? We've done more for the Jungle than—"

"Calm down, we won't get rid of you that easily. Narcotics will be disbanded, yes, but you and your men will be transferred to the Sixth Division."

Biagio turned pale.

Sixth Division: the Street Crime Taskforce, a former experimental section of the Crime Squad set up to fight the phenomenon of youth gangs, small networks of pushers, and a whole series of minor offences. Dealing mainly with surveillance, stakeouts, and operations in tough areas with a high crime rate. On paper, at any rate. In reality, for Biagio and his men it would be like going from the national soccer championship to kicking a ball around the local sports field. Being in the Sixth meant chasing small fry, being tied to a particular territory, and having much less freedom and autonomy. The taskforce consisted of about fifty officers in plain clothes, working mostly at night. For him and his men it was nothing less than professional suicide: hunting down the *pandillas*, the gangs of Latin American youths who infested the southern outskirts of the city.

"Tell me you're joking," Biagio said.

"No, we have a top class Crime Squad, Mazzeo, so don't underestimate the taskforce. You'll be in a special team dealing with those fucking *latinos* who are causing us such trouble, but you'll be an integral part of the Sixth division and—"

"So we'd have to play babysitter to Dominicans and Ecuadorians, would we? Do you see me talking Spanish, giving lectures to snotty-nosed kids?"

"Three members of the Trinitarios and MS13 murdered in the last six days, do you think that's child's play?" the commissioner retorted. "These are criminal gangs pure and simple. And I wouldn't be so fussy with a charge of homicide and corruption hanging over me. We're doing you a favor, Mazzeo, in case you haven't realized that yet, because the way things stand you really should be transferred to prison and put in solitary. Just use your head and agree."

"Forget it."

"Think about it."

"No, I don't want to think about it. You can't treat us like this, I won't stand for it."

Irene Piscitelli stood up and walked to the door with a folder under her arm. "Excuse us for a minute," she said to her colleagues. "Mazzeo, come outside with me, I have something to show you."

Surprised, Biagio followed her out.

Irene said nothing until they entered her office.

"Please close the door."

"They've given you a nice office."

"I'm more important than you think. So, I'm trying to get you out of this mess and you're being fussy?"

"Why did you arrest Claudia?"

"To make it clear to you that you have no choice: you have to deal with me if you don't want me to send you all to prison. How long do you think it would take us to cancel the agreement I made with Verri? I just have to click my fingers and you and your people will all end up behind bars."

"Bullshit," Biagio replied, scratching his throat.

Irene fiddled for a few seconds with her iPad, then turned it and pointed to the screen. "Do you recognize him?"

It was a black and white video. It showed two SUVs lined up at a traffic light, one black—the one in front—and one white. The film seemed to have been shot from above. The man in the black vehicle got out and started beating on the window of the car behind him, a Porsche Cayenne. Then he started hitting the window with something metallic until he smashed it. He dragged the driver, a young man, out of the Porsche, pinned him to the ground, and started punching him repeatedly.

Biagio gave a start. Shit, he thought, remembering the rich kid he'd beaten up the week before, whose only offense had been to keep sounding his horn to get him to move.

Irene froze the image just as a patrol car entered the frame. "Do you recognize that?" she asked with a smile.

Biagio realized he was finished.

They had put the decision to the vote. Oscar's proposal won.

"Boys, we're doing a stupid thing," Giorgio said, shaking his head. "This way we risk screwing things up even more."

"Giorgio, the majority has won. And this is what we've decided. It's the only thing we can do."

"Biagio wouldn't agree."

"But Biagio isn't here, dammit! Can't you get that into your head? He's behind bars! We're alone, and it's the only thing we can do if we want to save Claudia."

"Giorgio, we don't have a choice this time," Vito said, placing a hand on his herculean shoulder. "Those people really are going to kill her. And I don't want to be in mourning for anybody else."

"Well?" Oscar said, putting on his jacket. "Are you with us or not?"

"I have a bad feeling about this, boys, it isn't—"

"Stay here, then, we'll go," Oscar said, walking out. The others followed him, their faces taut.

"Shit," Giorgio spat, standing up and collecting his pistol. He followed his comrades, even though he knew they were screwing up big time.

"Well?" Irene insisted.

"It's not me."

"No?"

"Did you see how he punches? That's not my style."

She laughed and sat down. "Have a seat."

"I prefer to stand."

"Your choice." She passed him some papers. "Take a look at these."

Biagio looked through them and felt himself die. They were doping tests done on hair samples from Claudia, Vito, Oscar and Luca. They were all positive for cannabis and cocaine, with levels, in the case of Claudia and Vito, that indicated possible addiction.

"What are you trying to—"

Irene again turned the tablet toward him and clicked on another video.

This time the shot was from a satellite, and showed a plot of land with a farmhouse in the middle. Biagio knew the place well: it was where they were hiding the cocaine stolen from the Calabrians.

"Shall I give you a summary? You can see various cars driving away from the building and coming back. One is registered to Inspector Giorgio Varga, another to Vito Filomena. What's in that farmhouse, Mazzeo?"

"Nothing. Wine, and tools for the harvest. We decided to invest in vineyards."

"Really? Then you won't have any objection if I send some of my men to take a look around?" She lifted the receiver.

"Wait."

She put the receiver down.

"You can't—"

"I know you don't know much about bank accounts, statements, and tax audits, but take a look at these documents." She passed him another pile of papers. They were the bank statements of all the members of the pack. Biagio understood immediately.

"So there's a—"

"An investigation of your financial affairs in progress, yes. And all kinds of interesting things are being discovered."

"How—"

"It doesn't matter how. Now this, on the other hand, is a file on the disappearance of a criminal named Dante Carrisi. He was an informer of yours. Do you know anything about it?"

"No."

"Strange. An eyewitness says he saw Vito Filomena driving Carrisi to the industrial park, and coming back on his own."

"He's wrong."

"Hmm, not according to his cell phone records. But do you want to see the pièce de résistance?"

No, I just want to disappear, Mazzeo thought.

"Here it is."

She clicked on another video: this one was taken at night, and vehicles and people looked green against a black background. It showed a number of masked men with police bibs killing some people lying on the ground, then loading blocks of cocaine into a van. One of the men removed his ski mask: it was Biagio.

His heart skipped a beat.

Irene froze the video on the image of his uncovered face. "That's the best one, isn't it?"

"Who are you really?" Biagio asked in a thin voice.

"Come on, sit down. We have a whole lot of things to talk about."

Verri and De Rosa were smoking nervously.

"Do you know what Piscitelli wants from him?" the commissioner asked.

"No. And frankly I don't give a damn. I just want to solve this thing about Bucciarelli before it's manipulated politically in order to attack some people and defend others. You know as well as I do that it would be a godsend for someone's electoral campaign. But we have to think about how to handle this. A police office killed by his own men besmirches the whole department, and right now we can't afford that. Not with the six-monthly reports to determine funding coming up. We can't let this thing come out, you know that. It's so absurd, we'd all lose our jobs. I'm almost certain that Biagio is guilty, but I must think of all my officers. If it all gets out, it would be suicide for the police department of this city. Because in the end it wouldn't be only Mazzeo who paid, but also all the honest police officers who have nothing to do with this mess he's made, damn him."

"We'd be covering him yet again, you do realize that?"

Verri stubbed out his cigarette on the burn-studded photograph of the Minister of the Interior that hung on the wall. Among the police officers in Headquarters, it had become the habit to manifest their disapproval for the umpteenth bureaucrat who had raised their expectations and then abandoned them. "I know, Giovanna. But we have to think of the greater good. Is it better to cover up a homicide, or to allow half the department to be investigated and leave the city without protection?"

"What about Claudetti?"

"Piscitelli is acting on behalf of the ministry, let her deal with him."

"Let's hope she manages to persuade Mazzeo, then."

"I don't think he can afford to be too fussy this time. And the woman's a shark."

Biagio gave her back the photographs of the three corpses with the severed hands. He was speechless. He had assumed she wanted him to do something unsavory, but nothing like this. Irene was sending him to his death.

"You can't ask me to do this."

"I'm not the one who screwed up, Mazzeo, you are. And you did it all by yourself. You're a crooked cop, dammit, do you really have so many qualms? I'm not asking you to do anything you haven't done before."

"And if I get my fingers burned?"

"That's your business. There won't even be a document to show that I was involved in all this. You'll be on your own."

"In other words, I have no guarantee except your word?"

"Precisely," she said with a smile. "No document, no written agreement, no judge. You'll be on your own."

"If I agree, you have to let Claudia go."

Irene burst out laughing. "Forget it. She stays in prison. She'll be my insurance. For all I know, you might run away as soon as I release you. While the operation is ongoing, Inspector Braga will stay behind bars, in solitary."

"My family, my boys. If I agree, none of them must be involved."

"Hold on a minute. Obviously the agreement includes them. Don't think you can do this by yourself, Mazzeo."

"They mustn't be involved, dammit. I don't want any of them to know anything about this. Either we do it my way, or you can go to hell."

Irene stared at him in silence for a few seconds, then nodded. "Okay. I promise you we won't involve them and that I won't tell them anything."

"And what if I fail, what'll happen to Claudia?"

"She'll stay in prison. And the others will follow her. No result, no benefit. I can't prevent the law from taking its course, I want that to be clear from the start. And I want it to be clear too that one phone call from me and they'll all be behind bars. One phone call."

"You're using my family to force me to agree to this madness. That isn't an agreement, it's fucking blackmail."

"Of course it is. That way you'll know how all the people you've screwed over the years have felt. Well?"

Biagio was rubbing his knuckles compulsively, immersed in his thoughts. As if trying to give him a push, Irene picked up the telephone and dialed. "This is Special Agent Piscitelli. Please proceed with the transfer to prison of Inspector Braga. Immediately."

Biagio watched her as she hung up. "Don't you disgust yourself?"

"You people disgust me. None of you are innocent. It's true, you prevented a turf war between dealers in this city, but what methods did you use? You're hardly the person to preach to me, Mazzeo . . . I'm waiting for an answer. How long do you think someone like Claudia will last in prison?"

Biagio nodded. "Okay."

"Okay, what? I want to hear you say it."

"I'm in."

Irene smiled. "I knew we'd reach an agreement."

"But I have conditions."

"Let's hear them."

Two officers had bundled her into a police car and set off for the penitentiary. Mindful of Biagio's words, Claudia hadn't put up any resistance. She was afraid, of course, but she knew that right now there was nothing she could do to change the situation. What scared her most wasn't ending up in prison—although a cop in prison is always at risk—but leaving the team without a leader. With her and Biagio behind bars, the pack was adrift. Neither Oscar nor Giorgio were leaders, and Vito, Zeno, and the others weren't level-headed enough to make the right decisions under stress.

"What the fuck is that guy doing?" cried the officer at the wheel.

Claudia looked through the metal grille at the white Fiat Punto that had stopped just ahead of the police car, blocking the traffic.

"Hey, move your ass! What the hell—"

His words were cut off by a terrible smashing sound. A black Ducato van had hit the left-hand side of the car full on, sending it crashing against the guardrail.

Claudia was flung against the window. When she managed to sit up again, she saw the door of the van open and some masked men get out with submachine guns in their hands. She yelled to the two officers to do something, but one of them had lost consciousness while the other had hit his head, which was now bleeding. Two more masked men got out of the white Punto.

Claudia realized she was screwed.

A moment later the masked men opened fire.

Biagio and Irene came back into Verri's office after more than half an hour. This time it was Biagio who had a folder under his arm.

Verri opened his arms wide in dismay. The ashtray in front of him was filled with cigarette butts and a blanket of smoke hung in the room.

"I know, excuse us," Irene said, sitting down, before he could make any protest.

"Where's the commissioner?" Biagio asked.

"She left, she had things to do . . . Well? Did she manage to persuade you?"

"Yes," Biagio said. "But I have conditions."

"Let's hear them."

"Carmine Torregrossa."

Verri immediately turned up his nose. Torregrossa was a former colleague of Biagio's, dishonorably discharged over charges of serious brutality.

"I want him to be transferred back here and assigned to the Street Crime Taskforce with us."

"Out of the question. You remember what happened when I was forced to suspend him?"

"That was a long time ago, and I'll make sure—"

"No," Verri said, digging in his heels. "And don't—" He broke off for a coughing fit. His throat was burning from an excess of cigarettes and he was forced to pour himself a glass of water. "As I was saying, get it out of your head."

"I think that all things considered, captain, we can meet him halfway," Irene cut in. "I'll take care of expediting the transfer forms."

"But—"

"I'll vouch for him," she said, passing a hand through her long silky hair.

Verri shrugged. Going against Irene Piscitelli would mean contravening orders from the ministry. "All right. But, Biagio, keep him away from drugs and alcohol, for everyone's safety. If he does anything stupid—"

"He won't."

"Next?"

"You have to leave me another week before my transfer. I don't want to be suspended, or given sick leave. I have to be operational, stay in Narcotics, and utilize its resources."

Verri blew smoke from his nostrils and nodded his consent.

"And I won't have to report on my actions or my men's to anyone."

"Do you also want the keys to the city and a licence to kill?"

"Yes or no?"

"One week. Anything else?"

"No."

"Did she tell you how Spada's murder will be handled?"

"You'll use him as a scapegoat," Biagio said, making no attempt to conceal the scorn in his voice. "He'll be portrayed as a crooked cop."

He really didn't like the idea of besmirching his mentor's reputation, but right now he couldn't do anything about it.

"It's the price to pay to stop the investigation and prevent—"

"I don't want to hear any more bullshit. Let me sign whatever I have to sign and I'll go."

"We ought to hear what the commissioner has to say."

"Commissioner De Rosa won't make a fuss," Irene said, "not if she wants to hold on to her job."

"We have more important things to think about now. This is the duty report on what happened that night, as we spoke about it before. Read it and sign. Vito Filomena was with you that night, he'll have to sign too. Will he do it?"

"Of course."

"Good. And remember to drop by the armory downstairs and pick up a replacement service pistol, since yours is still with Forensics. I'll call the commissioner."

Biagio nodded his agreement and signed, while Verri's footsteps echoed in the room.

The officer in the passenger seat managed to open the door but couldn't get out because it was blocked. He took out his Beretta, pushed his colleague's body down, and opened fire through the smashed window, forcing the attackers to retreat.

"We have to get out of here!" Claudia cried.

"Stay down!" the officer retorted, shooting at the windscreen and kicking it to secure a way out. But all at once he stopped: he was out of bullets.

The attackers yelled something and Claudia saw him put his weapon down on the floor.

The car was surrounded by the five masked men, who kept them covered and yelled to them to give themselves up.

One of the hitmen unblocked the back door and pointed the sub-machine gun at Claudia, who closed her eyes, certain that she was done for.

As Verri had ordered him, Biagio went downstairs to the central armory and asked the officer on duty to provide him with a temporary service pistol to replace his own. It didn't take long: Verri had already sent down his instructions. Biagio just had to sign a few papers, check the weapon was in good working order, and count the ammunition in front of the officer.

Once he had finished, he went into the toilets. In his hand he had a small transparent plastic bag with the personal effects that had been confiscated from him following his arrest. He put his shoelaces and belt back on, fixed the heavy steel bracelet to his wrist, put the keys to the Alfa in his pocket, switched on his BlackBerry and, after turning it around in his fingers for a few seconds, slipped onto the ring finger of his left hand a big platinum ring, a small war trophy he had decided to keep to remind himself what being a leader involved: repressing your own feelings.

He washed his face for a long time with cold water. The cell phone kept vibrating with text messages about missed calls. He put it in his pocket without even glancing at the messages. He had more important things to do right now.

As he dried his face with paper towels, the door of the toilet opened and Andrea Claudetti, the Homicide inspector who had arrested him, came in. Seeing Biagio, Claudetti gave a start.

"What the fuck are you doing here?"

"Free, you mean?" Biagio said with a smile, throwing the paper in the bin and rubbing his hands. "What did I tell you?"

"But the judge already signed the—"

"I wanted to thank you for the welcoming committees you've been sending me for the past few nights," Biagio went on, placing his pistol and handcuffs on the sink.

"Have they reinstated you?"

"You bet they have."

In his frustration, Claudetti launched a punch that hit Biagio glancingly on his right cheek, sending him slamming into the wall.

Biagio cracked his neck and smiled. "I was waiting for that," he said and hurled himself at Claudetti.

The attacker hadn't fired because he didn't want to kill her. He needed her alive. He grabbed her by the arm and forced her out of the car.

Even in the thick of the action, Claudia realized that if they succeeded in taking her it was all over: her men would hand back the cocaine to save her, and that would mean the end of everything. She couldn't allow that.

As the masked man pushed her toward the Ducato, she kneed him in the groin, then brought him to his knees with an elbow to the head. She made a dash for the cars that were lined up waiting to pass. Running with handcuffs on wasn't easy, but despair had put wings on her feet.

The attacker got up again, groaning with pain. He heard the wail of sirens in the distance. They didn't have much time, they had to get her at all costs. When he was a few yards from her, he flung himself at her, sending her slamming against one of the cars. He hit her on the back of the head with the butt of his submachine gun, knocking her unconscious, then hoisted her onto his shoulder, walked back to the van, and handed her over to the other two, who bundled her inside.

In the meantime, the two who had gotten out of the Punto were still firing at the police cars, covering the other men's escape. The one who seemed to be the leader gave a whistle, as a signal to go: more cops were arriving.

The kidnappers melted into the paralyzed traffic.

Officer Pella had chosen the wrong moment to take a leak. As soon as he opened the door of the toilets, Claudetti came crashing into him. The Homicide inspector, being a former rugby player with an impressive physique, dragged the officer to the ground, crushing him beneath his weight.

"What the fuck!" Pella cried.

"You have to watch out for flying assholes," Biagio said. He dragged

Claudetti off Pella and kicked him in the stomach, knocking the breath out of him.

"Hey, what the hell—"

"Shut up and get out. This is between the two of us. He fucked my girlfriend."

The young officer made himself scarce.

"That was for my stay in the cells. Are we quits or do you want some more?"

"Go fuck yourself," Claudetti muttered.

Biagio kicked him in the balls. "That's enough now, Claudetti, my patience is over." He pinned him to the floor and grabbed him by the throat. "You know what your problem is? You've watched too many Hollywood movies. But this isn't a movie, and you aren't Clint Eastwood. Whatever you're thinking, forget it. Stay away from me and my men, don't force me to move up to the next level."

He looked intently at him for a few seconds, then let him go. He was about to call Oscar when his cell phone started vibrating. It was an officer close to the gang.

"Hey, Rianna, what's up?"

"Biagio, at last! Something bad's gone down!"

Biagio immediately froze, half closing his eyes and preparing to receive yet another blow. "What the hell is it now?"

"An armed group attacked the car that was taking Claudia to prison. They opened fire. Shit, it was like a western! They took her away. One of the two cops with her was seriously wounded, I don't think he'll make it to the hospital alive."

"Who the fuck—"

"I don't know. Guys in masks. From the way they acted I'd say they're professionals."

"Please keep me up to date."

"Sure."

Mechanically, Biagio pocketed the cell phone. He tried to slow his breath, but it was impossible. The Calabrians had beaten him to it. If he wanted to save Claudia, he had to deal with them. He quickly requested a car and tried again to call his men. They had to sort out this mess as quickly as possible.

The van stopped inside an abandoned warehouse.

"Let's wake this bitch," said one of the masked men. "I'm damned if I'm going to carry her again. She almost dislocated my shoulder before."

"Hey, wake up!" said the other one, slapping her. "Get up, dammit!"

Claudia shook herself abruptly and instinctively moved back, banging her head against the wall of the van.

"Nearly shit yourself, didn't you?" the man asked.

Claudia rolled her eyes. "You—"

The man took off his hood. It was Oscar.

"Come on, hurry up," he said, helping her to her feet. "We have to get out of here right now."

"What the fuck have you done?" she asked after a few seconds of total bewilderment.

"We saved your ass, you ungrateful bitch. The Calabrians called us, saying us that if we didn't give them the coke, they'd kill you in prison. We couldn't allow that."

He helped her out of the van and took off her handcuffs. As he did so, the white Punto drove into the warehouse and the three men inside took off their masks.

They were Giorgio Varga, Vito Filomena, and Zeno Marinoni, who had been hit by the cop in the police car.

"How is he?" Oscar asked.

"It isn't serious, but he does have a bullet inside him," Giorgio said, supporting his wounded colleague. "We have to get somebody to take a look at him." He turned to Claudia. "Are you all right?"

"Yes, but—"

"There's no time now," Oscar said, grabbing a jerry can of gasoline and starting to sprinkle it over the Ducato and the Punto. "We have to scram. Get in the cars."

They all did as he said, apart from Vito. It was he who had shot the cop. Now his hands were shaking, and he was deathly pale.

"Hey, what the fuck's gotten into you?" Giorgio said, shaking him.

"I killed him. I killed a cop. I'm in the shit."

Frenzied messages were coming in on the police frequency, all about escaped fugitives and an officer down. It wasn't clear if he was dead or not. But Giorgio had witnessed the scene and knew it was serious.

"We'll deal with that later. Right now, we have to get out of here. Come on, get up."

"I . . . I killed him."

Giorgio slapped him. "We don't know that you killed him. Now get up, for fuck's sake. Or do you prefer to stay here and get yourself put inside?"

After a bit of hesitation, Vito did as he was told, but he was still in a state of shock. He knew he had done something terrible and screwed things up for all of them. He had freed Claudia, but at a very high price: the life of an innocent cop. Now they had to protect their backs not only from the Calabrians but also from their colleagues. Not to mention Claudia: she was a fugitive now, and they had to hide her.

If only they'd listened to me, Giorgio thought as he bundled Vito into the car and got in the driver's seat.

Oscar and Luca finished pouring the gasoline. They set fire to a few balls of paper and let them fall to the ground. The flames began to swallow the Punto and Ducato used for the assault.

The others got in their cars and sped away. Nobody spoke.

It should have been a walkover. But now they were in the shit up to their necks.

Biagio parked the Alfa Romeo in a working-class district on the outskirts of town, outside one of the pack's hiding places, a complex of garages. Safe inside the garage, he took one of his coded cell phones from a drawer and then, copying it from a small sheet of paper, dialed the one number he had for Pugliese's syndicate: it was the one he had used to talk about the cocaine delivery.

After a few rings, he heard someone pick up, but there was no reply. Caution personified, he thought.

"You know who I am, don't you?" Biagio asked.

Silence.

"I assume you do. Why did you need to kidnap her?"

"Kidnap who?"

"Don't fuck me around. My colleague. You screwed up, you killed a cop."

Silence.

"Why? What do you think you solved?"

"I don't know what you're talking about."

"I've had enough of these games. Wasn't it you who—"

"No. What do you want?"

Biagio had to sit down.

"Well? You're wasting my time. And the more time passes, the more at risk you all are. Where's the cocaine?"

"Forget the cocaine for now," Biagio said, regaining control. "I want you to send two messages to Pugliese in person. One: no more threats or reprisals, because I intend to negotiate. But if he hits any more of my people, then to hell with negotiations, we'll be at war. Two: I want to talk with him directly. Find a way to put me in contact with the big boss because I won't deal with anyone else about this. Either we do it this way or everything blows up."

Silence.

"We have to reach an agreement as soon as possible," Biagio went on. "This tension is bad for business."

"We'll call you on this number," the other man said, cutting him short, and hung up.

Biagio almost flung the cell phone to the ground in anger. He sat down at a desk, took several deep breaths, and cracked his neck.

Then he took out his BlackBerry and called his men. Nobody replied.

He went back to the Alfa. He opened the trunk and threw in a large bag with cash, a change of clothes, and a shotgun. In a false bottom, he hid a small bag with a little amphetamine, in case he needed it, and then got in the driver's seat and set off for Oscar's house.

The SUV with the darkened windows entered the garage and the shutter was lowered behind it. Vito gave a start and vomited on the floor. It was the third time he had thrown up.

"Hey, are you all right?" Claudia asked, crouching by him and massaging his broad back.

"No, fuck it. I'm not all right. I killed a cop."

"You don't know that, Vito."

"What got into you, huh?" Oscar cried, coming out of the little bathroom in a corner of the garage. "Why the fuck did you shoot at head height?"

"Hey, take it easy," Giorgio intervened. "Now's not the time—"

"Take it easy? Have you gone crazy? The agreement was that nobody would get hurt. We were supposed only to fire at the car, for Christ's sake. And this dickhead fires at a cop."

"But he was firing at us!" Vito roared, getting to his feet. "He'd just hit Zeno. What the fuck was I supposed to do?"

"Anything, just not kill him!"

Giorgio helped Zeno to sit down and ordered Luca Zorzi, another member of the team, to bring him the first aid kit. He'd treat his friend himself: involving someone from outside, however trusted, was a risk they couldn't take right now.

Giorgio went into the little bathroom to wash his hands. As he turned off the faucet he heard a sharp slap. He turned abruptly and came out just in time to see Vito collapse to the floor.

"What the fuck are you doing?" he cried, grabbing Oscar by the shoulders and moving him away from Vito.

"That asshole screwed it up for all of us! Leave me alone!"

Giorgio shoved him away, sending him crashing to the wall.

"Who was it who came up with the fucking plan in the first place, huh? You. So don't blame him if everything got fucked up. If we'd used our heads we wouldn't be in this situation right now."

"No! If he hadn't killed a cop we wouldn't be in this fucking situation."

"And what was he supposed to do? Let the guy keep shooting at us? He saved my ass, and Zeno's too, in case you've forgotten that."

"Why don't you try explaining that to the judge who'll put us inside?"

"You should have left me where I was," Claudia said, helping Vito to his feet.

"Like fuck we should have," Oscar roared, switching on his cell phone. "They'd have killed you, Cla. And I'm sick and tired of being shot at. After the old man, nobody else should get hurt. Biagio would have done the same, I'd bet my life on it."

"We can't change things now," Giorgio said, "so calm down. We have to think about how to avoid any more screw-ups."

"It's best if I give myself up," Claudia said.

"Don't talk crap," Vito retorted. "It wouldn't serve any purpose, except to get you a sentence as accessory to murder or something like that."

Giorgio took the first aid kit and made Zeno strip off. "It's going to hurt," he said.

"You deal with getting it out, I'll deal with the pain."

"Try not to scream. We can't allow ourselves to be discovered."

As Giorgio cut into the wound in search of the bullet, Oscar's phone started vibrating.

"Hello? . . . Yes. . . When? . . . Okay . . . "

"Who was it?" Claudia asked.

"The lawyer. They've released Biagio."

"What?"

"They've just released him," Oscar repeated.

"Shit, now who's going to tell him about this fuck-up?" Vito asked.

His colleagues stared at him without a word.

Stefania was surprised to see him come home at this hour. She opened the door, went to him, and embraced him. "Did you forget something?" she asked.

"No, I just have to take a look at a document," Claudetti replied, kissing her on the forehead.

"You don't look good. Hey, that's a bruise! What have you been up to?"

"This? It's nothing. A little argument."

"Someone you arrested?"

Claudetti smiled. "In a way, yes."

"Hey, tell me the truth," she said, freeing herself from his embrace and pressing her fingers to his chest. "Don't make things difficult for yourself. It takes too much of a toll when you do?"

He looked at his wife, forcing himself not to lower his gaze. "You remember the officer who came to the house a few nights ago?"

She nodded.

"He's dead. Killed by another officer, the one he was investigating and trying to stop."

"Shit. But what's all that got to do with you?"

"He asked for my help and I refused. And now he's dead."

"Oh, shit. Listen, you have two children, *we* have two children. I need you, don't think—"

"Hey, calm down, do I look nervous to you?" he said, taking her head in his hands. "I assure you there's nothing to worry about. The last time somethig like this happened, I was up against politicians and important people, that's why I got fucked. But this is just a crooked cop, believe me. Just an administrative matter."

"We won't be in any trouble?" she asked him.

"No."

"Promise me."

"I promise," he said, smiling. "Come on, make me a nice cup of coffee, I'll be with you right away."

She kissed him on the lips and went back inside the house.

Claudetti set the burglar alarm and then took a glance around the neighborhood. Not noticing anything unusual, he went inside. He had his coffee together with Stefania and let her persuade him to have his wound treated. He played a little with the children, then shut himself up in his study with the folder Bucciarelli had given him before he was killed.

You told me there was enough in here to bring him down, he thought, opening the file on Narcotics. I hope you were right.

The shutter went up and Biagio stepped into the garage. He looked at them one after the other. None of them was able to sustain his gaze.

When he saw Claudia, Biagio raised his hands to his head. "What the fuck did you do?" he asked in a thin voice. "Do you have any idea?"

Giorgio went up to him. "Those bastards called us and said that if we didn't hand over the coke, they'd kill her as soon as she entered the prison."

"Shit. They knew she'd been arrested?"

"Yes. We couldn't risk them taking her. We put it to the vote. The proposal to help her to escape won."

"Killing a cop, Christ!" Biagio roared.

"That was an accident," Oscar said. "The plan was to fire only at the car. One of the two cops fired at us, and Zeno was hit. We had to fire back, Biagio."

Biagio passed his hands over his tired face. He was incredulous, certain that as soon as Irene Piscitelli found out she'd tear up their agreement and send him back behind bars. "Who shot him?" he asked.

"I did," Vito said, ashen-faced. Biagio saw that his hands were shaking.

"I can't believe it. What the fuck were you all thinking?"

"We didn't know what to do, Biagio! You were in the cooler, and we didn't know if and when you'd be released. Verri suspended all of us. Those bastards were breathing down our necks. We knew you would never have wanted us to hand over the coke, there was only one thing to do to save Claudia. It went wrong, but that wasn't how we planned it."

"Went wrong? Now we have a fugitive on the run, we have to protect a cop who almost certainly killed another cop, and at the same time we have to save our asses from the Calabrians and stand guard over two hundred kilos of cocaine. I'd say 'went wrong' is a bit of an understatement, Oscar, don't you think? We're all going to end up behind bars, for fuck's sake!"

"Well, there's at least one positive side," Zeno said, befuddled by the whiskey and painkillers he'd taken to ease the pain of his wound.

"And what the fuck would that be?" Biagio snarled.

Zeno smiled. "We already have a five-a-side soccer team for the inter-penitentiary championship."

For a moment they all stared at him as if weighing up whether or not to take out their pistols and finish him off. Then Biagio burst into a loud peal of laughter that soon infected all of them.

"Get this idiot out of my sight," he said. "What a fucking mess. Tell me at least you didn't leave any traces."

"Did you lose any blood?" Claudia asked Vito. "On the ground, I mean."

"No," Giorgio said. "I checked."

"Was anyone else wounded?" Biagio asked.

"No, nobody else," Oscar said, lighting a cigarette. "How come they released you?"

"Claudetti didn't have a fucking thing on me, and I managed to persuade Verri and De Rosa. But now we have to figure out how to deal with this screw-up." He had no intention of telling them about Irene Piscitelli and the agreement they had come to, especially after this latest disaster.

"What about the Calabrians?" Luca asked.

"We'll deal with them later."

"How do you want to proceed?" Giorgio asked.

Biagio was silent for a few moments, stroking his bruised knuckles. "You'll take Claudia to the safe house, making sure that nobody follows you. Extreme caution. We have to hide you, sweetheart, until we find a solution."

"Okay," Claudia replied.

"Vito, the same goes for you: low profile. Oscar and Luca, you'll see to that. You mustn't set foot outside the house, understand? Not for any reason in the world. We'll make sure you have secure cell phones, and we'll take shifts to guard you, but nobody, I repeat, *nobody* must leave the house unless I tell you. Got that?"

"Yes," Claudia replied.

"Vito?"

"Got it, chief."

"It probably won't take them long to discover that it was us. So all the others have to continue with a normal routine. You must stay visible, deny any involvement, and be as calm and relaxed as you can."

"How the fuck can we—"

"Christ, just find a way or we're all done for!"

Nobody replied.

"This is very important: for the period of two hours before and after the assault you need cast-iron alibis. Involve your families. They'll have to testify that you were all together, and that they saw you talking, maybe about the collective suspension, agreed?"

They all nodded.

"Zeno, do you need a doctor?"

"No," Giorgio said. "I took the bullet from his back. I also have some antibiotics. He has to take quite a few, but he's fine for now."

"It's better that way, because you really have to disappear."

"In what sense?" Zeno asked

"Leave the jungle. If they pick you up with a gunshot wound in the back, then we can already start to take bets on that inter-penitentiary championship."

"You need me, Biagio!"

"No. We need you to get the hell out of here. If they pick you up it won't take them long to put two and two together. Do you want all the others to end up inside?"

"But—"

"He's right, son," Oscar cut in.

"Another thing: you mustn't tell anyone that it was you who helped Claudia to get away. And when I say anyone I mean even girlfriends, wives, and children. Don't even talk about it among yourselves. There could always be somebody listening. We have to behave as if it really was the Calabrians who took her, okay?"

"Is that our story?" Giorgio asked.

"I don't know. It may be. For now, do as I say."

"Maybe I should just give myself up," Vito said, wringing his hands.

"Bullshit. Don't say it even as a joke. They know perfectly well you didn't act alone. If you give yourself up, they'll come and get the others too."

"What if you left me somewhere, as if they'd let me go or I'd managed to get away?" Claudia suggested.

"Too dangerous. This thing has to handled properly, we need to calculate all the variables. Let's hope that cop doesn't die, but if he does, the Department will stop at nothing. If they found you, they'd give you the third degree until they got something out of you that'd put them on our tracks, you can be certain of it."

"So what do we do?" Luca asked.

"What I said. Claudia goes to ground in the safe house. Vito and all the others resume your normal lives. And Zeno goes away somewhere."

"Shit, that way there are too few of us to protect my house. We've taken all the families there."

"You did the right thing," Biagio said, slapping Oscar on the back. "I called Carmine earlier. He'll be here on the first flight he can get. He's coming to give us a hand. Luca, you'll go pick him up at the airport."

"Sure."

"Even with him, there are too few of us," Oscar said.

"Look, we're just wasting time," Biagio said. "Get ready, all of you. Five minutes and we're out of here. Please: make sure nobody follows you. Giorgio, Oscar, Vito, and all the others who took part in the operation, take your SIM cards and burn them. Also change your cell phones and let me have the new numbers as soon as possible. Now go."

They all headed for their cars. Biagio grabbed Giorgio by the arm and took him aside.

"Whose big idea was this disaster?"

"Oscar."

"Christ! And the bruise Vito has on his face?"

"That was him too."

"Oh, great. First he sends you to slaughter and then he gets pissed off."

"The problem is Vito. He's in shock and feels guilty. We shouldn't leave him alone, I'm afraid he'll do something stupid."

Biagio gave him a glance. Vito was wandering through the garage, disorientated. He was a shadow of his former self.

"Okay. I'll deal with him."

"What is this business about Verri?"

"Too long to talk about now."

"And this mess here? Do you think you can sort it out?"

Biagio snorted. "I don't know. I'll try to pin it on the Calabrians, but I don't know if Verri and the others will buy it. Not after Bucciarelli."

"Hey, chief, I'm sorry about Sonja."

They hugged. "Thanks, son."

"And how are you?"

"Like shit. But I can't allow myself to think about it. Especially now."

"I'm sorry, Biagio," Giorgio said again. "I tried to stop them, but—"

"Right now take Claudia to the safe house. Tonight, I want to see both you and Oscar."

"Okay."

"Vito, come here!"

Vito walked up to Biagio, who gave him a little smack on the cheek. "All of you were involved in this screw-up, okay? The others are as much to blame as you are."

"I'm sorry, Biagio, I . . . He'd shot Zeno, and was about to—"

"It's over now. We'll sort it all out, as we always do. Just come here."

Biagio gave him a big hug, continuing to whisper to him that they would get out of this together. He couldn't see the cold stare cast at them by Oscar, who was watching them from inside one of the cars.

Bucciarelli had done an amazing job. Inside the "Mazzeo file," Claudetti had found three CDs on which the deputy commissioner had saved photographs and audio and video recordings on Biagio Mazzeo and his team. Claudetti started to look through the images and saw a whole bunch of them that aroused his curiosity: they all showed the ex-cop who had been Mazzeo's mentor in the company of a man whom Bucciarelli had identified as Boran Paja, an Albanian coke dealer he claimed was in business with Mazzeo. According to Bucciarelli's notes, Mazzeo's team used the former cop to interface with the Albanian and negotiate the supply and sale of coke in the city. From the photographs, taken at different times, it was clear that there was something between the ex-cop and the dealer: was the motive for his murder linked to drug trafficking?

"It could be," Claudetti whispered as he read a note by Bucciarelli that also indicated Paja as one of Mazzeo's informers.

Apparently you can't attack Mazzeo head on, he said to himself, but there's nothing to stop you from attacking his men. You can use them to bring him down. And Paja might be the right man to destroy them

Because there was one thing he was sure of: Mazzeo had to pay.

Roberto Messina made his way through the crush of his colleagues, trying to get to the end of the corridor. From the way they looked, it was obvious the situation was very critical.

"No, you can't come in," said one of his oldest colleagues, barring the way to the intensive care department.

"Is he alive?" Roberto asked.

"Yes, but—"

"But what?"

"He's in a bad way, Roby."

Roberto leaned against the wall and for the first time in many years he prayed, begging God to spare the life of his younger brother.

Carlo had just had a child and couldn't go like this.

"Who the fuck was it?" Roberto snarled.

"We don't know yet, but it must have been professionals helping the woman to escape."

"They told me she's a cop, is that right?"

The old officer nodded.

"Who the fuck wants to free a cop who's been arrested? And why?"

"We'll deal with that later. Now we have to wait for Carlo to wake up. Because he will wake up, Roberto. He will wake up, got that?"

Roberto nodded, but he had the distinct feeling that his colleague was lying to him just to calm him down.

Even though he was the younger brother, Carlo had always been the more sensible of the two, the one who had started a family, who had bought a house, who lived for his wife and their child. Roberto, on the other hand, was still a little boy for all his thirty years and the job he did. He lived in a rented room, didn't have a regular girlfriend, and loved having fun and getting back home at dawn. And that was what made him feel so guilty: it should have been him in that car, on that damned highway. Right now, the doctors should be trying to keep him alive, not Carlo.

I shouldn't have asked them for that change of shift, he thought, raising his hands to his head. If I hadn't come back at five in the morning, I wouldn't have had to ask them to put you on instead of me.

"What happened" asked a woman's voice.

Roberto immediately looked up. It was his mother, Olimpia. He hugged her.

"There was an accident," he said. "Carlo got hurt. They're operating on him now."

He felt her stiffen.

"How . . . how did it happen?"

"He was shot."

"What? Who? Who shot him?"

"I don't know."

Olimpia Messina was no ordinary woman. She had brought up two sons on her own, working and trying at the same time to be a mother and father to them. She was a tough woman with a will of iron, proud of how she had brought up her boys. They were everything to her.

"Was he on duty?"

"Yes."

"But he shouldn't have been on duty today," she said, puzzled. She knew all about her sons' shifts, and given the job they were in she always telephoned before and after to make sure they were fine.

Roberto wondered if he should lie to her. "I know. I asked him to swap shifts with me. I should have been there, not him."

Olimpia drew him to her. "He's a strong boy," she said, reassuringly. "He'll pull through."

"Yes, mother."

"Don't waste time here, all we can do is wait. Go, Roberto."

"Where can I go?"

She freed herself from his embrace, took his face in her hands, and looked into his eyes. "What do you mean, where? To find the man who did this to your brother."

Roberto Messina stood motionless for a few moments, then nodded and did what his mother had ordered.

Giorgio and Claudia walked into the apartment where she would have to hide.

"Shit, I still can't believe it," she said, collapsing on the couch.

"You'd better get used to the idea," Giorgio replied, raising the blinds, but leaving the curtains closed. "And you have to do it fast. Do I need to remind you again of what you mustn't do?"

"You've already told me ten times, Giorgio."

"It's important, Cla. If they find you, we're done for."

"They won't find me."

"No, not if you follow what I told you to the letter."

"Okay, but how the fuck are we going to get out of this situation?"

"I don't know, but we mustn't let our instincts get the better of us. We have to let everything cool down and then deal with it calmly. Now that Biagio is out, it'll be easier to handle this thing."

"Easier? Maybe you're forgetting the Calabrians."

"Of course not. But maybe with this other mess, the cop we killed, even those bastards will think twice before showing their faces again. All the attention will be on us, not on—"

"You told me you didn't kill him."

"I saw it, Cla. Vito hit him right in the head. That poor guy won't make it, trust me."

"Christ," Claudia whispered, passing her hands through her hair. "You shouldn't have done it, you—"

"Hey, they would have killed you, okay? This isn't a gang of fucking Nigerians we're talking about, or some other assholes, this is the 'Ndrangheta. These are people who have hitmen everywhere. They could have had a couple of prison guards take you out. We had to minimize the risk."

"I . . . I don't know what to say."

"Don't say anything. You'd have done the same for any of us. That's how it works."

She wondered whether, if the roles really had been reversed, she would have had the courage to carry out an operation as brave and foolhardy as the one her colleagues had mounted.

Giorgio removed his jacket and took a look around, checking the pantry and the refrigerator.

"I'll have to do a bit of shopping for you and—Cla!"

Claudia had slid to the floor, seized by what looked like an epileptic fit. She was panting, and shaking convulsively as if she were very cold.

"Hey! Look at me. Breathe, dammit. Breathe!"

Giorgio had been a soldier in Special Forces before joining the police and realized immediately that she was experiencing what the doctors called post-traumatic stress. He knew there was only one thing to do. He struck her on the neck with the edge of his hand, knocking her senseless. Then he stripped her and took her in his arms.

Claudia woke with a start when she felt the jet of hot water from the shower. She shook herself, realizing that she was suspended in the air, held in Giorgio's big arms.

"What the fuck—" she tried to say, but Giorgio told her to keep quiet.

Giorgio was bare from the waist up, his jeans soaked. With his shirt off, he looked even more muscular. "Close your eyes," he said.

Her anger and embarrassment faded, and she closed her eyes.

He crouched and, still holding her tight, rested her on one of his legs. She huddled against his chest, and abandoned herself to the caresses of the hot water, which seemed to release her. Giorgio started massaging her head and hair. He raised the temperature of the water until it was almost boiling hot, and Claudia moaned and clung even more to him.

"Shhh," he whispered, running his big hand over her face.

"It's wonderful," she murmured, completely abandoned to his reassuring physicality and the warmth of the water.

Then Giorgio abruptly switched the mixer faucet to cold and put his hand over her mouth. Within a few moments, an icy rain was falling on them. Claudia tried to struggle, but Giorgio's arms and hand held her still. This torture went on for nearly a minute, then Giorgio switched back to hot. The icy water didn't seem to have had any effect on him.

Claudia was so breathless, she couldn't even speak. Her mind had all at once recovered its lucidity, and after those frozen jets, the heat of the water gave her a heavenly sense of well-being.

"I'm sorry, but that's what you needed," was all that Giorgio said. She still clung to him, driven by a sense of gratitude and dependence she could barely understand.

"Do you hate me?" he asked.

"No," she murmured. "That's enough, though. The attack has passed."

"No. It'll come back if we don't continue."

Ice again. Then fire. Ice and fire. And again . . . And again . . .

When whatever energy she still had seemed to have abandoned her body, Giorgio massaged her, washed her hair, and then carefully dried her, completely without any inhibitions. Totally abandoned, she let him do it, even when he again took her in his arms and carried her out of the shower stall. He wrapped her like a child in warm towels, laid her on the bed, calmly dried her, then covered her with soft blankets.

With her eyes half closed, already in freefall toward sleep, Claudia watched him as he undressed in the semi-darkness with his back to her. She looked at his broad back and the tattoo that covered all of it. He turned to her for a second, completely naked. She caught herself quivering.

"Now sleep," he said, and left the room.

Claudia Braga didn't have time to wonder about the sensation she had felt suffuse her private parts a few moments earlier, because she immediately slipped into a deep sleep.

Dangerous Lies

Biagio walked out of the shower stall in the bathroom of his apartment. His BlackBerry had been vibrating for more than ten minutes, but he had avoided answering, knowing perfectly well who was trying to reach him.

"Hello?"

"At last, dammit!" Irene Piscitelli said. "You gave me your word and you already screwed up!"

Biagio took a towel and threw it on. "What the hell are you talking about?"

"What the hell am I talking about? You fucked up big time, don't you realize? I mean, have you gone crazy? How am I supposed to save your ass after that Wild West gunfight?"

Inwardly, Biagio cursed his men. "I'm sorry, but I don't follow you. What is it I'm supposed to have done?"

"This is no time to fuck me around, Mazzeo. It really isn't, believe me."

"I don't understand, Piscitelli."

"Claudia Braga was helped to escape by a bunch of people who attacked the police car that was taking her to prison. They opened fire, and one of the officers in the car was fatally wounded. Do you realise what you've done?"

"Are you pulling my leg?"

"Are you telling me you had nothing to do with it?"

"Do you think I'd be so stupid as to pull a stunt like that? After the agreement we made? What the hell would I gain?"

Silence at the other end.

"Are you still there?"

"So who was behind it?"

"You tell me, dammit. Where's Inspector Braga?"

"I just told you. Someone helped her to escape."

"Helped her to escape or abducted her?"

"I don't know."

"Use your head, Piscitelli. It could only have been them. They want to force me to cooperate."

"Pugliese?"

"Who else?"

"He can't have gone quite that crazy."

"Clearly he has, because I had nothing to do with this thing you're telling me about. But are you sure it's true? Are we sure it isn't a made-up story to put me to the test?"

"Unfortunately, it isn't. There's an officer in the hospital fighting for his life, though the doctors say he won't make it."

"Christ. So what do I do now?"

"Carry on as per the original plan, I guess. We don't have much time, and after this fuck-up we have even less."

"Maybe I should try to find Claudia."

"Forget it. Just try it and I'll put you back behind bars!"

"But—"

"No fucking buts. I'll deal with her. You see to Pugliese."

"What about Verri? I assume he also thinks I was involved."

"I'll sort him out, dammit. You just go ahead, and don't make me regret it, or I'll drop you like a ton of bricks. Understood?"

"The press must be onto it."

"We won't mention Inspector Braga. We'll just say that a criminal was helped to escape, and that for the moment we can't release any other information in order to safeguard the investigation."

"Do you think you'll be able to keep it secret?"

"If your colleagues want to hold on to their jobs, yes."

"Okay. Keep me updated."

"You too."

Irene hung up. Biagio passed a hand across the steamed-up mirror and looked at his own reflection. His life rested on so many lies that now even he found it difficult to tell truth from falsehood.

He rubbed his hands over his stubbly cheeks. Sonja had liked it when he let his beard grow. That thought was enough to reawaken his grief at her death.

"You can't do anything for her now, you have to protect the living," he whispered, stroking the ring that had belonged to Ivankov, the man from whom he had stolen it. "You have to protect the living and avenge the dead."

He felt a cold rage rising inside him, sweeping away the memory of Sonja.

He went into the bedroom, opened the bag and took out the shotgun, which he laid on the night table. Then he took out some clothes and the confidential file on Domenico Pugliese that Irene Piscitelli had given him.

He got a beer from the refrigerator, ignoring the photographs of himself with Sonja, sat down, and started studying the file.

According to the Organized Crime Directorate, Domenico Pugliese, sixty-four years old, was one of the most wanted men in Italy. He had created an empire that went from Reggio Calabria to Milan by way of Piedmont, swerved toward Liguria, came to rest on the French Riviera, and then leapt to Switzerland, from there extending like a spider's web to Germany and Holland and as far as Canada and the United States, not to mention Australia, where it was practically on home territory. The more he went through the pages, the more Biagio realized that he had made enemies of the wrong people.

Don Domenico was no ordinary crime boss: as a member of the Santa, the inner circle at the top of the 'Ndrangheta, he represented the elite of the organization.

Biagio felt a shiver of cold reading the words of the prosecutors:

The Santa is a particularly dangerous branch of the Calabrian Mafia. It grew up in the 1970s after the first 'Ndrangheta war with a very specific aim: to take over the State from the inside. Members of the Santa may have contacts with non-members, including individuals who have sworn allegiance to the State, such as police officers, carabinieri, politicians, and magistrates, many of them Freemasons. Unlike normal members of the 'Ndrangheta, who are bound only by the rules and oaths of the organization, members of the Santa are allowed to become Freemasons, which gives them more room for maneuver within the State establishment and enables them to build relationships of mutual interest with the political classes and even infiltrate the political field themselves. Where the ordinary member of the 'Ndrangheta needs intermediaries to approach people from the banking, business, and political worlds through the Freemasons, the member of the Santa becomes those people. If the common member does not even speak with power, the member of the Santa is power.

"My God . . . " Biagio sighed, scratching his throat.

The file claimed that Pugliese was one of the leading representatives of what might be described as a *"liquid Mafia" for its ability to infiltrate everywhere, duplicating the same organizational model as the original 'Ndrangheta in places very far from those in which it was born. Investigations suggest that Don Domenico Pugliese, with his very high rank in the Calabrian organization, heads a kind of maxi-Mafia above the simple 'Ndrangheta, with its own organization and autonomous rules devoted to the development of indissoluble links with political forces of both coalitions and with national and international business, spread through the well-oiled mechanisms of the Masonic lodges.*

But the judges of the Organized Crime Directorate went even further, maintaining that the 'Ndrangheta was in a state of constant evolution: in reflecting the ups and downs of the economy it had been forced to change continuously, and several Prosecutor's Departments suspected that Pugliese had taken the Santa to an even higher level, a kind of superior commission, known as the Vangelo, to which few members had access, and which included both members of the Santa and high-ranking officials of the State. According to some members who had turned State's evidence, Domenico Pugliese was currently overall head of the Provincia, the governing structure established after the second 'Ndrangheta war to resolve conflicts and coordinate the organization and the management of all the families, including those in international territory.

Biagio closed the file. The more he read, the more his stomach was in knots. Partly because there was something he knew that wasn't in that file. Domenico Pugliese was dead, and his empire had been inherited by his son, Natale, who had just triggered a new 'Ndrangheta war. The war Biagio Mazzeo had to stop.

Roberto Messina switched off his car engine and continued on foot to the scene of the crime. He took out his gold badge and pinned it to his chest for the benefit of those police officers who didn't know him.

"Hi, Roby," said one of the inspectors who was waiting for Forensics to finish their examination. "I'm sorry, son. How's Carlo?"

"Not well. They operated on him, but he's still in a critical state. Do you have any idea what the fuck happened?"

The inspector looked around the area. "From what the witnesses have said, the car stopped when a white Punto suddenly braked in front of them. A second later, a black van hit the car on the left-hand side, sending it against the guardrail. At that point, some masked men got out of the van and started shooting. They also had accomplices inside the Punto. They forced your brother and his colleague to lower their weapons and took the woman away. As they were leaving, your brother managed to open fire, hitting one of them. They shot at him and then left. It's unbelievable."

"The one he hit—did he kill him?"

"We don't know. He hit him in the back, but his accomplices managed to get him away."

"Have Forensics found anything?"

"No hard evidence for the moment."

"Who was the woman?"

"Roby, I really can't—"

"Come on, this is my brother we're talking about. A fellow cop."

"Okay, but we mustn't let this get out. There are strict orders to keep this away from the press and—"

"I'm not the press, Gianfranco. I'm his brother."

"She's one of Mazzeo's team."

"A Narc?"

"Precisely."

"Why was she arrested?"

"Something to do with drugs."

"Do you think it was Mazzeo who got her out?"

"No. When the attack happened Mazzeo was at Headquarters. It can't have been him."

"Who, then?"

"I don't know, but we'll find out, I promise you."

Roberto nodded and looked around. "I'll leave you my number. If anything emerges, I'd like you to let me know."

"You aren't looking to do anything crazy, are you?"

Roberto smiled and slapped him on his shoulder. "Me? Of course not," he said, and left.

As he walked to his car, Biagio saw a young black boy on a BMX break away from a group of young people dressed in full hip-hop fashion who were staring at him curiously, and cross the street toward him.

"Hey, chief," the boy called to him. He must have been fourteen at most. Was he going to ask him if he wanted to buy some grass? Biagio wondered. That would really put the finishing touches to the evening.

"What is it?" Biagio said, keeping an eye on the others, who were still staring at him from the other side of the street.

"A guy asked me to give you these," the boy said, stopping his bike a few inches from Biagio's combat boots and holding out a closed fist.

Biagio frowned and then held out a hand to the boy, palm upwards. The boy dropped some metallic objects into it.

"They're bullets, aren't they?" the boy asked, excited.

Biagio's blood froze. The bullets fell to the road, jingling. With one hand he pulled the boy off the bike and thrust him behind his back, with the other he took out his pistol and aimed it straight ahead. The kids on the sidewalk opposite ran off, screaming, at the sight of the gun.

"Hey! It was nothing to do with me, I didn't—"

Biagio grabbed him by one arm and shoved him up against the door of a parked car. "Shut up," he said, looking around at the other parked cars. He didn't spot any threat, any suspicious person. "Who the fuck gave them to you?" he asked, lowering the gun.

"A guy with sunglasses. He gave me fifty euros."

"What?"

"Yes, crazy. He said you'd come out of that building, he told me to wait for you and give them to you, then he went away."

"Did he also ask you to tell me something?"

"Yes. That he didn't like the little joke with the redhead. What does it mean?"

"Anything else?"

"No. He said you'd understand."

"And he didn't tell you anything else, are you sure?"

"I asked him if they were real, and he said no, it was only a joke."

Of course they are, Biagio thought, putting his pistol back in its holster. "Okay. Do you know what this is?" he asked, taking out his badge.

"Shit!" the boy said. "That means I don't get to keep the money, right?"

Biagio smiled and hit him on the nose with the badge. He loved the new generations. "No, you can keep the money. But it's best if you don't tell anybody about this, got that? And advise your friends to do the same, or they can forget about dealing in this neighborhood, understood?"

"Loud and clear, chief."

"Good. Now get out of here."

The boy break-danced back to his bike, then took off his little hat and bowed by way of farewell

Biagio shook his head and picked up the bullets from the ground.

They were 7.62s, the kind used in AK-47s and some submachine guns. The kind that had killed his mentor Santo.

He looked around for a few more seconds, then got in his car and sped away with his heart pounding. "Message received, you bastards," he said, hands gripping the wheel.

They stared at Boran Paja on the monitor linked to the hidden camera in the interrogation room.

"Did he resist arrest?" asked Carmen Brancato, the deputy commissioner who supervised the Homicide division.

"No," Claudetti replied, folding his arms. "All he did was ask if we were sure about what we were doing."

Carmen laughed. "Did you find anything on him?"

"Unfortunately not."

"What about his lawyer?"

Claudetti smiled in disgust. "One of those who charge three hundred euros an hour."

"Only the best for our dealers," Carmen replied, staring at the papers on her desk: documents and photographic material photocopied from Bucciarelli's file. Claudetti had hidden the originals in a safe place. "You know, don't you, that none of this constitutes evidence of a crime. It was all speculation on Bucciarelli's part, and he isn't here any longer to testify."

"I know. But you have to admit it's circumstantial evidence of a kind. I hope showing him the photos will lead him to say something compromising."

Brancato started beating the fingertips of her right hand on her folded arms, nervously. "Have you already called his lawyer?"

Claudetti shook his head.

"How about the prosecutor? Have you informed him?"

"No, I thought of working on him a little myself, without external interference. Do you think that's feasible?"

She sighed. It was obvious she didn't like it: the code for criminal procedure obliged them to inform the arrested man's lawyer as soon as possible. Paja's would be able to accuse them of not following the procedure, and that would create tensions with the prosecutor and the examining magistrate.

"I advise you to do it this way: have a look at who's on duty and wait for whichever magistrate you think can help you. Just make sure it's someone who has no ties with Mazzeo."

Claudetti nodded. "And what about his lawyer?"

Carmen looked at her watch and then again at the monitor. She reached over to the laptop on which the interrogation was being recorded and stopped the recording.

"I'll drop by in two hours' time and realize I was so absent-minded that I forgot to record the interview. I'll come in to tell you and I'll also ask you to inform his lawyer, having previously told you I would do so but having been prevented by a more urgent case."

Claudetti smiled. "Thank you."

"I'd do more, Andrea, but with the National Crime Bureau hanging around Headquarters, and De Rosa and Verri out for blood, I have to be careful. And remember, rumors travel fast here, and Mazzeo is a police officer. He'll hear soon enough that his protégé has been arrested, it may even be Verri who tells him, that wouldn't surprise me at all. So expect him to send for Paja's lawyer at any moment. Until that happens, I repeat, you have at most two hours before informing him."

"Perfect."

"I saw a bit of a crowd. Did you arrest somebody else?"

"Yes, his bodyguards. Two of them have records."

"Run the usual checks on all the computer records. Maybe if we're lucky we'll find a few pending charges to validate the arrest."

"I'll have that done right away," he said, and left the office. Outside the interrogation room he joined Diego Gatti, with whom he had carried out the arrest.

"Free hand?" Gatti asked.

"Yes. We have a couple of hours."

"Do you think that'll be enough?"

"The important thing is that he doesn't speak with Mazzeo or any of his men. That's why we have to make sure the bastard is never alone. There always has to be one of our people keeping an eye on him and stopping him being approached by anybody who isn't one of us, okay?"

"Don't worry, I'll see to that."

"Any news about the search of his house?"

"The boys are still there."

"Tell them to turn the house upside down. If they find something, anything, I'll immediately ask the examining magistrate to put him behind bars, that way it'll be harder to communicate with him, even for Mazzeo. One other thing: check everything you can on his men. Fingerprints, etcetera. With a bit of luck we might come across something in records."

"Consider it done."

"Any news about the wounded cop?"

"Nothing for now. He's still hanging in there, but they don't hold out much hope."

"The bastards."

"Do you think Mazzeo was behind it?"

"When the car was attacked, he was with me, so it wasn't him personally. But it could have been those sons of bitches he surrounds himself with . . . I'm going in now, there's no time to waste."

"Destroy him."

Claudetti went in and closed the door.

"I've been in here for half an hour," Boran Paja said. "Have you called my lawyer?"

"Of course," Claudetti said, sitting down opposite him.

"So where is he?"

"Maybe he's finishing his dinner, give the poor man time to digest."

"Bullshit."

Claudetti laid out on the desk the photographs showing Paja in the company of Biagio Mazzeo's mentor Santo Spada.

"What's this?"

"Spada was killed a few days ago in a somewhat violent manner, as you can see," he said, putting down the photographs of the corpse taken by Forensics.

Paja didn't bat an eyelid, Claudetti had to grant him that.

"Well?" Paja said.

"Do you know anything about it?"

Paja laughed. "I want to see my lawyer."

"He's on his way, I told you."

"Until he gets here, I won't say anything that could be used against me."

"Come on, Boran, we aren't in America."

"Could you bring me some water, inspector?" Paja asked in a voice dropping with contempt.

Claudetti held his breath. It was clear that he was provoking him: Paja wasn't some two-bit thug, he was a major trafficker, who knew how to screw up an interrogation and an investigation.

"Of course, but first tell me about your relationship with Santo Spada."

Paja uncrossed his legs and leaned across the desk. "I'd like to call my lawyer in person."

"Let me get this straight," Claudetti said gravely. "You'd like to use your cell phone, the one we confiscated from you?"

"Precisely."

Claudetti laughed in his face.

"You know I'm one of Mazzeo's informers, don't you?" Paja said.

"Even informers can be charged with murder, Boran," Claudetti said with a wink.

Paja rolled his eyes. "Is that what I'm being accused of?"

"I don't know. You tell me."

"What the hell does that mean?"

"What was your relationship with Santo Spada?"

Paja smiled and shook his head. "If that's the way you want it, cop. I invoke my right to keep silent."

Claudetti smiled back at him. He hadn't imagined, even for a second, that Paja might cooperate. What he was interested in was keeping him as far as possible from Mazzeo. "It's going to be a long night, then," he said, joining his fingers behind his neck.

Biagio was on his way to Vito's place. He knew the boy needed him, and it was best not to leave him alone. He was just parking near the apartment building where Vito lived when his phone vibrated. It was the phone on which the Calabrians were supposed to contact him.

"Yes?"

"Make a note of this address," said a voice with no trace of a Southern accent.

"Okay, got it."

"Listen carefully. Be there in half an hour. Turn off all cell phones and any device that could trace your movements. Go to the address alone, you won't run any danger. It's not in our interests to hurt you."

"That seems a little too—"

"I repeat: alone. You don't need weapons, you don't need anything. Come in, talk with us and then go. Make sure you aren't followed. If you are, pass the hangar, sound your horn, and then go. If you aren't, sound your horn twice as soon as you arrive."

"Okay."

"Don't do anything stupid," the voice said, and hung up.

Shit, they're all we need, Biagio thought. He sent Vito a text message, saying he would see him later, and switched off his cell phones. He drove through two red lights and did a three-point turn to make sure nobody was behind him, then headed for the highway and took the exit toward the industrial park. Destination: the freight yard.

He hadn't told anybody where he was going. This time he would do everything alone.

Vito Filomena believed in the pack. He believed in it so much that he had had a panther's head tattooed on his back. He loved his brothers. He would have done anything for them. That was why he had shot that cop. Out of love. To prevent any of them from being wounded.

But he had opened fire to kill. In the excitement of the moment he had acted instinctively. And instinct had screwed him.

He rang the doorbell again. When he had received Biagio's message postponing their meeting, he had decided to pay his young son a visit.

The door opened and his ex-wife Ilaria stared at him in surprise. "What are you doing here?"

"I wanted to see him."

"It isn't your day."

"I know, but I need to see him, Ila."

"Has something happened?"

"No. I just want to see my son."

"I . . . It's not the best time, Vito. I'm with someone."

The judge had ruled that *his* apartment should go to Ilaria, and now that bitch was bringing her new flame here. Even just a day earlier, Vito would have gone crazy about something like that. But now everything had changed.

"I don't care. I just want to see the boy."

"Are you sure you're okay? Your face . . . That's a nasty bruise. Who have you been fighting with?"

"Will you let me in or not, dammit?"

She huffed and puffed, but eventually let him in. Vito headed straight for his son's bedroom. As he did so he passed a man of about forty, well dressed, a regular-looking guy. He winked at him and carried on.

As soon as he saw the boy in his playpen, he smiled and his eyes grew moist.

"Hi, there, kid," he said taking him in his arms and kissing him on his soft cheeks.

Nicholas replied with an incomprehensible noise and a smile. For a moment, all his problems vanished beneath the disarming force of that smile.

"What's the matter, Vito? I know you only too well. What happened? Are you in trouble again?"

He turned. She was leaning against the door post, watching him. With one hand, Vito grabbed the rucksack he had on his back and threw it to her.

"What the fuck's this?"

"Money. Thirty thousand."

"I'm sorry?"

"Close the door a moment."

She gave a grimace of disgust, but obeyed. "Okay, now it's obvious you're in trouble."

"Shut up and listen. It's thirty thousand in cash. You mustn't keep it here and you mustn't put it in the bank either. Hide some of it with your mother, your sister, anybody you're sure won't steal it from you. And make sure you don't spend it on bags and shoes, for Christ's sake."

"Why are you giving it to me?"

"For the boy. I want you to leave the city for a while."

"Oh, Christ, Vito! Again?"

"Shh, don't shout. It's peanuts compared to the money you will have, okay? Just think of it as an advance. For anything else, any problem, just ask Biagio. He'll sort it all out."

"Vito, what have you done?"

"Did you understand what I told you?"

"I . . . Yes."

"Good. Leave me alone for a few minutes with the kid, please."

Ilaria could see how strange he was. Gentler, calmer. Almost resigned.

"Will he see you again?"

He stared at her without replying.

Ilaria closed the door with a sigh.

That area of the merchant port had been abandoned for some years now after having been closed down several times for environmental violations. Now it was used as a dump for all the rusty containers or those they couldn't get rid of, the carcasses of ships, and the chassis of cars that thieves took there, dismantled, and then burned.

Ignoring the instructions of the man on the telephone, Biagio parked about a mile away. He wanted to see whether or not it was a trap.

He walked around a bit, pistol in hand, without noticing anything strange. There wasn't even a car anywhere near the container indicated.

Maybe you'll go in and they'll blow you up, he told himself. But he didn't believe that: the Calabrians had done a lot so far to get their cocaine back, it would make no sense for them to kill him. Not now, at least.

After looking around one more time, he headed to the container indicated to him on the phone. He leaned against the iron wall and tried to hear if there were any noises inside. He caught only the mechanical hum of an electric generator.

Overcoming all his reluctance, he took a deep breath, opened the door, and went in with his pistol pointed straight ahead of him.

The container was empty apart from a table in the middle on which stood a laptop computer. There were neon lights running off a gasoline-operated generator, so that the interior, which stank of rust and damp, was illuminated by a cold surgical light.

Biagio gave a start when he saw all the photographs and documents piled on the table and the floor. The images showed the members of the pack with their families. The documents were of the most varied kind: his men's matriculation papers and references, their children's school report cards, their wives' medical records.

Biagio felt his blood freeze. With his combat boots, he moved the photographs on the floor, and saw that some of them showed him talking with dealers or having dinner at an open-air stand with Sonja.

A sound made him jump. He saw that the computer screen had come on, and a Skype call was in progress. *Accept or refuse* said the caption on the screen.

The sons of bitches didn't trust you, he thought, accepting the call.

In a window on the screen appeared the half-length figure of a man in his forties.

"Biagio Mazzeo," the man said. "We meet at last."

"Who the fuck are you?" said Biagio pretending to be irritated. "I asked to speak with Pugliese, and in person." Maybe Pugliese didn't know who he was.

"One question at a time. It's safer to have this conversation on Skype, it can't be intercepted. They should have left you a chair. Please sit down."

"I prefer to stand. I repeat, where is Pugliese?"

The elegant man on the screen shrugged. "I'm sorry to have to tell you: Domenico Pugliese is dead."

"What do you mean, dead?" Biagio snarled.

"Dead, deceased, departed, passed on. How else would you like me to put it?"

"And who the fuck are you?"

"I'm his son."

"I had an agreement with your father. An agreement he broke."

"Hmm, there's a lot I could say about that. Did he break it, or did you when you killed ten of his men?"

"I didn't kill anybody, it was the Serbs who did that, quite rightly I'd have to say, given that you arrived without any money and carrying guns."

"What happened between the Serbs and us is none of your business."

Biagio didn't reply. At that moment he was thinking only of Piscitelli's words: *Force him out into the open if you don't want me to put your men behind bars.*

"Listen to me carefully," the man went on. "I had people watching that night, and I know you and your men intervened with your cops and killed my people, those who were still alive at least. You'd guaranteed the deal would go down, so don't fuck me around."

"It was you who opened fire first, idiot."

"Mind your language, cop."

Biagio bit his tongue, thinking of the photographs of the children. "What do you want?" he asked.

"First, my three hundred kilos of cocaine. I know you have them because there wasn't any seizure."

"Actually, there was, except it didn't come out in the press, you know how it is, the usual high-level deception."

"Bullshit, when your superiors arrived you'd already gotten rid of the stuff. I want those three hundred kilos, Mazzeo, and as you've seen I don't have any qualms about showing how determined I am. Did you look at the photographs?"

Biagio's legs were shaking. "You shouldn't have killed my man."

"It was the only way to make you understand that I'm not joking. I want my cocaine. And not only the three hundred kilos. I want another ten for every one of my men you killed. Let's say you killed five, so don't tell me I'm not meeting you halfway."

Biagio laughed in his face. He hit his temple with the barrel of his pistol. "You're crazy. I'm not giving you a fucking thing."

Pugliese also smiled. "No, Inspector, you're the crazy one. I won't take it out on you, but on the people close to you. Do you seriously think that shutting them up in Oscar Fortunato's villa is going to protect them? Or that pulling that Bruce Willis stunt on the street to help the dyke get away served any purpose?"

Biagio felt a shiver down his spine.

"Daddy screwed up, kid. I only wanted to save Claudia, and instead I shot a cop. A cop just like me, who'd never done me any harm. On TV they said he has a son the same age as you. They also said he's in a critical condition. Daddy isn't a murderer, Nico. But he is an honorable man. Nobody will ever be able to tell you the opposite."

Vito continued to cradle him for a few more minutes, savoring the sensation of that warm bundle of flesh against his chest. Then he put him back in the playpen and kissed him on the forehead. "See you soon, little man."

He went in the kitchen, where Ilaria and her man were eating.

"I'm going, thanks," he said.

"Wait, I'll see you out."

"Will you do what I told you?" he asked her when they got to the front door.

"Are we in any danger?"

"Let's say I'd feel better if you had a change of scenery for a while."

"How about you?"

"Don't worry about me. I won't be around for a while, but like I said, whatever you need, call Biagio. He'll see to everything, okay?"

"You really don't want to tell me what you did?"

Vito shrugged. "All I did was protect my family."

With this he left. Ilaria realized she had goose bumps. Something told her she would never see him again.

"Come on, who do you think you're dealing with?"

"This is between you and me, don't involve my men," Biagio replied.

"I'll be happy to oblige if you give me the three hundred and fifty kilos I'm entitled to."

Biagio took a few seconds to think. Pugliese had him over a barrel, and he was more dangerous than Irene Piscitelli: he knew where his family was hiding, and anyone who killed an ex-cop in the center of the city must have resources and nerve enough to do it again. Even supposing he agreed to negotiate with him, Biagio was a hundred and fifty kilos short.

"I want to talk in person, face to face."

The man on the screen shook his head. "We aren't playing games. Just give me the cocaine or I'll really be pissed off."

"You have to give me a bit more time. I need to convince my men."

The slightly distorted voice coming from the speakers of the computer replied that he didn't have time.

"But I don't—"

"You may not think so, but I've been very soft on you, Mazzeo. I could have had you abducted and tortured for hours until you told me where you have the cocaine. Actually, you're making me regret I didn't do that. My father was the boss, but now that he's dead I'm in charge, and I won't have any qualms about sweeping you away if you don't give me what I want. I don't think that's so difficult to understand, or am I wrong?"

"If you really represent the 'Ndrangheta, why are you doing all this for three hundred fucking kilos?"

"It's a matter of principle, Inspector. I won't let anyone screw me around, let alone a cop."

"I need at least three weeks."

Pugliese let out a harsh laugh. "Three weeks? I'll give you three days. I don't want to hear any more bullshit. Three hundred and fifty kilos, all in one go. Call the number you know for details. In three days I want *my* cocaine. All of it."

"Wait, I can't—"

"I'm not waiting a fucking minute. And get this into your head: for every day's delay, I'll kill one of your men or a member of their family, understood?"

"Filthy son of a—"

Pugliese smiled. "Oh, and Mazzeo, you can keep the photographs." He hung up, and a second later had vanished.

Biagio grabbed the computer, hurled it to the floor, and stamped on it with his combat boots.

When his fit of anger was over, he heard a noise behind him. He spun around, raising his Beretta, and saw a hobo give a start and put his hands up.

"What the fuck do you want?" Mazzeo said.

"I . . . I . . . Do you have a cigarette?"

Biagio let out a little laugh and walked up to him without lowering the pistol. "I don't smoke. Do you have anything to drink?"

"Right pocket."

Biagio gave a grimace of disgust. "Forget about my putting my hands in there, old man."

Shaking as if possessed, the man took out a metal flask and held it out to Biagio.

"Whiskey?"

The man nodded.

Biagio unscrewed the top and poured the liquid over the photographs.

"Hey!"

Biagio cocked his pistol and the old man swallowed his disappointment. "This'll teach you to mind your own business," Biagio said, throwing the photographs and the documents from the table onto the floor. "Give me a light."

With the old man's lighter Biagio set fire to the photographs and documents. He watched them burn until they were black as soot, then pointed to the electric generator.

"If you know what to do, you can sell that for no less than five hundred euros."

"Are you serious?"

"Bet your ass I am. But you've never seen me."

"With these cataracts, I'd find it pretty hard to recognize you."

"Good for you. Now get away from the door."

Biagio went out, looked around, and ran toward his car.

"Shit," he snorted as he got in the car. He was almost starting to miss Sergej Ivankov. At least he played away. Pugliese's clan, on the other hand, were here, all around him.

Yes, but where? he wondered. He had no idea. The only thing he knew was that three days were nothing. He'd never be able to get so much cocaine together. His one chance was to stop Pugliese some other way. But to do that he had to know who he was dealing with. And right now he knew almost nothing about him. So he called the man who had introduced him to the Calabrians and told him they needed to meet right away.

Someone had to sacrifice himself for the team. And it could only be him. He had thought about it for hours on end, but hadn't come up with any other solution. He had to turn himself in. Assuming it was he who had fired the shot. If he turned himself in of his own free will now, while that cop was still alive, there was still a chance he wouldn't get life. He'd tell them he'd been behind the assault. He'd trusted to a bunch of immigrant punks who'd taken off and left him in the lurch. He'd be able to hold out even if they gave him the third degree, he was sure of that. The pack wouldn't understand.

Vito parked outside Headquarters. He switched off the engine and drummed on the wheel.

Open this fucking door and get out now or you'll never do it, he told himself.

"Come on, get out," he whispered.

He opened the door and got out of the car.

The night air was cool. The patrol cars going in and out gave him a feeling of security, but at the same time a sense of loss. He took his bill-fold with his gold badge from his pocket and stared at it, feeling a kind of betrayal.

It's over, my friend.

He cast a final glance around, then walked toward the entrance, determined to turn himself in.

Gabriele Barranca was a respected civil lawyer specializing in company law. He was a handsome man in his fifties, distinguished, elegant, cultured, strong connections in high society. On the surface, at least. In reality, he was a member not only of the Santa, but also of the Lombardia, the name given to the high command of the 'Ndrangheta in Northern Italy, for which he also managed the mutual fund used to help the families of members in prison, pay for their lawyers, and deal with general expenses. It was Attorney Santini, the Panthers' lawyer, who had introduced Barranca to Biagio Mazzeo. Like Santini, Gabriele Barranca was a member of the regional council, although for an opposing party. They had needed to meet in order to resolve some tensions that had arisen between the Panthers and the local branch of the 'Ndrangheta. Barranca was a skillful mediator and had quickly come to an agreement with Biagio. The Calabrians and the Panthers could coexist, as long as their spheres of interest did not clash or overlap.

Since that meeting, Biagio had had no further problems with the Calabrians. In fact, he had often cooperated and lent his services to Barranca's syndicate, in particular by using his contacts to protect some of the members who were behind bars, and when he had had to find a buyer for the three hundred kilos of Serbian cocaine it was Barranca he had phoned, asking to meet. Over lunch, he had asked the lawyer if he was interested. Barranca had kindly declined the offer, but had put him in contact with a family who would surely be tempted by such an investment.

Barranca was ten minutes late for the appointment. He arrived in a Mercedes, escorted by another car, which was unusual for their meetings. When he got out and came toward him, two men followed him.

"What's the matter, don't you trust me?" Biagio asked.

"Things are getting nasty around here," Barranca said with a smile. Then, indicating the men escorting him: "Orders from upstairs, don't go thinking I like it."

The two men shook hands.

"Do you want them to search me too?" Biagio asked.

"If you don't mind. You'd set their minds at rest."

Biagio shook his head. Very slowly, he took out his pistol and placed it on the hood of the Alfa. Then he opened his arms wide and let himself be searched by one of the two bodyguards.

"Okay," the man concluded after a careful search.

"Sorry about this, Biagio."

"No problem. Let's go."

They walked to the construction site that Biagio had chosen as a meeting place and sat down on one of the benches the workers used in their lunch break. The two bodyguards stopped some thirty feet away.

"So, Biagio, it isn't hard for me to guess the reason for all this urgency."

"Pugliese," Biagio said.

"As I imagined."

"I'm in shit up to my neck. What the fuck's going on?"

"A revolution, a civil war, I don't even know what to call it. How much do you know?"

"I know that deal I proposed to you that I diverted to the Puglieses, on your advice, went down the tubes. Those bastards killed the Serbs and tried to take all the cocaine. I was forced to intervene to stop them, and had to confiscate the consignment."

Barranca shook his head in dismay. "I think it's best at this point if we put our cards on the table. Did you kill his men?"

Biagio looked at him in silence for a few moments, uncertain whether or not to reply, then nodded almost imperceptibly.

Barranca half closed his eyes, sighing.

"Shit, I gave the Serbs my word of honor," Biagio cried. "You told me this Domenico Pugliese was someone who could be trusted. As a reprisal for my confiscating his cocaine, he killed one of my men, bang in the middle of the city, for fuck's sake. And as if that wasn't enough, I try to negotiate with this scumbag and find out he died!"

"I'd say 'was killed' is more accurate."

"Whatever you like. Anyway, I find myself negotiating with his son, who apparently has a screw loose because all he does is keep threatening me and my men. What the fuck is he thinking? Does he want to start a war with the police?"

Barranca slowly lifted his right hand. "May I speak?"

"That's what you're here for."

"To start with, Natale Pugliese, the son, was the person who ordered the murder of Domenico, the father."

"Great," Biagio said ironically.

"Let me speak, because this is a very delicate matter. For a whole series of reasons I'm now going to explain, your 'deal' happened during a rather unpleasant period for our organization." Barranca lit a cigar. "I think you'd agree that our presence here in the North has been an established fact for years."

Biagio nodded.

"Domenico was one of the smartest members we've ever had. With his father's help, he was one of the first to lay down roots here, at a time when the North was like another continent. Anyway, to cut a long story short, he built an empire here. In Lombardy alone, there are more than twenty branches and, believe me, that's an incredible result. Thanks to his intelligence, Don Domenico scaled the heights of the organization, so much so that this year he was promoted boss of bosses, an annual appointment, the most important one we have and—"

"Okay, I get the idea. You had a hard-on for the son of a bitch. But what the fuck are you getting at?"

"Be patient for a minute. A few years ago he went back to the South, more precisely to Africo, his native village, because now the Organized Crime people were hot on his heels. He left his son in charge here in the North. A hothead, someone who acts on instinct—"

"No kidding!"

"—rather than thinking, but intelligent all the same. Do you know what the Lombardia is?"

"Your high command here in the North?"

"More or less. As you know, the family is the basic unit of the organization. A family generally controls a small town or a neighborhood, depending on the size, right?"

"I am a police officer, in case you've forgotten."

"I'm only saying it in the spirit of clarity. If there's more than one family in an area, they form a branch. The Lombardia is a structure linking all the branches in the North. It's a kind of coordinator that has the task of keeping relations and contacts with Calabria, known as the Provincia or the Mother House, to which it is subordinate."

"In other words, the South tells the North what to do."

"Precisely. The Lombardia federates the branches all over the North, and members can belong to one of the inner groups like the Santa or the Vangelo, but they always take their orders from Calabria. Always. That was the categorical imperative that Domenico gave his son when he put him in charge of the High Command."

"But . . . ?"

"But the son isn't the father. Natale has always criticized the way the organization is run, seeing it as culturally backward."

"He wants independence from Calabria. Well, well, a Mafioso who supports the Northern League."

Barranca smiled ruefully. "Let's say he's always had the idea of becoming independent of the Provincia. The Calabrian top brass refuse to see the members of the Lombardia as being of equal importance, and that doesn't go down well with him. He wants to be the one who makes all the decisions regarding his territory, not leave it up to old men hiding in San Luca."

"He thinks he's a fucking Lucky Luciano."

"Right. He wants precisely what happened between the Sicilian and American branches of Cosa Nostra: a clean break. Though if you think about it, that's what led to the downfall of the Sicilians."

"So what happened?"

"He started to work in that direction, concentrating power in himself and those branches that support him, increasingly excluding the Mother House. He had various warnings from his father, until he went one step further and killed him. Since he already had the unconditional support of thirty branches and considered the North powerful enough to scare the South, he committed that crazy act of killing Don Domenico as a declaration of war. When I put you in touch with the Puglieses, Domenico was still boss. But by the time the thing with the Serbs happened, Natale had already killed his father, and he was the one who ordered the massacre."

"But why?" Biagio asked.

"To demonstrate his ferocity and his power."

"And why did he kill Santo?"

"To demonstrate to the Provincia that he isn't joking and that he can even attack police officers. It's a signal to all the families that oppose him: I'm prepared to start a new Mafia war if you stop the cells in the North from breaking free of the Calabrian yoke. I'm ready to draw the attention of the cops and of public opinion, which will make trouble for everyone, unless things are done the way I want."

"Christ. But what do the people in San Luca say about it?"

"They're knocked for six. Kill your own father, a boss of bosses? It's unimaginable. There was a previous attempt to break away, and it was put down with a lot of bloodshed. But to start a Mafia war right now would have damaging repercussions for everybody, not only at a national level. The political situation is too confused. Until the political context is stabilized, starting a war without solid protection from above means risking everything."

"So what's happening now?"

"For now the South is taking its time. Natale has lots of people on his payroll, police officers, magistrates, politicians and businessmen, who are equally useful to the Provincia."

"So the higher-ups are losing their grip and letting him do what he wants?"

"No, of course not. At first, when he demonstrated his intention to break his ties with the Mother House, they isolated him, excluded him. It's a social thing, like not inviting you to a wedding or christening to make it clear to you that you're *persona non grata*."

"And how did he react?"

"Let's say he reacted badly," Barranca said with a frown.

"How badly?"

"First, I forgot to tell you that above the General Manager, which is Natale's rank, there's a General Director." He stopped for a theatrical pause, as if he were in a court room. "Or rather, there *was*, because Natale had him killed and took over his post."

"Fuck!"

As he was about to walk through the entrance to Headquarters, Vito felt himself being grabbed by one arm and pulled aside.

"What the fuck are you doing?" Oscar said, forcing him to do an about-turn. Cristiano and Manuel, Oscar's men in the Traffic Police, fell into step on either side of Vito as if they were his escort and walked him to the parking lot.

"Leave me alone, dammit!" he cried, shaking off Oscar.

Oscar elbowed him in the stomach, leaving him breathless.

"Hold him up."

Cristiano and Manuel supported Vito and bundled him onto the back seat of Oscar's SUV.

"I was right not to trust you, dammit," Oscar said, grabbing him by the throat. "What the fuck were you thinking?"

"Not here, Oscar," Manuel said, looking around. "Let's move."

They all got in and drove away from Headquarters.

"You followed me."

"Thank God I did."

"You should have let me go."

"You were going to turn yourself in, weren't you?"

"Do you have another solution?"

"The one that Biagio gave you, idiot."

"You know as well as I do that hiding won't get us anywhere. They'll find out it was us. There's no point in us all paying. I was the one who fired the shot, I'll be the one who pays."

Oscar slapped him. "I don't want to hear any more of this crap, okay?"

"You're making a mistake, Oscar."

"Shut up."

"Where are we going?"

Oscar took out his pistol and pointed it at Vito's stomach. "Say another word and I swear I'll kill you right here."

Vito fell silent.

Barranca coughed and resumed speaking. "That was a signal to all the northern branches that Natale wasn't afraid of the South, and that anyone who opposed the split would be food for the worms. He's been planning this for years: first he won the favor of most of the Northern branches, using their respect for his father as a screen, then in the space of a day he had his father, the General Director, and five bosses of branches that opposed the split all killed, in effect taking power. You know the two murders that took place in Novara prison last week? That was him."

"He's an intelligent son of a bitch."

"You bet he is. He's young, don't forget, just like most of the Northern members. Many were born here, like him, and have never even been to Calabria, now that the initiation rites are carried out right here. This is *their* territory and they don't want to have to share any of it with the Southerners. Plus, you have to bear something else in mind: the economic factor. As I told you, Natale has a sharp brain: after his father left him in charge here, he took over all the labor rackets involving illegal immigrants, and now he practically has a monopoly in earth moving, cement mixing, digging, demolition, and so on."

"In other words, he has enough money to afford to buy the consent of the other Northern families."

"I'd go further: he's already done it, as well as buying practically half of the Regional Council. Plus, you're forgetting one thing: Expo 2015. That's worth millions, and the Lombardia is involved up to its neck. All the contracts belong to the Lombardia, all the work is done by the Lombardia, so why on earth send the money south? Want another example? I don't know how the hell he did it, but a few days ago, on a technicality, the Supreme Court dismissed all charges in one of the biggest trials of Northern members of the 'Ndrangheta in the North. All the accused have links to Pugliese. There are more than a hundred of them, and they're all likely to be set free. And one more? Two days ago three emissaries from the South were sent to negotiate with him. He killed them and cut off their hands. The quintessence of diplomacy, don't you think?"

"Christ," Biagio said. "So now I'm in the middle of a Mafia war."

Barranca sighed. "I'm sorry, son. In normal circumstances the 'Ndrangheta would never have killed your man. But these aren't normal circumstances, and maybe this isn't even the 'Ndrangheta anymore."

"What the fuck do you think is going to happen?"

Puffing at his cigar, Barranca shook his head. "I haven't the slightest idea."

Biagio rubbed his platinum ring almost compulsively. "And what about you? Where are you on the chessboard?"

Barranca shrugged. "I'm at risk. I represent tradition, the past, all those rules the new generation has grown tired of having to respect. I've always been one of those most loyal to the Mother House, and I've never supported the breakaway wing."

"What about them?" Biagio said, indicating the two bodyguards with his chin. "Were they sent from the South?"

Barranca nodded.

"What do you advise me to do?"

"Take your time, if you can. Negotiate."

"No," Biagio snorted, throwing his head. "I can't take my time, and there's no way to negotiate with that bastard. He wants three hundred and fifty kilos of cocaine immediately."

"Which puts you in a difficult position."

"I'm in a trap, no doubt about it. Even if I did what he says—which I don't have the slightest intention of doing—I might find the Southerners against me."

"There is that risk, yes."

"But if I don't take sides, he'll play target practice with my men."

Barranca shrugged.

"Shit! Do you know who actually killed my man?"

"No. My relations with Natale are very sporadic. We only ever talk over the phone. He never informs me of his moves. Apart from that, Biagio, I'm a member of the Santa, I have more contacts with the executive than the military, if I can put it that way."

Biagio stroked his knuckles nervously. "In other words, you can't do anything to help me."

"Unfortunately, no."

"Not even have a word with him?"

"It wouldn't be any use, my friend."

"Fuck, now I understand why he's so interested in our cocaine. The bosses in the South have cut off his supplies to make it clear to him that drugs are still their thing. They're trying to isolate him. So, either he goes through other channels and finds new suppliers—"

"Which would be a lot more expensive."

"—or he plugs the gap with *my* haul."

"And meets the demands of the Northern market for a few months," Barranca concluded. "Yes, that's it."

"Son of a bitch," Biagio snarled. "He worked this all out months ago."

Barranca nodded, expelling the smoke. "Except that neither you nor I knew that."

"That's why he wants me to work for him, to get him more coke."

"Drugs are still the most immediate source of cash, Biagio. Obviously, money comes in from contracts, extortion, loansharking, but not at the same speed. Drug trafficking is their ATM. It's obvious he targeted you: for him, you represent a quick and sure source of income. If he loses customers in the drug market, he loses money and credibility." Barranca gave him a pat on the back. "For what it's worth, I'm really sorry, Biagio."

"No, I'm grateful, I know you exposed yourself by coming here. You respected our friendship, and I really appreciate that. But I'd like you to go even further. Any information you can find out about him, any rumors about where he is, anything, let me know immediately. I'd consider it a personal favor and I'd be in debt to you." Biagio squeezed his arm.

"I'll do what I can. Anything to stop the power-crazy bastard."

Biagio nodded and let him go.

Christ, what the fuck do I do now? That son of a bitch wants to slaughter us, and if I do what Piscitelli wants, he'll kill us one by one. As if that wasn't enough, we have to hide a fugitive and a likely cop killer . . .

Biago stood up and looked at the city at the foot of the hill. A restless wind was blowing, trying to seep into his bones. The thoughts in his head were ugly ones.

Claudia woke, unsure where she was. The fact that she was naked didn't make things any better.

"Shit," she whispered, passing her hands through her hair. She had just remembered that she was in the safe house.

She covered herself with a sheet and called to Giorgio. There was no answer. She found a note from him in the kitchen, saying he would be back later with clothes, cigarettes, and other provisions.

She got dressed, thinking of what had happened under the shower. She'd had some kind of attack, thanks to all the guilt she felt after the fiasco her colleagues had dreamed up. They had risked their lives for her. Vito might even have ruined himself forever for her sake.

If only they knew, she said to herself as she put on her shoes.

Her mind was awhirl with thoughts. She knew her life would never be the same again. She wondered when she would see her son again. *If* she would see him again.

The answer to that question terrified her.

She looked around in search of something to do, but couldn't find anything. She decided to go out onto the terrace to breathe a little fresh air and look at the city. But when she tried to open the door, she realized it was bolted.

Giorgio had locked her in.

Biagio entered a pub, sat down at an isolated table, and ordered a rib of beef two fingers thick surrounded by mountains of fries lightly sprinkled with salt, which he washed down with a pint of Guinness.

At last a decent meal, he thought as he bit into the soft juicy meat, which was almost raw, the way he liked it.

After a few minutes, he was joined by Giorgio and Oscar.

"Where's Luca?" Biagio asked.

"He went to pick up Carmine from the airport," Giorgio replied. "The others are at Oscar's house, on guard with Mirko and the others. I preferred to leave them there."

Biagio nodded. "You did the right thing. What about Zeno?"

"I sent him to his relatives in Sicily," Oscar said.

"Good. And Claudia?"

"She's in the safe house. She had an attack of nerves. The stress. She's better now. I thought I'd sleep there tonight, I don't feel like leaving her alone."

"I think that's an excellent idea."

"I know it's a stupid question," Oscar said, embarrassed. "But how are you?"

They broke off when the waiter came to take Oscar's and Giorgio's orders.

"How am I?" Biagio repeated, cutting the meat.

"Shit, Biagio," Oscar interrupted, pointing at the steak. "That beef's so rare, a vet might still be able to save it."

The three of them burst out laughing.

"What were we saying? How am I? I feel guilty. About Sonja, about Santo. That's obvious, isn't it? And I'd definitely be better if my men hadn't attacked a police car, shot a fellow officer, and freed a prisoner I now have to hide."

Silence.

"I know," Oscar said. "But to give them the cocaine would be an even worse screw-up."

"Eat in peace, Biagio," Giorgio said. "We'll talk about it later."

Biagio took a swig of the Guinness and finished eating. He pushed away the plate and wiped his mouth. "How about you. Did you do what I told you?"

"Yes. All the families are at my house. Fuck, it's like Christmas dinner."

Biagio smiled. "How are the kids?"

"Oh, for them it's a party. They're together, playing, joking."

"And the women?"

"Worried. But they cook to relieve the tension, watch reruns of *Sex and the* City, and thank you for the case of Chardonnay you had delivered along with the flowers."

"It seemed the least I could do."

The waiter returned with the two pints for Oscar and Varga. The three of them raised their tankards.

"To Santo," Biagio said, looking them in the eyes.

"To Santo," Oscar and Varga replied.

Biagio finished the fries and started stroking the platinum ring. "Have you had any problems?" he asked. "Has anybody threatened you? Have you had the impression that you were being followed?"

"No," they replied.

"Have you had any other contact with the Calabrians?" Oscar asked.

Biagio seemed to hear the metallic jangling of the bullets on the asphalt and Pugliese's voice threatening him. "No," he lied. There was no point in getting them even more worried than they were. "But that doesn't mean we should lower our guard. On the contrary."

"My house isn't exactly the safest place."

"You need to be patient for a few more days, my friend. I know perfectly well it's a pain in the ass, but we have no alternative. Your house is the biggest of all. I told Luca to find another, maybe outside the city. A villa, a farmhouse, whatever. But it's easier to keep watch over a single house than ten different ones."

"That's a fact."

"And right now we need to stay together, united."

The others nodded.

"Among other things, as soon as Carmine arrives he'll give us a hand. He'll be crazy too, but he's good."

"Christ, we certainly need him," Oscar sighed.

"Carmine Torregrossa," Biagio said, his eyes smiling. "We've been friends since we were kids. He was a little boy in my neighborhood."

"Hold on a second, wasn't he the guy who was thrown out for brutality?" Giorgio asked.

"Right. But he wasn't thrown out, he was transferred to the asshole of the world, one of the quietest towns in Italy, down in Sardinia."

"Was he in Narcotics?"

"Yes, it was before you'd arrived."

"I'm sorry, am I wrong or was he the one who used to come in stoned to work?"

Biagio and Oscar shook their heads.

"No, it wasn't exactly like that," Oscar said.

"How do you mean?"

After a swig of Guinness, Biagio said, "The story you know is a lie, it's just an excuse Verri dreamed up with the press and his colleagues, actually he was kicked out because of that mess with the serial rapist, you know about that, don't you?"

"No."

"There was this fucking rapist of young girls, all minors. He had already raped six or seven girls, the whole city was looking for him, we were heavily involved in Narcotics because he drugged his victims and we couldn't figure out where the fuck he got the drugs from, because it was a substance that was quite rare. In the end, Carmine nabs him in the act, thanks to a tip-off. First he slaps him around, then he tries to crucify him to the wall. By the time they stopped him, he'd already planted a nail in one hand."

"Fuck!" Giorgio said, frowning. "I see you know a lot about it."

"Well," Biagio admitted with a smile, "I was with him when he did it."

"Jesus Christ, I was sure of it. And what were you doing while he was trying to crucify the guy?"

Biagio shrugged. "I was holding him still."

Giorgio almost choked on his beer. Biagio and Oscar burst out laughing.

"You're pulling my leg, right?"

Oscar shook his head. "No, but it was all a little bit more complicated than the way Biagio just told it. Practically the whole city was up in arms about that bastard, partly because one of the victims was the niece of the prefect, so you can imagine the pressure. Verri had given everybody free rein, and obviously had sent Narcotics on ahead. These two dickheads had been on amphetamines for a week when they caught him, so you can imagine the state they were in: two pit bulls on steroids and methedrine, foaming at the mouth and out for blood. Santo was still working then, he was in charge of Narcotics."

"Yes, we were in big trouble," Biagio said. "The rumor was going around at this time that the bastard would kill his victim because he knew he was going to get caught, he could feel the cops breathing down his neck."

"So what happened?"

"We burst in and catch him with his pants down, I take the girl away, and when I come back in I find Carmine with a hammer and nail in his hands. Like I said, we were out of our heads, doped up to our eyeballs, we hadn't slept for days, and so I hold him still, he was a fucking Bulgarian. I was convinced he just wanted to scare him." Biagio burst out laughing at the memory. "But the asshole really does hammer a nail into him."

Giorgio shook his head. "Holy fuck."

"Santo comes in and literally kicks our asses, and along with Franco and Rino tries to pull the nail out of that animal's hand while two other cops take us away. Hell, I remember Rino actually fainted at the sight of all that blood."

"How did you manage to get away with it?"

"The old man was clever. He took my pistol from me and used it to shoot into the guy's wounded hand, then put the hammer in his other hand. But Verri didn't swallow it, and rumors started circulating, you know how it is. Santo only had two years to go to his pension, and he accepted early retirement, with a big cut in his severance pay. I came out of it clean because the old man took all the blame with Verri, and because the prefect did everything he could to cover our asses. I was put behind a desk for a few months, then sent back out on the street. But everyone knew Carmine was out of control and that he was the one who'd lost his head, so Santo couldn't stop them transferring him, there was nothing he could do: one of us had to pay, and they chose Carmine. They spread the rumor that he had drug problems to divert attention from that crucifixion thing."

"What a fucking story," Giorgio sighed.

"Right. That time the old man saved our asses and our careers."

"And what happened to the Bulgarian?"

"In the end, the magistrate made a deal with his lawyer, reducing the sentence in return for dropping charges of police brutality."

"How long was he in jail?"

"Two months, I think," Oscar said. "Then we had him stabbed to death by a gypsy."

"Right," Biagio said. "Anyway, that's Carmine. But don't let it sway you, son, that was a special case, and the circumstances were unusual. He's one of us, trust me."

"Sure, you just have to keep him away from hammers," Oscar said, again triggering a wave of hilarity.

"Okay," Biagio said, drumming his fingers on the table. "Now let's get to the questions you came here to ask me."

The two men stared at each other in embarrassment.

"I know why you wanted to see me, and you have every reason. Where do you want to start?"

"Bucciarelli," Giorgio said, after a moment's hesitation. "Why did you kill him?"

Biagio twisted his neck sideways, making it crack, as if he had just absorbed a hard blow. "Because he'd tried to ally himself with Barberi, he was determined to make us pay, and didn't give a damn about the risks involved. He was ready to end up in jail just to bring the squad down and put us all behind bars. Barberi called me and explained in person what Bucciarelli had in mind: he was about to sabotage us with the press and the Prosecutor's Department. It was urgent, I had to stop him right away. So I organized the raid with Vito, since the two of you were busy, you with Anna and you with your family. I didn't want to disturb you."

"What about Barberi? Does she know?"

"She agreed with me, she knew all about the plan and gave me the go-ahead. I have her support in this, and you can imagine how reluctant she was to be so tied in with the squad. But there it is. We now have a prosecutor working for us."

"How on earth did she agree to it?"

"Because she was also scared of Bucciarelli. He had material on her and her, how shall I put it, her *collaborations*. And a prosecutor who collaborates with crooked cops, well, that's not the best thing for advancing your career."

"Fuck," Oscar sighed. "And how do they plan to handle your—"

"The Commissioner will hold a press conference tomorrow," Biagio said with a smile. "You'll hear for yourself."

"And what about the Calabrians?" Oscar asked, stroking his bald head.

"It's all my fault. I underestimated this Pugliese and his syndicate."

"You know what I can't quite figure out?" Giorgio said.

"Shoot."

"How they can kill for three hundred kilos of cocaine. Obviously, a lot do. But such a high-profile murder of an ex-cop linked to cops who are still on the force, and in a major division? Anyone who can do something like that must have only two reasons: either he's on his uppers and is desperate for cash, or else he's—"

"Untouchable," Biagio said, getting in ahead of him. "And apparently that's the way it is: he's untouchable."

Oscar and Giorgio both cursed.

"What do you plan to do?" Oscar asked.

"Are we going to give back the coke?"

Biagio looked at them. They were scared. They had seen with their own eyes where his overreaching had taken them and they didn't want to repeat the same mistake. He could read it in their faces. His error had been to keep them in the dark about the risks they were running.

"No. We aren't giving back the coke. Not for now, at least."

They looked at him as if he was crazy.

"But—"

"I know you may think it's a mistake, but giving it back now would be an even bigger mistake."

"Why?" Oscar asked.

Biagio didn't reply because any answer from him would have meant a thousand more questions he had neither the desire nor the time to answer.

"Biagio, why would it be a mistake?" Giorgio insisted.

"I ask just one thing of you. However absurd it may seem, it's the best thing to do right now: I ask you to trust me."

"But we do trust you, Biagio," Oscar said.

"No, if you trusted me you wouldn't ask questions."

The two said nothing. Doubt had started to erode their trust in their chief. In their eyes, he had changed, he was more introverted, weaker than usual. Biagio was aware of that.

"What about Claudetti?" Oscar asked. "Do we let him get away with it after all he's done?"

"No, he'll pay. Not now, there are more urgent things to do. But if Claudetti has decided to play dirty, we have to keep an eye on him and stop him from making things too hard for us. Not like we did with Bucciarelli, obviously. We have to tread carefully right now."

"So what do we do?"

"I don't know. We'll think about it when the time comes . . . Well? Do I have your trust?"

"I'm with you," Giorgio said.

"Me too."

"On my conditions?"

"On your conditions," Oscar replied.

Biagio heaved a sigh of relief. "Good. I promise you won't regret it. I won't make any more false steps, any mistakes."

"Another mistake could get some of us killed," Oscar said.

"I know. It won't happen."

"Just one thing, Biagio," Oscar went on. "What did you do with the Chechen woman? The blonde."

Biagio's lips stretched in a smile. "Vatslava? I handed her over to Paja, asking him to sell her to a trafficker. She'll become a streetwalker, Albanian style. It's what she deserves."

Oscar nodded. "So at least as far as the Chechens are concerned we're done, we shouldn't expect any more reprisals or threats?"

"No, we're safe."

"Good."

They ordered three rums and sat in silence for a few minutes. When the waiter brought the rums, they drank a toast to the memory of Sonja.

"Right, we still have one thing to discuss: Vito. What the fuck happened there?"

Oscar's face darkened. "The dickhead wanted to turn himself in. I guessed he wanted to do something like that, so I had Cristiano and Manuel follow him, and when we realized he was going into Headquarters we stopped him. It was a near miss. The kid's running wild, Biagio."

"Where is he now?"

"At home. With Manuel and Cris keeping guard on him, in case he tries again. I'm scared we've lost him."

"I think you're exaggerating," Giorgio said.

"Like hell I am! You didn't see his eyes. He looks like someone who can't wait to confess."

"Vito's tough, he'd never do anything like that."

"Like fuck! He'd already have done it if we hadn't stopped him, Biagio. He disobeyed your orders. He was about to screw things up for us even more."

"Even if that was so," Giorgio said, "as far as he was concerned, he was simply taking the weight off us."

"By taking all the blame himself? Come on. What would he have said when they asked him where Claudia is?"

Biagio and Giorgio exchanged glances.

"So what do you suggest?" Biagio asked.

"We're in a bad situation, boys. The Calabrians, this thing with Claudia, the other cops who are already looking at us as murderers. We can't take any chances. If we lose sight of him for a second and he gives himself up, we're fucked. If they give him the third degree he'll contradict himself and end up confessing everything, and at that point it'll all be over. They'll turn him, and Vito knows too much."

"So what do we do?"

"I say we eliminate him," Oscar said.

Boran Paja woke with a start, feeling the cold water soak his hair.

Andrea Claudetti burst out laughing and put the empty glass down on the table. "Wakey-wakey," he said, sitting down. "I think you needed a good wash."

Paja cursed in his own language, then nervously brushed his wet hair back.

"So, did it help to sleep on it? Do you have anything to tell me about Santo Spada or Biagio Mazzeo?"

"Where's my lawyer?" Paja asked, wiping his face with the sleeve of his jacket.

"I think he probably fell asleep, or maybe he said, okay, let's leave him in Headquarters, it's only one night anyway. I mean, the food's pretty good here, don't you think?"

"This is harassment. I want my lawyer."

"I don't know what to say, I did call him. If he doesn't come, I don't see what business it is of mine."

"Let me talk to Mazzeo, then."

"Forget it."

"Then go fuck yourself."

Claudetti's slap knocked him to the floor. "Oops, I'm sorry. There was a fly on your cheek, did I get it?" He stood up and dragged Paja to his feet.

Paja instinctively pushed him away, making him knock the back of his head on the wall.

This was what Claudetti was waiting for.

The door opened and two uniformed officers rushed in and pulled Paja off.

"Not good, Boran," Claudetti said with a smile, straightening his creased jacket. "The code calls it *violence to a public official*. You can go to prison for that, you know."

"You provoked me, you bastard!"

"Me? What did you boys see?"

"The suspect attacked you, Inspector."

Claudetti opened his arms wide. "You see?"

Beside himself by now with the stress of the wait and Claudetti's humiliating treatment of him, Paja tried to hit him again, earning himself a knee in the balls from one of the two officers.

"What do you want us to do with him, Inspector?" one of the two asked, handcuffing Paja.

"Put him in the holding cells. I want him in a single cell with some-one keeping an eye on him. Nobody's to speak to him apart from me or Inspector Gatti, otherwise you'll have me to deal with personally, understood?"

"Absolutely. Get up, you piece of shit."

Claudetti watched as the two officers took him away and then sat down at the table in the little room.

Boran Paja would talk, he was sure of it. It was just a matter of time.

"You've gone crazy!" Giorgio said.

"Giorgio, he cried all the time I was driving him home. Does that sound like someone who'd hold out under interrogation?"

"Oscar, we can't—"

"Wait, chief. Did you say you'd settled the Bucciarelli thing? Great. What happens if someone questions Vito about that night? What if they see the state he's in and decide to test him for drugs? You know how much coke he snorts."

"Oscar," Giorgio retorted, "you do realize you put him in this situ-ation?"

"Fuck, I didn't tell him to shoot at head height, I already told you!"

You can't save them all, said a voice inside Biagio's head.

"Giorgio," he said, "this time Oscar's right."

"You're joking, right?"

"Listen to me. Verri called me earlier about the business of the assault on the police car. I have an alibi because I was with Claudetti at the time, but what about the two of you? He wants to question us tomorrow. We could decide not to show up, but he'd interpret that as an admission of guilt. And if we do show up, if Vito submits to ques-tioning, can you guarantee me he'll keep his mouth shut?"

"I . . . Of course not, but that doesn't mean—"

"If he blabs, we all end up inside. And if we end up inside, who'll protect our families from the Calabrians?"

"I don't . . . " Giorgio sighed and threw his head back. "Shit, it isn't possible."

Biagio and Oscar exchanged cold glances.

"I'm sorry, but we have no choice," Oscar said. "It's the simplest thing to do. The most painful, but the simplest."

"If we do something like that, we're finished. Nobody will ever trust us again."

"Who says we have to tell the others?" Oscar said.

"What do you mean?"

"He's in a fragile state, Giorgio, they've all seen him. He might decide to end it all."

"Do you really want to do something like that?" Giorgio asked Biagio.

"I can do it if you like," Oscar said.

"No," Biagio said. "I'll do it."

They stared at him in surprise.

"Are you sure?"

"Yes."

Because there was one thing that Giorgio and Oscar didn't know about: Piscitelli. If Vito confessed his involvement in the assault, the National Crime Bureau would torpedo the agreement it had made with Biagio. They'd send him back behind bars and proceed with charges against the whole squad. It was up to him to shut Vito's mouth.

"Biagio, I don't think you're in any condition to—"

"I said I'll handle it. I'm the one who got you in this mess."

"That isn't true, you—"

"And I'll resolve it."

"But—"

"Listen to me very carefully. Nobody must ever, for any reason, talk about this, understood?"

Giorgio lowered his eyes. He'd heard those words before.

"Is that clear?"

The two men nodded.

"Good. Oscar, go back home and keep your eyes open. Giorgio, stay with Claudia and calm her down. You'll have to stay close to her—as soon as she finds out she'll feel even guiltier."

"Okay, chief."

They finished drinking in silence and Oscar stood up. "Okay. I'm going now."

"Be careful and call me if there are any problems. We'll get out of this soon."

"I hope so."

"I'm also going, Biagio," Giorgio said.

"We have no choice, son."

"I know." He paused and looked intently at Biagio. "Is there something you want to tell me?" It was as if he knew everything about Piscitelli, Pugliese, the ultimatum.

You're just imagining it, Biagio told himself.

"No, son. I have nothing to tell you."

"Are you sure you can do it?"

"I have to do it."

"Do you want me to come with you?"

"No, I want you to go to Claudia."

"Okay. Call me when you've finished."

"Stay calm."

Alone again, Biagio ordered another rum. He removed the platinum ring and turned it in his hands. Silently, Biagio toasted the memory of Sergej Ivankov.

"I won, Ivankov," he whispered. "In the end I won."

Roberto Messina motioned to his mother to come closer. Olimpia rose from the bench and joined her son in the waiting room.

"Coffee?" he asked.

"A double, if there is one."

He inserted a few coins in the machine.

"Any news, ma?"

"No. But they've told me it's best not to hold out too much hope."

"Jesus. How are Chiara and the boy?"

"Chiara came on her own, but I sent her away after an hour. She's in pieces, and couldn't stop crying."

"Did they let you see him?"

"Just through the glass. He's so full of tubes, it's scary."

"Here . . . I'm sorry, ma. What about his colleagues?"

"I sent them away. They were acting as if he was already dead, they were getting on my nerves. You look tired, you should sleep a little."

"I can't close my eyes. If I try, I see . . . No, I want to stay awake."

"What about you? Any news?"

"Yes. The person the bastards helped to escape was a police-woman."

Olimpia raised an eyebrow. "A policewoman?"

"Yes, a crooked one. She's part of a squad of sons of bitches who are all going down big time."

"And who do you think helped her escape? Her colleagues?"

"I don't know."

"You have to find out."

"I will, I promise."

"They shot my baby."

"Ma, it's best if you go home now. I'll stay here."

"No. I want to be here when he wakes up. I don't care what the doctors say. Carlo will wake up, I know."

"Of course he'll wake up."

He hugged her, then walked with her as far as the intensive care department. They sat down together on the bench and Roberto put his arm around her shoulders.

"I don't care if it was cops who did it. You have to punish them anyway."

"I know."

"You have to do it for your brother and for your nephew. And you have to do it for me."

"I will do it, ma."

They sat there in an embrace, waiting for sleep to catch up with both of them.

"What is this mess with Claudia Braga?" asked the Voice over Skype. "What the hell happened? Are you trying to screw everything up, for Christ's sake?"

"I don't know," Irene Piscitelli replied, staring at the screen. "Mazzeo had nothing to do with it, he can't have had anything to do with it. He was still in the cooler and didn't talk to anybody except me. And when the assault happened, he was in Headquarters. It wasn't him."

"Then who the fuck was it?"

"I can only think of one person capable of doing something like that."

"Pugliese?"

"Who else?"

"Shit. That means you have to act even faster."

"I know."

"How did it go with Mazzeo?"

"Fine."

"So he's still on the job?"

"Absolutely, yes."

"Excellent. And Verri?"

"He's in agreement, he knows that this way we all win."

"Good, good. We know you have reservations about him, but we don't. We firmly believe this has to be done, and that he's the one to do it. On condition that . . . "

Irene raised an eyebrow. "On condition that what?"

"Boran Paja."

"He's one of Mazzeo's informers, if I'm not mistaken."

"Precisely. Claudetti, the cop who arrested Mazzeo, has brought this Paja person in and is putting him through the wringer. Why do you suppose he's doing that?"

"Shit," Irene said. "Okay, I'll deal with it tomorrow."

"The sooner you deal with it, the better. This Claudetti could complicate things."

"Right now, I'm writing the Commissioner's speech for tomorrow's press conference. You needn't worry about Paja. He's a solvable problem."

"All problems are solvable, you should have learned that by now."

"That's true. I'll deal with it, guaranteed."

"Okay . . . No cream today?"

"Goodnight."

"Goodnight, Irene."

Biagio knocked at the door of Vito's apartment. Cristiano opened.

"You can go," Biagio said. "I'll stay with him."

Oscar's two men stood up, put on their jackets, and made to go out. First, though, they handed Biagio a pistol.

"It's that asshole's," Cristiano said, pointing at Vito, who lay sprawled on the couch in front of the TV, staring into space. "You know how he is."

Biagio nodded, removed the magazine, and placed the weapon on a chest of drawers.

"What the fuck's going on, Vito?" Biagio asked as soon as they were alone.

"It was the best thing to do, Biagio. It *is* the best thing to do."

"Oh yes? And you think that knowing you were behind bars, the Calabrians wouldn't have tried to get to you? You would have screwed things up even more, because they'd have used you to put pressure on you. How many fucking times have I told you, you have to think of all the consequences before you make a move?"

Silence.

"Switch off that fucking TV or I swear I'll shoot it."

He switched it off.

"Stand up. Let's go get a bit of air."

Vito stood up, grabbed his jacket, and made to take his pistol, but Biagio stopped him.

"No. It's better if you leave it here until you clear your head."

"Don't you trust me anymore?"

"Would you trust yourself after you screwed up the way you did?"

They exchanged a long look.

"Now move your ass," Biagio said. "I need some fresh air."

They took Vito's car. Biagio had said he didn't want to drive.

"Where should I go?"

"Where you buried Omar."

"Why on earth? What the fuck has Omar got to do with anything?"

"He was Bucciarelli's key witness. Verri, De Rosa and I sorted every-thing: Bucciarelli will pass for a hero who was killed in a shootout with a dealer. I want to get whatever I can for myself and wipe out all the things that tie us to him and all the shit we did to cover ourselves. And the kid's body would cause us nothing but grief if it was discovered. All it needs is for someone to accuse us of having killed him and we're really fucked."

"Okay, but why now?"

"Because I want you to dig. That way you'll learn not to screw up again. And now shut that fucking mouth."

"I—"

"Shut up and drive."

*

They reached the place. It was a wooded area, lit only by a sliver of moon. A gloomy, menacing spot.

They got out of the car.

"Show me where you buried him," Biagio said.

They walked for about a hundred yards, until at last Vito pointed at the ground. "I think it's here."

"Are you sure?"

"Yes, I'm sure. But how am I going to dig? With my hands?"

Silence.

Vito laughed. "You don't want to dig up a body, do you? You just want to add one."

Biagio took out a pistol. "I'm sorry, son. Get down on your knees."

"I knew it. I knew it from the first moment you came in through the door. And you know the strangest thing? I'm pleased. Better dead than in prison. And if I have to die, I want it to be you who does it."

"On your knees, Vito."

"All I wanted was for you to be proud of me, Biagio. I wanted to save Claudia, I wanted to protect the family."

If only you had known what Claudia did, son, you wouldn't be in this mess now, Biagio thought. But now it's too late.

"I wanted to protect all of you."

"Me too. Now get down on your knees. Don't make it any more difficult for me than it already is."

"The kid."

"You don't even need to say it. We'll take care of him."

"He had a son too."

"Who?"

"The guy I shot."

"I don't want to hear any more about that. Close your eyes, Vito."

"Promise me you'll kill the bastards who murdered Santo."

"They're already dead, they just don't know it yet."

"Okay . . . I . . . " he stammered, imploring Biagio with his eyes.

"Shh. I'll deal with everything. Now close them."

"Goodbye, chief."

Biagio screwed up his eyes and breathed out deeply. "Goodbye, son."

*

"Hey, you look upset," Claudia said as Giorgio came out of the bathroom, his skin still damp. "Is there something you want to tell me?"

"No. It's just the situation, that's all."

"How's Vito?"

Giorgio tried to avoid her gaze. "It's hard for him. But he'll get over it, don't worry."

"I'm scared, Giorgio. I'm scared that this time—"

"Shh. Don't even say it. We'll get through this somehow. We always do."

She gave him a firm hug, then punched him in the side, taking him by surprise. "Never try to lock me up again, asshole," she said with a smile.

"Go to bed, you idiot."

"Good night."

"'Night."

Giorgio watched her as she withdrew to the bedroom, wondering how she would react the following day to the news of Vito's death.

Biagio had Ronny drop him outside Oscar's villa. He got out of the car and told Ronny to wait for him.

He moved a few steps away and dialed Oscar's number.

"Biagio?"

"I'm outside your house. Come out. Alone."

A few minutes later Oscar came out and together they walked along the sidewalk.

"What's Ronny doing here?" Oscar asked.

"I had him come and pick me up."

"How did it go?"

They turned the corner, slipping into the dark side of the street. Biagio stopped.

"Did you make it look like a suicide?" Oscar asked.

"I didn't kill him."

"What?"

"Vito's alive, I pardoned him."

"Are you joking? How the fuck are we going to—"

Biagio turned and pinned him to the wall. "Listen to me carefully.

This is what I decided. I made him promise he wouldn't do anything else stupid, and when you have a gun pointing at your head you don't lie."

"How can you trust him after—"

"I trust him, period. He won't betray us, I guarantee it. I vouch for him."

"But I trust you, it's *him* I don't trust, dammit! You should have done it, Biagio. Or rather, I should have done it, for Christ's sake. You couldn't do it, could you?"

Biagio again saw Vito on his knees, his eyes closed, the tears falling down his cheeks. He saw the shaking in his hands and heard his heavy breathing. He felt the pistol becoming too heavy. And then, somehow, the presence behind him of Sonja, Santo, Stefano Zara, all people he had loved and who had been sacrificed on the altar of his ambition. Not even Ivankov's ring could chase away those ghosts.

"He won't betray us, got it?" he said, shaking Oscar. "And I'll tell you something else, don't you dare touch him. He knows he screwed up and he just wants to make up for it, and I'll help him to do that. Before, in the pub, you told me you would trust me. Well, keep trusting me, Oscar."

Oscar shook him off. "I think you're going to regret it, Biagio."

"If he makes one false move, you can kill him yourself. I promise you."

"Shit. Okay. Where is he now?"

Biagio replied with a wicked smile.

"Where is he?" Biagio asked the owner of the massage parlor, which became a brothel at night. It wasn't a classy place, like the Dolcenera owned by his former friend Donna, but something more rough and ready, a quick fuck and off you go.

The madam, a forty-year-old blonde in a négligé, swayed her hips ahead of him down a corridor lit by a muted red light, opened a door, and leaned against the door post.

"What's he celebrating?" she asked. "Birthday or promotion?"

Vito was fucking a black girl from behind, while a redhead and a blonde, kneeling on the bed, were playing at putting their breasts in his mouth and pulling him by the hair. The more he arched, intoxicated with pleasure, the more the panther tattoo on his broad back seemed to come alive. The girls were scratching him and he was panting like a wounded animal. At the foot of the bed, two empty champagne bottles and the butts of joints.

"Neither," Biagio replied. "He just needed to let off steam."

"Well, those three will help him do that, you can be sure of it. How about you? Don't you want to relax?" She put a hand on his crotch. "For you, it's on the house."

"Another time, darling," he said, slipping a roll of banknotes into her bra and moving her hand away. "I'll be back for him tomorrow morning. Tire him out."

"Don't worry. Tomorrow you won't recognize him."

Biagio slapped her ass, threw a last glance at Vito lost in the throes of lust, and left.

He had told him why he couldn't kill him. Because of the sense of guilt, of course. But also because he would be more useful to him alive. Neither of them had anything more to lose. Vito's fate was to end up in prison or die. Unless . . . unless Biagio involved him in his plan. And that was what he had done. As soon as he had told him what they would have to do and what Piscitelli expected of them, Vito had thrown up. When he had also revealed to him what Pugliese wanted, and what he was prepared to do to get it, Vito had started shaking like a leaf and thrown up again.

"It's madness!" he had said, wiping his mouth.

"You'll do whatever I tell you to do."

"We can't do something like—"

"Either that or a bullet in the head," Biagio had replied. "Choose."

Vito had chosen to follow him. But Biagio needed him level-headed, determined, vicious. He needed Vito as he had once been, not the ghost he was now. That was why he had taken him to the brothel. To clear his mind of the assault on the police car. To stop him thinking.

Before getting in his car, he sent Giorgio a text. Then he stared for a few moments at the screen saver on his cell phone, which showed him and Sonja together, embracing and smiling.

He went into the image gallery of the BlackBerry and deleted the photograph.

He started the car and drove home, trying not to think of anything. But every time he looked in the rearview mirror he seemed to see *her* eyes. And there was nothing he could do to delete them.

Giorgio read Biagio's text: *Changed my mind. Not doing it. I'll deal with him. I'll keep him close. Trust me.*

He heaved a sigh of relief and went back to bed.

The officer on guard hit the bars with his nightstick, waking Boran Paja with a start. "Wake up, handsome," he said, opening the cell door. "You have a visitor."

Two officers handcuffed him and escorted him upstairs to the Homicide offices. In the room where he had been interrogated a few hours earlier, he found Claudetti waiting for him, a cryptic smile on his face.

"Where's my lawyer?" Paja asked as soon as the two officers had forced him to sit down facing the inspector.

"He's taken the day off," Claudetti replied, motioning to the two officers to leave them alone.

"This violates my rights."

"One of your men we arrested has talked."

"Bullshit."

"He had a previous conviction for rape. Or rather, he assaulted a girl and at the time we weren't able to nab him. We had nothing on him. We had his fingerprints and his sperm, but no DNA or prints in our records to match them to."

"I don't understand what—"

"Yesterday the first thing I did was have your men's prints taken, along with samples of their DNA, all authorized by the prosecutor, in other words it was all above board, because according to the judge's report "the subject was within the physical parameters indicated by the victim of the assault," and boom! Your man's fingerprints matched the prints left on a stick the victim had used to defend herself. In less than a week I'll also have the result of the DNA test, and he knows there's no way how he'll get out of it then."

"I don't—"

"But you know what the clincher was? The girl he assaulted was the daughter of a carabiniere. Do you know what that means? How long do you think he'd survive in prison?"

"You're bluffing. Which of my men are you talking about?"

"You know."

"None of them will ever go against me. Nobody talked, it's impossible."

Claudetti smiled. "He hid that rape thing from you, didn't he?"

The door opened and Deputy Commissioner Carmen Brancato came in. "What has he decided to do?" she asked Claudetti. "Cooperate?"

"I don't think he's quite grasped yet what a mess he's in."

"You're both lying. And you're violating my rights. I want to talk with my lawyer."

"In a minute," the deputy commissioner replied. "Your friend is in a very uncomfortable position. Given the gravity of the charges hanging over him and the delicacy of the matter, he's decided to cooperate."

"He can't—"

"Witness Protection Program, Boran," Claudetti said. "He's telling us more about you scumbags in the Albanian Mafia than we really want to know."

"You're all—"

"Make it clear to this animal that we aren't joking," Carmen ordered, folding her arms.

Claudetti smiled sardonically. "Just what I wanted to hear."

He grabbed Paja by one arm, pulled him to his feet, and shoved him out of the room and into the corridor.

"Mazzeo will kill you for this, you know?" Paja said.

Claudetti grabbed him by the hair and pushed his face up against the window of another interrogation room, forcing him to look inside. There, some uniformed officers were trying to pull a man in civilian clothes off Klodian Uri—one of the men closest to Paja—who was on the floor, handcuffed, the right side of his face covered with an enormous hematoma, his lips split.

"The man they're holding back is the girl's father, the carabiniere," Claudetti whispered in his ear, squeezing Paja's against the glass. "And not just any carbiniere, he's a colonel. Now do you believe me, asshole?"

Paja cursed in his own language.

"If you're intelligent, you'll cooperate with us, and maybe I'll be able to put you in the program and save your ass."

"This may all be staged, you're trying to screw me over, I know you!"

"Before the colonel interrupted us, because obviously we informed him that we'd found the animal who raped his daughter, Klodian was telling us everything about how you went from trafficking girls to dealing cocaine. He listed names, dates, the murders you committed to wipe out the competition. And he's barely started. He'll tell us anything just to get our protection, because he knows that otherwise he's a dead man. As soon as the colonel leaves here he'll put a price on Klodian's head. How long do you think it'll take him to find someone inside ready to cut off your friend's dick?"

Paja did not reply.

"And how many crimes will he have pinned on you by the time he's finished talking? Because you have quite a few skeletons in your closet, don't you, Boran?"

"What do you want from me?" Paja asked after a few seconds.

"Mazzeo," Claudetti replied. "I want that son of a bitch."

Around five in the morning, Giorgio was awakened by Claudia's screams. He leaped to his feet, then stopped to listen. She was crying.

Nightmares, he thought. He wondered if he should check on her and give her a hug. He decided not to. Each person has to confront his own demons alone if he wants to defeat them. He had learned that from personal experience. And he wanted Claudia to defeat hers as soon as possible. So he went back to bed. As soon as she was asleep again, he got up and went to look at her. He covered her properly and lightly touched her face with his fingers.

You just have to hold on, girl, he thought. It'll pass.

He realized that he wouldn't get back to sleep again tonight, so he opened the sports bag he had brought from home, put on his sweatsuit and shoes, along with his bullet-proof vest and his .22, hiding everything beneath a thick hooded jacket, and left the apartment, locking Claudia inside.

He loved the silence and calm of the Jungle at night. It helped him to think. He was thinking now about why, when they had asked Biagio if he had any news of the Calabrians, he had lied, saying no. It might have deceived Oscar, but not him. And Biagio had lied again when he had asked him if there was anything he had to tell him. *No*, he had replied, as if determined to keep him in the dark, even though he had always been his shadow.

As he ran through the city, he wondered why Biagio was smothering them in lies. But he couldn't find an answer.

Untouchable

The boardroom at Headquarters, where press conferences were held, was filled with journalists. Unusually, Commissioner Giovanna De Rosa and Deputy Commissioner Nicola Santangelo, the head of the Crime Squad, did not sit down at the table. De Rosa picked up the microphone, looked around at the packed room, and began speaking.

"If you 'll all sit down, I think we can start . . . Silence, please . . . First, let me say that this is only a statement, therefore neither I nor the deputy commissioner are prepared to give interviews or answer your questions, although we will certainly do so later. As you all know, investigative work never stops, and right now we are hard at work trying to clarify all aspects of this sad business. Before anything else, I want to thank you for coming, given the absurdly short notice and the unusual hour, but we've been in the eye of the storm these past few days, and it's only now that all the pieces are in place and we have a fairly accurate picture of what happened . . . Could somebody please turn out the lights?"

She aimed a remote control at a projector and on the white wall behind her a photograph of Valerio Bucciarelli appeared.

"Today is a particularly painful day for all of us," she said, her face glazed with sorrow, "because we are mourning the death on duty of a colleague, a friend, and I would go so far as to say a hero. Deputy Commissioner Valerio Bucciarelli, who supervised the Narcotics division, was killed two days ago in an exchange of gunfire with a wanted drug trafficker of Nigerian origin named Oyo Balewa."

She pressed a button on the remote and the image of a young Bucciarelli in uniform appeared side by side with the mugshot of the Nigerian.

"Why did I say just now that Valerio was a hero? Because it's true. Our officer was working undercover to capture this fugitive, and on the night he was killed he was in a hotel room where he had arranged to meet with him for a drugs deal. Some details still have to be clarified, but something went wrong, and the deputy commissioner was attacked. When the team supporting him burst into the room, the exchange of fire, in which Valerio was fatally wounded, had already begun. His men tried to save him, and were unable to prevent the criminal from escaping. Unfortunately nothing could be done for Deputy Commissioner Bucciarelli . . . You can only imagine the enormous grief we are all feeling. Right now, we are in close contact with his family, his wife and his two wonderful children, whose daddy has been taken away from them. Personally, as a woman and as a mother, even more than as a law enforcement officer, I can assure you this is a very difficult time for us, one in which it is hard to find answers. As professionals and as human beings, we ask you to respect the privacy of that poor family . . . Valerio Bucciarelli died in the performance of his duty, with courage and contempt for danger. Our city and its police department have lost a great detective and a tireless worker . . . "

She broke off, overcome with emotion, and the journalists applauded.

Nicola Santangelo stroked her shoulder to console her. She passed him the microphone and asked him to continue.

"I'd also like to say a few words. Valerio was a trusted colleague of mine, and as you know, under his supervision the Narcotics division has achieved truly remarkable results. I share the grief over this loss, which is more human than professional, and send my sincerest condolences to Gloria and her children. But the law cannot and must not stop. Immediately after the murder—which a board of internal enquiry is still investigating—we launched a manhunt throughout the region, and I have to tell you that we almost experienced a second tragedy within our department. When two officers of the Traffic Police tried to detain the fugitive at a roadblock, he opened fire on them and drove on. This gives you some idea of the dangerous nature of the individual. This time, though, he didn't get away with it: the two officers gave chase, and there was a second exchange of fire, in which the criminal was killed. Obviously, this news is of no comfort to us. We would have liked to bring the murderer to justice, but his violent nature prevented us from doing so. Further details will be provided for you later, given the delicacy of the operation and given that other individuals will continue, operationally speaking, the late deputy commissioner's work. In fact, all my respect, as an officer of the law and as a man, goes to those men who find themselves engaged in proceeding in this investigative work in order that Valerios's sacrifice should not have been in vain. The Narcotics division, the Crime Squad, and the whole of the police department will ask the mayor and the prefect to declare a period of public mourning in order to honor the courage and dedication of a great servant of the State. Thank you."

Amid a roar of applause, the two of them left the room, refusing to answer the reporters' questions, most of which concerned the mysterious assault on a police car the previous day.

In a corner of the room, Andrea Claudetti found it hard to move even a single muscle. He couldn't believe they had really done it. He felt a burning sense of powerlessness. It was only now that he fully realized who he was fighting and what forces were at work.

Irene Piscitelli, who was behind him, watched him leave the room with reporters hot on his heels. There was a satisfied smile on her face, like that of a bashful theatre director hiding among the audience and watching the actors take the applause for his work.

Biagio woke with a strange sensation of danger. He sat up in bed and rubbed his eyes. As soon as he put his feet down on the floor, he became aware of the reason for this strange anxiety. The shotgun he had put down on the night table the previous night was no longer there. Maybe you hit it in your sleep and knocked it down, he thought, holding his breath and looking down at the floor in the morning light.

There was nothing there.

Under the bed, he told himself. He checked, but it wasn't there either. The rifle had disappeared. Who the fuck came in? How did they find me? Was it—

A noise from the living room gave him the answer. He went to the chair where he had left his jacket, hoping that whoever had taken the rifle hadn't noticed the holster with the pistol under the jacket.

Tell me it's there . . .

It was.

Biagio unfastened the safety catch and, trying to make as little noise as possible, cocked the pistol. He took a deep breath, trying to cut out the thousand questions whirling around in his head. He had to create a void, leave room for instinct. His life depended on it.

After a few seconds, he made up his mind. Slowly, he walked to the bedroom door, then slipped into the small corridor that led to the living room and advanced with his pistol held directly in front of him.

It could be one of the Serb hitmen, or one of the Calabrians who had come to get him. He had far too many enemies.

He had to wipe away a drop of sweat that had slid into one of his eyes, and in doing so his foot knocked over a broom he hadn't noticed in the semi-darkness.

Shit, he thought, trying to grab it as it fell.

He didn't succeed.

The broomstick hit the floor, and from the living room he heard the sound of someone getting up quickly and also knocking something over.

To hell with the surprise, Biagio thought, launching himself into the room, ready to open fire.

She had managed to persuade them to give her an office. And not just any office. A large room on the top floor complete with computer, air conditioning, and a panoramic view of the city. On her desk, she had all the material gathered about Biagio Mazzeo and his team. The more she read and sorted the papers, the more she smiled: Mazzeo didn't have the slightest idea of the shit that might fall on his head if he dared to screw her over.

Irene Piscitelli stood up, went to the window, and looked out at the fog-shrouded city. Cops called it the Jungle because of its high crime rate and the state of almost total neglect from which it suffered. The police department was short of at least three hundred officers, and lacked technical back-up and even parking spaces.

But she wasn't here to listen to their complaints. She was here to clean things up. She put the files away in a drawer and locked it. She did the same with the door when she left the room. She headed toward the elevator, and as she waited for it she wondered how Andrea Claudetti would react when he was ordered to release Boran Paja, the dealer he was trying to use to nail Mazzeo.

The Beretta's sights framed a tall sturdy man standing with his back to the door.

"Don't move!" Biagio cried, making him freeze before he could reach out his hand to the little table where he had placed the shotgun. "Put your hands up and turn around very slowly!"

The unknown man obeyed, and as he turned Biagio saw that he was smiling.

"So? Who do we have to crucify?"

Biagio heaved a sigh of relief. "You great big son of a bitch!"

"Are you always so nervous this early in the morning?" Carmine Torregrossa asked, recovering his can of beer from the table.

"Christ, Carmine, it's seven o'clock!" Biagio said with feigned contempt, lowering his pistol.

"What can I say?" Carmine retorted, knocking back a generous swig of beer. "The pineapple juice was finished."

Biagio dropped the Beretta on the couch, went up to him, and clasped him in a big hug, slapping his huge back.

"Fuck, you've lost weight," Carmine said.

"And you're even bigger, you fucking gorilla! You don't know how happy I am to see you. How was the journey?"

"Forget it. The whole flight they tried to palm bottles of perfume and all sorts of useless crap off on me. The only thing they didn't try to sell me was an anti-hemorrhoid cream."

Biagio smiled and punched his friend's broad chest—Carmine Toregrossa had been a rugby forward. "Look at those muscles, I'm envious, dammit. And you've even got a great tan, you bastard."

"I came straight from Paradise."

"So I see. Fuck, so I see. And what about this thing, you big queen?" Biagio pulled Carmine's little goatee beard.

"Oh, let that be. Women like it."

"You old dog . . . Coffee?"

"You bet."

"Coffee and beer, I can't believe it. You haven't changed a bit."

"But what about you? Since when have you been sleeping with a rifle? I had to take it away from you because I was afraid you wanted to fuck it, or have you gone over to the other side and are now sticking it up your ass?"

"Very witty. How the fuck did you get in?"

"What's his name—Luca?—gave me the keys."

Biagio nodded.

"Nice kid. He also painted an interesting little picture of the situation. You haven't lost the knack of getting into trouble, chief."

"No, I haven't, but this time I went too far," Biagio said, raising his eyebrows, as he put the coffee pot on the boil.

"You mean Domenico Pugliese?"

Biagio looked at him and frowned.

"I couldn't sleep so I read the file you had next to you."

"Yes, him and a thousand other problems."

"Well, to avoid any misunderstandings, I brought my hammer with me."

The two of them laughed like little boys.

As soon as the coffee was ready they drank it, exchanging jokes and indulging in shared memories that reaffirmed their friendship. It only took five minutes of chatter and leg-pulling to make them feel as if they had never been parted.

"Fuck," Biagio said. "I thought being transferred to Sardinia would have knocked some sense into you, but now I realize that's mission impossible."

Carmine smiled and then looked him straight in the eyes. "Now that we're done with the bullshit, tell me what I missed and who we have to kill."

This time there was no irony in his voice.

Biagio sustained his gaze for a few seconds, then nodded and told him everything.

Irene went downstairs to the high-security holding cells and asked the officer in charge which cell the Albanian was in.

"Oh, Paja isn't here. They took him upstairs last night and haven't brought him back."

"Last night?"

"Yes."

"Claudetti?"

"Yes, the order came from him."

"Shit," she said, running up the stairs, hoping that it wasn't too late.

*

"Santo was like a father to us," Carmine said, as soon as Biagio stopped speaking.

"Yes, he was."

"I'm sorry, my friend. About your girl, about Claudia, and all the others."

The thought of Claudia reminded Biagio that he had to call Paja. He tried to do so, but couldn't get through to him. Ever since they had released him, he had tried to call him to clarify the matter of Claudia and to make sure that Vatslava had received her punishment.

"Who's on our side in this?" Carmine asked, dragging him away from these thoughts.

"Augusta Barberi, the prosecutor who helped me nail Bucciarelli. Verri will do what he can, and then I don't know. Vito, obviously, but nobody else. I want to keep the others out of this, it's too dangerous. There are a lot of favors to call in, but I don't have a lot of time to do it. Those bastards are breathing down our necks. Including the National Crime Bureau."

"Whatever you have to do, Biagio, and I mean *whatever*, I'm with you, you know that."

Biagio sighed. "I'm sorry I had to call you in just to help me out of this mess."

"All these years, Biagio, you've been sending me money as if I'd never left. But even apart from that, I'm with you, I always have been."

"I know, and you know how much it means to me."

"But right now the question is: how the fuck do we get out of this situation?"

Biagio did have an idea, but he knew his friend wouldn't like it.

Irene walked into Claudetti's office but found it empty. She tried Homicide's interrogation room, but that was empty too.

"Shit," she said under her breath as she walked along the corridor.

She entered the office of Deputy Commissioner Carmen Brancato without even knocking.

"Yes?" Carmen said, taking off her glasses.

"Do you know who I am?"

"National Crime Bureau," was all that Brancato said.

"Precisely. Where is Boran Paja, the dealer arrested by Claudetti?"

"Why?"

Irene smiled. It wasn't a friendly smile. "So now you're asking me the questions?"

Carmen shrugged. "You're on my territory, in case you'd forgotten."

"Well? Or do I have to call the Commissioner to get an answer?"

"Paja was transferred to prison last night, as ordered by the examining magistrate."

Irene heaved a sigh of relief. If he was in prison, it'd be much easier to shut him up.

"You see?" Carmen said. "You didn't need to kick up such a fuss."

"Go to hell," Irene said, and walked out.

Carmen shook her head and picked up her cell phone.

"Andrea? . . . She was just here. You were right. I told her you took him to prison, that should give us a few hours' head start . . . Yes . . . Oh, Andrea? Try to make him talk, okay? I can't stand that bitch, I really want to stick it to her . . . Great. Talk to you later."

"Thank you," Olimpia said, taking the coffee the unknown woman was holding out to her. "Do we know each other?"

"No. I only just heard what happened. I'm sorry. Can I sit down for a second?"

Olimpia nodded. "I thank you. How on earth did they let you through?" She pointed to the entrance of the department, which was guarded by two uniformed officers.

"They know me."

"Are you a patient here?"

The unknown woman touched her bruised face and split lips. "No, I'm only here for a checkup."

"Who's the bastard who beat you like that?"

"Forget about it."

"Is he worth it?"

They looked into each other's eyes and immediately recognized each other as strong women who weren't easily beaten.

"Yes, as long as I let him believe he is."

Olimpia returned her smile. "I'm sorry."

"These things happen. Have you heard anything about your son?"

"The doctors are meeting now. They're supposed to be operating again later. Not that they hold out much hope. They told me not to have unreasonable expectations."

"Damn. What a ridiculous business. Do they know who did this to him?"

"They're working on it. But I have a kind of feeling there were other cops involved."

"Are you joking?"

"No. They attacked that car to free a policewoman they were taking to prison. I'm sure it was her colleagues."

"Incredible."

At that moment, the door of the room where the surgeons had been meeting opened and one of them called Olimpia over.

"Excuse me, I have to go."

"Of course. Do you need anything, clothes, things like that?"

"You're very kind, but my other son will bring me a change of clothes and the rest. Thank you. I haven't even asked you your name. I'm Olimpia."

"Donna. Pleased to meet you. Go, don't let me keep you. Best wishes for your son."

"Thank you."

They shook hands, and then Olimpia ran to the little room. Donna stared after her for a few seconds, then left, saying goodbye to the uniformed officers by name. They knew her well because she was the person closest to Biagio Mazzeo. Or rather, she had been for a long time. Now everything had changed. And Olimpia, in her eyes, wasn't only a distraught mother. On her personal chessboard, she might become a queen thirsty for blood. That was why Donna hoped that Carlo Messina wouldn't survive the operation.

Boran Paja had finished the pack that Claudetti had left him the night before. He tried asking the cop guarding him for a cigarette, but unfortunately he didn't smoke.

Shit, the only cop who doesn't smoke and he's with me, he thought, throwing himself back down on his bed, his body tingling with nerves.

He hadn't slept all night. His mind was a jumble of unpleasant thoughts and recriminations. Claudetti really had nailed him, and he'd finally agreed to apply for the Witness Protection Program. He'd had a preliminary interview with a deputy prosecutor named Corrado Tortora, who had tested his willingness to cooperate. He'd fed him a few things about Mazzeo as indication that he was in a position to send him and all his squad to prison, but then he had clammed up. He needed guarantees, black and white assurances about his future. A new life, a passport with a new identity. He had relatives in England and the United States who would be happy to receive him.

They had taken everything from him—cell phone, wallet, jewelry— and he hadn't been able to call his lawyer, let alone his men. Claudetti had taken him away after the interview and locked him up in this safe house, afraid that Mazzeo or one of his guys could get to him. When he had asked if he could speak to his lawyer, Claudetti had replied, "Why do you need a lawyer? If you don't trust me, how can you think to put your life in my hands? Because that's what you're about to do, Boran."

He'd had to agree with him. Klodian had defamed him, and Paja knew he was liable for multiple life sentences thanks to that son of a bitch. He had no choice but to betray Mazzeo. He knew that if he ended up in jail, Mazzeo would have him eliminated for that very reason, to stop him spilling the beans about him and his men.

As far as he's concerned, he thought, you're a dead man. As soon as he knows you're talking, he'll use every means possible to make sure you don't get to your trial alive.

The agreement with Tortora stipulated that his father, Dazin, be transferred from prison to a detention home where Mazzeo had no contacts. For years Mazzeo had been using his father to put pressure on him.

"What happens if you can't get me into the program?" he remembered asking Tortora and Claudetti.

"Then you'll have to give me something big that I can really use," Tortora had replied. "If you do that, I'll put in a request to transfer you to a special prison, with a big reduction in your sentence." It was clear from these words that he could screw him over as and when he wanted, because he was only a little paper boat adrift on the impetuous ocean of the law.

Claudetti had also asked him if he'd been behind the assault on the police car the day before. Paja didn't even know what he was talking about. He had then asked him a whole series of questions to figure out if he was lying, but Paja hadn't contradicted himself.

"Why, what happened?" he had asked Claudetti.

"Claudia Braga was arrested. Mazzeo and his men mounted an assault on the police car taking her to prison, released her, and fatally wounded one of the officers in the car."

Paja had said nothing. That was the same lady cop Mazzeo had asked him to . . .

"If he's prepared to do something like that for a colleague," that bastard of a cop had said, knocking the breath out of him, "imagine what he might do to shut the mouth of someone who could send them all to prison. I'm all you've got, Boran. Remember that."

Paja closed his eyes and tried to get to sleep.

"What do you mean he wasn't transferred there?" Irene yelled. She was in her office, speaking on the telephone with the warden of the penitentiary where they were supposed to have transferred Boran Paja.

"Like I said. We don't have any registration for—"

Turning white, Irene hung up. "The son of a bitch!"

She dialed another number: Biagio Mazzeo.

"Yes?"

"How much does Boran Paja know about you?"

"What? Why are you—"

"Answer me!"

"I don't know. Quite a bit."

"Enough to get you in trouble?"

"Will you tell me what's happening?"

"Answer, dammit."

"Yes."

"Okay. I'll deal with it. I'll call you back as soon as I've resolved this. I'm saving your ass, Mazzeo. I hope for your sake it's worth it."

She hung up without even waiting for his reply. Every minute was precious. Because if Paja wasn't in jail and not even the examining magistrate knew where he was, there remained only one option: Claudetti had admitted him to the Witness Protection Program.

When Biagio entered the office, Attorney Santini came to greet him. They embraced and Santini expressed his condolences for Sonja and Santo.

They sat down and Biagio got straight to the point. "You said you had something for me."

"Yes," Santini said, taking a document from a drawer and passing it over to him. "It's his will. He asked me to let you have it if anything happened to him. I thought it was best to give it to you as soon as possible, I don't know, just in case there was something, how shall I put it, compromising in it."

Biagio read it quickly. His heart almost stopped beating when he read the last sentences: *Take care of yourself, son. You owe me that. I've never told you this, but you've been like a son to me, and I'm proud of you. Drink a toast to me and stay alert.*

"Would you like me to leave you alone for a few minutes?" Santini asked, embarrassed, seeing Biagio's hands shaking.

Biagio shook his head. He placed the handwritten sheet on the desk and put his hands in the pockets of his jacket. "When did he give it to you?"

"This may seem strange to you, but it was just over a week ago."

Biagio nodded as if to himself.

"He left some property and a little cash to his wife and son, but you'll inherit the Bang Bang and most of the rest, Biagio."

"They aren't for me."

"I know. But you'll be the administrator of his property." Santini searched in a drawer. "To tell the truth, there's also another letter. This one. It's for her. Do you want to give it to her?"

Biagio felt uneasy, but he nodded and took the white envelope. "Have you already informed her?" he asked.

"Not yet. I wanted to see you first and hear what you wanted to do."

"You did the right thing."

Biagio continued staring at the white envelope. He felt his hands trembling inside his pockets, and a vein on his temple had begun to throb.

"I'm sorry, Biagio."

Biagio nodded. "Can I keep it?" he asked, picking up the will.

"Of course."

He folded it and slipped it into his wallet.

"A drop of scotch?" Santini asked, as he usually did when they met.

Biagio had always refused, but this time he accepted, slipping the envelope for Santo's daughter into the inside pocket of his jacket.

"What do you intend to do with her?" Santini asked after they had drunk.

"What he asked me: I'll take care of her. Only, this . . . this is a difficult time for me and the boys."

"I heard. If you don't mind me saying so, I think she ought to know her father is dead."

"He never told her he was her father. We always kept it from her."

Santini nodded, understandingly. "Sooner or later you'll have to tell her, Biagio, she's no longer a child."

"I know."

"What should I do with the money? Should I handle the forms for the inheritance?"

Biagio nodded slowly.

"Listen, about Sonja. Have you informed her relatives?"

"No."

"Someone ought to. Would you like me to do it?"

"Yes. I'd also like them to have some money, but I don't want them to know anything about me."

"I can tell them it was money she put aside, if you like."

"Okay. I'll send it to you through one of the boys."

"All right . . . I don't like that look, son. What's the matter?"

"Maybe it's time for me to make a will too."

Santini turned pale.

"Yes?" the Voice replied.

"We have a problem."

"We have or you have?"

"There's no time for these little games, this is serious."

"Let's hear it."

"Paja."

"Well?"

"Claudetti got in ahead of me. Witness Protection."

"Christ. How much does he know about *our* inspector?"

"Enough to bring him down."

"If he goes down, so will half the force, including you, you know that, don't you?"

"He won't go down."

"And how do you propose to solve the problem?"

"I need to know where he took him, which safe house he's in."

"Oh, God. You know that'd be going right outside the law, don't you?"

"I thought we were at war."

"We are."

"All's fair in love and war. Get me that address and I'll see about stopping him."

"Are you sure of what you're doing?"

"Do you have anyone else apart from Mazzeo who'd be able to stop the war?"

"No."

"Then get me that fucking address before it's too late."

"You know that any blame—"

"Will fall on me, I know. The address. That's all I ask of you if you want to see this operation through."

Silence.

"Well?"

"Speak to you soon."

Irene hung up and stared at the Jungle through the window of her office. If she didn't move fast enough, she thought, she would completely lose control of this assignment. And if that happened, not only Mazzeo and his pack would end up in prison. She would too.

Roberto Messina entered the bar where he had made an appointment with two colleagues from his squad. There they were, in plain clothes, waiting for him.

"Hi, any news?" asked Mariano, the younger of the two, embracing him.

"I spoke with my mother on the phone earlier. They're due to operate on him in less than half an hour. It's a delicate operation."

"Let's hope for the best," said Angelo, the oldest of all of them.

"Is there anything we can do?" Mariano asked.

Roberto looked at his two colleagues. The relationship that bound them was very close, molded by the uniform they wore and by an episode that had united them indissolubly.

It had all begun one evening when Mariano and Angelo had been ordered to take to hospital a dealer who had been wounded while resisting arrest. The orders were to keep an eye on him. And that was what they had done. A pity that the doctor had refused to allow them into the little room where the wounded man would be seen to. They had complained, but the doctor had kicked up such a fuss about violation of privacy and other crap like that, they had decided to drop it and wait for him outside. After more than half an hour's, wait they had become suspicious because of the lack of noise from inside the room. They had knocked at the door but there was no answer, just total silence. They had forced their way in and found the doctor and the two nurses on the floor and the dealer gone. They knew their blunder might cost them their jobs, so they had decided not to raise the alarm. Not right away, anyway. They had called Roberto and Carlo Messina and had asked them to help find the fugitive. The two brothers had been perfectly well aware of the risk they were running, but they had helped them.

It had actually been Carlo who had found the dealer as he was leaving his neighborhood in a custom-built car. There had almost been a shootout, but Carlo had put a stop to things before it got to that, and had then called his brother to help him take the scumbag to Headquarters. The two Messinas had saved their two colleagues' asses, and Mariano and Angelo had gotten away with a dressing-down and two months behind desks.

Now the time had come to repay that debt, and the two officers knew it.

"Yes, I might need a hand. The guys who . . . who shot Carlo may have been cops."

"What?"

"Mazzeo's men."

"Oh, shit," Mariano said.

"And what do you want to do?"

Roberto rubbed his forehead. "First, I need to be sure it was them. And if it was, I want to give them what they deserve."

Angelo and Mariano nodded, grim-faced.

"Can I count on the two of you?"

They exchanged tense looks, then Mariano said, "You don't even need to ask."

Squinting in the sunlight, Vito left the brothel. Biagio was waiting for him, leaning on the Alfa, his arms folded.

"Morning," Vito said. "I need a coffee. And also a new dick, I think."

"Christ, you stink of pussy from a mile away. How was it?"

"Intense," Vito said, getting in the car. "I already took a shower, do I really stink of pussy?"

With a little laugh, Biagio started the car.

"What does Oscar say?"

"That I have to keep you on a leash."

"After last night, leash, whip, and handcuffs are words I never want to hear again."

"Christ. Did they use a leash? Really?"

"Drop it, I'm trying to forget about it. So, has he pardoned me?"

"I've pardoned you. I hope it was worth it."

"I'll do whatever you want, Biagio. I swear."

"Good."

"Where are we going?"

"To organize a war," Biagio replied with a wink.

Biagio stared at the white envelope. He turned it over and wondered if he should read it, if he'd be doing right by Santo if he did. His conscience told him he shouldn't, but he had a strong desire to discover what his friend had wanted to write to her. It couldn't have been easy for him to write to a daughter who didn't actually know that he was her father, and Biagio wondered how his friend could have found the right words.

He succeeded in overcoming that impulse and put the envelope in his jacket pocket. For now, he knew he had to keep her far away from the Jungle. And above all from him. Anyone close to him was in great danger and he knew he couldn't protect everybody. But the problem wasn't her, it was her mother. Knowing her, as soon as she heard about Santo's death she would show up, asking for money. She didn't give a damn about her daughter, she was only interested in money to buy herself drugs. She said she was clean, but that was bullshit. Santo might have believed her, but he didn't.

That's all we needed, Biagio thought, sipping a large cup of bitter coffee as he waited at a café table for Vito to come back from the bathroom.

Carmine Torregrossa came in and headed straight for Biagio's table.

"Did you manage to get some sleep?" Biagio asked.

"Not much. I find it hard if there isn't anybody around to sing me a lullaby."

"Asshole. How do you find the SUV?"

"Quite a machine."

"Hey, I don't want to see even a scratch, got that?"

"As long as nobody shoots at it, you have no need to worry."

Vito returned and Biagio made the introductions. He was about to get onto the subject of Pugliese when Vito's cell phone started vibrating.

"Excuse me . . . Hello?"

Vito listened in silence for a few moments. His two colleagues saw a grimace of incredulity on his face, then one of anger. They exchanged questioning glances then looked back at Vito.

"Wait . . . No, don't do anything . . . I'll be right there . . . "

He hung up and stared at Biagio.

"What the fuck's the matter?" Biagio asked.

"Claudetti," he said in dismay. "He's having my apartment searched. That was my neighbor."

"What? Christ, tell me you don't have any coke there."

Vito lowered his eyes.

"Vito!" Biagio cried, getting to his feet and grabbing him by the back of his neck.

"No! I don't have anything!"

Biagio slapped him. "Good. That piece of shit."

"You think he found out something about—"

"No, definitely not. He couldn't have. It must be something connected with Bucc—"

Now it was Biagio's cell phone vibrated. He picked up, also listened for a few seconds, mumbled a thank you, then hung up.

"They're searching my place too," he said in a thin voice.

He looked in a daze at the other two, then tipped the table and all its contents onto the floor.

They had asked her if she wanted to see her son before he went into the operating room. Obviously she had said yes. They had made her put on a gown, gloves, shoes, and a mask, and only then had they let her in. "Just five minutes," they had said to her. "That'll have to do," she had replied.

Olimpia Messina approached her son's bed. He was as pale as a corpse. Dozens of tubes were attached to his body, and the machines that were monitoring him hummed continuously.

"Don't touch him," the doctors had said.

How can you tell a mother not to touch a son who may die? Olimpia had said to herself, seeing him so fragile and helpless. She would have given her life to save him.

"Darling," she whispered. "Can you hear me? You can't abandon us. You must hold on. For the child. For me."

In a few seconds, Carlo's whole life—Carlo who was so sensible, so lovable—flashed before her eyes. She had brought him up well, everybody told her that. And now someone was taking him from her.

She heard knocking on the glass. She turned and saw one of the doctors signaling to her that her time was up.

"Carlo," she said in a harder tone, turning back to her boy. "If you love me, if you love your son, you must hold on." Then, moving even closer: "Because if you die, I'll have all those who did this to you killed. All of them. Do you want me to become a murderer?" She touched his face lightly. "Hold on."

She placed a kiss on his lips and left the room. She hadn't shed a single tear. As far as she was concerned, it wasn't she who should be crying. It was the people who had made Carlo end up on that bed.

Giorgio read the name of the deputy prosecutor who had signed the search warrant: Corrado Tortora. He cursed. A tough magistrate who had it in for crooked cops, one of those who saw police officers not as colleagues, but as errand boys. Claudetti had chosen a good ally.

"Satisfied?" Inspector Diego Gatti asked with a smile.

"As always when I make myself a new enemy," Giorgio whispered, rolling the warrant into a ball.

"Do you have anything to declare?"

"Of course. Suck my dick."

Gatti laughed. "You're all going to end up inside, Varga."

"Bullshit," Giorgio snarled.

"Inspector, look here!" one of the officers called.

Gatti joined them in the bedroom. The officers had smashed through a plasterboard wall, behind which was hidden a steel rack containing dozens and dozens of automatic weapons—pistols, shotguns, submachine guns—along with ammunition.

"What are these?" Gatti asked Giorgio.

"They're for foxhunting," Giorgio said, at which all the officers present in the room burst out laughing. But it was true: the weapons were all licensed for sport, hunting or personal defense. The really interesting toys were elsewhere.

"Get the fuck out of our way, Varga," Gatti ordered brusquely.

Giorgio went back to the living room and answered a call from Vito.

"Giorgio, at last."

"You've chosen a bad moment, Vito," Giorgio whispered. "They're searching my apartment. I got a call from the building supervisor half an hour ago and—"

"Not just yours. They're searching all our places, Claudia's, Santo's, Biagio's and mine."

"Fuck. Claudetti?"

"Yeah."

"What fucking reason does he have? How did he manage to get authorization?"

"They arrested Boran Paja."

Giorgio froze, at a loss for a moment. Then he walked out onto the landing. "Are you sure?"

"Yes. Listen, Biagio said not to kick up a fuss, to let them carry on without provoking them, he'll sort it all out, understood?"

"Yes."

"Talk to you later."

Giorgio hung up. First the blanket searches, now the arrest of Paja.

Did Claudetti's line of attack depend entirely on him, he wondered. I hope not, or we're really fucked.

"Hello?"

"I thought you were going to deal with it."

"What the hell are you talking about?"

"Claudetti. He's had all my men's homes searched, including mine."

"Shit. Tell me you don't have drugs lying around that would incriminate you."

"No, we're fine on that. But a blanket search . . . What the fuck's going on, Piscitelli?"

"I'm dealing with it. He won't get anywhere, believe me. You just think about what you have to do."

Biagio hung up and got back in his car. Vito closed the file on Pugliese.

"Christ," he said in a low voice, looking up at his chief. "Have we really got this son of a bitch breathing down our necks?"

"You ain't heard nothing yet," Carmine said.

"How do you mean?"

"There's only one way to stop these people," Biagio said. "And you won't like it."

Walking into his apartment, Biagio didn't feel anger so much as a sense of nakedness, embarrassment, almost shame. Even though he didn't spend much time here, this was still his home. Now it was upside down. They had ruined furniture, trampled on the memories of a lifetime. They had searched through his underwear, torn the kids' drawings off the walls, slashed open the mattress, and thrown all his clothes on the floor.

The kitchen was a disaster: on the floor were broken plates and glasses, as well as food that had been thrown there. He even thought he could smell the drug-sniffing dogs they had brought in, hoping to find even a few grams. They had found nothing.

Claudetti's men had tried to humiliate him by turning his home upside down and pissing on his clothes: the acrid stench of urine was unmistakable. That did make him angry.

Biagio sat down on his exercise bench and tried to slow his breathing. In the past he would have killed over a humiliation like this. But now he had to put his ego aside.

He removed a few barbells, lay down on the bench, and began a series of lifts. His muscles were burning, but it was what he needed. Pain, effort, adrenaline. They were escape valves for the anger and hate he had inside.

Having finished the last series, he had a look to see if there was anything salvageable among his clothes. He stuffed some underwear and a few pairs of jeans into a sports bag. The suits—they were what really concerned him, given that Sonja's funeral was the following day—were the things those cops had most enjoyed pissing on.

"You can all go fuck yourselves!" he cried, kicking the mattress.

As he sat down behind the wheel of the Alfa, his BlackBerry vibrated. It was Oscar.

"What's up?"

"Carlo Messina, the officer in the car. He didn't make it. He died in the OR a few minutes ago."

Biagio half closed his eyes and laid his head back against the headrest. "Christ . . . "

"This changes everything, Biagio."

Biagio found it hard to breathe. "No, it doesn't change a damn thing," he replied, icily. "Keep doing what I told you."

"A cop has died, Biagio."

Biagio hung up and rubbed his head with his hands.

It's done, my friend, he told himself. If you want to save them, you have to step over that corpse too, you have no alternative.

He took a deep breath and started the car.

She was kneeling on the floor, her hands on the edge of the toilet, head bent forward. Giorgio was holding her hair back to stop it getting dirty.

"Are you feeling any better?" he asked.

She was still retching and panting, but she nodded.

A few minutes earlier, he had told her that the young officer had died. He and Biagio had decided that it was better she find it out from them than from the TV news.

He helped her get to her feet and wash her face.

"It's my fault."

"Don't talk crap, you're not to blame."

Claudia hugged him, wetting his T-shirt with her tears.

"We'll sort it all out, sweetheart," he said, stroking her hair.

"We killed a cop. What have we become?"

Giorgio couldn't summon up the courage to answer that question.

Andrea Claudetti forced his way through the mob of his uniformed and plainclothes colleagues outside the mortuary. It didn't take him long to spot Roberto Messina, the dead officer's brother, since everybody was hugging him and expressing their condolences.

Claudetti approached one of the older officers, whom he knew, and they exchanged a few words, then he walked over to the hospital's parking lot, where he lit a cigarette and smoked in silence.

Roberto joined him a few minutes later, followed by Mariano and Angelo. "Inspector Claudetti?" he asked.

"Call me Andrea," Claudetti replied, holding out his hand. "My condolences. I'm really sorry."

"Thank you. Beppe told me it was urgent."

"Yes. I know now's not the best moment, but—"

"Biagio Mazzeo. Beppe said you had information about him."

Claudetti could see the spark of vengeance in the young man's eyes. From the pocket of his jacket he took the A4 sheets of Bucciarelli's file on Narcotics and passed them to him.

"I don't have proof, but I think it was Mazzeo's men who attacked the police car and killed your brother."

Roberto stared at him in astonishment.

"These notes are by Deputy Commissioner Bucciarelli. He was investigating his own men, but Mazzeo killed him to keep him quiet. Don't believe the bullshit spouted by De Rosa: Bucciarelli didn't die a hero. He died because he was investigating Mazzeo. He died because of these papers. They're doing everything they can, short of breaking the law, to isolate me, but I tell you this, I'm going to nail that bastard."

"Why do you say he's behind it? What makes you think that?"

"The fact that it was Claudia Braga in that car, for a start. Read the file and then you'll have an idea who these sons of bitches are. You'll realize that what happened is perfectly consistent with their way of operating. They aren't cops, they're criminals."

"Why are you telling me all this?"

"Because your brother didn't deserve to die. I can't let that pass. I want to put those bastards behind bars, every single one of them. And I may have a card up my sleeve that'll help me do just that. But I need a hand."

"I don't—"

"I'm not expecting you to trust me immediately. Read the file, and ask your older colleagues about me, and about Mazzeo and Bucciarelli. Then if you think, as I do, that that bastard is behind Carlo's death, call me."

He held out a business card. Roberto took it and gave it a quick glance.

"I'm really sorry. Forgive me for disturbing you at this time, but I felt I had to."

Roberto nodded.

She was already standing there waiting for him, staring at the lights of the city, arms folded, her loose hair blowing in the wind.

Biagio got out of the car and approached her.

"Claudetti," he said, looking down at the Jungle below them. "Have you dealt with him?"

Irene took out the frequency scrambler and switched it on. "Not yet."

Biagio opened his eyes wide. "What the fuck do you mean, *not yet*?"

"A cop died, Mazzeo. An innocent young man who was simply doing his job. He was carrying out orders, orders that came from *me*."

"What can I do about that? You know perfectly well I was in Headquarters when that happened. I'm sorry for him but—"

Irene turned and stared into those icy eyes of his. "I'm about to save your ass from Claudetti. I'm covering for you *again*. I can do that for the higher goal, of course. But I can't just pass over a homicide for which I feel responsible."

"What do you want me to tell you?"

"Look me in the eyes and tell me you had nothing to do with the assault on the police car."

Biagio held his breath and looked her straight in the eyes. "I had nothing to do with it."

"And your men?"

"Neither did they. Christ, what the hell are you thinking?"

"Are you sure?"

Biagio nodded.

"I want to hear you say it."

"Neither I nor my men had anything to do with that officer's death, happy now? It was Pugliese's doing, and now you're wasting my time. That son of a bitch has abducted one of my officers and I don't want him to kill her."

Irene nodded. "Then go and do what you have to do."

"Get that ball breaker off my back. Because if you don't do it, I'll be forced to, and believe me you wouldn't like it."

He got back in his car and drove off.

Irene stood there in silence, staring at the lights of the city. She switched off the machine and dialed a number on her cell phone.

"It's me . . . Yes . . . We can go ahead . . . Yes, state funeral . . . I said we can go ahead. Get me that address."

She hung up and dried a tear the wind had driven down her cheeks.

"Ma?"

Olimpia looked up at her son.

"There's someone here who'd like to see you. Her name is Donna."

Olimpia nodded. "Show her in."

Roberto admitted the woman with the bruised face to the mortuary, which was empty now except for his mother, still sitting on a wooden bench.

"The undertakers took him away," Olimpia whispered.

Donna took her hands in hers. "I know we don't know each other but, believe me, if there's anything I can do, anything . . . "

"Thank you."

"I mean it, if you like I can deal with the paperwork," she said, indicating a bundle of documents lying on the bench. "I've done it before, unfortunately."

Olimpia gave a weary smile and picked up the papers. "These aren't the documents from the undertakers. Those I already dealt with. Do you see this? My son says this is the man who killed Carlo. Look at those eyes."

Donna stared at the photograph of Biagio and her breath failed her. "Why do you have his photograph? What do you intend to do?"

"Do you really want to know?"

"Of course."

"No, better not. You wouldn't like it."

"I know what you're thinking and I think I can help you," Donna said.

He had agreed with Luca that he would be present at Sonja's cremation. He owed it to her. He felt he had to accompany her on that final journey.

But he had had to change his plan at the last moment when one of Pugliese's men had called him. "Mazzeo, time's passing, where's our cocaine?"

"I still have two days," he had retorted. "Leave me alone."

From a distance, Biagio flashed his headlights so as not to startle his men, and a few seconds later parked in front of the farmhouse.

Cristiano, Ronny and Franco were on guard outside. They greeted him and asked him how come he was there.

"I wanted to be sure you're not blowing all that coke," he said ironically as he walked in. Ronny and Cristiano remained outside while Franco accompanied him down into the cellar.

Halfway down the stone steps Biagio saw the huge table with the blocks of cocaine on it. It was an incredible quantity, and seeing it all together was frightening.

Biagio walked around the table, looking at it as if hypnotized.

"Crazy, isn't it?" Franco said. "You could feed a city."

"You bet," Biagio replied, without taking his eyes off the drugs.

"I never thought we'd pull it off."

"We were great, Franco."

At what price, though? Biagio thought. Two hundred kilos of extremely pure cocaine, stained with the blood of dozens and dozens of people, including Santo.

Those two hundred kilos for which they hadn't had any qualms about killing and breaking the law could easily become at least eight hundred if they could find someone good who was prepared to cut it. Eight hundred kilos of coke at retail price meant something like a hundred and sixty million euros. Now that the Calabrians from the South had cut off supplies to those in the North, there would be an incredible demand for coke in the Jungle in a few days. And they had the supply. It was there, in front of his eyes, in all its snow-white splendor. What to do? Submit, give it up, and then give themselves up, or raise their heads and fight?

A hundred and sixty million euros, Biagio, the cocaine seemed to whisper to him. With that money you can build an empire.

"Is there reception for cell phones down here?" he asked Franco.

"Fortunately yes."

"Perfect," he replied, letting his fingers glide over the cocaine as if it was a beautiful naked woman. "Franco?"

"What is it, Biagio?"

"Do you trust me, my friend?" he asked without turning around.

"Of course, Biagio. What the fuck are you talking about? Why shouldn't I trust you?"

"Have I ever disappointed you, Franco?"

"No, Biagio, never," Franco replied, embarrassed.

"So if I tell you that nothing will happen, and that you'll die old and rich, do you believe me?"

"Of course, Biagio."

"Good. Go home, Franco."

"What?"

"Tell the others to do the same. Take your things and go home. Rest."

"But . . . what about here?"

"I'm here."

"Alone?"

"Yes. Nothing will happen tonight, don't worry."

Franco stared at him in confusion, then shrugged. "Whatever you want."

After a few minutes Biagio heard the cars start up and drive away, leaving him alone with the cocaine.

Surrounded

Oscar closed the door of the garage, glanced at the Harley, and threw himself down on the bench. He needed physical exercise to get rid of the tension.

After half an hour of weights, he heard someone knocking at the door. "Pull it up, it's open," he called out, wiping the sweat off him with a towel.

Ronny and Cristiano, his two subordinates in the Traffic Police, came in.

"Hi, boys, everything okay?" he said, grabbing a dumbbell and starting a series of biceps exercises.

They leaned against the wall. "Will you tell him or shall I?" Ronnie asked Cristiano.

"Tell me what?" Oscar asked, breaking off his exercises.

"Biagio. He came to the farmhouse last night. On his own. He said we could go, that he'd stay there and guard the coke."

"He did?"

"Yeah," Cristiano replied.

"Why would he do that?"

The two young officers shrugged.

"Who was there with you?"

"Franco. Biagio talked to him."

"Is he still asleep?"

"Yes."

Oscar nodded. This was quite strange. He picked up his cell phone and tried to call Biagio. "He's switched it off," he said, more to himself than to them.

"Did we screw up by leaving him on his own, chief?" Ronny asked.

I hope not, Oscar thought.

"You know, we thought maybe he needed it, after Sonja and Santo . . . "

"Take turns here, and don't tell anybody about this for now. Maybe you're right, he just needed to be alone and he went there to keep guard, because he has insomnia, and let you catch up on your sleep."

"Right," the boys replied. "So what do you want to do?"

"I'm going to him to see what's happening," Oscar said, standing up and putting on a sweatshirt.

"We're coming with you."

"No, I prefer you to stay here. The safety of the family before anything else."

The two of them looked at each other, then nodded.

Once they had left, Oscar sat down on the bench and put his hands together.

Why did Biagio want to be alone? he wondered. He didn't have a good feeling about it. He took a steel strongbox the size of a shoebox down from a shelf. He tapped out the combination on the keyboard, and when it opened took out a large semiautomatic pistol and slipped it in one of the pouches on the motorbike the dealer had given him to replace his beloved Harley, destroyed a few weeks earlier by Ivankov's men. He tried again to call Biagio, but the cell phone was still off. Then he called Giorgio.

"Oscar?"

"Hi, son. I don't want to scare you but I have a nasty feeling"

"What do you mean?"

"Biagio went to the farmhouse last night and sent Ronny, Cristiano and Franco away, saying he'd keep guard over the load by himself. The boys did as he said. In itself, that's strange enough. But when you add that now he has his phone switched off, it starts to be quite worrying. Do you know anything about it?"

"No, nothing."

"Okay. Listen, I'm going there to see what's going on."

"I'm coming too. I'll see you there."

"All right."

Oscar sat there for a few seconds, thinking, then got up, put on a leather jacket, and pulled up the door.

A hundred yards from the farmhouse, Oscar stopped and pushed up his sunglasses to see more clearly. He hadn't been mistaken. There was no vehicle parked near the farmhouse.

What the fuck's going on? he thought, taking his pistol from the bag and releasing the safety catch. Behind him he heard a 4x4 approaching. He turned and saw it was Giorgio.

"There's nobody around," Giorgio said through the car window as soon as he drew level with his friend.

"Right. I smell a trap."

"Are you armed?"

"Only this toy," said Oscar, showing him the pistol.

Giorgio slapped one hand on the steering wheel. "Get in. We'll go closer in this."

"Now I feel better," Oscar said, picking up the shotgun Giorgio had left on the passenger seat.

They parked some twenty yards from the building and got out with their weapons in their hands. They split up and walked around the stone colonnade. There was nobody in sight. They met up again at the entrance, and made up their minds to go in. The door was open. Giorgio pushed it without making a noise and went in, pointing his pistol in front of him. Oscar followed him in, shotgun raised. They descended the steps, but by the time they were halfway down they'd already realized that there was nobody there. Nor was the cocaine.

"We can't hide this from the others," Oscar said.

"I know."

"And believe me, they won't like it."

Giorgio nodded. He knew Oscar was right. At a difficult time like this, the disappearance of the cocaine could be the last straw, the thing that set them against each other.

He was awakened by the sensation that someone was watching him. He wasn't wrong. Claudetti was sitting at the one table in the room, eyes fixed on him.

"Fuck, you scared the life out of me," Paja said, sitting up in bed and rubbing his eyes.

"Slept well?"

"Go fuck yourself. Well, any news?"

"Deputy Prosecutor Tortora is talking right now with the people who matter. They're evaluating your case."

"I hope they get it right."

"Are you sure you can give me what I promised them?"

"You can count on it."

"It'd be best for you, because I've made sure you have an incentive to cooperate."

Paja frowned. "What do you mean?"

"I've made sure Mazzeo knows you're cooperating with me."

Paja turned white and leapt to his feet. "Why the fuck did you do that?"

"Sit down."

"You've sentenced me to death, you piece of shit!" Paja yelled, going right up to Claudetti. "Do you know who we're talking about? Do you know the kind of things he can do?"

Claudetti sent him sprawling back on the bed with a left jab to the jaw. "I told you to sit down."

Paja touched his jaw and gave him a look full of hatred.

"Now I'm sure you'll cooperate. And you'd better tell me everything, you know why? Because you're right: Mazzeo would be willing to do anything to stop you testifying against him. That's why if you want to save your ass the only way is to talk, to say everything, anything, even the most insignificant thing." He threw him a notebook and a pen. "There. I advise you to start writing to refresh your memory."

"You're a son of a bitch," Paja said, shaking his head contemptuously.

"Write. And do it quickly. Every minute that passes is a minute of freedom you give that bastard, while you're stuck in here like a rat in a trap."

Boran took the notebook between his fingers, lifted it in the air, and dropped it to the ground. "I can't write," he sneered.

Claudetti smiled and took a small voice recorder from his pocket. "I expected that. That means I'll have to transcribe it."

Paja swallowed. "Once Mazzeo's behind bars—"

"Hey, slow down," Claudetti said, with a nasty little smile on his lips. "This isn't just about Mazzeo."

"What do you mean?"

"The prosecutor and I have realized that the only way to save your ass was to raise the stakes."

"In other words?"

"His squad. We want to put them all inside for association with organized crime."

The first was Manuel. And he got himself a slap for it.

"Say that again, and as God is my witness I'll tear your balls off with these hands!" Vito said, on the point of hitting him again.

Giorgio pushed him away. "Keep your voice down! The kids are upstairs. And keep your hands where they are."

"I know you're all thinking it," Manuel said, defending himself. "It's clear he took the coke. Two things could have happened: either he's run away and plans to keep it for himself, or he's given it to the Calabrians. The stress has driven him crazy! Whatever he's done, he didn't consult us. What do you call that?"

Carmine, who had remained silent so far, sunk in his armchair, now stood up. With two quick strides he reached Manuel and hit him with a punch to the jaw so strong that Oscar thought he had killed him.

"Christ, if you broke his neck, we're fucked!" Luca said, going to the aid of his colleague.

Vito smiled, fascinated.

"Goddammit, I'd rather die than listen to any more of this bullshit!" Carmine cried, glaring at all of them. "The thought that he betrayed you shouldn't even cross your mind, you fucking ingrates! After all he's done for you? After you screwed up the way you did? You have to be thankful he didn't dump the lot of you, you sons of bitches."

Looking at the gleam in Carmine's eyes, Giorgio understood now how he could have tried to crucify that rapist. "Manuel was scared and didn't think before he spoke," he said, going up to him. "Nobody here is saying that Biagio betrayed us or robbed us. But you have to admit it's very strange. Just as it's strange that he's not answering his phone and we can't get in touch with him."

"He knows how to take care of himself," Carmine replied.

"I'm not saying that," Giorgio said, without taking his eyes off his.

Oscar intervened and separated them with some difficulty. "Giorgio's right, Carmine. Nobody's accusing Biagio, but we have to do something to find him or to figure out what the fuck's going on. Vito, have you called Headquarters?"

"Yes. Nobody there has seen him."

"And there was no sign of him at his apartment or Sonja's," Giorgio said.

"Shit!" Oscar cried. "Where the fuck is he?"

Silence fell over the room.

It was broken by Giorgio. "There was nothing to suggest there'd been any shooting. And you all know that Biagio wouldn't just let himself be taken, without retaliating."

"Maybe he doesn't want to be found," Luca said.

"Or maybe he's testing us," Carmine said.

A dozen pairs of eyes turned to him like laser gunsights, but he didn't lower his gaze a fraction of an inch. It only took him a moment to realize they didn't trust Biagio anymore.

When the tension had dropped, Carmine moved aside and sent Biagio a text telling him that the meeting had gone badly.

Just as I imagined. Tell Oscar and Giorgio I want to see them for lunch, Biagio replied. Carmine wondered what the hell Biagio had in mind, and why he had asked him to hold this pointless meeting in the first place.

Someone knocked at the door. Claudetti told Paja to shut himself in his room.

Paja held his breath.

Claudetti heard a woman's voice. He smiled and opened the door, admitting a tall, slim, beautiful young woman, smartly dressed, with long chestnut hair and gray eyes. He winked and led her to Paja's room.

"Hey," the Albanian said. "You brought me a hooker. Thanks, it was a nice thought." He went up to her. "What's your name?" he asked, stroking her silky hair.

She kneed him in the balls and shoved him to the floor.

"Boran, let me introduce Inspector Ariana Manisci from the Organized Crime division."

"Bitch," Paja gasped, from the floor.

Ariana responded with a kick to the stomach. "Shut up, worm," she said in Albanian.

"Ariana is of Albanian origin, as you just heard. She has two degrees, and works in liaison with Europol. I imagine that, unlike you, she can write. She's a trusted officer and is giving me a hand with the interrogations of your men, those who can't speak Italian."

"And why the fuck have you brought her here?"

"Don't you get it yet?" Claudetti said with a smile, pulling him up and straightening his crumpled clothes.

"No."

"If I'm going to nail Mazzeo and his Narcotics squad for criminal association, I need the cooperation of colleagues who deal with organized crime. To be specific, you're helping them and Deputy Prosecutor Tortora to break up the Albanian Mafia in this city, and they're helping me to put Mazzeo and his squad behind bars. I know the Narcotics division is in cahoots with Albanian criminals, and you're one of the biggest. Criminal association and links with foreign criminal organizations: those are the kind of charges that give the judges a hard-on, and I want them to come in their underpants."

"Have you gone crazy? That wasn't the agreement!"

"The agreement has changed. If you want to be in the Witness Protection Program, that's what you have to give us. Unless you want to give up the idea, but then you'd have to face a trial for murder, drug trafficking, and slavery, or alternatively . . . "

"What?"

". . . Mazzeo and his men."

"You're crazy if you really think—"

"Seems to me he doesn't want to understand," Claudetti said to Ariana.

With feline speed, Ariana twisted Paja's right arm behind his back and pushed him out of the room.

"Open the door!" she ordered the plain-clothes officer on guard, who hastened to obey.

She shoved Paja outside, making him fall on the sidewalk. He stared at her, disoriented, as he got back on his feet.

"There. You're free. Now go deal with Mazzeo and your family. I e-mailed them your request to enter the Witness Protection Program, with your signature at the bottom. I bet your uncle Adem can't wait to take you in his arms. Good luck!"

She closed the door.

Claudetti looked at her admiringly. "Coffee?"

"Great idea."

When the coffeemaker started purring, they heard knocking at the door.

Ariana opened and cried, "There's a little orphan here, looking for a home!"

Boran Paja glared at her.

"So, did you think it over?"

Paja lowered his eyes.

Ariana Manisci opened wide the door and stood aside. "Come in, you piece of shit."

From the rented BMW, Irene Piscitelli watched Boran Paja go back inside the safe house. She took out her cell phone, dialed a number, and identified herself. "I need to know who signed the form for the use of an unmarked black Fiat Bravo."

"License number?" the operator asked.

She gave it to him.

"Wait a moment."

As she waited, Irene filled the time by touching up her make-up in the rearview mirror.

"Special Agent Piscitelli?"

"Go ahead."

"Inspector Ariana Manisci."

"Division?"

"First."

"Organized Crime."

"That's right."

"Thanks a lot," Irene said and hung up. Organized Crime means only one thing, she thought. Claudetti is taking his investigation up a notch.

She shook her head and texted the address of the safe house to a number on her contact list. She liked Claudetti, with his unquenchable thirst for justice. But she wasn't a social worker: she was a police officer who had realized that concepts like justice and law are very relative, especially when you reach a certain level of power.

She threw a last glance at the house, then set off for her hotel. This assignment was becoming more stressful every day, she told herself. She really needed a relaxing massage.

As he waited for the tailor from whom he'd bought the suit for the funeral to fix the hem of the pants, Biagio went into an Argentinian restaurant and ordered beef ribs with a side order of grilled vegetables. A song was playing by an Italian girl singer Biagio didn't know, and he immediately fell in love with it. The voice reminded him of Nina Simone and Billie Holiday, and the swinging, soulful song made forget his grim thoughts.

When Giorgio, Oscar and Carmine came in, he was dipping a piece of bread in the red juice of the beef.

His men sat down around the table.

"I think the animal rights people are going to kill you before the Calabrians," Oscar said to break the tension, pointing to his plate.

"Especially if you keep eating the animals while they're still alive," Carmine said, eyebrows raised.

Biagio smiled. "Anyone wants a bite, go ahead and order, it's on me. But not Carmine."

Carmine laughed, and started leafing through the menu.

Oscar shook his head. "After what happened last night, I couldn't eat a thing. I pass."

"You?" Biagio asked the others, ignoring Oscar's barb.

"Nothing, thanks."

"I will," Carmine said. "What he had, plus a mountain of fries with mustard and mayonnaise."

"A mountain," Oscar said. "Forgive him, he read too many Tex Willer comics when he was a child,"

"When he was a child? Shit, he still reads them, are you joking?"

"Now I understand a lot," Giorgio said.

Biagio looked at his colleagues and drummed with his fingers on the table. After the wave of laughter, their faces had turned grim again. "Well? I thought you told me you would trust me?" he began in a cold tone staring at Oscar and Varga.

"Where's the coke, Biagio?" Oscar asked.

Biagio stared at him and nodded. "The coke, the coke . . . " he repeated as if to himself. He took out his pistol, placed it on the table, and slid it toward Oscar. "Why don't you point that at me and ask me again, while you're about it?"

Carmine shook his head. "I told you guys."

"Come on, Biagio."

"Don't give me that. Just point the gun at me, Oscar. Do it."

"Why do we always have to make spectacle of ourselves?" Giorgio cried in exasperation.

"Will you point it at me, Inspector?" he asked Giorgio.

Giorgio put his hand on the pistol and slid it back to Mazzeo.

"Biagio," he said, "nobody's accusing you. But put yourself in our shoes: we're nervous, we're forced to hide in Oscar's house with our families, I have to be a guard dog to Claudia, we're scared, and we don't know anymore—"

"You don't know what?" Biagio said irritably, putting the Beretta back in its holster.

"If . . . if we're doing the right thing."

"The right thing? Put it this way: the best thing to do isn't always the right thing."

"What the fuck does that mean?" Carmine asked.

"You told me you would trust me. Either keep trusting me or grow some balls and tell me to back off." He looked at them in turn with his Arctic blue eyes. "Well?"

Oscar and Giorgio nodded.

"Incredible, I'm burying my girl this afternoon, and my men are accusing me of stealing the cocaine. What a fucking day!"

"Don't take it like that, Biagio," Giorgo said. "We—"

Biagio raised one hand to silence him. "Let's stop right there. That cop who was killed, Messina, Carlo Messina. I spoke with the people upstairs and managed to divert suspicion from us to the Calabrians, don't ask me how."

"So we're out of trouble now?" Oscar asked.

"Yes, but let's stay on our guard. We still have the Calabrians to deal with."

"Still no word from them?"

"No," Biagio replied. "By the way, I managed to get assigned a two-officer patrol car to keep an eye on Oscar's house twenty-four seven, with three shifts. Obviously, it isn't much, but at least it's a signal that may discourage them from showing their faces. Was everything okay last night?"

"Yes," Oscar replied.

"Good. Oscar, a couple of things: the men who were supposed to be guarding the load, move them to the villa. There'll be too many of them, but it's better that way. Here's three thousand euros. It's my own money. Please don't make that face. Use it for the family: buy new games, do a little shopping, get a few gifts for the girls. Hire some fucking magicians or clowns to entertain the kids, okay?"

"I can't accept it, because we don't take—"

"Christ, take it, period. Another thing. The weapons we used for the job—"

"Look, I know you told me to get rid of them but in all this mess we haven't had time yet."

"Good for you. Move them to your house. Lock them up in the cellar. I want them all there."

"Why?"

"I want to have them all within reach in case something goes wrong."

"But it's an arsenal."

"Do you think we're defending ourselves from a bunch of Cub Scouts?"

Carmine laughed.

"Okay. Look, I'm sorry about this business with—"

"Forget it. We have to move on. Go now, I'll see you in church."

"Biagio, Claudia told me to give you a hug. She's sorry she couldn't come."

"Thanks. Tell her I'll call her later. Now go."

Biagio remained alone with Carmine. "They don't trust me anymore," he said.

"With all due respect, partner," Carmine replied between mouthfuls, "you aren't exactly doing all you can to gain their trust."

"The less involved they are in this business, the better it is for all of them. I'm just protecting them."

"They don't see it that way, they feel excluded."

"I can't do anything else now."

Carmine shrugged and bathed his steak in spicy oil.

"We have to talk, Carmine."

"Mmm. I know that tone."

Biagio gave a wicked little smile and told him what he had in mind. Listening to him, Carmine lost his appetite.

The church was practically empty. It had been Biagio who had wanted it that way. He had no desire for either a flashy ceremony or demonstrations of false affection, with people just there to show their faces and look good in his eyes. What he needed was to know that his people were with him. And they were all there, apart from Claudia and Zeno. The ten officers recruited by Mirko were watching the house, along with the patrol car with two officers on board. The whole pack was here.

The mass had been going on for less than five minutes when Biagio heard murmurs behind him. He turned and saw that some of his men were pointing to someone: Donna, his childhood friend. She looked very elegant and was wearing dark glasses that covered most of her face and the bruises. She had sat down a few benches away from his, on her own.

Biagio felt his flesh creep. "Let me through," he whispered to Giorgio.

"Biagio, now's not the time to—"

"I said let me through, dammit!"

Giorgio had to do as he was told.

Biagio left his front-row seat and, heedless of the fact that the ceremony was in full flow, headed straight for Donna. He grabbed her brutally by one arm and pulled her in the direction of the exit.

"But—"

"Don't say a word."

Once outside, he tore off her sunglasses and threw them to the ground. "What the fuck are you doing here?"

"I wanted to say goodbye to her for the last time."

"Is that a joke?"

Donna looked at him with head held high. "You want to hit me?"

Biagio pushed her against the door of the church and pressed a finger to her forehead. "You have no right to be here. You're the last person who should be here, because if she's dead the fault is—"

"You killed her, Biagio," she said calmly.

Biagio frowned. "What?"

"After you hit me you went to her and killed her. Do you really think you can lie to me?"

He pushed her again and her back slammed against the door. "Have you gone crazy?"

"I called the hospital, the hours coincide, Biagio. And I can read it in your face."

"Be careful what you say. You're playing with fire, you ugly bitch."

"I'm going back into the church now and attending the rest of the mass."

"You aren't doing a fucking thing."

"If you stop me, I'll spill the beans. I'll tell them you killed her. How do you think they'll take that?"

Biagio felt as if he couldn't breathe. "You . . . you fucking whore."

"Listen, I'd like to go back inside," she said, her voice almost cracked with remorse. "I wish I hadn't done what I did, but I can't do anything about it now. I'm sorry, I really liked her. And I want to say goodbye to her. If you don't let me go in, I swear to God I'll tell them. All of them."

Biagio retreated, the veins on his neck swollen, his hands shaking. "I . . . I . . . You shouldn't have said that, Donna. You made a big mistake." He shook his head contemptuously and spat on the ground, then opened his arms wide. "Do what the hell you like." He turned and headed toward his car.

"Stop it and come inside, Biagio."

Not listening to her, he started running, as if pursued by his ghosts.

"Biagio!" Donna cried.

No, he wouldn't listen. He got in the Alfa and set off with a screech of tires.

"Biagio . . . " Donna whispered desperately, her tears running freely now, ruining her make-up.

Fuck all of them, Biagio thought, stopping at a traffic light and swallowing an amphetamine pill. He took off his jacket and arranged the holster on his belt. After a few seconds, he felt the pill kick in. His muscles tightened, his senses stretched to the maximum, blood flooded his muscles. As soon as the green light came on, he set off at top speed.

Boran Paja's apartment had been sealed by the police. Claudetti had beaten him to it. If that asshole had money and drugs at home, Claudetti must have found them. But if he had, he wouldn't release him, Biagio said to himself as he tried to force the lock. It was harder than he had expected, and he gave up.

Think, Biagio, think. What the fuck's the point of going in if the cops have already been here? And Boran isn't so stupid as to hide money or drugs where he lives. Think, where can he have put them?

"Fuck, I have no idea!" he cried out loud. Wound tight with anxiety, he ran downstairs. His family doubted him, he had run away like an idiot from the funeral of the girl he'd been crazy about, and he had started looking for money and drugs in preparation for a war . . . Everything was falling to pieces, his whole life. And the more effort he made to prevent that, the more shit he was in.

As he approached the exit, he saw a young guy walking cautiously toward the building. The mirrored glass prevented him from looking inside, but Biagio recognized him and his heart skipped a beat. It was one of Paja's men, one of those Claudetti apparently hadn't managed to arrest or maybe had had to let go.

Biagio hid, took out his pistol, and waited for the Albanian to pass him.

Much to his surprise, the man didn't go up to the second floor, but down to the basement.

Biagio smiled and followed him.

Giorgio tried to call him. No answer. Cell phone still off. "What did he tell you?"

Donna shook her head. "Nothing, we just argued, he was . . . out of it, the stress maybe, the funeral, I don't know. Maybe he just needed an excuse to leave. He's not the kind of guy who'll admit he can't handle things, you know."

Giorgio nodded and drummed with his fingers on the wheel of the SUV. "Do you have any idea where he might be?"

"No."

"He isn't himself," Giorgio sighed. "And when he's like that, he turns dangerous."

"I know."

"It was him, wasn't it?" he asked, lightly touching her bruised face. "*He wasn't himself* . . . "

Giorgio shook his head. "I'm sorry, Donna."

All through the service he had been wondering where the hell Biagio had gone. He had seen Donna come back into the church and stay until the end. When they had gone out, they had all embraced her and asked about Biagio. She had said he hadn't felt up to staying: too painful, he had said.

But Giorgio hadn't bought that. "I have to find him," he said.

Donna placed her hand on his massive leg. "You've always been his guardian angel," she said with a hint of tenderness in her voice. "But not now, darling. I think it's best you let him be. He needs to be alone right now. You know how he is."

He knew that Donna was right, but he felt an ugly sense of foreboding eating away at his brain.

"How's it going at Oscar's?" she asked, changing the subject.

"Quite well, but we miss you, Donna. The kids keep asking after you, and the girls too. This tension between the two of you affects the whole family. Can't you find a way to resolve it?"

She smiled sadly. It struck Giorgio that Biagio's stress level could be measured by the number of bruises he had given her. It was painful to look at her in this condition. "I'm sorry, but it's a really shitty time for us," he said. "We've gotten in trouble with the 'Ndrangheta."

Donna threw her head back and let out a curse. "Christ! The 'Ndrangheta?"

"Yeah. They were the ones who killed Santo. Now we all have prices on our heads. And these are people who don't have any qualms about hitting innocents or family members. I think you should get out of the city for a while, Donna."

"But—"

"You might also be a target of theirs. The way things are right now, we can't protect you. Do you have somewhere you can go?"

She lit a cigarette and lowered the window. "Yes."

"With Biagio in this state and the rest of us walking around with our guns at the ready, maybe it's best if you leave the Jungle for a while."

"Okay," she sighed. "This thing about the cop who was killed. Were you involved in that?"

He looked at her without replying, then nodded.

"My God. Why?"

"It was an accident. But it's a long story, forget about it. How did you get here?"

"In a taxi."

"I'll take you home."

"All right."

As Giorgio drove, Donna withdrew into an impenetrable silence.

Seeing him come back up from the basement with a sports bag over his shoulder, Biagio realized he had been right. He could stop him there and then and take it from him, but he didn't do so. If the idea he'd had was right, this son of a bitch would do all the work for him. So, as soon as he left the luxurious building and got into a Seat Ibiza, Biagio got in his Alfa and followed him.

When, twenty minutes later, the Albanian knocked at the shutter of an underground parking garage, he made the mistake of yawning, closing his eyes, and stretching, now decidedly more relaxed since he was almost safe.

But he wasn't. Biagio came up behind him, put his left forearm around his throat, and pointed his pistol at his right temple. "Don't do anything stupid," he whispered. "As soon as they ask who you are, answer normally or I'll kill you."

"Who is it?" a man's voice asked in Albanian from inside.

"Jeton," the first man replied. "Open up."

As soon as the other Albanian pulled up the shutter, Biagio pushed the first one inside and, taking the other man by surprise, hit him full in the face with the grip of his pistol, making him collapse to the ground.

Then he raised the pistol in front of him, sweeping the garage in search of others.

He found them. But not the way he'd been expecting.

"What the fuck!" he exclaimed at the sight of three bodies of men on the ground and a half-naked girl covered in bruises trembling in a corner.

One of the two Albanians was about to throw himself on a revolver left on the floor. Biagio kicked him in the mouth and at the same time kicked away the weapon. He followed this up with a kick in the balls to make him understand who was in charge.

"On your feet and against the wall!" he ordered the two men. "Keep quiet and nothing will happen to you."

The girl didn't seem to understand him.

"Tell her to keep quiet," he ordered one of the two.

The man obeyed.

From the looks they were giving him, Biagio realized they knew who he was, and that was a good thing: they were aware that he wouldn't think twice about shooting them if they did anything dumb.

"On your knees, both of you," he said. "Hands behind your heads."

With one hand he lowered the shutter, then threw a glance at the three bodies on the ground. There were visible knife wounds on their faces. Looking more closely at them, he recognized them. They were all Paja's men: he had seen them with him in the past.

"You couldn't come to an agreement about how to divide your loot, is that it?" he sneered, approaching the closet at the far end of the garage, still with his pistol pointed at them. He opened the door and found a number of large bags. He opened one at random: it contained money. A lot of money.

A warehouse for money and drugs. But these are little fish, whatever possessed Paja to tell them where he hid the money? He dug his own grave, Biagio thought. Then he understood: it wasn't Paja who had sent them.

He walked around the bodies and aimed the pistol at the two Albanians. "You know who I am, don't you?"

The two men nodded.

"Good. You have only one way to get out alive: tell me the truth, okay?"

"Yes."

"Who sent you here?"

"Adem Paja," replied the one he had followed from Boran's place.

"Who the fuck's he?"

"He's Boran's uncle. The guy who supplies us with the drugs."

"And why did he send you here?"

"To get the money and drugs out before the cops got here."

"Why on earth should the cops come here?"

"Don't you know?" the other man asked contemptuously.

"No, I don't," he lied.

"Boran's cooperating with the police. Adem received a document from them. Boran has betrayed us, he's helping the law to screw us all over."

"The Witness Protection Program?" he asked, his mouth twisted.

"I think that's what it said, yes."

He threw a glance at the girl, who was still sniveling, then turned back to the two men. "And so some of you decided to stay with this Adem, and others thought it best to screw him over too and run away with the money. Did you two win?"

They nodded.

"You, get up," he ordered one of the two, the one who had remained on guard in the garage. "Take the bags, all the money and the drugs, and put them on the floor, there, very slowly. And you, boy, lie down on the floor, hands behind your back."

Biagio first pinned him down with one knee, then quickly hand-cuffed his wrists without removing the pistol from the back of his neck even for a second. Finally, he gave him a little slap, and told him that if he behaved he would survive. "How are we doing over there?" he asked the other, who was piling up the bags.

"It's a terrible move, cop," he replied. "Adem is really bad."

"No, Adem is really scared, take it from me," Biagio said, approaching the girl. He took her chin between his fingers and looked in her eyes. "Calm down, sweetheart," he said to her in a soft voice.

Her pupils were dilated, but not because of drugs: she was terrified and those bastards had beaten her till she bled.

"Tell her to calm down, in a few minutes I'll let her go, she'll be free," Biagio said to the one who was lying on the floor. "Try to tell her anything else and I'll put a bullet in your head."

The Albanian translated.

"Got that?" he asked the girl.

She nodded.

"Now you have to listen to me very carefully," he said to the guy on the ground. "What did you tell me your name was?

"Jeton."

"How about you?" he asked the other man, whom he still had covered.

"Gojtar."

"Good. Jeton, I'm taking your phone now and calling this fucking Adem, and we'll see about—"

A shot rang out in the garage.

Instinctively, Biagio threw himself on the ground, aiming the pistol at the Albanian, but saw him fall back against the wall and collapse to the ground with a hole in his head.

He moved his pistol to the girl, who was crying and shaking, holding a revolver aimed at the other Albanian.

"Shit!" Biagio cried. "Tell her to put the gun down or I'll kill her."

Jeton translated tensely.

As if in a trance, the girl shifted her gaze toward Jeton and walked up to him, without deigning even to glance at Biagio. She raised the gun in her small, trembling hand and aimed it at Jeton.

Biagio hit her on the back of her head with his pistol.

"Christ!" he cursed, his eyes moving wildly from one side of the garage to the other. He was in a complete daze.

Giorgio rang the bell to let her know he had arrived and then opened the door.

"When are you going to stop locking me up?" Claudia asked, her eyes red with tears.

"Maybe when you bring me breakfast in bed."

Amused, Claudia punched him in the chest, the only result being that she hurt her hand.

"So it didn't go well?" she asked, referring to the funeral.

Giorgio had called her earlier to bring her up to date and make her feel less alone.

"No, it didn't."

"Any news of Biagio?"

"No."

"Shit. God knows where the fuck he is."

"Maybe he just needed a breather."

"That isn't like him."

"A trauma like the deaths of Sonja and Santo one after the other, well . . . That can bring even someone like him to his knees, Claudia."

"Oscar called me earlier. He told me the bastard who hit Donna really did a job on her. Did you see her? Was she that badly beaten?"

"Yes," Giorgio said, avoiding her gaze. In order not to get Biagio in trouble, Donna had made up a story that it was a client who had hit her. "She isn't a pretty sight."

He unzipped his jacket, took off the holster with his pistol, and put it down on a shelf.

"What about the coke?" she asked. "What do you think he did with it?"

Giorgio shook his head. "I don't know. I'm going to take a shower."

"Okay."

He closed his eyes under the hot water and waited for his breathing to slow. He had to rid himself of the tension that had knotted his muscles. He too was starting to lie. To protect Biagio and to protect himself.

He let the water fall over his powerful back. He wondered if it was right to confide in Claudia the doubts and unpleasant thoughts he had about Biagio. If she hadn't been in this mess, maybe. But not now. He hadn't even been able to tell her the truth about Donna.

While he was lost in these doubts, the door to the stall opened and Claudia stepped naked into the steam-shrouded shower. She looked at him without batting an eyelid, then took a step forward and placed her hands on his marble chest.

"Cla—"

"Shhh, Inspector," she said in a hoarse voice, letting her hands run over his legs and sucking one of his nipples. "You know I'm your superior, don't you? I order you to fuck me."

"But—"

"Do you intend to disobey me, Inspector?" she asked with a wicked look in her eye, grasping his cock.

Giorgio stared at her, unable to contain his mounting excitement.

"No, Chief Inspector," he said, grabbing her by the buttocks, lifting her, and gluing his lips to hers.

Biagio put on a pair of leather gloves, partly raised the shutter, and moved the bags to the trunk of his car. From the weight of some, it was clear they contained weapons. When he finished, he closed the packed trunk and went back into the garage.

"Listen to me carefully," he said to Jeton, bending down. "Do you have a cell phone?"

"Yes."

"Do you have a number for Boran's uncle?"

"Yes."

"Under what name?"

"His own: Adem."

Biagio searched his pockets and confiscated the phone. "Good. Now you have two choices: either you cooperate with me, or I knock you out and leave you here, and you'll wake up to find a whole lot of cops around you asking you what the fuck happened. Which do you choose?"

"I'll cooperate."

"Good boy."

Biagio crouched down and looked at the girl. He did not dare imagine what violence they must have perpetrated on this innocent-looking young girl to lead her to commit a cold-blooded murder.

"What did you do to her and why?" he asked Jeton.

"She was a girl we brought here. We were keeping her hidden before sending her out on the street. We bought her two weeks ago."

"She's survived of a week of hell, is that right?"

Jeton lowered his eyes and nodded.

"Where are her papers?"

"I think they burned them."

"Sons of bitches."

She reminded him of Sonja. Like her, she was blonde, young, and very pretty. Maybe it's fate, he told himself, calculating the pros and cons. Maybe this is how you must honor her death.

He bent down, took her in his arms, and loaded her over his shoulder. He raised the shutter a little more and leaned out to see if there was anyone around.

There was nobody.

He laid the girl on the back seat of the car then went back inside the garage. With a handkerchief, he picked up the gun the girl had used to fire the fatal shot and wiped her fingerprints off it. He also cleaned any other surface he remembered having touched and then pulled Jeton to his feet.

"No tricks, okay?"

"Don't worry."

"Open your hands."

The man obeyed. Biagio put the revolver in his handcuffed hands.

"Now close them. Good."

He kneed him in the small of his back, making him lose his grip and drop the revolver to the floor.

"There. One more reason not to tell anybody what happened here, understood?"

"Bastard!"

Biagio pushed him outside, loaded him into the passenger seat without taking the handcuffs off, and, holding him tight by the throat, put the belt on him with his other hand. He pulled down the shutter, cleaning the handle with his handkerchief. He got in the car and sped off.

"Olimpia?"

"Yes," she replied.

"Hi. I checked it out. You were right."

"So it was him?"

"Yes."

"The same man who beat you up?"

"The same."

"He deserves it, Donna."

"I know."

"Can you tell me where I can find him?"

Donna was silent for a few long seconds.

"Yes, I know where he is."

Biagio stopped the car in the highway's emergency lane.

"Why did you stop?" Jeton asked.

"Are you fast?" Biagio asked removing the little hat he had put on him to cover his face. "Well? Are you fast?" he asked again, snapping open the seatbelt.

"What the fuck are you talking about?"

Biagio shifted him to the side, took off his handcuffs, and aimed the Beretta at him. "Take off your jacket."

"W-what?"

"Take off your fucking jacket."

Jeton obeyed.

"Good. Now get out of the car."

"But—"

"Get out!" he repeated, cocking his pistol.

It was already dark and cars were zooming past on the highway. Jeton got out and Biagio followed him, the arm with the pistol hanging by his side.

"How many yards do you think it is from here to the other side of the road?" Biagio asked.

"I . . . You don't want . . . "

Biagio aimed the pistol at him. "There's only one thing you can do: run."

"No, I beg you, I . . . "

Biagio pressed the gun barrel further in and pushed Jeton to the edge of the first lane. "It's just a matter of calculating the time properly. If you reach the other side alive I'm done with you, you're free. If you refuse, I'll take you to Headquarters and give my colleagues in Homicide the address of the garage. The choice is yours. Well?"

The man vomited. "I beg you, no . . . "

"What about the girls you've thrown on the street?" he said, fixing him with an icy glare. "Have you ever listened to them begging you?"

After a few seconds Biagio grabbed him by the hair and pulled him up, the barrel still sunk in his back. "Now that you've freed yourself, you'll be even lighter. It'll be a walkover. Run!"

"No! I beg you, I'll do anything!"

"The places where you hid money and drugs," Biagio breathed in his ear. "It doesn't make sense that the Pajas would have only one. Tell me where the others are and I'll let you go."

"But that way—"

"Do you prefer running?"

Jeton realized he had no choice and gave him the addresses of two warehouses.

"Are they being guarded?" Biagio asked after memorizing the information.

"No. We were supposed to go there and clean them out after that garage."

"Are you sure there aren't any others?"

"Yes, I'm sure, dammit."

"Congratulations," Biagio said and gave him a push that sent him tottering onto the first lane.

Jeton was about to turn back toward Biagio when he saw a Fiat Punto coming at eighty miles an hour. To avoid it he darted toward the second lane, the central one.

He never got across it. The driver of a truck just then overtaking mowed him down without even realizing. When he stopped at the next service station to take a leak, he noticed the blood and dents on the front of his truck and thought: Fucking dogs, they just keep getting bigger and bigger.

"Roberto?"

"Hello, Ma. How are you?"

"Fine. I know where he is."

"I . . . Okay, tell me."

"You mustn't get this wrong, darling."

Silence at the other end of the line.

"Roby?"

"I'm here. I know, Ma, I won't make a mistake."

"Okay. Listen carefully . . . "

Biagio woke the girl a quarter of an hour later. He tried to calm her with gestures, made her put on Jeton's jacket, and gave her six hundred euros, telling her she was free.

She had been too long in captivity to believe it, so he had to grab her by the arm and push her out. On her hand he wrote in pen the telephone number and address of a nun who would help her, then hugged her and kissed her on the forehead.

Still in a state of shock, she burst into tears and clung to him as if she didn't want to leave him anymore.

He pointed to a taxi parked in a lay-by and then at the address he had written on her hand.

The girl nodded between her tears and ran to the white cab. As he watched her say something to the taxi driver and get in, he wondered if he had done the right thing. The best thing would have been to kill her, he thought, and you know that perfectly well. She's a witness, even though she killed that scumbag, and she could get you in trouble. But

Biagio had had enough of murders and violence. The more he tried to get out of this whirlpool, the more he was sucked in. He leaned the back of his neck against the headrest. His heart was pounding and he felt a paralyzing sense of anxiety. But he couldn't let himself go. To stop meant to die.

He started the car and set off.

Safe in one of the pack's garages, he stared at the contents of the bags he had taken from the Albanians: thirty thousand euros in cash, four kilos of coke, two kilos of ecstasy, fifteen of heroin, three revolvers, two baseball bats, and a sawed-off shotgun.

Not bad, he thought. The problem is to figure out what to do with it and how to eliminate the Boran Paja problem.

The answer came to him when he switched on his BlackBerry and found a strange message from an anonymous number. He smiled. It didn't take him long to reconfigure the situation in the light of that message. He called Leonardo Verdini, his man in the penitentiary, and gave him some instructions, then sat down and waited, staring at the money he had recovered.

After about ten minutes he received a call from Verdini's number. But when he picked up, it wasn't Verdini at the other end, but Dazin Paja, Boran's father.

"Biagio."

"Dazin, I'll skip the pleasantries. Your son has turned rat."

Silence.

"You're wrong."

"No, I'm sure of it. Listen to me carefully. Make a note of this number. It's your brother Adem's."

"How do you know—"

"Shhh. Do as I say." Biagio dictated a cell phone number. "Call him, he knows the situation Boran is in. Decide between you what to do and then tell him to call me on this other number. Tell him I know how to resolve the situation. Did you get all that?"

"Yes," Dazin replied grimly. "Now I understand why they're about to transfer me."

Shit, just in time, Biagio thought, heaving a sigh of relief.

"Be quick about it, we have to sort this out in a hurry before he sends your whole family to prison."

He hung up and prayed that he was still in time.

Ten minutes later, his other cell phone started vibrating.

"Hello?"

"Hello," began a voice with a heavy Eastern accent. "You're—"

"No names."

"How did you get my number?"

"The boy gave me your number, and I tried to get to you before my colleagues," Biagio lied. "Luckily, I made it."

"What do you want?"

"I know how to resolve the situation."

"How?" Adem Paja asked.

Biagio told him.

"And what do you want in return?"

He had no intention of telling him that he had already taken an abundant reward. "Nothing. You'll owe me a favor. How did Dazin take it?"

"He started crying. I've never heard him cry before."

"I'm sorry. You know you have to act fast, don't you?"

"I know."

"And you also know that your brother is under my protection, right?"

Biagio had no idea how Dazin might take what was a barely veiled threat: *If you try anything stupid, your brother is dead.*

"Don't worry."

He hung up and thought of his plan, rubbing the platinum ring.

She had cast a spell on him. As he drove, vivid images of what had happened in the shower crossed his mind. He was licking her breasts, entering her, feeling the curve of her back; she was scratching his, slapping him, trying to bite him as if driving him on to fuck her harder, without any inhibitions. He was kissing the dragon she had tattooed on her side, which climbed her back and then descended into her ass. Intoxicated with passion, he was biting that ass, then turning her abruptly and squeezing her pussy between his lips, sucking, enjoying hearing her come. Their hands were intertwined. She was trying to stop him, but he continued, drowning her in pleasure . . .

He blinked as if trying to stop that X-rated video he had in his head. He realized he had lost control for the first time in his life. He had completely abandoned himself to sex and to the frenzy of a woman who fucked with the aggressiveness and violence of a man. He felt that it was wrong to make love with her, that Claudia was clearly running away from something. Her sexuality was a mystery to him. He couldn't use her just to let off steam, he had told himself. But it hadn't taken him long to realize that the only person being used in that shower had been him. Claudia had let herself be carried to the limits of pleasure, and even beyond, by his strong, perfect body. And he had left her breathless, knowing it was what she wanted: to lose herself in sex, to stop thinking. And he had pleased her. But had it been the same for him, or had there been something more as he had sunk into her and made her scream? He was afraid of finding out.

Biagio had called Carmine to get help in emptying the Albanians' warehouses. They hadn't encountered any problems and once they had finished they had gone straight to one of their own garages, where they had unloaded all the stolen merchandise.

They stared at the loot: ninety thousand euros in cash, forty-two kilos of heroin, seven of cocaine, three of ecstasy, and, apart from the weapons found in the first of the garages, two Kalashnikovs and a dozen semiautomatic pistols.

Carmine sank his hands into the pockets of his jeans and shook his head. "Fuck, if you'd confiscated all this shit in an official mission, they'd have promoted you."

"Promoted me?" Biago retorted, massaging the knuckles of his right hand. "Do you think I give a damn? I just want this whole thing to be over as soon as possible."

"How do you intend to use it?" asked Carmine pointing to the drugs.

Biagio took a deep breath, then told him.

"Can I confess something?" Carmine asked once his friend had finished outlining his plan.

"Shoot."

"Sometimes you really scare me."

"Did you get all that?" Roberto asked his two colleagues.

Angelo and Mariano nodded.

"Nobody's forcing you to do it, boys."

"Don't say that, even as a joke," Mariano said. "That bastard killed one of us. Carlo was a brother. The son of a bitch has to pay."

"And he will pay," Angelo said.

Roberto Messina nodded and distributed the pistols with erased serial numbers that one of his informers had gotten for him along with the stolen car parked near the building where Biagio Mazzeo lived.

As he waited for Biagio to return home, Roberto heard his mother's words in his head: "Show you're a man, Roberto. Avenge your brother. Kill that piece of shit. Do it for him and for me."

He nodded to himself. He wouldn't betray his mother. The murder of Carlo would be avenged soon.

Biagio parked his Alfa outside the apartment block. He had barely gotten out of the car when he felt a pistol aimed at his side.

"I swear if you make the slightest move I'll shoot you," Mariano said.

"Don't tell me—" Biagio said.

A Ford Fiesta stopped a few feet from them and he was pushed inside.

"Try anything stupid and I'll kill you here," Roberto said by way of greeting, pointing a semi-automatic at him, while Mariano stuffed him into the back seat, searched him, and confiscated his Beretta.

"What the fuck are you doing?" Biagio asked, disorientated. "Who the fuck are you people?"

"We're the good cops," Mariano said, and hit him on the back of his head with the grip of his pistol. Angelo put his foot down on the accelerator and sped off, heading out of the city.

Biagio came to. He was lying on the ground, on a dirt road, his hands cuffed behind his back. He had to close his eyes because the lights of the Fiesta were aimed at him. The three unknown men stood around him, weapons in their hands.

"What the hell do you want?" he asked.

Roberto Messina responded with a kick to the stomach, knocking the breath out of him. "I ask the questions, Mazzeo."

Their faces were uncovered. That meant their intentions weren't good. Biagio spat on the ground and looked up at Messina. "What do you want to know?"

"Why did you kill my brother?"

"Who the fuck is your brother?"

This time it was Angelo who hit him.

"Carlo Messina, the police officer your men killed on the highway. My brother. Tell me why."

"We didn't kill anybody, who fed you that bullshit?"

Roberto cocked his gun, crouched, and pressed the mouth of the barrel to Biagio's forehead. "Last chance. Why did you kill him my brother?"

Biagio sustained his gaze. "I don't think it's a good idea to kill a cop," he said.

"You're not a cop, you piece of shit," Roberto retorted. "You're a murderer."

Biagio laughed. "Oh, yes? Then you're just three dickheads."

Mariano and Angelo exchanged amused glances, then turned pale when they felt something hard coming to rest against the backs of their necks.

"Put down the gun and free me, or your friends are dead," Biagio said with a smile.

Roberto turned and saw two masked men aiming weapons at his colleagues, who lowered theirs.

"What the fuck—"

"Surprise, surprise."

"But—"

"I'm losing my patience. Put down that fucking pistol or *my* friends will shoot."

The masked men forced Mariano and Angelo to lie down, then tore the pistol from Roberto's hands and knocked him to the ground.

"Where are the keys?" one of the masked men asked.

"Go fuck yourself."

The unknown man kicked him in the balls. "Well?"

"I have them," Angelo said. "Right-hand pocket."

The masked men took out the keys to the handcuffs and freed Biagio.

"Good, good," he said, getting in the Fiesta. He recovered his pistol and came out releasing the safety catch. He looked around. They were outside the city, in an agricultural area. Not a single light anywhere. Open country. The ideal place for a murder.

"So you're the brother of the colleague who was killed?" he asked.

"Don't dare call him a colleague, you bastard."

"Who sent you? Was it Claudetti?"

Roberto didn't reply.

Biagio pointed to Mariano and said to his men, "Kill him."

"No!" Roberto cried.

Biagio pinned him to the ground with his boot and pointed the pistol at his head. "Tell me, dammit, or I swear I'll kill you one by one!"

"Yes, he has a file on you and all the shit you've done. He's going to bring you down, which is what you deserve, you bastard."

Biagio pulled him to his feet and shoved him against the trunk of the Ford. "Listen to me carefully, boy, I didn't kill anybody. Claudetti is a fanatic who's gotten it into his head he has to bring me down, for whatever fucking reason, but he doesn't have a thing. He's so desperate, he tried to use you to get rid of me, don't you understand that? He's using you, you asshole."

"But Claudia Braga, your partner, was in that car."

"That's true, but do you think I'm so stupid as to start a massacre in broad daylight on a fucking highway?"

Roberto said nothing.

"I'm sorry about your brother, and I understand how pissed off you are, but we had nothing to do with his death."

"Who was it, then?"

"That's a good question," Biagio said, letting him go.

As the masked men took him away, Biagio checked his cell phone and sent a few texts.

"You did well, damn you," said the man at the wheel.

"I can't say the same for you guys. A few more minutes and they'd have killed me. And take off that mask, you look scary!"

Carmine removed his ski mask and winked. "Better now?"

"Oh, no, shit, you look even scarier. Mind putting it back on?"

Vito burst out laughing in the back seat. "Carmine's right, Biagio. You're really good."

"When you're in shit up to your neck, either you start eating it or you learn to swim."

"Or else you make someone else eat it," Carmine said.

"Fucking right," Biagio replied. "How are you, son?"

"It hasn't been a walkover," Vito said. "Fuck, his brother . . . But I'm okay, chief. Claudetti's going too far, though."

"He'll pay soon enough, you can be sure of that. Please, I don't want you to tell the others about this thing with the Messinas, understood?"

The two of them nodded.

"Where should I drop you?" Carmine asked.

"Take me to her," Biagio replied, massaging his knuckles.

She opened the door and let him in.

"Scotch?" she asked.

"No," he replied, looking around. "I assume you think I should thank you, or am I wrong?"

She shrugged. "I warned you what was going on. Those cops would have killed you. Yes, maybe you should thank me."

Biagio bowed his head and frowned. "No, I don't think so. You're just trying to make up for what you did to Sonja but, believe me, it's better if you just forget it, because you'll never be able to come to terms with what you've done."

"I just wanted—"

"You shouldn't have come to the funeral, Donna. It was a really bad idea."

"What happened to the boy?"

"He's still alive, if that's what you're asking me."

"But he didn't—"

"Yes, he'd have killed me. About that you were right. But I won't thank you."

"I don't want thanks."

"What do you want?"

"I don't know. To go back to the way we were before, I know it's impossible, but at least let me come close to you."

"Forget it. I won't kill you and that's quite something, trust me."

"Would you really kill me?"

"It's what you deserve."

"Biagio—"

"Never show your face again," he said before leaving. "And don't make me come back."

Donna collapsed into an armchair and stared into space.

When the elevator doors opened on the floor where his apartment was, Biagio saw her.

She was sitting on the floor, back against the door, eyes closed. He felt a pang in his heart and found it hard to breathe. "Sweetheart?" he called out, unable to restrain a smile.

She raised her head abruptly. Her blue eyes opened wide. She was the same as ever, the same lively little pest. She leaped to her feet, ran to him, and jumped up, wrapping her legs around his back.

Biagio felt a sense of peace and happiness flood over him. He hugged her tight and moved her blonde hair away from her forehead, kissing it. "How are you, sweetheart?" he asked the girl. She was fourteen, as thin as a nail, with a diamond in her nose and an expensive lipstick she couldn't afford. She was wearing a pair of All Stars that didn't match, one green and the other red, black stockings, a pair of frayed denim shorts, a black Nirvana T-shirt, and a leather jacket with badges of skeletons and musical groups. Her thin wrists were covered in silver bracelets.

"Biagio," she whispered in that melodramatic and unconsciously comical tone that always touched his heart.

"How long have you been waiting here?"

"Two hours. I was late for Sonja's funeral. Everybody had left."

Her eyes misted over and he clasped her to his chest, stroking her head. "Calm down, I don't want to see tears, okay?"

She nodded.

"Who brought you here?"

"I came on the bus."

"Let's go inside," he said, putting his arm around her shoulders and picking up the green canvas bag she had left by the door. He shuddered at the mere thought of the risk the girl had run. Because she was Santo's daughter. Nicky.

Nicky had always been part of the family. In fact, she was the mascot of the pack, had been that ever since the boys were unmarried, childless greenhorns, had always been the center of attention. Biagio was her godfather, and she called Santo uncle, not knowing that he was her father. Santo had always wanted to keep it hidden from her: he had made a pact with Giada, her mother—a former businesswoman who had destroyed herself with coke and had become one of his informers—which stipulated that he would pass her a reasonable amount of money every month on condition that she kept his paternity secret. It had worked. As for the second part of the agreement, that of coming off the coke, she alternated periods of detox with months of total dependency, during which Biagio or one of his men was forced to go and fetch Nicky and take her to Santo's or Oscar's. If Biagio had had a euro for all the dealers who supplied Giada and whom he had beaten up and made swear they wouldn't sell her anything more, he would have been a millionaire. At the end of his tether, he had seen to it that one of them had ended up dead in a dried-up canal. The rumor had gone around the city in record time. After that, all the dealers in the Jungle kept away from Giada, and so she had changed cities, taking Nicky with her. But Nicky regularly ran away from home. As far as he was concerned, the cops were her family. She reminded Biagio of himself at the same age, partly because of another characteristic: Nicky was a born thief. And with the passing of the years, that peculiarity had grown, so much so that the Panthers had had to intervene several times to get her out of trouble. Her stealing was a cry for help. But Santo had never wanted to take her away from her mother or even entrust her to anybody. He loved her, and he always said that it wasn't right for him to upset her life. So what at the beginning had been merely an appeal for help soon became a compulsive habit. You could forgive that lively, good-humored little mite anything. Her enjoyment of life and her ability to make people smile were disarming.

In the last few years, she had sworn everlasting love to Biagio, who pampered her like nobody else. She creased him up whenever she described their wedding, where they would celebrate it, what menu they would choose. Whenever she ran away from home and came to the Jungle, she always dropped into the Bang Bang or Headquarters, and spent a few days together with Biagio and Sonja to catch her breath. Then there were the intimate evenings, when she and Biagio were alone, and he was everything to her. Those evenings happened at least twice a month, sometimes more if Giada was going through a bad patch and Nicky didn't want to stay at home.

Biagio loved his friend's secret daughter. But despite the fact that he was more than happy to see her, now really wasn't a good time.

There was nothing to eat in his apartment and everything was upside down, so they decided to have dinner out and then go to Sonja's. Biagio took her to a fashionable restaurant with redbrick walls and exposed pipes. He had chosen it because in his current situation he was at less risk of attack in crowded places.

"Where is Giada?" he asked as she looked at him with her doe-eyes.

"The bitch took a room in a swanky hotel, but I don't think she has the money to pay for it. She never cared a damn about Santo, she's here only because I kicked up a fuss."

"How is she?" Biagio asked, stroking his nostrils.

"In a bad way," she replied, hiding behind the menu.

Biagio smiled. She had put on vintage glasses that looked huge on her small face.

"And how are you?" she asked.

"I . . . " he began, turning his gaze away. He could lie easily to anybody, but not to her.

"Listen, let's do this: for tonight we give each other a present. We don't talk about Sonja or Santo. We pretend nothing happened, that it's just you and me, okay?" As she spoke, she nodded several times, as if agreeing with herself.

With those big glasses, Mazzeo couldn't look at her without smiling. "Okay, sweetheart. What are you going to eat?"

"How does it work here?"

"They bring you a pizza as big as your glasses . . . "

"Great," Nicky said, half closing her eyes and pouting.

" . . . with at least four different flavors, cut into slices, so you can taste different kinds."

"Cool! I bet you're on a diet, right?"

Biagio winked. "I'm always on a diet, sweetheart."

"In that case I'll have: pizza with truffles, provola and cooked ham, pizza with potatoes and tuna, pizza with gorgonzola and pears, and to end with, something not too heavy, pizza with mushrooms, sausages, rocket, and onions!"

Biagio burst out laughing. "I missed you, you know?"

They continued talking and pulling each other's legs, until suddenly Biagio stopped, pricking up his ears. On the radio, they were playing the same song he had heard at lunchtime in the Argentinian restaurant.

"I'm crazy about this song. Do you know who the singer is?"

"You bet I do. Nina Zilli. The song's called 'Per Sempre.'"

"It's great. I love it."

She took his hand in hers. "Please," she said, fluttering her eyelashes, "can we make this our song, just ours?"

"Of course, sweetheart," Biagio said, winking.

They sat in silence for a few minutes listening to the song, holding hands like a couple of lovers.

In the safe house where Deputy Prosecutor Corrado Tortora had had Boran Paja put while waiting for a response to his request to go into the Witness Protection Program, the Albanian was killing time playing poker with the police officer on guard. He was in a bad mood because—apart from this whole shitty situation—he kept losing. "How long are they going to take?" he asked the officer, referring to the pizzas they had ordered half an hour earlier.

"Calm down, partner," the officer replied.

"Shit, I'm hungry," Paja cried, throwing his cards in the air.

"I said calm down."

"When the fuck is Claudetti coming?"

"We have a change of shift in ten minutes, relax."

"But didn't he tell you anything else when he phoned? Don't you know what they've decided?"

"Paja," the officer said, changing tone, his face turning grim, "he didn't tell me anything, I told you. Keep calm. In ten minutes he'll be here and you can ask him directly, so stop breaking my balls."

At that moment, the doorbell rang.

"There, I just hope you're one of those people who keep quiet when they eats."

The officer stood up, grabbed his pistol, and bent to look through the spyhole.

He gave a start. Three masked men were aiming rifles at the door.

"Get down!" he cried, throwing himself to the floor.

A fraction of a second later, the men opened fire, reducing the door to shreds.

In the incredible roar of the shots and in haste to take shelter from the storm of lead and fragments, the officer slipped and lost his Beretta.

"Don't even think about it," cried one of the three men in a heavy Eastern accent as the cop made to recover his weapon. "Hands behind your head!"

The officer had a wife and two small children. He didn't have the slightest intention of playing the hero for Andrea Claudetti. He obeyed.

The man hit him on the back of his head with the grip of his rifle, making him lose consciousness, and then went out, leading the way for his companions, who were pushing a shaking and incredulous Boran Paja.

"Try anything stupid and you're dead," they said to him. In Albanian.

Paja could do nothing other than obey.

The men loaded him into a van that was waiting for them outside the house with its engine running, cried to the driver to leave, and disappeared as quickly as they had arrived.

The pizza delivery boy kept his shaking hands up for a few seconds longer, as if paralyzed. The boxes that had fallen to the ground were already wet with urine.

Nicky was eating like a professional wrestler. She wiped off the traces of pizza and when the waitress removed her plate she winked at her and said, "Appearances can be deceptive, my darling."

"Would you like something else?" the girl asked, embarrassed.

"Why, do you think we're too fat for a little dessert?"

The waitress blushed and came back a few seconds later with the dessert menu.

"Nicky, give her a break," Biagio said, when the poor girl walked away after taking the orders. He was stroking the ring on his finger.

"Is that new?" Nicky asked, ignoring his reproach. "I've never seen it on you before. Did Sonja give it to you?"

Biagio looked at the ring. "No . . . It's a gift from an old friend."

Just then, one of his cell phones vibrated.

It was the encrypted number. A text message. *One down.*

That was all.

He put the phone back in his pocket, and the dirty reality he had so far succeeded in keep away from this beautiful evening descended on him like a dead weight.

"Trouble?" Nicky asked, lowering the menu and noticing the cold look in his eyes.

Biagio stared at her. He thought of the white envelope lying in the pocket of his jacket: Santo's legacy to his daughter. He ought to open it and read it, or maybe wait a little longer before giving it to her. What was written in it might hurt her.

This isn't any of your business, an inner voice told him. It isn't down to you to decide.

But her security and happiness mattered to him. To find out in one fell swoop, while she was still in mourning, that the person she was mourning had been her father would be a devastating blow. And to discover that her godfather had been the indirect cause of his death might break her heart.

"No, sweetheart," he reassured her with his roguish smile. "Everything's fine."

When the desserts arrived, Nicky played with the spoon, suddenly silent.

"What is it, sweetheart?"

"Biagio, I'd like to see him."

For the first time he saw her as what she was: a little girl. No irony in her voice, no adult mask. Just a sad and frightened fourteen-year-old.

"Sweetheart, maybe it's better not to—"

"Please. I loved him a lot. One last time."

Biagio sighed. "All right. Tomorrow."

As she devoured her dessert, Biagio told himself that he ought to send her away, send both her and her mother back home, far from him and his violent world. That was the best thing to do, for him and for them.

But he couldn't. In the turbulent ocean of hatred and violence that had become his life, Nicky had appeared like a benevolent wind. He couldn't send her away. He had an almost physical need for her, because he felt that if she went away he would go crazy, unable to bear all the pressure that seemed to be crushing him. She calmed him, exorcised his inner demons. He had known very few people who could do that.

He shuddered when he realized that all the others were dead.

Andrea Claudetti glanced at his watch, which made his wife even angrier.

"You've put up with me for too long, is that it?" she cried, throwing the photographs at him. "You want to leave, don't you? That'd be the easy way out. Too easy, dammit!"

The photographs fell to the floor. There were a dozen of them, showing him and Ariana Manisci having a coffee together, laughing, joking. In one, they were hugging. It had been nothing but a simple embrace between colleagues. But Stefania didn't see it like that.

"Who the fuck is that whore? You have to go to her, is that it?"

She started hitting him. The twins were crying in the next room, but she didn't seem to notice.

"I already told you. She's a colleague of mine, we were just having a coffee and talking about a case."

The fact that Ariana was so attractive certainly did nothing to lessen his wife's jealousy. That afternoon, Stefania had found an envelope addressed to her in the letter box. Inside were the photographs, along with a message: *Keep an eye on your husband.*

"A coffee? What case are you working on?"

"Mazzeo, what else?"

"You promised me you'd drop it, but the photographs have today's date. So either you were lying to me yesterday, or you're lying now!"

Claudetti realized he had painted himself into a corner. "Stefi, for God's sake, calm down! You're making a big fuss about nothing!"

"Oh, do you call these nothing?"

"Yes!" he screamed in exasperation, making her jump. He was twenty minutes late. He should already have been at the safe house to take over from his colleague, but he was still here, having spent the last two hours justifying himself over something that made no sense. Of course he had seen Ariana after they had interrogated Paja together, and they had had a coffee, but only to discuss the details of the case and decide how to move ahead on the charges of criminal association. He had hugged her because she had told him that she had applied for an important post in Europol and had been accepted: she would be leaving in a few months.

"Don't you understand? It was Mazzeo who sent you those photos, to cause trouble between us, to get back at me!"

At that moment his cell phone started vibrating. Stefania got to it first. And went red. It was Ariana Manisci.

"Oh, look who's calling you at eleven in the evening. It's because of her you have to go out, isn't it? Don't talk to me about guard shifts! You have to see that whore, you bastard!"

"Pass me the telephone, please," Claudetti said, as calmly as he could.

Stefania threw it at him out of spite. "Go, then, go fuck your girlfriend!" she cried, turning her back on him and going to check the twins, cursing in Sicilian.

He waited until his wife had left the kitchen, then replied.

"Ariana? Everything okay?"

Hearing her reply, his eyes widened and his face turned pale. He hung up, grabbed his jacket and his pistol, and ran to the entrance. When he opened the door he gave a start and retreated, brandishing his Beretta, his eyes wide, the breath knocked out of him. "Christ!"

In front of the door to his house lay a body, face downwards.

"Stefi, stay inside!" he cried, stepping over the body and checking, pistol in hand, that there was nobody out on the street.

His wife's screams made it clear to him that she had not listened to him. Claudetti shook her, pushed her inside, and ordered her to call an ambulance.

Then he threw himself on the body and turned it over. He shuddered. It was Boran Paja. With a knife in his heart.

"No . . . no, no, no . . . damn!" he moaned, falling to his knees.

"So, what's new?"

"Claudetti's been neutralized."

"Tell me how."

Irene did as the Voice asked.

"That thing with the photos was really a touch of class."

"Thank you," she said with a smile.

"But the business with the body? Wasn't that a bit much?"

"That was something Mazzeo arranged with the Albanians. It was over the top, which is the way he and the individuals he works with are. I told you he's a hothead and acts too much on instinct."

"Don't start, please. At the very least with these tactics he's diverted attention from himself and his squad and shifted it to the Albanians. That strikes me as a brilliant move."

"I haven't changed my mind about him."

"You just have to make sure this whole thing works out."

"Yes, sir!" she replied ironically.

"Carry on and remember that you're doing all this for a higher purpose."

Higher purpose my ass, she thought as she ended the Skype call. She stood up and looked out at the lights of the city from the big window of her office, wondering if she was doing the right thing.

Giorgio was sitting in the glider on the porch of Oscar's house with his little niece sleeping in his arms.

Oscar put a blanket over her. "Is she asleep?" he asked in a low voice.

"Like a log," Giorgio replied, stroking her hair.

Oscar leaned back against a column with a beer in his hand. "Where's Biagio?"

"I have no idea, he hasn't answered my phone calls."

"Mine neither. What's happening to him?"

Maybe you should tell him the truth about Donna for a start, Giorgio told himself. But a second later he decided not to. He wanted to talk about her with Biagio in person first.

"I don't know, Oscar. Maybe he's in shock, maybe he's disappointed with us or feels guilty. Really, I have no idea."

"I keep going over it in my head, but I just can't figure out this business of the coke. Why won't he tell us what he did with it?"

Giorgio shook his head.

"I don't think he's in his right mind," Oscar went on. "That's the impression I get anyway. I understand he's grief stricken and exhausted, but this is too much." He pointed to the villa. "How long do you think we can carry on here like this?"

"I don't know," Giorgio said, kissing the child and standing up. "Listen, I'll take this little one inside, then I'll go. I'll drop by my apartment, and then go to Claudia's."

Oscar smiled and watched him go back inside with the child held tight in his arms. He wondered how they'd all be able to adapt to normal life again after this interlude of forced cohabitation. For now, the girlfriends and the children had become dependent on that family atmosphere, the routine, the sense of protection this closed environment gave them. Having someone looking after their safety and happiness kept them free of worries and complications. It was rather like being on vacation. But not for the Panthers. They were hiding like wounded beasts in a cave, fearful of the dark and the cold, and above all terrified of the other animals. And Oscar knew perfectly well that soon those other animals would appear to demand their tribute of blood and try to enter their cave. Very soon.

Going to the funeral had been only an attempt to get close to them, as had been her manipulation of Olimpia Messina. In this tense situation, in which the family was forced to hide, Donna knew they all needed her. For years she had been their point of reference, a shoulder to cry on, a friend to go to for advice and opinions. And now that point of reference had vanished. Exiled from their world.

When they had clashed outside the church, Donna had seen a murderous gleam in Biagio's eyes that had scared her. That was why she was here now, in the car, outside Giorgio's house. Talking with him a few hours earlier, she had detected a glimmer of bewilderment in him. Maybe he too was starting to see Biagio in a different light. Now that her friend had threatened her, Donna had to protect herself and the only way she knew how was by twisting the truth and manipulating people.

Giorgio would become her life insurance.

Slowing down to park, Giorgio saw a Mercedes flashing its lights. As he parked, he saw it was Donna.

"You managed to drive," he said, getting in the car.

"Yes, though I'm stuffed full of painkillers," she replied, lighting herself a cigarette.

"Is everything okay?"

She nodded.

"Why are you here, Donna?"

"All evening I've been thinking over what we said."

"And?"

She pulled a face and breathed out the smoke. "I realized it was right to tell you."

"Tell me what?"

She looked him in the eyes. "Biagio killed Sonja."

"I'm sorry?"

"That's the way it is, he switched off the machines that were keeping her alive."

"Come on, Donna."

"He killed her, Giorgio."

"No, it isn't possible."

"And yet that's the way it is. After he hit me that night, he went to the hospital and killed her."

"I'm sorry, but why would he do that?"

"Because she'd become a burden to him. Someone they could use to put pressure on him. You know how well I know him. It's how he's started to think. He's changed."

"I don't believe—"

"Think about it: how did he react to her death?"

Giorgio reflected. It was true: when they had told him Sonja was dead, his reaction had been cold, almost detached, practically no reaction at all.

"As if he already knew," Donna said, almost as if reading his mind. "That's how he reacted, isn't it?"

Giorgio nodded.

"I don't know exactly what happened to him, but something changed him."

Ivankov, Giorgio thought. He was the one who changed him. Biagio wants to become like him. That's why he wears his ring. And it's like that fucking ring was a curse, possessing him. Yes, it's like Ivankov possessed him.

"He's cut off a part of himself," Donna went on. "Will he do the same to me? Or Claudia, or even you? Who knows? But do we have to let him do it? Do we have to act like puppets in his hands?"

Giorgio stared at her without answering. "He killed Sonja," he said in a thin voice. This time it wasn't a question.

"Precisely," Donna said, while inside she thought: Now you're mine too.

To eliminate all the people closest to him by setting them against him. To isolate him. To take from him all he held most dear. To smash his system of values and his desires. That was her plan. And she was doing everything she could to carry it out.

"Why did you decide to tell me?" Giorgio asked.

"Did he tell you anything about the brother of the cop who was killed?"

"What should he have told me?"

"He found out that you guys were behind his brother's death, and he was about to kill Biagio. I think they've made a pact now. Did he really not tell you anything?"

Giorgio shook his head.

"He's becoming dangerous, elusive. How many lies is he telling all of you? Do you even realize?"

He sighed. "Yes."

"Those of you who are close to him had to know. He even killed the person he loved the most."

He was on the verge of doing it to Claudia, he thought. And Vito too.

"I might be next," Donna said, pointing to her bruises. "And if that happens, I want someone to know the truth."

He took her by the arm, pulled her to him, and hugged her tight. "I won't let it happen, don't worry."

"I just want you to be careful, Giorgio, you and the others."

"I know. Thanks for telling me. It can't have been easy."

Donna burst into tears and shook her head. "No, it wasn't easy at all. I'd just like him to be the way he was before."

Giorgio knew that wasn't possible. People can't turn the clock back. They change, they evolve, for better or worse. But once the process of transformation has begun, they can't turn back. Not people like Biagio anyway.

"Now you have to do as I said: leave the Jungle until we sort out this mess, okay?"

Donna nodded.

Giorgio kissed her on the forehead and promised her that he wouldn't let Biagio do anything to her. "Now go."

He got out of the car and watched her disappear into the night. He would have liked to vanish too. But he couldn't. His family needed him more than ever.

Nicky was so exhausted, that she fell asleep in the car. Biagio decided they would sleep in Sonja's apartment tonight.

As usual, he drove around the block a few times, trying to spot any likely threats, but didn't see any. He climbed the stairs with Nicky in his arms.

I'll ask Mirko to be her bodyguard while she's in the city, Biagio thought. He didn't want to give the girl up. He had no desire to go back to his apartment and find it empty of life and full of ghosts. He needed human warmth.

He laid her on the couch, took off her shoes, covered her with a big plaid blanket, and arranged a cushion under her head. "Sweet dreams," he whispered, kissing her cheek.

He closed the bedroom door and called Giada, Nicky's mother.

"Hello?" she replied in a hard voice.

"It's Biagio."

"Shit, at last you call! Thanks for warning me, eh? I had to find out from the newspapers, you bastard."

"Calm down. And stop talking as if you cared."

"What do you want?"

"Nicky's with me. She's sleeping here tonight."

"As far as I'm concerned, you can keep the little bitch."

"Careful what you say, now's really not the time."

"When will I see my money?"

"What money?"

"The inheritance money, what else?"

Biagio was alienated by her pettiness. Santo wasn't even buried yet and she was already concerned about the money. What was he thinking the day he fucked her? he thought.

"It isn't your money, you whore: it's Nicky's."

She laughed. "I want that money, Biagio, or I'll tell her everything."

Biagio breathed in, trying to calm down, thinking about the one-sided agreement with which this bitch kept them in check. "I have to talk with the lawyer about the will and the other things."

"Hurry up about it. I'm not leaving here until I get my money."

"You'll get it."

"Good. Where is the little bitch?"

"Stop calling her that. She's asleep."

"Listen, I need an advance."

Biagio shook his head. Fucking cokeheads, he thought. They're all the same. "We'll talk about it tomorrow, I have to go now," he said and hung up.

As he undressed, he thought about what awaited him. The truth, the one he couldn't admit to anybody except himself, was that he was fucking afraid of what was about to happen. He stared at the ring. Paradoxically the person he now felt closest to was the one who had brought him to his knees and tried to destroy him. But he too was a ghost.

Sometimes I get the feeling I've become a ghost too, Biagio thought as he lay down and stared up at the ceiling in the darkness of the room. Because this place feels more than ever like hell.

The pistol on the night table was there to demonstrate how concrete that thought was.

Claudia sat down at the table, a towel around her still damp hair.

As she watched Giorgio move lightly and casually around the modern kitchen, she lost herself in the beautiful jazz version of "Tainted Love" by the Stella Starlight Trio he had put on as a background.

A few seconds later he served her.

"Risotto with shrimp and orange . . . Chicken with yoghurt and harissa with carrots in argan oil . . . Mafalda with rocket pesto and salmon . . . Strips of chicken with zucchine, ham and saffron . . . Salmon with citrus fruits and an excellent organic Sicilian white wine from vines grown on land confiscated from the Mafia . . . A mix of east, west and middle east. Enjoy your meal, Inspector."

Claudia stared at the whole thing open-mouthed. "This is a joke, right? Did you really make all this?"

Giorgio winked as he sat down.

"I had no—"

"Food should be honored in silence," he said with a smile.

Claudia started eating and realized the dishes didn't just look good, they tasted amazing. "Where the hell did you learn?"

"Oh, here and there," he replied cryptically. The fact was, every year, adding vacations and hours owed, he put aside a whole month in which he disappeared and nobody knew where he went. He left for the Far East: Japan, Thailand, India, China, Vietnam, Indonesia. It was his tonic. Everywhere he went, he had a new animal added to the big tattoo that covered his back. During that month he would study martial arts, immerse himself in Eastern meditation, and learn the secrets of the local cuisine.

"Hell, we've known each other for years and I never knew you could cook this well."

"What other people know about us is our weakness, what they don't know is our strength."

Claudia put her hands together and gave a little bow. "Thank you, oh wise man of the mountains."

"Claudia."

"Yes?"

No, you can't tell her. Not yet.

"Would you like a little salt?"

"No, it's fine like this, everything's delicious." She noticed his somber expression. "Are you all right?"

He smiled. "I'm absolutely fine, don't worry."

The area was swarming with officers, ambulances, and Forensics people examining the crime scene. From inside the house, Claudetti told himself they might as well save themselves the effort: Paja hadn't been killed here.

"Hey, Andrea, are you listening to me?" Deputy Prosecutor Tortora said, clicking his fingers.

Claudetti turned and nodded. He was surrounded by the people he had to explain this fiasco to: Tortora, Deputy Commissioner Carmen Brancato, Ariana and her partner, Diego Gatti.

"I don't understand how the fuck it could have happened," Tortora went on. "Do you realize the mess you've gotten me in?"

"Yes, Corrado, I know. And I'll take whatever blame I have to, but Christ, give me a break." He turned to his superior. "What about the officer? Any news?"

"Just concussion, nothing serious," Carmen replied. She wasn't angry with him, she was on his side: Mazzeo and his men had to be punished, they had known from the start that something like this might happen, and it was no reason for her to abandon Claudetti.

"The problem isn't the officer, luckily," Tortora resumed. "But how the fuck did they find him, Andrea? How? Did you let him make a call?"

"No."

"Are you sure?"

"Hell, yes."

"The officer said they were Albanians, he must have called them somehow. But they knew he was cooperating with you, which means someone told them. Did he by any chance leave the house on his own? Say something, for Christ's sake!"

Claudetti met Ariana's guilty eyes. "It was Mazzeo who tracked him down, not—"

"What the fuck has Mazzeo got to do with it? Answer my question: did he leave the house, yes or no?"

Claudetti sighed. "For a couple of minutes he—"

"Fuck!" the prosecutor cried, kicking away a chair. He walked out cursing.

Ariana was about to speak, but Claudetti stopped her with a gesture: there was no point in her also paying for this.

"Verri will be here soon," Carmen said. "It's best if you prepare a line of defense, or he'll eat you alive. I'm going to phone to see if there's anything new from the safe house. Diego, try to find out if the neighbors saw anybody leaving the body. Andrea, I advise you to make yourself a coffee: it's going to be a long night."

"Thanks, Carmen."

When they were alone, Ariana gave him a hug. "I'm sorry, I should never have let him out."

"No, it's not your fault. Paja had nothing to do with it, he didn't call or anything else. It must have been Mazzeo, somehow."

"There's no need for you to cover me, I want whatever blame is due to me and—"

"Shhh . . . " he said placing a finger on her lips.

At that moment, Stefania appeared in the kitchen with one of the twins in her arms, and froze when she saw what was happening.

"Stefi, don't—" Claudetti began, freeing himself from the embrace.
She turned abruptly and left, slamming the door.
"Shit," Claudetti sighed, closing his eyes.

She was waiting for him on the veranda, her arms wrapped around her pullover to keep warm.
"Done?" she asked as soon as he came level with her.
"It wasn't him," Roberto said, leaning against the wall.
"What do you mean?"
He slapped the wall angrily. "He had nothing to do with it. The other cop, Claudetti, simply used me."
"But . . . why should he have used you?"
"Because he wants to see Mazzeo dead. Maybe he knows he can't arrest him and he thought I could get rid of him for him."
"But that policewoman was in the car. She was the one they helped to escape, wasn't she?"
"Ma, the whole thing is more complicated than it seems."
"Meaning what?"
"They didn't help her escape. She was kidnapped. The cops were in trouble with the 'Ndrangheta, who kidnapped the woman to take revenge on Mazzeo."
"The 'Ndrangheta?"
"That's right. It was the Calabrians who killed Carlo."
Olimpia stared at her son, unable to say another word.

A Pact with the Devil

The morgue was no place for a young girl. But given that Biagio was holding her hand, nobody dared to say anything.
Biagio thanked his colleague for showing him the body on a steel stretcher in an isolated room. He told him that they wanted to be alone for a few minutes.
"No problem," the man said as he closed the door. "Call me when you've finished."
"Are you sure about this, sweetheart? If you've changed your mind, it's fine by me, believe me."

Nicky shook her head, without letting go of his hand.

"Your choice."

He lifted the white sheet and uncovered Santo's face. In the stillness of death, it looked swollen. But it was him, with his tufted mustache and his big good-natured face.

Nicky felt a pang in her heart. The tears started running down her face.

Biagio put his arm around her and drew her to him. "You mustn't be afraid, little one," he said, without taking his eyes off his friend.

"Did he suffer?" she asked.

Biagio saw again the tide of cartridges around the bullet-riddled body. "No," he replied.

She wiped her tears, looked at the body again, and smiled. "You know, I've never seen him without a hat before."

Biagio also smiled, sadly. "You're right. Without his Borsalino he looks like a different person."

"Why didn't you tell me he was my father?" Nicky asked.

Biagio gave a start. "What? You . . . you . . . "

"I've always known, Biagio."

They stood there in silence for a few seconds, Biagio digesting this revelation.

"Was it Giada?" he asked, unable to conceal a hint of malice in his voice.

Nicky shook her head. "No. I found it out by myself. I understood from the way he looked at me, the way he talked to me, pampered me . . . I just knew. I've always known."

Biagio was speechless. He would never have expected that she knew.

"I don't know, sweetheart. Maybe he thought it was right that way. What about you? Why did you always keep this inside?"

"I thought that if he wanted things to be like that between us, he had his reasons. I was afraid that if I told him, he would be more distant. And then all of you would be the same. I'd rather have died."

Biagio hugged her tight. "We would never have been distant, Nicky."

"Can I . . . can I touch him?"

Biagio nodded.

She put her hand to her father's face and caressed it. "He's cold."

"He's at peace now, Nicky. And he'd prefer it if we didn't think about him, I'm sure of that."

"Can I stay alone with him for a few minutes?"

Biagio weighed up the request. It wasn't the most appropriate thing for a young girl's psyche, but Nicky wasn't just any young girl, and she had just demonstrated that.

"Okay. I'll be right outside."

On his way out, he was intercepted by the pathologist. "Biagio, can I bother you for a moment?"

"Go on."

"You know that in cases of such a violent death a post mortem is only a formality, don't you?"

Biagio nodded slightly.

"But we were forced to perform one on Santo too, for bureaucratic reasons. And we discovered that . . . "

"What?"

"I've been trying to make up my mind whether or not to tell you, but . . . Santo had cancer. A large tumor, at an advanced stage."

Biagio turned pale. "Are you sure?"

The doctor nodded.

"I had no idea. He . . . he never said a word."

"That's what I assumed. But I thought it was right to tell you."

"Yes. Yes, thank you."

Why did you never tell us anything, old man? he wondered, feeling a deep sense of alienation. But the answer wasn't long in coming: because he was ashamed. We're *men*, we don't like to appear sick and weak. Am I right, old man?

Biagio wondered how his friend had felt, knowing his days were numbered. He wondered how he had been able to face the disease alone, and he cursed himself for not having noticed anything. And he felt even more hatred toward Pugliese: Santo knew he was dying, he could have said he was ill and gotten himself out of that mess with the Chechens and spent his last months with the people he loved, including Nicky. Instead he had continued to fight shoulder to shoulder with the Panthers. Santo Spada hadn't betrayed his own nature.

Nicky came out of the room, putting an end to his thoughts. Biagio bent and kissed her on the forehead, hugging her to his chest. "Are you all right?"

"Yes. Thanks for bringing me. It . . . it was important to me."

"Your father was a good man, a brave man."

"I know . . . Now let's go."

As the speakers pounded out "Living Proof" by Black Water Rising, sending electricity coursing through him, Biagio lifted the heavy bar with the dumbbells in the offices of the Narcotics division. To train himself, to feel his muscles grow in volume, to take his body beyond its limits had always given him a sense of security and stability. He had always taken it for granted that working on his body, on his muscular mass, on his physical strength, also strengthened his spirit, his ego, his force of will. The pain, the adrenaline, the testosterone, and the endorphins were able to placate his inner demons and discipline his savage soul. That had been his credo ever since he had been little more than a child: if you appear strong, you *are* strong.

He put down the bar and felt the blood suffuse his muscles.

The door of the room opened, interrupting his thoughts. It was Nicola Santangelo, the head of the Crime Squad. "Everything's fine, Biagio. Verri has checked and he says you can go."

Biagio nodded. Verri had summoned him to ask where he had been the previous night at the time when it was presumed that Boran Paja had been killed and dumped outside Claudetti's house. Biagio had a cast-iron alibi: he had been having dinner with Nicky at the time, and there were lots of people who could bear witness to that. He was unassailable. Having left all the dirty work to Boran's uncle's men absolved him of all blame. Even Verri must have been convinced that the Albanian Mafia was alone responsible for the murder, and yet he had brought Claudetti in and interrogated him, putting him in the cooler to teach him a lesson.

"Nico, is Claudetti still in custody?"

"Yes, he's still downstairs. What are you thinking?"

Biagio smiled. "Nothing, don't worry."

Not even she understood what was happening between them. She felt that it was wrong, that it was simply an attempt to run away from her own problems, her own sense of guilt. And yet, however strange he might seem to her, he was handsome. In the past she had been with men, but since she had gotten together with Sara, Giorgio was the first, and nobody had stirred her blood the way he had. Maybe she had drawn close to him partly because she felt guilty: when she had betrayed the pack, she had also betrayed Giorgio. But beyond her personal motivations, she had discovered that he was a passionate lover, as voracious as the wild animals tattooed on his back.

The previous night, he had joined her half an hour after that delicious dinner, and they had done it again. This time it had been even better. More violent and more animal, because he seemed to be trying to pour all his anger and anxiety into her, forcing her to submit and bending her to the fury of that perfect body of his.

Neither of them had asked too many questions: they had united their solitudes in an attempt to mitigate the stress and the fear, finding an outlet in ecstasy. Claudia felt the need to be physically destroyed in bed in the hope of collapsing into a sleep without dreams, because otherwise, as soon as she closed her eyes, she relived the assault on the police car.

But sex was only a fleeting palliative.

That night too she had woken with a start, screaming. Giorgio had hugged her to him, asking her what was happening, but she had not found the courage to tell him. She couldn't.

The truth was that Claudia was fighting with herself. It wasn't an easy battle. She hadn't done coke in a long time: that was another of her demons that was constantly knocking at her door like a drunken violent husband. So far she hadn't opened the door again. She had tried to plug her ears, to distract herself. That was why she wanted to be with Giorgio: when she was close to him, her demons kept quiet as if they were afraid to present themselves. But in spite of that, abstaining from coke was tough. She was the first to be surprised that she was still standing.

You're steady on your feet because you made a promise to Biagio, she told herself, doing press-ups on the floor. You gave him your trust, even though he seems changed. You gave him your word, and after what he did for you, you can't disappoint him, even if it means making enemies of the others. You know he'd never hurt anyone in the family. You know that because he forgave you, and now your life is his, remember that.

She hoped Giorgio would be back soon. When she was with him

everything was simpler. She could even pretend to be a normal person, not a fugitive.

Biagio had entrusted her to Mirko. Nicky was walking along the street, head held contemptuously high. It wasn't bad going around with a seven-footer as a bodyguard.

When she saw a record shop, she asked Mirko if they could go in. She wandered between the shelves and after a few seconds found the Nina Zilli CD containing the song that Biagio liked. She threw a glance at the assistant, who was busy at that moment. With an almost automatic reflex, Nicky looked around: no cameras, and she was out of range of the other customers' eyes. She stared at the photograph of the singer on the cover and swore to herself that Biagio would have that CD come what may.

"Jump that red light," Giorgio ordered.

"Why?" Vito asked.

"Just do it."

Vito obeyed and sped through at sixty miles an hour, gaining curses for at least six generations.

"You people are going to get me killed one of these days. Why did you make me do that? Are you in a hurry?"

Giorgio's only response was to take out his pistol and cock it. "We're being followed."

"Fuck. Who is it?"

"I don't know. There are two of them. They've been behind us since we left Oscar's house."

"What do we do?"

Giorgio tried to call Biagio, but there was no reply. "Shit," he whispered. Reluctantly, he called Carmine.

"Hi," he replied. "Were you missing me?"

"Oh, sure. We need a hand. Do you have a car?"

"Yes, Biagio's 4x4. What's going on?"

"Trouble. We're being followed."

"Where are you?"

Giorgio told him where they were heading. "If you're at Oscar's house, there are a few toys in the basement that could come in useful."

"Okay, I'll be right there," Carmine replied, hanging up.

"Exit and take the highway."

"What are you thinking?"

Giorgio turned to his friend and smiled. "Do you have good insurance?"

Vito threw his head back. "Oh, fuck!"

Biagio went downstairs to the holding cells and stopped in front of the one where Claudetti was being kept. As soon as he went in, the first thing he did was make sure he put the bugs out of use.

"I told you if you kept breaking my balls you'd end up behind bars."

Claudetti sat up on his mattress and glared at him. "Fuck off, Mazzeo."

"What does Verri say?" Biagio asked.

"Are you pulling my leg? Don't you know?"

"No."

"They threw me out of Homicide. I may lose my job and be put on trial for misrepresentation. So he can fuck off too. But it's you I have to thank for this, isn't it, you son of a bitch?"

"You should have listened to me."

"You're nothing but a murderer. First Bucciarelli, then Messina, now Paja. You disgust me."

"And yet right now I'm your only chance."

"What the fuck do you mean?"

"I can get you back in Homicide through the front door."

Claudetti laughed. "Bullshit."

"Listen . . . " Biagio said, and presented his proposition.

Listening to him, Andrea Claudetti felt his blood run cold.

"Stop here," Giorgio said as soon as they had entered the industrial park. "Do you have any toys in the car?"

"*Nada.*"

"It doesn't matter. Go on for another two or three hundred yards, and stop there, in full view."

"Shit, are you trying to use me as bait?"

"Are you scared?" Giorgio teased.

"Like hell I am. Let them so much as come close."

"There won't be any need, I'll get them from behind. Do as I said."

He got out of the car and ran behind a row of containers, cursing himself for having left the big bag with the guns in his 4x4.

He tried again to call Biagio, but the telephone seemed to be off. Shit, he said to himself, glancing at the street. Two minutes later, he saw the SUV that had been following them come into view. It passed the row of containers and stopped fifty yards from Vito's Audi TT. Two big men in dark clothes got out. They were carrying automatic weapons. Vito was shrewd enough to put his pistol on the ground and raise his hands.

Covered by those metal walls, Giorgo started running, hoping to get there in time.

The person in front of him wasn't a man. He was the Devil. And he had just asked him to sell his soul. In return, he'd get his life back, he'd be in charge of Homicide again. Not just that. He'd get respect and honor. Plus the knowledge that he'd stopped a monster and avoided a war. Better still, an enviable position and a secure future for his children. But in return he would have to follow Mazzeo. He would have to become like him.

"I'm just asking you to become what you are: a cop. The alternative is to do a few months inside and then say goodbye to the uniform. You can forget the street, you can forget ever investigating. Is it worth it, do you think?"

"You're asking me to ally myself with you, Mazzeo, do you realize that?"

"I'm not becoming your ally, no way. In fact, things between us won't change. No, I'm not asking you to forgive me, to pass over what you think I've done or shit like that. I'm just asking you to postpone our war for the moment. I have a score to settle with you, and when this business is over you can be quite certain I'll come to find you, without my badge or my pistol."

"No. You won't."

Biagio laughed. "What makes you think that?"

"Let's say I agree, what happens?" Claudetti asked, changing the subject.

"We stop that son of a bitch and you get a promotion."

"Why should I trust you?"

Biagio shrugged. "Let's put it this way: what do you have to lose right now?"

Claudetti didn't answer that. "Was it your idea to put me on the list of suspects for the death of Boran Paja?"

"The way I see it, you incriminated yourself, acting behind the backs of your superiors, pissing them off totally. That's why you're in here now. Verri has thrown you down the toilet and pulled the chain. To everyone, you're just a ball-breaker who let the witness he was supposed to protect be killed. However strange it may seem to you, I'm your one hope of salvation."

"Are you really sure of everything you've told me?"

"One hundred percent. I'll be the one who'll take all the risks, I swear it on the heads of my men."

"I don't believe you," Claudetti said in a weary voice.

Biagio took out the keys he had been given, fiddled with the lock, and opened the cell door wide. "Do you believe me now?"

Claudetti stood up and made to walk out. Biagio landed him a left hook to the chin with all the force of his two-hundred-plus pounds behind it. Claudetti fell to the floor without knowing what had hit him.

"That's to make it clear that even though we'll be working together you mustn't hope to get off lightly when we've finished," Biagio said, waving the painful hand with which he had hit him in the air. "Get this into your head: I'm only doing this because I need you."

"When this is over I'll put you inside, Mazzeo," Claudetti muttered. "That's a promise."

Biagio held out his hand. After a moment's hesitation, Claudetti grabbed it and let him help him to his feet.

"You know what you're asking me?" Claudetti asked.

"To show some balls and let those bastards know who's boss."

Claudetti shook his head. But he did so with a smile on his lips.

"Where's the other guy?" one of the two brutes asked in broken Italian.

"I left him in his car. Who the fuck are you and what do you want?"

"Where's Mazzeo?" the other man asked. Vito guessed they were Slavs, but wasn't sure of which nationality.

"Who wants him?"

As his only response, one of the two shifted the barrel of his pistol to aim at the Audi and fired two shots, smashing the rear window.

"Hey! What the fuck—"

The other Slav punched him full in the face, knocking him to the ground. "We ask the questions. Where's Mazzeo?"

"How the fuck should I know?"

They exchanged glances and said something in an incomprehensible language.

"Want to bet your memory will come back if I shoot you in the leg?" said the bigger of the two, aiming his weapon at one leg. "Right, Radovan?"

The other didn't reply. The Slav turned and saw that Radovan was lying senseless on the ground.

"Radovan?"

He felt something press against the back of his neck and heard the click of a gun being cocked.

"Toss it," Giorgio said.

The Slav turned abruptly, trying to elbow him, the result being that he got the grip of the pistol on his nose. Giorgio tore his weapon from his hand and hit him with a kick to the cheek that threw him to the ground, the breath knocked out of him.

Vito threw himself on the man, pummeling his face with punches.

"Enough, Vito. Vito! Enough, for Christ's sake! You're going to kill him!"

"That's exactly what I want to do," Vito said, unperturbed. "He ruined my car, the son of a bitch,"

Giorgio had to grab him by the throat and pull him off before he really did kill the man.

"Control yourself, for fuck's sake! All those steroids are frying your brain!"

"Fucking Albanians!"

"They aren't Albanians, idiot," he said, letting him go with a push. "Radovan is a Serb name."

"Serbs? Fuck, the guys with the coke?"

"That's quite likely," Giorgio replied, searching them. "Take a look in their car, see if there's anything that might interest us."

Searching in their wallets, Giorgio realized he had been right: Radovan and Stefanovi were both Serbs. He knew that meant only one thing: more trouble in store.

Biagio was about to start the car and leave Headquarters when his BlackBerry started vibrating: Giorgio.

"Hey, handsome!"

"Fuck, Biagio. I've been trying to get hold of you for an hour."

"I was in a place where there was no signal. What is it?"

"Vito and I were followed by a 4x4 with two guys on board. We took them to the industrial park and forced them out into the open. Now they're here, lying unconscious at my feet."

"Who the fuck are they?" Biagio asked with a frown.

"Serbs."

"Jesus!"

"Right. What should I do?"

Biagio threw his head back against the headrest and closed his eyes, swearing.

"Is it just you and Vito there?"

"No. I called Carmine when you didn't pick up. He just got here."

"Did you find anything on them?"

"Weapons, and some photos of you with your home address and the address of the Bang Bang on the back."

"Sons of bitches!"

"They're the guys with the coke consignment, aren't they?"

"Yes, I think they are."

"So what do I do?"

Biagio let a few seconds pass, then said, "Kill them."

"What?"

"Kill them."

"Biagio, maybe I didn't make myself clear."

"No, you made yourself very clear. Kill them."

"Chief, are you losing it?"

"Do you trust me or not?"

"What's that got to do with it? I can't just—"

Biagio hung up.

"Shit!" Giorgio cursed at the phone. He redialed Biagio's number but the answerphone came on immediately. He had moved away to talk uninterruptedly. He called again, but Biagio was still busy with another conversation. On a sudden intuition, he turned abruptly to his friends and at that moment saw Carmine hang up on a call, put away his cell phone, and take out a pistol.

"Nooo!" Giorgio cried, running toward him.

But it was too late.

Carmine gunned down the two Serbs in cold blood.

Giorgio closed his eyes while the echoes of the shots bounced around him, amplified by that artificial amphitheater of containers.

He heard Donna's words in his head: *I don't know exactly what happened to him, but something has changed him . . . He isn't the same anymore . . .*

He kept his eyes closed and concentrated on his breathing. When he heard steps, he opened his eyes again.

"Any problem?" Carmine asked, still holding his gun.

Giorgio stared at him in silence for a few seconds.

"No," he replied. "No problem."

Corrado Tortora had taken the rest of the day off. He was in a foul mood, given what had happened the night before. He had no desire to meet the eyes of his colleagues and superiors in the Prosecutor's Department who would remind him of the extent of his defeat. So, after a brief, stormy meeting at Headquarters with the prefect and some police bigwigs to figure out what had happened and how to arrange the matter with the press, he had gone straight to the sports center to shake off his anger and tension by swimming.

When he came out of the showers he found Biagio Mazzeo in the changing room.

"How was the water?" Biagio asked with a smile.

"What the fuck are you doing here?" Tortora asked, stiffening. They were alone in the room. "And how the hell did you find me?"

"I'm a man with a thousand resources," Biagio replied with a shrug.

"What the hell do you want?" Tortora asked curtly, opening his locker and changing.

"I don't know, I saw that Verri managed as usual to cover up this Paja thing by pinning all the blame on the Albanians. To the press, the murder will be presented as a settling of scores within the Balkan underworld. And it's true, because that's exactly what it was."

"Of course."

"And in spite of all your insinuations, I have a cast-iron alibi that proves I had nothing to do with any of this."

"Bullshit."

"Let me finish. So, the Albanian Mafia was solely responsible for the murder: case closed. But I know it wasn't like that. Boran Paja was an informer of mine. Many of my operations bear witness to the fact that Paja was a trusted confidant, with everything above board. Whereas what you and Claudetti did wasn't exactly legal."

"You can't—"

"What would happen if I told the truth to the journalists, but above all: what would happen if *this* got to them?" He threw a document on the bench where Tortora was sitting.

Tortora picked it up. It was Paja's request to be taken into the Witness Protection Program, in which it was clear that while waiting for a response he was being protected by the judicial authorities. It was proof that at the time of his murder Boran Paja had been under the protection of the State.

Tortora turned pale.

"How did you get—"

"That's not your problem. Well? You know, I'm in a dilemma: I can be content with the official version, or I can raise a great ruckus and have an investigation opened into the death of my informer whom *you* couldn't protect."

"I didn't—"

"Of course, of course, not you personally, I know. But speaking from a technical and legal point of view he was entrusted to you, because this is your signature, right? What would happen if this became public knowledge?"

Silence.

"Tell me, what would happen if I accused you of having let a key witness of ours in a major international drug trafficking investigation be killed, an investigation we've been working on for years and which was still in progress at the time of his arrest?"

Biagio passed him a report from Narcotics on an investigation in which Paja was indicated as key to the success of the operation.

Tortora slumped on the bench, defeated.

Biagio smiled and slapped him on the back. He took the document from his hands and folded it back into his jacket pocket. "You people acted in a very dubious way, moving in an area that wasn't quite legal, and you got a witness killed in a safe house. You're a good man, and I think you're also ambitious. Do you really want this stain on your reputation? This is a matter for the Law Council, Tortora."

"What do you want?" Tortora asked in a thin voice, blinking nervously.

Biagio stood up and squeezed his shoulder. "You'll know in due time," he said, leaving him alone with the crushing knowledge that he had just sold his own honesty.

In the restaurant, the customers were talking and joking in over-loud voices, but he didn't seem to mind. He was thinking about his plan, which was becoming clearer in his mind with every hour that passed in spite of the fact that everything seemed to be going against him.

He made a long series of telephone calls and then stared at two uniformed police officers who were just finishing eating and getting ready to start their shift. He signaled to the girl who had taken his order and told her that he would pay for his colleagues' lunch. He heard one of his cell phones vibrating in his pockets. He hoped it wasn't Pugliese's men.

Danger avoided. It was Adem Paja.

"Hi," Biago said. "Good work."

"Thanks. But I'm calling you about something else."

"I'm listening."

"Someone has robbed me. He killed my men, and one of them was found crushed under a truck."

"What's that got to do with me?"

"I was wondering if you knew anything about it."

"How do you mean? Are you accusing me?"

Biagio half closed his eyes and held his breath, waiting for the answer.

"No, not at all. I just want to know if you can help me to figure out who it was."

Biagio sighed with relief. "Okay. But it'll cost you."

"No problem. I just want back what was stolen from me."

"Did you have a feud with anyone?"

"No."

"Okay. Send me details and addresses by text and I'll see what I can do."

Biagio hung up and drummed his fingers on the plate thinking of how to solve this problem too, but he was interrupted by the arrival of the two officers. After a little chat to thank him for the lunch, they left. Deep inside Biagio envied them. When they had finished their shift and taken off their uniforms, their only concerns would be to help their wives with dinner or, in the most tragic of cases, to finish their children's homework. An easy life, without problems. Right now, it was something he could only dream about.

The waitress came to serve him, bringing him back to reality.

As Biagio was starting to eat, Giorgio rushed in. He came straight to his table and sat down in front of him, scowling.

"What will you have?" Biagio asked after a few seconds' embarrassed silence.

"I'm not here to eat. What the fuck's going on, Biagio? What is this business with Paja? Who killed him? Were you behind it? And what about Claudetti?"

"That's a lot of questions, let me eat in peace, then we'll talk. Come on, have something."

"I told you I'm not hungry, I just want to talk. What the fuck's happening to you, Biagio?"

Biagio shrugged and continued chewing. Then, indicating the plate: "We'll talk afterwards, right now I'm eating."

Giorgio kept staring at him. Then he reached out an arm and with one sweep of his hand threw the plate with all the food to the floor, making a great racket. "Now you've finished eating," he said.

Waiters and customers turned, but nobody dared to say anything. Biagio looked at him, stunned, then gave a little laugh and signaled to the waitress. "Unbelievable," he said, cleaning his mouth with a napkin. "All right then, go on. What do you want to talk about?"

Giorgio waited while the waitress cleaned things up, then leaned forward across the table and said, "Why did you have the Serbs killed? Do you think that was a sensible thing to do?"

"Better them than you, don't you think?"

"Are you serious?"

"Hey, you assured me you would trust me, so do it. Have a bit of confidence in me, and don't go having doubts."

"Biagio, wake up! You had those two killed, just like that, as if it was nothing. Without questioning them, without even knowing what they wanted, how many there are, and without calculating what might happen now."

"Who says I didn't?" he asked, looking around.

"What? In three seconds?"

"Being a leader means—"

"I don't want any of that bullshit. Biagio, look at me: you have to listen. You have a problem, you aren't thinking, you aren't clearheaded. First the coke, and you don't tell us what the fuck you're doing. Then Paja. Now the Serbs. And look how nervous you are. Are you stoned too? I know you have the deaths of Sonja and Santo to cope with. Okay, I understand that, but you need help. This way you're going to get us all killed."

"Have you finished?" Biagio asked with a lopsided smile, putting his fingers together. "So you really think I'm losing it, that I'm, what? Improvising, acting on impulse, that I'm not right in the head? Is that it?"

"No. The problem—"

Biagio beat his fingers on his chest. "I don't have any problem. You're the one with the problem, son, and it's a problem of trust in me. I've always taken care of all of you, and I still am, even if you think the opposite."

"How can I trust you if you don't tell me what you're thinking?"

"Do you realize you're ruining everything?" Biagio asked in a thin voice.

"No, chief, you're the one who's ruining everything. And you know why? Because you've stopped trusting your family."

Biagio shook his head, disappointed.

"Ever since you've been wearing that ring of his everything has changed, Biagio. Ivankov is dead. *Dead*. Leave that business behind you."

"This is the last time I'm going to say this, Giorgio. Look me in the eyes."

Giorgio leaned closer and did as he was told.

"I have everything under control, and I'm fine. Everything is the same as usual, and *none* of you will get hurt if you continue to do what I tell you. Got that?"

"Biagio, tell me what's going on or things are over between you and me."

"Giorgio, please—"

"I want to know what's going on, and I want to know *now*."

Biagio realized with infinite pain that Giorgio was the sacrificial lamb. His eyes misted over without his being able to do anything about it. Then he sat back in his seat, scratching his throat.

"Okay. Get out!"

"I don't—"

"*Get out!*"

Giorgio felt that something between them had broken forever. He was afraid of Biagio's eyes, because the last time he had seen that look he had killed one of the people closest to him. Giorgio realized it would be his turn now.

"I'm sorry, Biagio," he said, standing. "But I'm doing it for—"

"Get the hell out of here," Biagio said without looking at him.

Giorgio Varga left the restaurant with the devastating awareness that he had just lost a brother.

Biagio had had to swallow the deep disappointment, the aching sense of loss, he felt after his encounter with Giorgio. He couldn't allow himself to be disheartened. Not at such a difficult time.

"Here they are," Carmine said, distracting him from his thoughts.

Biagio joined his friend at the entrance to the warehouse, and watched the cars approach. These dickheads all seemed to have adopted the kind of SUVs associated with American gangsters: a BMW X5, an Audi Q5, a Mercedes and so on, a parade of truly bad taste.

"Are you sure these are the men you want to trust?" Carmine asked, raising an eyebrow. "Shit, have you had a look at them?"

Biagio watched as the dealers got out of their cars. He didn't exactly like the idea, but turning to them was the only way to reverse the situation with the Calabrians.

"I know," he said. "Discretion isn't their forte, I admit, but they are reliable. Anyway, it's not as if I had a choice. And appearances can be deceptive."

He signaled to the men in the cars to pull up and join them inside the warehouse.

"Eyes open, okay?" Biagio said, giving Carmine a slap on his broad back.

By way of reply, Carmine put the shotgun over his shoulder.

One after the other, the ten men entered the warehouse, looking arrogant and suspicious. None of them was older than thirty-five, most were black or mixed race, and they looked daggers at each other. They had come unarmed, one single representative for each ethnic group, as per the rules imposed by Biagio.

They handed their cell phones over to Carmine, who locked the door and escorted them, shotgun in hand, to the ten chairs arranged in a circle around the table in the middle of the warehouse, on which Biagio sat perched, his arms folded. On the table, within easy reach, was another shotgun, in case any of the criminals had the idea of getting too close to the forty kilos of heroin that were lying on the bench. Leaning against a wall, Vito was chewing gum and keeping an eye on the dealers, a pistol in his hand and a shotgun beside him.

"Good evening, gentlemen," Biagio began, ignoring their whistles and their excited expressions at the sight of all that heroin. "Sit down and don't talk. This is school."

"School?" said Swami, the Pakistani. "Who the fuck ever went to school?"

"And here was me thinking you were a college graduate," retorted Carmine, giving him a slap to make it clear they weren't joking. "Just sit down, you scumbags."

The men obeyed and sat down at a certain distance from each other as if they had difficulty breathing the same air. Behind their backs, Carmine watched them warily: he might be the pleasantest man in the world, but when he was serious he had a look that scared even hardened criminals like these.

In a way, all ten of them worked for Biagio, even though they were in competition with each other and in some cases—like the Africans—hated each other's guts. When Biagio, in order to put a stop to wars between gangs of dealers, had divided the Jungle into neighborhoods, he had entrusted to each of them a district where they could deal. Gambians, Algerians, Macedonians, Tunisians, Nigerians, Pakistanis, Romanians, Turks, and Bulgarians: to each ethnic group an area with well-defined borders and a series of rules, if they wanted to stay around. Whoever contravened any of the Panthers' directives was gotten rid of. Sometimes literally.

"Nothing to drink?" asked Petru, the head of the Romanians.

There was a bit of laughter, but Biagio silenced it with a glare.

"Are you here to do business or to cause trouble?" Vito asked angrily.

"Relax, I was only joking," Petru replied, raising his hands.

"Rule number one: just listen," Biagio said. "You'll talk when I tell you you can."

They didn't reply. Clearly, they had understood.

"As you can see, there's one representative missing from this meeting. Boran Paja, the Albanian. You know perfectly well that he was my protégé, and I also bet some of you already know what happened to him, and why."

This remark caused a stir.

"Paja has left a gap that will soon have to be filled by someone. The question is: who?"

The dealers stared at each other like boxers studying their opponents in a championship match.

"That's why you're here, to help me figure out who I can trust and who among you can most ensure me the security and reliability I was guaranteed by the Albanian. To put it briefly, I want to put you to the test. We've known each other for quite a while now, and you know that if you work by my rules you all derive benefits." Biagio smiled and opened his arms wide. "Let's put it this way: what I'm about to propose to you is a race. I'll set you some objectives. Whoever fulfils them better than the others will win the prize and take Paja's place, but even for all the others"—here he indicated the heroin—"there'll be a decent consolation prize."

He took the sheets of paper on which he had printed names, timetables, and addresses, and passed them to the gang bosses. One sheet for each dealer. He watched them reading—or trying to read—with expressions of curiosity and surprise on their faces. He whistled and then started throwing each of them a bag containing a kilo of heroin.

"This is to let you know how generous I am. Advance payment for services rendered, and the thirty kilos that remain here are the bonus for whoever distinguishes himself more than the others. Any questions?"

"I can't read," said Hafiz, the Nigerian.

Vito shook his head.

Biagio took the paper from his hands and started to read. Then, addressing all of them, he explained in detail what they had to do, and how, if they wanted to continue doing business with him.

"But those are—" said Krste, the Macedonian.

"Our enemies," Biagio said, cutting him short. "Do you want to carry on doing business? Obey my orders, and I'll deal with them."

"And what if we refuse?" asked Yahya, the boss from the Gambia.

"Our cooperative relationship ends here, and you go in my black book. Any more questions?"

Nobody opened his mouth, busy as they were in looking from the bag in their hands to the thirty remaining kilos.

"Is there anyone who wants to turn back? I have to know now. If I discover any of you trying to screw me around for any reason, I'll fuck you over big time, just as I did with the Albanian, understood?"

The ten men nodded.

"Then I guess you're all in the game. Good."

"What do we do with this stuff?" asked Swami, the Pakistani.

Biagio shrugged. "It's all yours, handsome, do whatever the fuck you want. I don't want a percentage or anything. It's your reward."

"What about the bonus?" asked Kaddour, the Algerian, his eyes shining. "Don't you want a percentage on that either?"

"No. If you win it, it's all yours. Obviously you mustn't tell anybody, I repeat, *anybody*, who gave it to you. Just keep to that rule, and it's easy money, boys."

Almost all smiled. In the current recession, heroin was coming back into fashion. In particular, it was the drug of choice among immigrant workers, who smoked it and relaxed into its languid embrace, wiping out their exhaustion and sending them into ecstasy before another day on the construction sites. A guaranteed high at low cost: a goldmine for the traffickers.

"But generous as I am, I won't show any mercy to anyone who does anything stupid. You've heard the rules, and I'm giving you impunity. You mustn't be afraid of reprisals or bullshit like that. If you do this, you're under my protection, understood?"

The men nodded, their eyes feverish with the desire to get down to work. Each of them knew he could do better than the others, and those thirty kilos meant a quantum leap for their respective gangs.

"Make a note of this number. If you have any problems call me here, okay?"

More nods.

"Good. I'd say we're though. Now get the hell out of here, and above all don't disappoint me."

As soon as the ten gang leaders had gone, Biagio, Vito, and Carmine moved the thirty remaining kilos to their hiding place, and Biagio called Adem Paja, Boran's uncle.

"Adem?" Biagio said.

"Yes, go on," Adem replied.

"I know who robbed you."

The Night of the Fires

When he got back home that evening, Nicky ran to embrace him and he felt better than he ever had before. She hugged him tight and winked at Mirko.

"Hi, chief, everything okay?" Mirko asked in a low voice, putting a hand on his shoulder.

"Yes," he said, putting down the shopping bags. "How about here? Anything to report?"

"Everything's fine," Mirko replied.

"Then you can go home," Biagio said, then, putting an arm around his shoulders, whispered: "Full alert tonight at Oscar's house, there might be a bit of movement. I want everybody to stay in the villa, nobody must go out, understood?"

Mirko nodded.

"And I want all the boys to dress warmly," Biagio added, a reference to bullet-proof vests.

Mirko turned pale. "Okay."

"Send three of your people here in two hours, I have to go out and I want them to stay with Nicky. And thanks, Mirko."

"No sweat. In two hours they'll be here, don't worry." He waved goodbye to Nicky. "Bye for now, you little tramp."

"Hey, be good or I'll beat you up," Nicky said, looking up.

Mirko left the apartment laughing, but with goosebumps on his arms.

Biagio was happy to be alone with Nicky. After such a shitty day he couldn't have stood the desolation of an empty apartment. He took off his jacket and holster and threw them on the couch. "So, I got everything you asked me for."

"Even the peanut butter?"

"Even that. But are you sure it's better to cook? Wouldn't it be quicker to order something?"

"You mean, like Chinese?" she asked, her eyes lighting up with joy.

"Why not? For me chicken with lemon and soy noodles with prawns, and please, no spring rolls: I don't want to spend all night on the toilet like last time."

"Yes, sir!" she replied, clicking her heels together.

His cell phone started vibrating. It was the encrypted phone. A text: *Time is running out. Get in touch or one of you will die. One every day.*

Biagio felt his blood run cold.

When he came back to the kitchen he found a gift package on the table, and the text message from the Calabrians disappeared from his mental radar. Nicky was smiling at him with those big Sixties glasses that made her eyes look huge.

"Don't tell me it's for me."

"Who else would it be for?"

Biagio gave her a kiss on her wide forehead and then started unwrapping the gift.

"As you can see I also had the package done, in case you suspected I'd stolen it. Although the thought did cross my mind, I admit."

Biagio laughed happily. "I love you!" he said, throwing her in the air like a little girl.

"Hey! Put me down!"

But he didn't put her down, he embraced her and covered her with kisses.

"Come on, let's put it on right now."

"You bet," he said, happy to dismiss all his problems from his mind thanks to Nicky's good humor.

Donna knew she was someone who never learned from her own mistakes. Especially when it came to Biagio. But with him there had been such a special relationship, they had been through so much together, that she couldn't accept the thought that it was over between them, not even after the scene in her house. She felt she had to try again. She couldn't lose the man she loved.

The elevator doors opened. As soon as she set foot on the landing, she heard music coming from Sonja's apartment. She slowly approached and heard the voices of Biagio and Nicky singing—out of tune and with lots of laughter—"Per sempre." She knew the song: she was crazy about the voice of the girl who sang it, it reminded her of her childhood and the colored singers she loved to listen to for evenings on end, but above all the words seemed written for her and Biagio.

Donna placed her hands on the door, listening to them singing and laughing happily. A tear streaked her face. She had hoped to find peace here, to refill the void that he had created inside him. But it wasn't the way she had thought. Biagio was happy, he had filled the space left by her and Sonja with this girl he loved like a daughter.

Donna realized she envied Nicky, and she was ashamed of that thought. From now on she was a defeated woman, someone who had nothing left. She hated herself for that. But it didn't take long for her to divert that hatred onto Biagio. *He* had distanced her from his life, preferring this irreverent young girl. Enough regrets and remorse, she told herself, wiping her eyes: she had to draw a line under that. Donna left, her eyes as cold as her heart.

The more time he spent with her, the more he realized just how much she had in common with her father: the love of food, the sparkling good humor, the always ready quips, the cheekiness, and the Westerns: she loved the spaghetti westerns of Sergio Leone, Sergio

Corbucci, and all the others, strange enough in a young girl, but something that made her all the more special to him.

Soon after the end of dinner the doorbell rang, and Biagio admitted the three men who would stay with the girl.

"What's with all this deployment of forces?" she asked him as he put his jacket on.

He smiled at the expression: she must have heard it on TV. He clasped her to his chest and gave her a kiss on the head. "Because you're my treasure," he said, "and treasures should be well guarded."

Nicky pretended to swoon and he had to support her. He walked her to her bed and told her he'd be back later.

"Should I be worried?"

"No, sweetheart."

He gave instructions to the three bodyguards, then left. That night he planned to act, to move the game forward and show what he was capable of.

The three cops stopped the 4x4 on the hill overlooking the city and got out. The Jungle was shining like a jewel, beautiful enough to take your breath away. They stood there staring out at the darkness around them, a darkness pierced by the lights of the buildings, the street lamps, the cars, the restaurants, and the nightclubs.

After a few minutes, Biagio checked the time on his watch. It was a few seconds to one. "Now," he said.

As if in response to that word, something in the distance started burning, assuming the shape of a fire. A few seconds later, another fire some hundred yards away lashed at the darkness. Then another further away, and then another, and so on.

"They kept their word," Carmine said, sinking his hands into the pockets of his jeans. "Who the fuck would ever have thought—"

"You bet they did," Vito retorted. "I'd have tracked them down one by one if they hadn't."

"And this is just the beginning," Biagio whispered, enjoying watching his hard-fought plan come to fruition.

Sure enough, after a few seconds, an explosion was heard in the distance, from the direction of the industrial park. Then two more blasts, and another . . . and another . . .

From this elevated point there was a perfect view of the Jungle, and you could clearly count the fires and the explosions.

"Shit, there must be more than ten," Vito cried, excited by the spectacle.

"Twenty," Biagio said. "Two incendiary attacks from each group."

He had given orders to the ten dealers to go with their men to the targets indicated by him and set fire to warehouses, earthmoving machines, garbage trucks, storehouses, and waste disposal facilities, as well as steal or sabotage diggers, trucks, and other mechanical vehicles used for construction and earthmoving. All the warehouses, the construction storehouses, and the trucks now in flames belonged to companies linked with Natale Pugliese and his associates. But it didn't end there. Right now, gangs of boys to whom he had promised the monopoly of small patches for dealing were bursting into bars, slot machine arcades, supermarkets, and various stalls in the fruit and vegetable market and attacking them with metal bars, Molotov cocktails, and paper bombs. The only rule he had given them was not to kill anybody. Apart from that, they had free rein to smash whatever they wanted.

"I'd give a lot to see his face right now," Vito said, his eyes sweeping over the various fires.

"If everything goes according to plan, you will," Biagio said.

Fire engine sirens started to wail, but they wouldn't be able to stop the fires: there were too many of them, and the construction sites now in flames would be unusable for months on end.

You shouldn't have killed Santo, you son of a bitch, Biagio thought, watching the flames consume Pugliese's enterprises. He glanced at his watch again. And this is just the beginning, he said to himself, turning.

"Let's go, or we might be late," he said to his men, walking to the 4x4. The night of the Panthers had only just begun.

After receiving the telephone call from his boss, local bigwig Rocco Neri dressed quickly and called his men: in his branch he was the man in charge of weapons and the hit squad, and right now the boss needed his help in escorting his family to a safe place.

When Neri had asked what was going on, his boss had replied, "We're under attack."

Neri had made a quick round of phone calls to call in the sleeper cells from those families linked to Pugliese, but as his Mercedes drove out through the electronic gate, three masked men emerged from a black 4x4, armed with Kalashnikovs.

Before Rocco Neri could reverse, the Mercedes had been riddled with bullets.

It was just after one in the morning when Deputy Warden Leonardo Verdini entered cell block 6. He slipped silently down the long corridor and stopped outside the cell where the Algerians the Panthers had put away a few months earlier were housed. He opened the door and left it slightly ajar. Then he did an about-turn and stopped outside another cell. He fiddled with the keys and opened this one too. Once the lock clicked, he headed rapidly for the exit of the cell block.

Algerian boss Malek Chebel and three of his men left their cell armed with improvised blades and headed without hesitation toward that of the Calabrians linked to Natale Pugliese. The Algerians burst in, weapons in hand, and stabbed the two Italian prisoners to death. It was quick and violent. Once it was over, they put the knives in the Calabrians' hands, as if to suggest that the men had killed each other in a quarrel.

Malek signaled to his men to leave as quickly as possible, and they went back in silence to their cell. A few minutes later, a guard entered the cell block, locked the doors of the two cells without even glancing inside, and went away again.

During this settling of scores, nobody in the neighboring cells had dared to say a word.

In appearance, it was a normal garage. But when the German shepherds from the Police Canine Unit entered, they went crazy, starting to bark and pull at their handlers, revealing the real nature of the place: a cocaine storehouse. This joint operation by the Narcotics and Organized Crime divisions, under the command of Chief Inspectors Andrea Claudetti and Ariana Manisci, led to a major drugs seizure. Ten kilos of cocaine plus quite an arsenal of weapons. Deputy Prosecutors Tortora and Barberi, who had signed the search warrants, were in seventh heaven: as Biagio Mazzeo had suggested, they had brought a reporter with them, promising her a scoop about the struggle against the Northern Mafia, and now they were strutting in front of the TV cameras. Claudetti, however, even though they were all smiling at him and congratulating him, wasn't enjoying it. This was the third raid of the night. In total, they had confiscated around thirty kilos of cocaine plus a basement fitted out as a laboratory for refining the drugs. They had arrested five men, all affiliated to Pugliese's syndicate, plus a few Romanian girls who worked as technicians in the laboratory.

Thirty kilos in one night. Enough to turn around a career. But he could take no credit for the operation. It had been Mazzeo who had given him the addresses and paved the way for him with the two prosecutors. He had simply asked him two things: to strike after midnight, and if there was any interference from the National or Regional Organized Crime Directorates to tell them to go to hell and continue with the raids. When Claudetti had asked him how he had come to know about these hideouts, Mazzeo had told him that he preferred his sources to remain secret. "How do you think I can persuade an informer of mine to cooperate with you after what you did to the last one?" he had said ironically.

"Come on, let forensics take care of it," Claudetti yelled to his team. "We have to go."

He still had one address given him by Mazzeo, and by now he knew he was on to a sure thing.

It was after two in the morning and in theory the pub should already have closed, but Biagio had asked a favor of the owner, an old acquaintance of his, to keep it open just for him and his men.

While Biagio, Vito and Carmine were sipping pints of Guinness, waiting for the people they had made an appointment with to arrive, Biagio's cell phone vibrated. A text. *Message delivered*, it said. The number was the one that Adem Paja was using.

Biagio smiled. The Albanians liked to display their muscle and since that afternoon when he had told Adem that it was Pugliese's Lombardia that had stolen his drugs, indicating a few prominent members of the organization, such as Rocco Neri, Adem had wasted no time in putting together a team to make it clear to the separatists that he was not the kind of person who could be fucked over so easily. Biagio knew what had driven him to act so quickly: the fear of losing the prestige he had acquired with years of sacrifice. His nephew Boran had started to cooperate with the cops and he had had to kill him, his brother was in prison, and he himself was a fugitive: any opposing criminal group might think that the Albanians were weak right now and try to oust them. The murder of Neri was about to indicate that Adem Paja still had control of the situation.

You've made yourself another enemy, Natale, Biagio thought, putting his cell phone back in his pocket. He barely had time to do so before another text message arrived. This time from Deputy Prosecutor Barberi: *Four raids, thirty-five kilos of coke, a Mafia war arsenal, and twelve people arrested including eight affiliated to Pugliese's syndicate. I love you, my handsome cop! Thank you!!!*

Biagio smiled. Apart from those four raids, there were actually another three. He had informed a contact of his in the Narcotics division of the Treasury Police about two apartments used as a heroin depot, and to a captain in the Narcotics squad of the Carabinieri with whom he had been friends for years he had passed a tip about a restaurant wine cellar where Pugliese's men hid pure drugs to be cut.

The list of the syndicate's hideouts that Attorney Barranca had let him have in return for the promise that he would get rid of Pugliese had turned out to be pure dynamite for the various law enforcement agencies. He could have carried out the raids alone, but he was thinking ahead. He wanted to accrue as much credit as he could among his colleagues from the different agencies, because he would need to call in a lot of favors when it came to the second part of his plan and the collateral damage it would involve.

"Claudetti has confiscated almost forty kilos of cocaine," he said.

"Shit, you've practically cleaned that son of a bitch out," Carmine said, raising his glass.

"You can say that again. Plus, the Albanians have whacked Rocco Neri, the guy who handled the military side of Pugliese's organization."

"What's the next move?" Vito asked. "Because frankly, I don't understand a fucking thing about what we're doing."

"And neither does Pugliese, that's for sure," Biagio said. "That's precisely the point: to strike hard, to hit it all at the same time, all in one night. To hit him from so many sides that he can't figure out where the attacks are coming from. With someone so powerful, it's the only possible strategy."

From outside, the attacks might seem random and small-scale, but Biagio had worked it all out down to the smallest detail. He had deliberately appeared weak to Pugliese to make him lower his guard, and then had attacked with all the anger and ferocity in his body.

"What do we do now?" Carmine insisted.

Biagio didn't reply. He couldn't reply. He couldn't tell them what would happen, because it was too great a risk to share that information with anyone else. Not because he didn't trust them, but because if Pugliese managed to get his hands on Vito or Carmine he would find a way to make them talk.

From a small bag, he dropped a dozen phones on the table. They were fake Chinese iPhones.

"Where the fuck did you find these?" Carmine said, laughing and turning one of them in his hands.

"I love the Chinese. These all have SIM cards with Hong Kong numbers and unlimited credit. I paid an arm and a leg for them, but having international numbers they're practically untraceable. Starting tonight, whenever there's anything important, I want us to communicate only through these, okay?"

At that point they heard heavy footsteps on the wooden stairs leading to the mezzanine where they were sitting, and they stood up.

The six newcomers were tough-looking men whose faces showed the signs of past fights and brawls. Vito greeted them with strong slaps on the back and powerful handshakes. It was he was who had recruited them from the gyms that he frequented. They were trained in martial arts and made their living as disco bouncers or debt collectors or bodyguards and security men in private bars and nightclubs. Strong, trustworthy men, accustomed to violence, who over the years had developed strong links with Narcotics: all of them dealt steroids under the protection of the Panthers. Now the moment had come for them to return the favor.

Vito opened a bottle of whiskey and poured a round for everybody, while

Biagio gave them the counterfeit iPhones. After a collective toast, Biagio told the six men what he wanted them to do for him. He overturned the contents of a sports bag onto the table. Pistols, Benelli shot-guns, MP5 submachine guns, handcuffs, clubs, fake police badges and bibs fell on the wood, shining in the dim light of the English-style spot-lights. Then he threw each of them a small wad of money. He saw them first turn pale, then start drumming nervously on the table. But they couldn't say no. Biagio could have them thrown in jail as and when he wanted. They would have to follow him in this madness.

When one of the bouncers informed Guido Sergi that there was a guy smashing up his Porsche Cayenne with a baseball bat, he ran straight out of the discotheque. The car was parked behind the club, in the area reserved for VIPs.

Guido, filled with coke and irascible by nature, went straight up to the animal who was destroying his SUV, his hands tightened into a fist, followed by the three young guys who were with him. He looked around, not so much for fear of having witnesses in case the situation got out of hand, but because it struck him that someone might be watching what for him was a humiliation, one of the classic things that can compromise a criminal reputation. But there was nobody in the parking lot except a few drunk young guys and a few hookers who had come outside for a little air.

"Hey!" Guido yelled at the unknown man in the leather jacket who was destroying his car.

The man turned, and found four semiautomatic pistols aimed directly at him.

"Toy guns, right?" Carmine Torregrossa said with a smile.

"What the fuck are you doing?" Guido said. "Do you want to die?"

He heard a shot behind him. Still keeping Carmine covered, he turned and saw one of his bodyguards on the ground, while three big guys with masks on their faces, identity badges on their powerful chests, and police bibs were aiming pistols at the backs of his other two men.

Before Guido could open his mouth, the baseball bat came down on his kneecap with all the force of Carmine's 260 pounds.

Guido screamed and fell to the ground, his knee broken. "Are you crazy?" he cried, his voice suffused with pain. "Do you know who I am? Do you know who my father is?"

As the two fake cops handcuffed the young man's bodyguards and loaded them into the black van, Carmine forced the end of the baseball bat into Guido's mouth. "Of course I know. You're the son of that piece of shit, Sabino Sergi. Are they members?" he asked, indicating the bodyguards.

Guido raised a hand from his smashed knee and showed him his middle finger.

Carmine took the bat from his mouth and launched another blow, aiming at the other knee.

"Yes! Yes! They're members!"

With one look Carmine ordered his three partners to load the third bodyguard, the one who lay on the ground, into the van too. "Now the two of us are going to take a little ride," he snarled, dragging him to his feet and pushing him inside the van, where one of the fake cops gagged his mouth with packaging tape.

Carmine got into the cabin and, as one of the fake cops reversed, he called Biagio.

"Biagio?"

"Hi. Got the beaver?"

"Yes, with three squirrels, as you predicted. All house-trained."

"Okay. Then bring me the beaver, and for the others follow the plan."

"Any news from the son of a bitch?"

"Not yet."

"He'll call."

"You can bet on it."

That night something went wrong with the provision of Deputy Prandelli's security guards. By two-twenty nobody had yet come to replace the Lancia outside his villa. A telephone call from the National Crime Bureau had been enough to persuade his guards to stay home, and now the deputy was without any protection. But of course, plunged as he was in an almost comatose sleep, he didn't know that.

He woke only when the light came on and he found himself surrounded by four masked men wearing police bibs and carrying guns.

"What the fuck—"

"Wakey, wakey," Vito said, giving him a violent slap.

"What the fuck are you—"

The deputy earned himself another backhander. Then Vito grabbed him by the arm and pulled him down onto the floor.

"Put something on and let's go," he ordered, aiming the Beretta at him.

Deputy Gilberto Prandelli, undersecretary at the Ministry of Economic Development and a prominent personality within the Justice Commission of the Chamber of Deputies, raised his voice. "What the hell are you doing? Who are you, and what are you doing here? Where's my security?"

"Just get dressed and come with us," Vito snarled, throwing him some clothes taken from a chair. "We're your security."

"Is this some kind of joke? I enjoy Parliamentary immunity, you know what that means?"

"Oh, shit, I'm sorry that changes everything," Vito said, carefully helping him to his feet. Once he was standing, he hit him with a hook to the temple into which he put all his hatred, exacerbated by the amphetamines he had taken just before bursting in. "That was for the four-hundred-euro pension you sons of bitches gave my mother," he screamed contemptuously, kicking him in the balls.

Two of the fake cops grabbed hold of Vito and pulled him off the deputy.

"Hey, what the fuck," one of them whispered in his ear. "He said to bring him in in one piece. Just take it easy."

But Vito wouldn't take it easy, he pushed them away and abruptly handcuffed this politician who was in cahoots with Pugliese. He had always known that Prandelli was rotten to the core.

"Where's my wife?" Prandelli moaned.

Vito's eyes lit up. "A good question." He shifted his gaze to the woman whom he had handcuffed and gagged a while earlier and who now sat shaking in a corner of the room, staring at them in terror. He glanced at the three toughs. "Hold him still for me," he ordered, his pupils dilated by the drugs.

"But—"

"He said not to do anything to him, he didn't mention *her*. Here she is, your little wife." He pulled the woman to her feet. He knew that the son of a bitch had managed to get her the perfect seat on the City Council: head of the Infrastructure and Public Works department.

Practically speaking, his wife was in charge of contracts, which, according to Biagio, were routinely awarded to the myriad of companies owned by Pugliese.

"This bitch is as guilty as you are," he said pulling out the cloth he had stuffed in the woman's mouth. She looked at him with terrified, imploring eyes.

He placed the barrel of his pistol to her forehead.

"I beg you, don't . . . don't hurt me," she stammered.

"Don't worry, darling," Vito said, smiling behind his ski mask. He turned to the deputy. "Tell me, how is she with her tongue?"

The man turned pale, tried to struggle, but the two toughs stopped him.

"I beg you, don't—"

"My mother begged you people too, telling you she couldn't cope and needed help. And what did you do? You took away her home, you and your revenue service."

"I had nothing to do with—"

"Nothing to do with it?" Vito said, unbuttoning the flies of his jeans. "Didn't you get our governor elected with the votes you asked Pugliese to deliver? Didn't you throw open the doors of your lodge to him? You're Pugliese's puppet."

At that name, Prandelli stiffened. "My wife has nothing to do with—"

"Oh, really? Isn't it your wife who decides on funding?"

Prandelli searched for the words but couldn't find them.

"Do me a favour, dickhead," Carmine cried, his eyes humid with anger. "Your wife goes to City Hall in an official car, with *three* of my colleagues carrying her Gucci handbag, while my mother had to go to the hospital by bus because I couldn't accompany her, busy as I was protecting your ass, *do you know that or not? And do you know it, bitch?*" he asked the woman, grabbing her by the chin. "Do you know what it means to come home from chemotherapy at the age of seventy-eight on a bus, holding your bag tight for fear some kids will grab your measly pension, while your son can't go with you because he's busy being stoned and spat at for *you people*? Well, whore, what do you have to say to that?"

"Hey, take it easy," one of the fake cops said. "We have to go now."

"No, not yet!" Vito said.

"Leave her alone," Parndelli said, weeping. "I don't—"

Vito struck him a backhander that split his lips.

"Now you're crying, are you? Are you scared of dying?"

The man nodded through his tears.

"When my mother died, I was outside the ministry beating up a crowd of workers who'd lost their jobs because of corrupt bastards like you. She'd left me a message telling me she was sick and asking if I could go pick her up, but I couldn't reply."

"I can give you money."

"Money? What the fuck do you want me to do with your money now? My mother died without seeing my son. What do you want me to do with your filthy money? Right now, she sucks me off and you watch."

"Nooo!" Prandelli cried.

One of the fake cops struck him with the grip of his pistol, reducing him to silence. But he didn't stop struggling.

"Keep him quiet," Vito said.

The men exchanged glances and obeyed: there was no way to make him see reason, and from their point of view he had right on his side. Let him answer later to Biagio, they thought as they pointed their pistols at the back of Prandelli's head and squeezed his neck in a herculean grip.

"Tonight you're going to spill the beans on that shitty Mafioso, but first . . . " Vito said, stuffing his cock in the woman's mouth while he pointed the muzzle of his pistol at her forehead ". . . she can show me how sorry she feels for my poor mother, and you look. If you just try to close your eyes, I'll break your teeth. Understood?"

"Please, no."

"*Understood?*" he screamed.

Vito saw the politician's perfect world crumble in contact with the brutality of real life. Prandelli nodded with lowered eyes.

"I told you to look, you piece of shit," Vito breathed.

The woman tried to retreat, but Vito pressed the barrel harder to her head and thrust his cock down her throat.

"Parliamentary immunity," he said, laughing to himself, hoping that Santo Spada, wherever he was, could see this. "Get on with it, whore."

When Oscar left the house with the pot of coffee for the two guys in the patrol car, he stiffened on seeing that there were now two cars out there. He approached the new one and greeted the officer who was standing by it, smoking.

"Good evening," the officer said.

"Good evening," Oscar said. "Who gave you the order for this surveillance?"

"Deputy Commissioner Santangelo, sir."

"And were you told the reason?"

"We only know that you received threats after the latest operations and drug seizures. That's all we were told, apart from keeping our eyes open and not letting anybody get close to the house."

"Two patrol cars on a Friday night, four officers," Oscar said, handing the officer the cup. "Deputy Commissioner Santangelo must really like us."

"Thanks, Oscar. I only know that Inspector Mazzeo insisted there had to be two cars outside here. We're in constant radio contact with the central switchboard and another car will drive by every half hour to take a look. There must be a valid reason why they've authorized this, given how understaffed we are."

"I see," Oscar replied, wondering why on earth Biagio had seen fit to increase the surveillance. "Boys, dial my number, for anything. If you need to use the bathroom, give me a call and I'll send someone to open up, there's no problem."

Ten men inside the villa keeping an eye on it, and four uniformed officers outside, on guard. This wasn't a house any more, it was a bunker. He was getting sick to the teeth of hiding and living in fear of being attacked at any moment. Right now, his one concern should have been to be with his sick wife, together with his daughters, before the lupus progressed further, condemning them to a life of pain leading up to an inevitable end. *I should be living quietly with Cristiana, letting her live out her last months in peace and serenity, and instead here I am, armed, with a houseful of cops. You promised to make as all millionaires, Biagio, and now we have to live like gangsters on the run.*

He took out his cell phone, intending to ask him what was happening.

"Hi, everything okay?" Biagio answered in that husky voice of his.

"I'm fine, but have I missed something?"

"How do you mean?"

"You had another patrol car placed outside the house. Why? Has something happened?"

"Let's say I feel calmer that way."

Oscar had the distinct impression he was hiding something from him. "Where are Vito and Carmine?"

"They're with me."

"Working?"

"Yes."

"What about us? Why do we have to stay here? Don't you trust us anymore?"

"Stop it, Oscar. Listen, I don't have time to talk now. Stay on guard there with your eyes wide open. I have a nasty feeling, and you know how much I trust my instinct."

"Biagio, there are fifteen cops keeping an eye on this place, what do you expect to happen?"

"I want my family to be safe, that's all."

"It is, but what about you? Where are you and what are you doing?"

"Don't worry. Say hello to the boys and take care."

Biagio hung up. Oscar stared at the cell phone. Now he was the one who had a nasty feeling.

Adem Paja's men proceeded to where Mazzeo had said they would find the car. In an old Fiat Punto abandoned near a field, the three Calabrians who had been Guido Sergi's bodyguards were tied hand and foot with black adhesive tape, and the same tape covered their mouths.

Without switching off the engine, the four Albanians got out of the Volvo XC60, shotguns raised They didn't deign even to glance at the Italians, they opened the trunk and found around fifteen kilos of heroin in a sports bag. *Their* heroin. Artan, the leader of the same group that had killed Boran, ordered one of his men to transfer the drugs to the Volvo, then, from a safe cell phone, called Adem.

"Hello?"

"It was just like the cop said, uncle. Three Calabrians and quite a bit of heroin. Around fifteen kilos, I think."

"Okay. Do what you have to, Artan."

Artan pocketed the phone, then, along with the others, aimed the

Kalashnikovs at the Punto and pumped it full of lead, tearing the Calabrians' bodies to pieces.

Biagio had assured Adem Paja that these three knew nothing, he had already interrogated them. They had simply obeyed Natale Pugliese's order to clear one of their storehouses. He had left them there, along with the drugs, as a personal favor to the Albanians. Adem hadn't doubted Biagio for a second, not after the way Biagio had acted to get Boran out of circulation, saving all of them in the process.

As the Calabrians' blood fertilized the ground, Artan and his men sped away from the field. None of them were aware of what they had become: pawns on Biagio's fatal chessboard.

In the files that Irene Piscitelli had passed to him to fill him in on who his enemies were, Biagio had discovered a whole lot of interesting titbits. For example that one evening the son of Sabino Sergi—a powerful local boss very close to Pugliese and his separatist project—had had a heated argument in one of his father's discotheques with a young Pole named Konrad Blonsky, over a woman. Both had powerful fathers behind them: the first a member of the 'Ndrangheta, the other a Polish Mafioso who was setting down roots in the North-East. The knives had come out, and before they were separated they had sworn to meet again a few days later and settle the matter once and for all. But when Blonsky the father had found out who exactly his son had made an enemy of, he had forced him to take a step back: the coke with which he was creating his own patch was supplied to him by the Puglieses, and making an enemy of Sergi meant saying goodbye to a secure supplier with a lot of firepower behind him. Artur Blonsky, who had sweated blood to establish himself in Italy and get rich, couldn't let his own business go hang because of a feud of his son's, not now that he had created a vast network of customers for himself. So he and Sergi had resolved the matter with a telephone call: Konrad would apologize personally to Guido for causing trouble in his disco and they would close the matter there, with their fathers present. But at the meeting Guido had said that a handshake wasn't enough for him, and so Artur Blonsky had had to stand by and watch his son being beaten up. When Guido had had enough, Sabino Sergi had swaggered up to the Polish boss and asked him if they were okay or if he had a problem. Swallowing all the hate he felt, all the slighted honor, Artur had replied that everything was okay and he had shaken the hand the Calabrian was holding out to him. Sergi had given him a pat on the cheek and had left with his son. When Konrad, weeping anger and blood, had sworn vengeance, his father had slapped him, telling him that the matter ended there: he would never allow all his efforts to be thwarted by a quarrel between kids.

But neither father nor son would ever be able to forget that humiliation.

And it was into that never-healed wound that Biagio Mazzeo had wormed his way.

Guido Sergi, abducted outside the disco, was sitting in the center of the container, hooded, a cloth stuffed into his mouth and his hands tied behind his back. His legs were free, but he wouldn't be going anywhere: both his knees were crushed. Carmine had had to lay it on thick to get him to answer Biagio's questions. In the end he had told them everything. Now he was moaning and groaning because with every minute that passed the pain in his shattered kneecaps seemed to get worse.

Outside the warehouse Biagio, Carmine, and the three fake cops were waiting, the three in ski masks and holding their MP5 submachine guns, Carmine with his beloved shotgun.

The Poles arrived on board two sedan cars a few minutes later. Apart from Konrad and Artur Blonsky, there were four of their bodyguards. The old man approached and shook Biagio's hand.

"I still can't believe it," he said, smiling.

Carmine threw a bag down on the ground: it contained two kilos of the coke they had stolen from Paja's storehouses. "Take a look at this and you'll believe it," he said.

"It's two kilos of cut cocaine," Biagio said, "ready to sell on the street. It has a market value of about three hundred thousand euros. I've respected our agreement, as you see."

Blonsky had a bag passed to him and handed it to Carmine. "That's two hundred and fifty thousand, as you asked."

Biagio nodded, signaling to his friend that there was no need to count it. Carmine loaded the bag with its contents in Biagio's SUV.

"From today we're in business, then," Biagio said. "I become your new supplier: coke, heroin, ecstasy, whatever you like. I'll do you very low prices compared with those that the Sergis did you, and if ever I have any problems, I'll put you onto a trusted supplier who'll give you the same prices as me. You'll be under my protection, and you won't have to worry about arrests or trouble with the police if you keep up to date with the payments and respect my demands. The first rule is that my enemies are your enemies. And Pugliese's syndicate is a fucking enemy of mine."

Blonsky nodded. "No problem. What about the other part of the agreement?" he asked, his eyes flashing with anger.

Biagio smiled and gave him a slap on the back. "Come," he said. He opened the container and led Blonksy and his son inside. He removed the hood from the prisoner and when Guido saw the two Poles, he started to struggle like a madman.

Konrad grabbed his chin between his fingers and forced him to look at him. "We meet again, you piece of shit."

Biagio placed a hand on his back. "A few minutes' patience. I still need him."

Artur Blonsky pulled his son away. "No problem, we have all the time in the world, right, Konrad?"

Konrad nodded and followed the men out of the container, excited by this imminent settling of scores.

"About the other thing, are we in agreement?" Biagio asked. "Can you assure me that you'll be able to do what I asked?"

"Of course. A whole lot of Poles work like slaves on those construction sites, it'll be no problem. As for the rest . . . " Blonsky smiled ". . . it'll be a pleasure."

"He's coming," Carmine said, noticing the clouds of dust raised by a Mercedes in the distance.

"Do they understand Italian?" Biagio asked Blonsky, pointing to the four armed Poles.

"Yes," Blonsky replied. Then, in Polish, he ordered his men to do whatever Biagio said.

"Okay, you wait inside," Biagio said to the two Blonskys, making them get back in the container. "Get out your guns," he ordered the criminals, himself also taking up an MP5. "And wait until I make the first move."

All nine arranged themselves behind the cars, weapons at the ready.

But there was no need to worry: Sabino Sergi had come alone, as Biagio had ordered. Not long before, he had called him and made him listen to his son's screams of pain as Carmine repeatedly beat his kneecaps with the bat: even the meanest father would have done anything to stop those screams. As if that were not enough, to make it clear to him that he wasn't joking, Biagio had told him the precise whereabouts of the field where the Albanians had killed Guido's bodyguards, and twenty minutes later he had called him again, telling him that if he wanted to get his son back in one piece, he would have to come alone, unarmed, to the place indicated.

Sergi, his face sweaty and tense, got out of the Mercedes with his hands up.

"Are you sure you're alone?" Biagio asked.

"Yes."

Not trusting him, Biagio ordered one of the fake cops to take one of the cars and drive around the area, to see if there was anyone lying in wait.

"On your knees," Carmine ordered. "Hands on your head."

Sergi hesitated. "Where's my son?"

Biagio slapped a hand on the steel wall of the container, and after a few seconds a cry of pain could be heard from inside. Guido.

"Bastards," Sergi breathed.

"Pull the slightest trick and you're both dead," Biagio said.

Sabino Sergi kneeled and put his hands on his head. While the others kept him covered, Carmine came up behind him and handcuffed him.

"You people don't know what you're doing," Sergi said.

Carmine laughed and pulled him to his feet, pushing him toward Biagio, who was putting on a set of brass knuckles. "Oh, I think we do, my friend," Carmine whispered in his ear.

"Do you know who I am?" Biagio asked.

Sergi nodded.

"Say it."

"You're the man who killed Sergej Ivankov."

Biagio's fingers slid over the Chechen's ring. "Correct. Say my name."

Sergi spat on the ground.

Biagio hit him with an uppercut to the sternum made all the harder by the brass knuckles. The crunch of broken bones could be heard.

"Say my name," he repeated, lifting him by the hair.

"Biagio Mazzeo," Sergi muttered.

"That's it," Biagio said with a smile. "And now you're going to tell me everything I want to know."

At first the Calabrian was reluctant to betray his associates: as usual in the 'Ndrangheta, they were all related. But when Carmine dragged him inside the container and the man saw the two Poles circling like sharks around his son, knives in their hands and vengeful smiles on their lips, as Biagio had predicted, he talked. Jesus, how he talked.

"Now if you're a man of your word let my son go," Sergi spat when they were outside the container.

"Who killed my man?"

"Let my son go and I'll tell you."

Biagio made a sign to Carmine, who tore off Sergi's left earlobe with nail clippers.

"Those who have ears to hear, hear," Carmine said with a laugh, throwing the piece of bleeding flesh between his feet.

The four Poles were startled by the brutality of the two cops. Biagio was in a hurry to bring this whole thing to an end, and whatever method he used to do so was legitimate. Besides, he was tired of having to deal with these arrogant Mafiosi who were so sure of their own omnipotence. As Sergi lay screaming on the ground, Biagio pinned him down with a boot on his chest and aimed the barrel of the submachine gun at his forehead.

"I'm not famous for being a patient man. Think carefully, because after the ears we move on to the balls. Who killed my man?"

"I don't know. All I know is that it was Natale who gave the order. I don't know, I swear!"

"And who the fuck does know?"

Sergi told him through his tears

Biagio took his cell phone from his pocket and asked him under what name Natale Pugliese's number was registered. Once Sergi had given him this last piece of information, Biagio dragged him to his feet, opened the container, and shoved him inside. "He's yours," he said. "Take all the time you need." He dialed Natale's number from Sergi's cell phone. When the call started, Biagio put the phone down on the ground and left the container. As he and his men got in their cars and left, from somewhere Natale Pugliese listened in horror to the inhuman screams of the two Sergis.

His first impulse had been to run away: to leave, to be alone without seeing anybody. And that was what he had done. He had taken the Ninja from the garage, switched off his cell phone, and sped away, without any particular destination in mind. He had needed to be alone with himself, to drive, to free his mind by riding fast on his motorbike. When he was too tired to continue, he had stopped in a hotel just off the highway and taken a room.

He had no idea how many miles he had traveled.

As if trying to stifle his thoughts and anxieties, he had taken off his jacket, his holster, and his T-shirt, thrown himself to the floor, and done exercises until he was breathless. Under the hot water of the shower, he had realized that he could go wherever he wanted and do all the press-ups in the world, but he couldn't run away from himself and his responsibilities.

Apart from Anna, your beautiful niece, what's forcing you to stay? Nothing. This is a world made up only of violence and death. Ste, Santo, Sonja, Ivankov, his daughter . . . How many ghosts do you still have to fight? he asked himself. Anna would be better off far from you and your world. You've put aside enough money not to have to worry anymore for her and her future. You can leave and not come back, leave everything behind. Thailand, Indonesia, India . . . You can go wherever you like.

He opened his eyes again and looked at the steam invading the plex-iglass shower stall.

Running away is for cowards, he told himself, sitting on the seat in the shower, his back against the wall. And you're running away, from Biagio, but also from Claudia and from what's happening between you. You may have called it a day with Biagio, but not with your family. They need you. Anna, Claudia, all of them. Even Biagio. There's nothing to say he won't change his mind. You don't understand why he's acting this way. Maybe he just needs help and he's too proud to ask for it.

The look in his eyes was that of a man ready to kill, an inner voice admonished him.

No, it was just the look of a desperate man. And I have to stop him, before it's too late. Then I could leave if I wanted, but before that we have to see this thing through.

He stood up and stretched, and the tattooed animals on his back seemed to come to life, twisting and leaping. As he dried himself, he tried to switch on his cell phone, but the battery was dead. He would call Claudia the next day, he told himself, before going back to the Jungle. Because he had decided: he would go back, and he would protect his family. With Biagio or against Biagio.

Sitting in the middle of the farmhouse where up until a few days earlier they had kept the cocaine, Biagio was waiting for Vito to bring Deputy Prandelli and his wife. He had asked Carmine and the fake cops to stay outside, without giving them a reason. He had done so because he wanted to be alone. With all the stress, and the fear of what might happen the next day, his resistance crumbled. From his jacket he took the white envelope Santo had left for Nicky and opened it. He was surprised to find two letters inside. And his surprise grew when he saw that one was for him. He frowned. He put the letter down on the table and started reading.

If you're reading these words, it means that as usual you couldn't mind your own business. But I'll give you the benefit of the doubt: you could have done it for fear of what I might have written to my little girl. You want to protect her, as I asked you, and you did it well. But this time, son, I ask you to trust me totally. Read your letter (this one) but leave Nicky's to her. There's nothing in it that can hurt her, believe me, and one day you'll understand (I hope) that what's between a father and a daughter is something that nobody else can understand, something too private to share with other people. Anyway, if you're reading this letter, damn it, it means I'm dead. Cancer or Ivankov, I don't know. But when that fucking Chechen showed up, I felt the need to write to you because there are some things I'd like to settle before going to shit blood in hell. One is Nicky. The second is you. You never asked me directly, but I know you want to know why I never told her I'm her old man: the answer is very simple, son. To protect her. I love you deeply, you and all the boys, you know. But there's something wrong in us. We love and protect each other, but we always end up wallowing in shit. That's not what I want for my little girl. She would have fewer problems staying with her junkie whore of a mother than with me. Because in the end the knot tightens for everyone, Biagio, and we've made too many knots. Far too many. Sooner or later they'll tighten, and I really don't want Nicky to be caught in the middle. My greatest regret is that I involved you in all that shit. You became worse than me, unfortunately, and that wasn't what I wanted. You were just a little boy who wanted to get out of that shitty neighborhood, and I helped you to do that, but in the process I turned you into a monster. I don't know why I did it. Maybe because I'd brought that faggot of a son of mine into the world. I was ashamed of him, or maybe I was more ashamed of myself, both for having had a little pansy and for not being able to hear him talk for two seconds without wanting to slap him. Daniele didn't deserve it, but I never managed to tell him that. I needed a real son, a boy I could see myself in, someone I could put all my hopes in, all my desire to give love, to be a father, I think. In the end, that's why we have children: to leave something of ourselves behind. And that's what I did with you. I raised you like a son, I protected you from the other cops and the criminals, I made you equal to me. Now, after Ste, after all the mess we got into, and now with these fucking Chechens, I realize it was a mistake. I look around and see a great family but one that has too many secrets, too many skeletons in the closet. That's not what I would have wanted. We had fun, we made money, but we couldn't stop at the right moment. Instead of stopping we kept crossing that line that was always shifting a bit further away every time, and us running after it like a bunch of assholes. Not Panthers, but assholes. Nicky was both a mistake and the best thing that ever happened to me. You have to protect her, son. From yourself and the others. Don't mix her up in our mess. Loving means also knowing when to give up, that's my final lesson. Jesus, I'm writing so much! But that's the way it is: when you're scared of dying, you turn sentimental. Anyway, listen to me. It's never too late to change. I never understood that, but you're not me. I have to go now. Think about what I've written, and take care.

Goodbye, son.

Biagio folded the letter with a pang in his heart and slipped it into his wallet. Nicky's letter he put back in the envelope, without even glancing at it, and put it back in his jacket.

A monster, he thought. Is that what I am? he wondered.

It's never too late to change . . .

That's how it is. I'm a danger to Nicky. I'm a danger to everyone. Just as I was to Sonja, Ste, and Santo. I have to disappear. I have to give them up, give up my desire to protect them. Is that what you asked me to do, Santo?

But he didn't have time to reflect too long on this. Vito had arrived with the two prisoners. The night of the Panthers had to continue.

Roberto Messina knew that Leonardo Sciglitano was the man in Pugliese's organization who dealt with homicide and revenge. But from what Biagio had told him, he was also the man responsible for his brother's death. Biagio had told him that it was actually Sciglitano who had led the assault on the police car, Sciglitano who had shot his brother.

And now he was just a few yards away.

"There he is, there he is!" Angelo said, stopping the car. "He's getting out."

"Take care you don't shoot the girl."

Mariano and Roberto pulled down their ski masks and got out of the car.

By the time Sciglitano noticed them, it was too late.

The two officers opened fire, hitting him in the legs and the side. Once he was down, Roberto walked to him and aimed his pistol at his face.

"This is for my brother, you son of a bitch," he snarled.

He pulled the trigger twice while Sciglitano's girl screamed, watching the execution from inside the car.

Roberto Messina stood there gazing down at the body as if in ecstasy.

Mariano pulled him away and they ran back to their car. Angelo set off again with a screech of tires, and they sped away. Roberto looked at his hands, which were shaking uncontrollably, and then, unable to hold back any longer, burst into tears.

Vito had brought Prandelli and his wife down into the cellar, their faces covered with black sacks, and forced them to sit down in front of Biagio, who had then motioned to him to leave them alone. Once Vito had left the room, Biagio had started to drum with the fingers of one hand on the table at which he was sitting, while with the other he played with the blood-smeared brass knuckles.

"Do you know who I am?" he asked.

Trembling, the two politicians shook their heads.

"Are you sure?"

"Are . . . are you a police officer?" Prandelli stammered.

"No. I haven't been a police officer for a long time. Maybe I never was."

"So what do you want from us?"

"Natale Pugliese and his whole organization."

In spite of the sacks, Biagio saw them stiffen.

He was about to say something when he got a text from Roberto Messina: *File closed. Thanks for the tip-off.*

No, thank *you*, Biagio thought with a smile, and replied that he was proud of him. That young officer had also become a pawn in his hands, like everyone in this nasty story. Using them, setting them one against the other, was the only way he knew to get out of this hell. And he *had* to get out of this hell.

"You see," he said, again addressing the prisoners, "I now have a problem. You don't want to talk because you're scared of Pugliese. And the only way I have to make you talk is to make you even more scared than he does. It's a matter of priorities. Are you with me so far?"

The two did not reply.

Biagio took out his pistol and fired two shots at their feet, making them jump and scream with terror. The woman urinated.

"Signora, what are you doing?"

"P . . . p . . . please let us go . . . " she spluttered through her tears.

"Nobody's coming to save you tonight, or even tomorrow. You're mine now. And you will talk." He pressed his pistol to Prandelli's ear. "Pugliese. Where is he?"

"I can't—"

Biagio pulled the trigger. The blast was so loud in that confined space that the shock of it knocked Prandelli to the ground. Biagio pinned him down and turned to the desperate woman. "Signora, I'm getting impatient. Either you talk or I really will hurt the two of you."

"I beg you! We don't know anything!"

Biagio pulled the black sack off her. She recoiled and blinked to accustom herself to the light. After a few moments, she saw Biagio in his black ski mask, and the big pistol he was aiming at her. She closed her eyes tight and started screaming.

Biagio slapped her. "Open your fucking eyes, bitch! Or, as God is my witness, I'll gouge them out of you!"

The woman obeyed, suppressing a scream of fear.

"Have you realized yet who you're dealing with?"

She avoided his gaze.

Biagio grabbed her by the throat, inserted the barrel of his pistol between her legs, and pressed it to her private parts.

"Do you realize who you're dealing with, yes or no?"

She nodded, unable to utter a word.

"Pugliese. All the contacts you have with him and his people. The names of all the judges, politicians, police officers, businessmen, and bankers who are in cahoots with him. Now."

"I don't know—"

"Tell your husband to talk, then."

"Gilberto . . . please . . . "

"Shut up," the man said from the floor.

"Oh, so that's the way it is? I have to play it the hard way, do I?" Biagio put the sack back over the woman's head. "Your choice."

He gave a shrill whistle and after a few seconds Carmine came down, carrying a jerry can of gasoline. He put Prandelli back on his chair and then tied them both together with packaging tape, whistling the theme tune from *The Simpsons* as he did so.

"I'm ready for the barbecue," Carmine said.

"This is your last chance," Biagio said. "Are you going to talk?"

They replied with moans.

Biagio made a sign to Carmine, who poured the gasoline over them.

"Yes, it's the smell of gasoline," Biagio said with a smile. "I've always liked it, how about you?"

The two screamed and struggled, but couldn't do anything.

"Who do I burn first?" Carmine asked.

"I don't know. Let's ask them. You first, Deputy, or your wife?"

"No, please!" the woman screamed.

"Mmm," Carmine grunted, lighting a cigarette lighter. "I really could do with a green pepper steak."

"Well, Deputy?" Biagio insisted.

"I . . . c . . . can't . . . t.. talk . . . "

"All right then, burn this piece of shit."

"Okay!" Prandelli shrieked. "Okay, I'll tell you everything!"

Biagio winked at Carmine. "Barbecue postponed. Start at the beginning and don't leave anything out." He switched on the voice recorder.

A few hours later, Biagio went outside, took the encrypted cell phone from his pocket, switched it on, and dialed Pugliese's number.

"You son of a bitch," Pugliese said as soon as he picked up.

"Like the fireworks?"

"Do you have any idea what you've done?"

"Remember those three days you gave me? Stick them up your ass."

"You'll regret this, Mazzeo. I'll—"

Biagio hung up on him and switched off the phone. He ordered Vito and Carmine to go back to the villa and try to sleep for a few hours. He would stay here with the five fake cops.

Once Vito and Carmine had gone, Biagio stroked Ivankov's ring and stared up at the starry sky. He realized that Santo had been right. He had become a monster. He was like a death sentence for the people closest to him.

But I'll change. Once this business is over, I'll change. I'll leave them free. I'll get Nicky and the others away. Enough violence, enough crime. And enough of the pack. I haven't been able to defend them, and they don't trust me anymore. There is no more fucking family. Everything's gone to hell. If I really love them, I have to abandon them.

Carlo's widow Chiara was sleeping at Olimpia's. She was too upset to be left alone, and for Olimpia, taking care of her and the child meant brooding less over Carlo's death.

That night, the boy wouldn't even hear about sleeping. Olimpia had taken him in her arms and gone down to the living room to look after him, leaving Chiara free to sleep upstairs.

That was how Roberto found her when he came into the house, with her grandson in her arms.

"How did it go?" she asked.

He came to her and embraced the two of them. "It's over. I killed him."

Olimpia sighed and kissed him on the lips. "I'm proud of you. You did the right thing, darling. I'm really proud of you."

Roberto nodded and looked at his brother's son. Suddenly he realized that killing Carlo's murderer had been no use: he still felt terribly guilty.

But now you'll be able to look your nephew in the face without lowering your eyes, he told himself. And you have Biagio to thank for that.

Everything is burning

Biagio woke with Nicky by his side. For a moment he wondered what the hell was happening, then he remembered that the previous night, when he had come back at dawn, he had woken up screaming and trembling after less than an hour's sleep. Nicky had tried to calm him and had stayed with him until he had fallen asleep again. Now, as he covered her properly and kissed her on one cheek, he tried to remember what his nightmare had been about. He couldn't, but he realized that they could no longer stay in this apartment. The presence of Sonja was too strong, and even though at the beginning he had thought that it might do him good, he was convinced now that it had been a mistake to be here.

He glanced at his watch: he had slept less than three hours. He had his usual large cup of strong bitter coffee and sent a text to Mirko, asking him to come and pick up Nicky and take her to the villa. He got dressed, and as he waited for Mirko he thought of the letter still lying in the pocket of his jacket. Nicky knew now that Santo was her father—or rather, she had always known— so he was more willing to give it to her. He just had to figure out if this was the right time or not.

This might be the last opportunity you have, he told himself. What happened yesterday was the first assault, but the war has only just started, and there's nothing to say you'll get out of it alive. Either you or the others.

A phone call distracted him from that thought. Claudia.

"Hi," he said, taking refuge in the kitchen in order not to make any noise.

"Biagio, sorry to disturb you."

"No problem. What's up?"

"It's Giorgio. He didn't come home last night. I tried to call him but his phone's off. I'm worried."

"Hmm . . . Do you know if the others have heard from him?"

"No. I mean, yes, I called them, but nobody knows anything."

"Okay. Listen, I know what might have happened. We had an argument yesterday about this Calabrian thing."

Silence.

"A difference of opinion, nothing serious. Knowing him, though, he may have wanted to be alone, to cool off."

"But—"

"Trust me, I'm sure that's what it is," he lied.

"Okay, but what do we do?"

"Nothing. Don't worry. I'll send Luca to keep you company until Giorgio gets back, okay?"

"All right."

As he was making another pot of coffee, he switched on the TV. They were talking about the "night of the fires," as they had already dubbed it. A woman reporter was saying that what had happened last night was quite incredible: more than twenty incendiary attacks had been carried out on construction companies and waste disposal facilities. The methods used were typical of organized crime, and it appeared that the attacks were linked to the murder of a well-known Mafioso, who had been killed in an ambush a few minutes before the fires were started. As if that were not enough, news, as yet unconfirmed, was coming in from the nearby prison of the death of two members of a Calabrian syndicate long established in the North. The Organized Crime Directorate had not yet released a statement, but it was clear— or so the reporter maintained—that some kind of showdown between Mafia families was in progress, families who had suffered heavy blows after the latest police operations, in which the combined forces of the Narcotics and Organized Crime divisions had seized large quantities of drugs.

Biagio looked at the TV with his arms crossed and a crooked smile on his face, wondering if the Poles were still torturing the Sergis.

In connection with these mysterious events, the TV news broadcast a flash interview with the candidate for regional governor, a man with a record as a tough Interior Minister, who—despite having maintained for years that the Northern Mafia was a myth—was making the fight against the Northern Mafia one of the main platforms of his election campaign. The candidate claimed that nobody had fought organized crime harder than he had, and that his administration, once elected, would stand firm against any kind of criminal infiltration.

Biagio switched off the TV in disgust: the former minister was a member of the same party as Prandelli, and his election campaign was paid for by the Puglieses.

He poured himself coffee and sat there thinking of his plan until Mirko rang the doorbell. He let him in, and when Mirko asked him if he had been behind what had happened last night, he evaded the question and told him he didn't have time to talk.

"Take her to Oscar's house as soon as she wakes up," he said, "and don't move from there until I tell you. I want the three boys who are downstairs to stay with you and go with you to the villa, understood?"

"Yes, Biagio, but are you sure everything's—"

Biagio grabbed his head in those hands of his. "Just tell me one thing, son: do you trust me?"

"What? I . . . Of course I do, chief."

Biagio knocked his forehead against his, then gave him a few slaps on the cheek. "Then continue to trust me and you'll see, this whole fucking mess will be over soon."

Mirko watched him put on his holster with the pistol and his jacket and go out. Hearing a noise behind him, he turned. Nicky was looking at him from the door of the bedroom, her face still swollen with sleep.

"Hi there, little thief, everything okay?"

She shook her head.

"What's up?" he asked, his face turning somber.

"It's Biagio. Last night he was screaming in his sleep that he would kill them all. I have a bad feeling, Mirko. I'm scared he's going to—"

"Shhh," Mirko said, going to her and stroking her back. "He's never disappointed us before, little one. And he's certainly not going to start now, so don't worry."

Biagio was eating a slice of toast when Deputy Prosecutor Pietro Magri of the Regional Organized Crime Directorate sat down at his table. He noticed that two officers who were with Magri had sat down a few tables away and had their eyes fixed on the entrance and on the other customers. These customers included Vito and Carmine, who were also keeping an eye on things.

"You want to tell me what the fuck's going on?" Magri said, playing with his gold cufflinks.

"What do you mean?" Biagio replied, continuing to eat.

"I mean you're playing a dirty war and screwing up other people's investigations, some of which have been going on for years. And you're doing it so casually that either you've finally gone completely crazy, or you have someone very powerful protecting you. I lean toward the second hypothesis."

"What makes you think I'm behind all this?"

"Don't fuck me around, Mazzeo."

"Aren't you ordering anything?"

"I'm not here to eat. Tell me what the fuck you want."

Biagio took a sip of red orange juice and stared at Magri, a prosecutor with political ambitions. "I can give you the biggest arms seizure of the last ten years."

Magri shook his head, a wicked little smile on his perfectly formed face, which gave off a strong smell of expensive aftershave. "Why so generous all of a sudden?"

"As you may know, the 'Ndrangheta has its eyes on some mines in the Congo where a mineral called coltan is extracted. It's a basic conductor for the whole electronics industry, used particularly in cell phones—"

"I know what it is."

"Good. Then you probably also know that it's quite rare, which makes it more valuable than gold. Pugliese has gotten his hands on it before all the other families and is taking control of the coltan mines in return for supplying arms from the Balkans."

All at once, Magri became really interested. He crossed his legs, pulling up his pants with his hands to maintain a severe crease, and looked Biagio straight in the eyes. "Tell me more."

"He gives the arms to the rebel troops who control the quarries, gets the coltan, and sells it to half the world at astronomical prices. All quite legal, apart from the initial investment. If it goes through, you're screwed, because he'll find a way to launder all those euros and you won't be able to do anything to stop him, and with the revenue he'll be able to undercut bids on contracts by forty percent until he's gotten control of this whole fucking region."

"And how come you know these things?"

"Does it matter? What I can guarantee is a huge haul. You'll be able to stop this traffic before it starts."

"And in return?"

Biagio told him, and Magri turned white.

"You're crazy! Why should I authorize something like that?"

"I'm not crazy. I'm just pragmatic. Think about it. How many lives could you save if you managed to stop that consignment from reaching its destination? We're talking about civil wars here."

Magri stared thoughtfully at his well-tended hands. "How many people are involved?"

"Here, about a dozen. After that, you'll have to start digging, or do you want me to do all the work for you?"

"Go fuck yourself, Mazzeo," Magri said with self-satisfied contempt.

Biagio smiled. "Is that a yes?"

"I'm not clear what you get out of all this."

He shrugged. "One less son of a bitch in my city."

"Bullshit."

"If you agree, I want you to use my team."

"Narcotics? Then you really are crazy."

"I'm not in Narcotics anymore. No, not my boys, a new team. Deputy Prosecutors Barberi and Tortora, and the task force on Pugliese, with Claudetti and Inspector Manisci of the Organized Crime division in charge. You'll be the director, and they'll be the actors."

"Why on earth would I do that?"

Biagio looked at his watch. "In two hours the ship will set sail and you can say goodbye to the seizure."

"Why have you told me this at the last moment?"

"Because I was afraid of moles. News like this—"

"What are you insinuating?"

"Nobody's immune from spies, Magri. Not even your department."

"I'll be damned . . . Okay."

Biagio took a paper napkin and wrote on it the number of the wharf and the name of the merchant ship onto which the containers with the arms had been loaded. He added Claudetti's telephone number.

"I'd get a move on if I were you."

"Do you know what you're going up against, Mazzeo? Do you know who Pugliese is?"

"I know who I am. And that's what matters."

"It's your funeral. Well? Is that it? Nothing in writing?"

Biagio held out his right hand. "Paperwork is for faggots. Old geezers like us just need a handshake, or am I wrong?"

After a moment's hesitation, Magri shook his hand. Biagio watched him hurry out of the bar, framed by his two men, his cell phone stuck to his ear. He glanced at his watch and wondered how long it would be before Pugliese made his next counter-move.

Giorgio drove into the underground garage of his building and parked the Ninja. He stretched his neck and back, tired from the journey: he had woken up at dawn to come back to the Jungle. He had made only one short stop to fill her up and have a coffee, and now he couldn't wait to have a hot shower before going to see Biagio.

As he lowered the shutter of the garage he heard footsteps behind him.

"Don't move and keep your hands where we can see them, Inspector," said an unknown voice in a tone that brooked no reply.

"There are three of us, Varga, don't try anything," added another.

He turned very slowly and saw three armed men who were keeping him covered. From the silver badges on their chests he recognized them as carabinieri.

"I don't understand," he said, almost in a whisper.

"You're under arrest, Varga. Don't cause any trouble. On your knees. Hands on your head."

"I've never seen you guys before," Giorgio said, suspiciously.

One of them showed him his badge: the Carabinieri's elite Special Operations Group. If they were involved, the situation must be serious. He kneeled down without offering any resistance.

"Do you mind telling me what you're arresting me for?"

"I advise you to remain silent, Varga," said the one who seemed to me the highest in rank. "You're in shit up to your neck."

One of them handcuffed him. They made him stand, and with their pistols in their hands they escorted him to an unmarked sedan that set off with a screech of tires.

One of the telephones started vibrating. It was the Chinese iPhone: Barranca.
"Hi."
"Is this a bad time?"
"Absolutely not," Biagio replied with a smile on his lips. "Go on."
"I know where they're supposed to be meeting."

In a single night the Lombardia organization, of which Pugliese was the head, had suffered a huge amount of damage. Thirty construction sites were out of use, as were the earthmoving machines and the waste disposal facilities. Fifteen of their clubs, garages, and supermarkets had been attacked and set on fire. Various members close to Pugliese had been killed in prison, while outside, Rocco Neri—the man in charge of the hit squad—and Guido Sergi's three bodyguards were food for the worms, slaughtered with Kalashnikovs in pure Albanian Mafia style. Added to that were Sabino and Guido Sergi, whose bodies, showing clear signs of torture, had been discovered in the trunk of a Mercedes outside the office of Pugliese's lawyer, Leonardo Sciglitano. In addition, their most highly placed man on the national political scene had disappeared along with his wife. There had also been more than five big drugs and arms raids on their warehouses. That morning too, the Carabinieri's Environmental and Food and Drink divisions had swooped on restaurants, bars, quarries, garbage dumps, and the few construction sites that had survived the flames, closing at least thirty commercial activities for serious irregularities and two quarries for environmental violations, and arresting a dozen associates. What's more, the Treasury Police, acting on a series of tip-offs, had closed down many of their video arcades and gambling clubs for lack of connection to the network, false invoicing, and expired licenses, not to mention the fact that many of the video poker machines had been fixed. And last but not least, a police task force under the aegis of the Regional Organized Crime Directorate had just put paid to the multi-million deal that would finally have given the organization a further massive advantage over the

Mother House: the exchange of arms for coltan. The police had stopped the cargo ship carrying the arsenal from the Balkans destined for the Congo, arresting another ten associates and bringing to its knees the entire structure that had advanced the money for the arms.

With crazed hordes of reporters roaming the city in search of news, and no respite from the police, the Carabinieri, or the Treasury people, the upper echelons of the Lombardia had decided to meet to figure out what the hell was going on.

They held their meeting in a social club, where Nino Mandalari, the new General Manager of the organization and the man closest to Natale, had gathered together the bosses of all the branches operating in the Jungle and the surrounding region. The situation was so serious that Mandalari neglected the age-old greeting rituals and got straight down to the matter in hand, outlining what he had been discussing up until a few moments earlier by telephone with Natale Pugliese himself, who at that moment was hiding in an unknown location.

Mandalari was tense and sweaty, as were his associates. Up until the night before they had felt as if they were the kings of the world, but now their network of protection and corruption seemed to have crumbled, leaving them exposed, defenseless, devoid of arms or drugs.

"Gentlemen, first of all, you mustn't worry about what's—"

The door of the room opened and a young man in a snazzy suit, Nino's son, came in, excused himself, went to his father and said to him in a low voice, "Pa, they've just called from the east side. Those fucking illegal Polish workers have rebelled, beaten up the engineers and the freight operators, put the trucks out of use, and blocked the construction sites."

"What?" his father asked, eyes bulging. "How many sites have they blocked?"

"Ten."

Nino Mandalari turned pale. Ten sites weren't so many in relation to the many enterprises they were involved in. But he knew perfectly well that rebellion is contagious, and the Poles might be joined by the Romanians, the Africans, and the Albanians, whose manpower they exploited to maximize their profits. He motioned his son to sit down. The ten bosses present at the meeting looked at him with suspicion and anxiety.

"Listen, I know the situation may seem—"

The door of the room flew open again. Three masked men in police bibs burst in, holding MP5 submachine guns.

"Everyone against the wall," they ordered. "Hands on heads."

The Calabrians obeyed without a word. While the three men kept them covered, Carmine came in, also masked and holding a shotgun. "Which one of you is Nino Mandalari?" he asked.

Nobody replied.

Carmine hit one of the Calabrians full in the mouth with the barrel of his shotgun. The impact was massive, and the criminal collapsed senseless to the floor, his mouth mangled. Carmine turned to the next man. "Which one of you is Nino Mandalari?" he repeated, brandishing his weapon.

"I am," a thickset man in his sixties said in a thin voice.

Carmine went up to him and gave him a slap. "Greetings from Biagio Mazzeo," he said. Then he started bludgeoning him with inhuman brutality. He didn't hit him on the head, only on the body and limbs, smashing his bones. The beating up continued for a few minutes while the other Calabrians watched powerlessly, still covered by the submachine guns held by the masked men. When Nino's son tried to intervene, Carmine set about him too, breaking his legs.

Then he pointed his shotgun at the men standing against the wall. "That's what happens to anyone who decides to stay with that faggot Pugliese, understood?"

Nobody replied.

Carmine approached one of them and hit him full in the stomach, making him collapse to the floor. "I didn't hear," he snarled.

The Calabrians all nodded emphatically.

"This is just a warning. Anyone who continues to support Pugliese will die. If you have a modicum of intelligence, hand him over to us, otherwise we'll keep wiping you out, one by one. Now which one of you is Belcastro?"

"I am," muttered a very thin man in his fifties. Carmine grabbed him by the neck, made sure he was the one whose photograph he had seen in the file Biagio had shown him, and shoved him outside.

"Everyone on the ground!" ordered one of the three fake cops.

The Calabrians lay down on the floor and a second later the masked men left.

Sitting at a table in a bar on the other side of the street, Irene Piscitelli had watched the whole scene with a cup of hot tea in her hands and a wicked smile on her lips.

During those hours Biagio's BlackBerry never stopped vibrating. The callers were mainly law enforcement officers begging for tip-offs, because the rumor had by now spread not only in every police station and Carabinieri barracks in the Jungle, but throughout the region: the former head of Narcotics was on to a sure thing, and could guarantee you a major haul and career advancement. To all of them he responded with hot tips about the Pugliese syndicate—always in return for something, though. But as soon as Carmine and Vito brought Mario Belcastro down into the basement of the farmhouse, Biagio switched off his cell phone: now it was up to him to show what he was made of. Again.

"Sit him down," he ordered, indicating a chair between Prandelli and his wife, whom he had resumed questioning a few hours ago. The marks of this latest violent interrogation were still visible on their gasoline-soaked bodies. He had forced both of them—pistol to their temples—to phone their respective secretaries and cancel all engagements on the grounds that they were indisposed.

"Here he is," Carmine said, giving Belcastro a slap once he was seated.

Belcastro was an accountant, a leading figure in the financial and administrative structure of Pugliese's syndicate. According to Prandelli, he was the only man who really knew Pugliese's turnover, as well as that of all the people who were in cahoots with him.

Biagio took the black hood off him and the man stared at him in fright. Biagio's face was uncovered and seeing those icy eyes of his, Belcastro's heart skipped a beat.

"Pugliese's finished," Biagio said, putting on a pair of leather gloves. "It's only a matter of hours. They're all abandoning him. They've realized it was a mistake to support him."

Belcastro nodded. His whole body was vibrating with fear. He was an accountant, not a soldier.

Biagio clenched his fists. "The question is: do you want the same thing to happen to you?"

Belcastro bowed his head in desperation. "W-what do you want to know?" he stammered.

"Everything."

The three carabinieri were even more crooked than the Panthers were. They worked for Pugliese, and like an idiot he had fallen into their trap. Three members of the Special Operations Group. If Pugliese had managed to infiltrate such an elite body, that meant he had immense power.

They had brought him to a garage, sealing his mouth with packaging tape. Handcuffed and covered by pistols, Giorgio had been unable to react. He had listened to them talk with Pugliese on the phone, and negotiate a price for this kidnapping.

He wants to use me as a bargaining tool, he reflected, tied to a chair, their eyes constantly on him. But maybe he doesn't know that Biagio has burned his bridges with me. If I'm the card he hopes to play, he's in real trouble.

Because the more he thought about it, the more Giorgio realized that if Pugliese got rid of him, he would only be doing Biagio a favor. Giorgio was the only one who knew the truth about Sonja and the beating up of Donna. He knew too many secrets. Now that they were on a collision course, all things considered he had become a dispensable pawn. Pugliese wouldn't be killing a comrade of Biagio's, but an inconvenient witness. Because if Biagio refused the exchange, Pugliese would never leave Giorgio alive, that was obvious.

Giorgio closed his eyes and wondered if he would ever again see his family.

The Treasury Police hadn't managed to get the ten men they'd arrested to tell them where they kept the cash from their illegal empire of video arcades and unauthorized gambling.

But Biagio had.

Belcastro told him. Just as he told him a whole lot of other things.

Biagio left the fake cops to keep an eye on the three prisoners, and went with Carmine and Vito to the warehouses indicated by Belcastro.

For hours, the three of them tore through the Jungle like madmen, pumped up with adrenaline and trembling with excitement, the van becoming ever heavier.

When they got back to the Panthers' central garage and emptied the last bag stolen from the Calabrians' stores, they stood and stared, speechless and wide-eyed, at the mountain of money.

Not even Belcastro knew exactly how much money there was in those warehouses. But he had said he was sure it was no less than ten million euros, maybe fifteen. In cash. It should have gone to Switzerland and from there—through a whole series of online transfers—to Brazil, where the syndicate was investing big time in preparation for the upcoming World Cup.

"Biagio, can I tell you something?" Carmine whispered, eyes still fixed on all those banknotes.

Biagio nodded, slowly. "Sure."

"I love you," Carmine said hoarsely.

Vito yelled for joy and dived onto the mountain of banknotes like Scrooge McDuck. It didn't take long for Carmine to join him.

Biagio and the boys were on their way back to the farmhouse. It was almost eight in the evening: they had taken longer than expected to gather the cash and hide it in the garage. As the SUV stopped outside the house, one of the cell phones started vibrating. It was the encrypted phone. Unknown number.

"Yes?" Biagio replied.

"Biagio," said Giorgio at the other end of the line. "It's me."

"Giorgio?" Biagio replied in surprise. "Why are you calling me on this—"

He heard a groan of a pain, and then Giorgio said "Biagio, they got me. Pugliese—"

"Giorgio, what—"

"You have something of ours and we have something of yours," said another male voice without any accent. Biagio had never heard it before. "Simple, isn't it?"

"What the fuck—"

"Shh. You've done enough to hurt the syndicate. Tonight we'll exchange your man for Belcastro and the drugs. All you have. And bring the money you've confiscated too. Try anything and . . . "

Another moan, even louder, reached Biagio's ears.

". . . and you'll get him back in pieces. Remember: Belcastro, the drugs and the money. And come alone. If we see any of your people, we kill Varga, got that?"

Biagio could do nothing but say yes.

"We'll tell you the time and place later. Don't try anything stupid, Mazzeo. Be good."

Vito and Carmine stared at their chief, who had turned pale.

"What's going on?" Vito said, tense.

"They've got Giorgio."

Carmine and Vito looked at each other in astonishment, not so much because of the disturbing news as because of the cold look in Biagio's eyes: it was as if he had been expecting that phone call at any moment.

"Shit. What do you want to do?"

Biagio told the two men how they would deal with this, raising his voice when they looked aghast.

"That's what we'll do, and that's it. It'll just be me, understood?"

"Whatever you say, Biagio," Carmine replied with a shrug, visibly worried. "But—"

His words were interrupted by the vibrating of Biagio's Chinese iPhone.

"Yes?"

"Biagio, it's best if you come to the farmhouse," said one of the fake cops. "Oscar is here and he's seen the hostages. He's beside himself."

"Shit," Biagio sighed, closing his eyes. "That's all we needed!"

"What the fuck is going on, Biagio?" Oscar asked in a calm voice, which made it all the more threatening, as soon as Biagio got out of his car. "Who the fuck are these people? What are you hiding from us?"

Biagio grabbed him by his coat and shoved him against the car. "What the fuck are you talking about?" he yelled in his face. "I'm not hiding anything! I'm just protecting you! I told you to stay in the house, I entrusted our families to you, for Christ's sake!"

"You're protecting us? It doesn't seem to me you're doing a very good job of that, you know? Or am I wrong, boys?" Oscar asked, turning to Ronny and Cristiano.

Neither said a word, but it was obvious they were of the same opinion as Oscar.

"Where's Giorgio?" Oscar asked.

Biagio looked at him wild-eyed, without replying and without letting go of him. One of his eyelids was twitching nervously.

"Where is he, Biagio? Nobody's seen him since last night. Should we be worried about him too? Should we already be writing him off? Because that's it, isn't it?"

Biagio landed him a violent slap that echoed like a whiplash.

Oscar didn't react. "So we can't even ask you a question now, is that it, chief? Sonja, Santo, Paja . . . and now Giorgio? They're playing target practice with us and we don't even know what the fuck is going on or what you're trying to do."

"You promised to trust me. You promised—"

"Tell me how the fuck we're supposed to trust you if—"

"If you think you can handle this thing by yourselves," he roared, letting go of Oscar and opening his arms wide, "go ahead and do it. I don't give a damn any more. Sort yourselves out. Do whatever you like. You're free."

He turned and headed inside the farmhouse, deaf to their calls.

Carmine placed a hand on Oscar's shoulder. "Oscar. Listen to me. Trust me. He knows what he's doing. It may not seem like it, but he does know what he's doing. You just take care of the families, the bodyguards, Claudia. Don't leave Claudia alone."

"What about him?" Oscar retorted. "Did you see the look in his eyes? Do you really want to let him go around like that? He's going to kill someone."

"We'll deal with him," Vito said.

"Oh yes, that's really reassuring."

"Oscar, listen to me," Carmine said. "All we know is that he's never betrayed us and has always protected us, right? He's Biagio. And he lives for us, you know."

"I don't think so. Who are the people he has in there?"

They exchanged a long tense look. A silence fell between them, a silence populated with doubts, recriminations, and unanswered questions.

"Okay, you don't want to talk either, all right," Oscar said, giving up. "I'll look after the family. You deal with him."

Carmine and Vito turned and ran after their chief.

"What do you think?" Oscar asked his colleagues.

"I don't know," Ronny sighed. "First the vanished coke, and we still don't know where that is. Then the blanket operation last night, now Giorgio disappearing . . . I don't know, I really don't."

Oscar looked at them, disorientated. "I'm going home. You two go check on Claudia. Let's give it a few more hours, then if Giorgio doesn't reappear we'll figure out what to do."

Everything was moving at supersonic speed. Once these events had started, it was only to be expected that sooner or later he would find himself crushed beneath their weight, with no possibility of breaking free.

"Biagio, what's the matter? Why are you so sad?"

He stared at Nicky. He had gone to see her because he needed her refreshing strength. He needed to see himself reflected in the eyes of someone who really trusted him. He needed to look at her one more time because tonight anything might happen.

"I . . . " he began, and broke off. He took her father's letter from his pocket and held it out to her. "Santo left you this. I don't know what it says, but I know it's something just for you. I wanted to give it to you, and I want you to read it, you decide when: now, in or month or in ten years . . . He loved you very much, Nicky."

She took the letter and turned it over in her thin hands. "I loved him a lot too."

"Come here," he said, and put his arms around her. He hugged her tight, as if it were the last time. "Promise me you'll take care of the kids and the girls.

They need you in this situation, you know. You have to make them laugh."

She nodded.

Biagio kissed her on the forehead and then whispered in her ear, "The person who killed your father is already dead, because I'm on my way to get him."

Nicky felt her blood run cold. There was something strange about Biagio's voice, it was the voice of someone who has been hurt too deeply and has grown mad with the pain.

"You mustn't—"

"Yes, I must. Promise you'll do what I asked, okay?"

"All right."

He ruffled her hair, then left, saying goodbye to the boys. The air was humming with tension, and they all looked at him with a mixture of skepticism and fear.

As he got in his car, his cell phone vibrated. It was a text telling him the place of the exchange and advising him to be alone.

Biagio thought about Giorgio as he drove to the farmhouse. He was the only one who knew about the Serbs, about Sonja and Donna. They were dangerous secrets that could destroy the family once and for all, now that all the cracks between them had grown exaggeratedly wide.

He's the sacrificial lamb, he thought. Is he worth more dead or alive?

He was afraid of the answer.

An hour later, Biagio stopped the van near the field they had indicated to him. As agreed, he flashed his lights twice, then got out, a .45 in his hand. He went to the back doors of the van, snapped open the lock, grabbed the gagged and handcuffed Belcastro by one arm, and pulled him out.

When he saw the lights of a car approaching in the distance, he forced Belcastro to his knees.

"Whatever happens, don't try anything stupid, or I'll kill you," he said without taking his eyes off the car, which stopped some sixty feet away. It was a big 4x4, with smoked windows. Three masked men got out, armed with pistols, shoving Giorgio ahead of them, his hands cuffed behind his back. The bruises on his face were visible even from that distance.

The three men approached with their prisoner. Two of them had their pistols aimed at his temples, while the third kept his by his side.

Giorgio was relieved to see his chief. He hadn't expected him to come, and yet he had. That meant that all was not lost.

"Are you all right?" Biagio asked, tense.

"He's all right," one of the three unknown men answered for him. "Did you bring everything?"

With a nod of his head, Biagio indicated the van. "It's all in there."

"Good. Then what are we waiting for?"

Biagio smiled and pulled Belcastro to his feet, pointing the .45 at his temple. "As I said, don't do anything stupid, you son of a bitch," he whispered in his ear, then pushed him forward.

Nicky had been locked in the bathroom for more than half an hour, turning the letter from Santo Spada, her father, over in her hands. She was torn as to whether or not to read it. Everything seemed to her so strange, so chaotic as to scare her. And she was afraid that what was written in that letter might disturb her even more. But she was only a young girl, and her curiosity to know more about that father who had never had the courage to reveal himself, to meet him again even if only through a letter, won out over these dark premonitions. So she read it. And started crying.

Santo had written everything she had meant to him, explaining to her why he had never told her he was her father. But when she read the last sentence, her tears of emotion turned to tears of terror.

This was what Santo had written at the end: *Even though I won't be there anymore, I know the love I have for you will remain inside you, protecting you. But now you have to promise me one thing, sweetheart: stay away from Biagio. This is my last wish: keep well clear of him, because he's a dangerous man. Even though I love him, he's nothing but a danger to you.*

Shaken by these words, Nicky wiped her eyes and wondered what her father had meant. Why on earth should she keep away from Biagio?

Biagio came to an abrupt halt and grabbed Belcastro's arm to stop him too.

"What's the matter?" one of the three masked men asked.

"Giorgio!" Biagio called.

Their eyes met and Giorgio nodded imperceptibly.

"I always loved you like a brother. You should have trusted me."

Giorgio stared at him in dismay and opened his mouth to cry out when Biagio's .45 shifted to aim at him. But the cry died in his throat, because Biagio fired twice, hitting him full in the chest and sending him lifeless to the ground.

When the going gets tough . . .

Better an evil experienced than a good unknown.
—GIUSEPPE TOMASI DI LAMPEDUSA, *The Leopard*

Extreme remedies

The three masked men stared in amazement at Giorgio's body. When they looked up at Biagio, he had again aimed his .45 at Belcastro's temple and had a wicked little smile on his lips.

"Change of plan," he said.

The doors of the van opened wide and eight masked men emerged, heavily armed, who arranged themselves in a halo behind Mazzeo.

"I'm going to say this just once," Biagio cried. "Put down your weapons."

The three men looked from Giorgio's body to the eight masked men and started cursing.

Oscar entered the room where Nicky slept to see if she was still awake. She had fallen asleep. He went close to her to cover her and noticed the letter next to the pillow. He immediately recognized Santo's handwriting. He picked up the paper and read it.

His eyes lingered over that last devastating sentence:

This is my last wish: keep well clear of him, because he's a dangerous man. Even though I love him, he's nothing but a danger to you.

It was Santo who had written that. Santo, the man closest to Biagio, his mentor.

He left the room in silence, that sentence screaming inside his head.

Biagio isn't what we think he is, he told himself. We should have stopped him a long time ago. Now it's too late.

"I'm getting pissed off. Put down your weapons."

Biagio retreated, while his men advanced with their MP5 submachine guns equipped with torches.

Pugliese's men dropped their weapons to the ground at the very moment Giorgio coughed and started writhing on the ground. The three carabinieri stared at him as if he were a zombie, but the fake cops forced them to their knees, handcuffed them, and shoved them in the van.

"Vito, take this piece of shit," Biagio said pushing Belcastro toward him. Vito loaded him in the van too.

Biagio and Carmine approached Giorgio, who was still writhing on the ground, his chest wet with blood.

"Sometimes they come back," Carmine laughed.

"What . . . what the fuck happened?" Giorgio muttered as soon as he had managed to catch his breath.

Biagio showed him the .45. "Have you never heard about bullets with a reduced force of impact or a low power of arrest, if you prefer?" He smiled. "Less gunpowder, less speed, and a rubber tip. They wound but they don't kill."

"A bit like Chinese contraband ammunition," Carmine cut in.

"Right, except that there the effect isn't deliberate," Biagio sneered. "These are used by armies for training without anybody getting accidentally killed."

Giorgio stared at him, still incredulous.

"As soon as they hit you, you fainted from the shock and the impact, which is still considerable. But you're alive, handsome."

"Hey, did you hear?" Carmine asked. "Do you want to put down roots here?"

"You . . . knew that . . . "

"Let's say I knew how it would go," Biagio said with that devilish smile of his, holding out his hand. "I wanted those guys to give themselves up, and I needed a diversion to take them by surprise. Did you really think I would kill you? Have we come that far?"

Giorgio seized his hand, and Biagio, groaning with the effort, pulled him to his feet and embraced him, heedless of the blood on his coat. "You didn't trust me, son," he said in a low voice, kissing him on the cheek and giving him a slap. "You broke my heart."

"I . . . "

"We have his accountant," Biagio went on, grabbing his chin, "and now we also have three of his men. We're bringing him to his knees, Giorgio. I'm fucking him over big time."

"Those three are carabinieri," Giorgio spluttered. "Special Operations Group."

Biagio gave a start. "What? Are you sure?"

"Yes," Giorgio replied, tearing off his T-shirt and verifying that Biagio was right: the bullets had wounded him, but hadn't made any holes in his flesh. "That bastard has men everywhere."

Biagio and Carmine exchanged anxious glances.

"Is there even one honest cop in this fucking city?" Carmine asked. "I'm not asking for much, just one, dammit!"

"Let's go now," Biagio said. "We'll deal with them later."

Giorgio had been the sacrificial lamb. They had taken him to the edge, pushing him out of the pack, isolating him in such a way as to make him a target for Pugliese. And so it had been: after Biagio had attacked him on all fronts, eliminating his associates, Pugliese had tried to strike back at him by using Giorgio, whom Biagio had deliberately pushed into his arms. But Pugliese hadn't been able to put pressure on Biagio, because Biagio had foreseen everything. What was more, he had arranged the chessboard in such a way that Pugliese had been forced to make that particular move. It had been a risk, because he had endangered the life of one of his own men. But it had been the only way to get his hands on some of Pugliese's men, those closest to him. All the same, Biagio had never expected to find carabinieri among them.

When he went down into the cellar of the farmhouse, Biagio looked at the three of them, tied to chairs next to Prandelli, his wife, and Belcastro.

"This place is getting crowded," Carmine said with a smile, sitting down on the table.

"You six know each other, I assume," Biagio began, walking around the prisoners. "Two politicians, three carabinieri from the Special Operations Group, and a reputed accountant. With people like you by his side, it's clear how Pugliese has managed to take control of this city. But tonight everything will come to an end. I've run out of time, ladies and gentlemen. This war will finish tonight, come what may."

He removed the gags from the three carabinieri.

"Mazzeo, you know who we are, do you realize what you're—"

Biagio punched the carabiniere who had spoken full in the face, sending him to the floor, with his chair following. The tension of Giorgio's fake execution had roused him to an insane fury, and he proceeded to beat the man so violently as to make the other prisoners shudder.

Carmine did not dare intervene: getting involved right now meant risking a beating himself.

After a few minutes Biagio spat on the floor and wiped his blood-stained hands on the face of one of the two carabinieri who were still conscious.

"Read," Biagio ordered Carmine, who read out the home addresses of the carabinieri from their identity documents.

"Do I have to take it out on your families to make you talk?" Biagio cried, his eyes burning with rage.

The two carabinieri exchanged terrified glances.

"If you were entrusted with a delicate task like kidnapping a police officer, that means you are people he trusts blindly, people who know his secrets. I want those secrets. And you'll give them to me if you want to get out of here alive!"

The prisoners looked at him in dismay. He had the look of a crazed animal.

As he waited for her to arrive, Biagio stared at his hands and saw that in spite of the fact that he had washed them carefully there was still blood under the nails.

Irene Piscitelli entered the club and came toward him, attracting lustful glances. She deserved them, he thought, looking at her slender body.

"We said we'd never meet in a public place," she said, sitting down at his isolated table.

By way of reply, Biagio took out his Chinese iPhone, inserted some earphones, fiddled with them for a few seconds, and then handed it to her. It was a video. A confession by the three carabinieri admitting their involvement with the Pugliese syndicate. They gave the names of politicians, judges, law enforcement officers, businessmen, and well-known professionals: the whole Lombardia system.

Irene watched and listened to the confession without a word, goosebumps on her skin. "How did you do it?" she asked, giving him back the phone.

"I can be very persuasive when I set my mind to it."

"Those names, I—"

"I'm not here just to deliver the names."

Irene raised an eyebrow. "What, then?"

"Those three are closer to that bastard than I imagined. They told me how I can get to him."

"Then why are you making that grim face? It's very good news, isn't it?"

"No," Biagio said, rubbing his grazed knuckles. "They told me how to get to him. But it'll be nasty, it'll go beyond the limits we set ourselves at the beginning."

"How far beyond?"

"Quite a way."

"Christ. Let's hear it."

Biagio told her, and she turned pale.

"Well, what do I do?"

"Is there really no other solution?" she asked nervously.

"Not now. There's no more time. My men are turning against me, I can't control them anymore."

Irene nodded. "Okay, but you can always—"

"I told you I don't have them anymore. This thing is exploding in my hands. This . . . " he said, tapping the cell phone ". . . is the last opportunity I have to get to him. I know as well as you how risky and dirty it is, but at this point why should I care?"

"Why should you care? Simply because you can't do a thing like that."

"What the fuck do you think I've been doing up until now? Charity work? If I turn back now, everything I've done will have been useless. After all that's happened, he's about to run away. He'll disappear if we don't stop him, and there's only one way."

Irene shook her head, biting her lips. "And would you be prepared to do something like that?"

"I've done worse."

She nodded. "Okay, dammit."

"Don't you need to talk to the people upstairs?"

"I am the people upstairs, Mazzeo."

"I know, but as far as all the rest is concerned, the names, the politicians, and the people who are my . . . *hosts*, I need to talk to *them*. We've come to the end of the race, Irene. My friend Barranca, Belcastro, the

Prandellis, the three carabinieri, and Sabino Sergi have given me the names of all the people involved. The jigsaw is complete now. We're at a level that's too high for us. We have to know what *they* want to do."

"I'll call right away and let you know."

"Tell them it's urgent. I have to move as fast as possible, we run the risk of losing him."

"I told you I'll call them right away."

"Okay, then I'm off," said Biagio heading for the exit.

"Mazzeo . . . "

He turned.

"Be careful."

Biagio nodded and left the club.

Verri looked at the time. It was almost one. "Who the hell is it at this hour?" he wondered, going to open. He looked through the spy hole and saw the distorted and therefore even more imposing image of Giorgio Varga.

"Giorgio, what's up?" he asked, opening the door.

"Sir, I need to speak with you," Giorgio said. As he was being escorted to the hospital, Giorgio had taken the pistol from one of the fake cops, knocked him unconscious, and stolen his car. He had almost fainted on the way here, but he *had* to know.

Verri gave him the once-over. He had bruises on his face and generally looked terrible. "Are you all right, Giorgio?"

"We have to talk," Giorgio replied.

Verri motioned him in. "What's the matter, son?"

"Biagio, sir. I have to find out what's going on."

"What are you talking about? How do you mean?"

"Chief, you have to tell me what you're all up to, or I'll do it."

"Do what?" Verri asked, bewildered.

"I'll kill him. I'll kill Biagio."

The woman and the child were crying when Carmine and the fake cop bundled them in the van. They hadn't even had time to figure out what was going on. The masked men had burst into the apartment in which they were hidden, disarmed the bodyguards, and abducted the woman and child.

"Are you going to kill us?" the woman asked Carmine through her tears.

He stared at her without answering.

"Please. What's going to happen to us? He's only a child!"

"It's not up to me, signora," Carmine retorted, folding his arms. "Now shut up."

Carmine realized that the boy was staring at him. For a while he tried to sustain the child's gaze, but couldn't.

The black van headed at great speed toward the farmhouse.

Irene Piscitelli parked the BMW in the underground garage of the hotel and got out, still tense after the telephone call with the Voice, and the subsequent one with Mazzeo. As she was about to activate the alarm, she felt something cold pressing against the back of her neck.

"Don't close it," Giorgio said, coldly. "Get in, and don't try anything."

"What?"

He pressed harder. "In the car. Now. Sit in the passenger seat."

All she could do was obey.

Still keeping her covered, Giorgio sat down in the driver's seat and closed the door.

"You're going to be sorry for what you're—"

Giorgio elbowed her in the stomach and, as soon as she opened her mouth to groan with pain, he stuck the barrel of his Beretta in it. "Now you tell me what kind of agreement you made with Biagio, or I swear to God I'll kill you."

Biagio parked the Alfa on the edge of the field, lit only by a sliver of moon. He switched off the engine, unhooked the holster with the pistol, and put it inside the glove compartment. He got out of the car, jumped over the fence that demarcated the field, and walked with difficulty across the freshly plowed earth. After about two hundred yards, he kneeled on the ground and put his trembling hands over his head. He remained motionless in the cold of the night, wondering if they would really come.

He found out a few moments later when he heard noises behind him. But he didn't turn, as instructed.

"You're alone, right?" an unknown voice asked.

"Yes."

"Unarmed?"

"Yes," he repeated.

A few seconds later, his head was covered with a black hood, his arms were cuffed behind his back, and something metal was pressed into his kidneys.

"Don't try anything stupid," the voice said. Then, in a tone of derision: "You're shaking. Are you scared?"

"Fuck off, you bastard," Biagio breathed. "Do what you have to do."

He was grabbed by the arm and forced to walk.

By the time Irene Piscitelli stopped speaking, Giorgio felt drained of all energy.

"Is everything you said true?" he asked, aghast.

She nodded.

"And where is he now?"

Silence.

Giorgio pressed the barrel of his gun into her ribs.

"He's with them," she sighed.

When the hood was removed, Biagio discovered he was in a hangar, on his knees, his hands tied behind his back, the barrel of a rifle pointed at the back of his head. They had taken away all his cell phones and searched him with electronic equipment to make sure he wasn't wearing a wire.

In front of him, four masked men sat on plastic chairs.

"We meet at last, Inspector," said the man furthest from him. He had a heavy Calabrian accent.

Biagio tried to speak, but realized that his mouth was too dry. Fear had dried his throat and lips.

The four men he had in front of him were the representatives of the four biggest families in the 'Ndrangheta. There before him sat the Mother House, the personification of the Calabrian Mafia.

"We've heard some very good things about you, Mazzeo, and I have to say you haven't disappointed us, you've behaved very well."

Not knowing how to respond, Biagio remained silent.

"Are you shaking, Inspector?" asked another man with an even more marked Southern accent. "You mustn't be afraid, we're among friends, aren't we? What did our mutual friend tell you? Did she scare you?"

The four men laughed.

"So, let's talk about serious things. Natale: have you managed to speak to him?"

"Yes. He's finished. When I let him hear his son's screams he gave up. He knows by now that everyone's abandoned him, and after last night's operation, the raids, the people arrested, he knows he's alone. He's being hunted by you, by me, and by his own men."

"Good. When will you see him?"

"He'll give himself up tomorrow."

"You know we're trusting you, don't you? The agreement was that you would arrest him alive, Mazzeo. Understood? *Alive.*"

"I know, but why?" Biagio asked, immediately regretting having asked the question.

"Why what?" one of the men asked.

"Why did you choose me?"

"It was Piscitelli who suggested you. She'd had her eyes on you for a while, she knew you were corrupt, that you'd committed murder, that you had contact with Barranca, in other words that you were more of a criminal than a police officer, and that she could have you by the balls, Inspector, as and when she wanted. She's a very bright girl. You were wrong to underestimate her."

"Why get me to do the dirty work?"

The men laughed.

"Does he deserve an explanation?" one of the men asked his companions.

"Well, after all he's done, I'd say yes."

"Natale had to be punished for the murder of his father, and for what he was *trying* to do, splitting from us, from the South. But this is an unusual time, Inspector. One government has fallen, another one is about to take over. The region that interests us is about to go to the polls. We couldn't afford a war, don't you see? If we'd been the ones to get blood on our hands, the politicians, the ones who matter, would have been forced to wage war on us, and we have no intention of see-ing that happen, not with the Expo almost on us and all the rest. With your help, we've made the public believe that the Mafia has been defeated in the North, and the arrest of Natale Pugliese will be the final proof of that."

"It's a political operation," Biagio said in a hoarse voice.

"You see? The boy's good. Of course, Mazzeo. What else? Now the businesses, the citizens, and the newspapers will be convinced that the Mafia has been wiped out. There won't be any more murders, there won't be any more attacks or reprisals. With the arrest of Pugliese it'll all be over, and we'll be able to carry on our affairs in peace. The loco-motive will be able to set off again stronger than before. You know why Piscitelli did business with us? Because we want the same thing: peace. That scumbag Pugliese, on the other hand, wanted war. If we'd risen to the bait, if we'd waged war on him, it would have been bad for every-one: for us, for the State, and for the police. Using her and her contacts, we've made everyone believe that it was the police that won, and the police *are* the State. Your arrests, your raids, have reassured public opinion. Piscitelli has been brilliant through all this, Mazzeo. She hasn't put her signature to a single document, has she?"

Biagio shook his head.

"Of course not. The National Crime Bureau used her, making her do the dirty work, putting pressure on her. There's nothing to prove that she acted on behalf of the ministry. As far as the law is concerned, she did it all herself. In the eyes of the law, there was no agreement with us, because there's no evidence."

"I . . . " Biagio stammered.

"We know, it's natural that you feel used. But when it comes down to it you saved your colleagues, didn't you? You stopped them all being arrested for criminal association. You also got something out of this, or am I wrong?"

"Never as much as you."

He heard them say something in dialect and then burst out laughing.

"Do you think we don't know about the money you stole from Natale?"

Biagio felt himself freeze.

"Don't worry, you can keep it. It's the price for the two hundred kilos of coke you gave us to seal our agreement, isn't it?"

Biagio felt himself flush, but was shrewd enough not to open his mouth.

When, the night he had remained alone guarding the consignment and had taken then the drugs as security for the agreement, they had told him that he would get it back, or at least pay him for it. But not at a reduced price like that.

Fucking Mafiosi, he cursed them under his breath.

"What's the matter?" they teased him. "Anything wrong?"

"The price isn't exactly the market one," he said.

The Calabrians burst out laughing.

"You really are a tough cookie. There you are, kneeling on the ground, handcuffed, a rifle pointed at your head, and you want to start haggling about the price? We could kill you right now and make you disappear forever, you know that, don't you?"

He smiled. "But you'll never get Natale that way."

"Are you trying to piss us off, Mazzeo?"

He shook his head. "No, I'm sorry. I'm grateful to you for the money."

"That's better. Did you bring what we asked?"

"Yes, they're in the pocket of my jeans."

He felt them searching him and someone took out the two memory sticks onto which he had copied the recordings of the interrogations of the carabinieri, Belcastro, and the two politicians, with all the names they had given him. All that could have led to the arrests of hundreds of people for criminal association. But Biagio knew there would be no arrests and no trial without their consent.

"We'll listen to these, and let you know who you can arrest and who you can't, understood?"

"Okay. One last thing. The Serbs."

"We already told you we'll deal with them. You've helped us to resolve this conflict, and we'll help you to resolve your problems with the Serbs and the Albanians. We can assure you that you won't have anything to fear from them."

Biagio nodded, satisfied that they would honor their agreement. That was why he had given the order to kill the two Serbs a few days earlier, why he had been so daring in his dealings with the Albanians: because he knew the Calabrians were protecting him.

"Do you have anything else to tell us?"

"You have to promise me that Pugliese will pay for the murder of my man," Biagio said, his voice steady and sonorous.

"How long do you think he'll last in jail after all the trouble he's caused us?"

"What about Piscitelli?"

"The agreement was that we would let you take him alive. She still believes in the law courts, and we're certainly not going to disillusion her. And in fact it won't even be us who'll do away with him, but the Serbs. Piscitelli won't be able to do anything either to us or to you, and the Serbs will finally have someone to take revenge on for that cocaine business. We all get what we want."

Biagio nodded, satisfied. "My family . . . "

"We will make sure personally that Piscitelli keeps to the agreement: nobody from your squad will be charged with any offence, they will all be free and clean."

"One thing I'd like to know. The candidate for regional governor. He's one of yours, isn't it?"

"Did you ever doubt it?"

Biagio sneered.

"We told you, Mazzeo. This was more a political move than a criminal one."

"Why, is there a difference?" one of the others said, arousing general hilarity.

"Get on with your life. Mazzeo. Have we been good to you, or are you starting to have a few qualms?"

In an instant, Biagio thought again of all he had done that week: he had ordered murders, kidnappings, beatings, deceived his own family, derailed investigations, and turned his back once and for all on his badge, doing business with ruthless Mafiosi.

"No qualms, gentlemen," he said.

"We like you, Inspector. You're a man of judgement and you know how to show respect, which is quite a rare gift these days. You are now under our Cloak of Mercy. Do you know what that means? It means you're untouchable, because you're *our* friend. Not everyone can say that, Mazzeo. If we ever need you again, can we count on you?"

He nodded. He knew that if he had said no, in a week's time they would kill him. Going into business with them was the only way to stay alive.

"And just to show you how fond we are of you and your squad, we know you've had a few little problems with this Claudetti. Do you want us to deal with him?"

Claudetti's destiny was now in his hands.

"No," Biagio replied. "Claudetti has only been doing his job. I'll teach him a lesson. Thanks for the offer."

"Your choice. We'll let you know about those names, then."

"What should I do with the three carabinieri and the politicians?"

"Once you've arrested Pugliese, let them go. We'll deal with them."

"Okay."

"One last thing, Mazzeo. What's the story with the murder of Messina?"

"How do you mean?"

"Please, we're not Piscitelli. Do you think we really swallowed the story that it was Pugliese who was behind that fiasco?"

"I—"

"You have to resolve that situation once and for all, have we made ourselves clear? *Once and for all.*"

Biagio remained motionless and silent for a few seconds, then nodded.

"Don't disappoint us, Mazzeo," said one of the Calabrians. "And give our regards to Piscitelli. Tell her we'll miss seeing her put cream on."

The hood was put back over Biagio's head. Then they made him stand up and took him away.

"I don't believe it," Giorgio said in a low voice.

"He did it for all of you, Varga. We would have arrested you otherwise. We had evidence that you were all corrupt, we could have put you inside for criminal association and gotten your families into trouble. Whereas now, all the evidence against you has disappeared, and there won't be any trial. Mazzeo has saved your asses. I was reluctant, especially knowing the state he was in after the deaths of his woman and Spada. But he just put his head down and charged. He really must love you guys very much."

"Why didn't he involve us?" Giorgio asked, more to himself than to her.

"Because he wanted to protect you. It was a dirty, clandestine operation. All the risk was on his shoulders, and he knew that. He didn't want you mixed up in it, so that he could protect you in case something went wrong."

"What kind of police officer are you? Aren't you ashamed to be a puppet of the 'Ndrangheta?"

"Come on, Varga, do you think you can really defeat the Mafia in this country when it's actually in power?"

"How long have you been dealing with them?"

She withdrew into a lofty silence, and he had to threaten her again with his pistol to make her talk.

"Forever, but heavily since the Duisburg massacre. We were under enormous pressure from the European Community to stop the bloodshed. They were afraid the feud might spread abroad, and we had to prevent that. We had to stop the war, and fast. It was only natural to establish contact with them. But once you start dealing with them, you can't stop."

"You disgust me."

"I love my country, Varga. And though you may make that face, I am protecting it. You can't not deal with these people, they're too powerful these days. If we hadn't done what had to be done, a war would have broken out. Strange as it may seem to you, I've saved a lot of lives. And I'm going to arrest Pugliese."

"You used Biagio like a puppet."

"We used each other, and we've all won, Varga. All of us. Mazzeo was the only card we could play. Pugliese had to be stopped, we couldn't wait. Dealing with that crazy cokehead was impossible."

"Whereas dealing with the old guard wasn't, is that it?"

"Use your head, Varga. If we'd done things according to the rules, it would have taken us at least two years just to set up a serious investigation. Two years, can you imagine? In a week, your friend did what we would have done in three or four years."

"That doesn't justify—"

"I'm not interested in justifications. I'm paid to avoid wars and innocent victims."

"Did Verri know about your pact?"

"No. He's a pragmatist, but he's old school, he would never have agreed."

Giorgio sat there in silence for a few seconds, then said, "Listen to me. Whatever you and Biagio agreed to, keep to it. Otherwise I'll come looking for you and kill you."

"Remember who you're—"

Giorgo aimed the pistol at her temple and cocked it. "I'll find you and kill you, got that?"

She nodded, terrified by his icy look. He got out of the car, overwhelmed with guilt.

As soon as they had taken him back to his car and left, Biagio crumpled on the seat, abandoning himself to the shakes that he had tried to curb throughout the encounter. In a cold sweat, devastated by the tension, he had vomited bile and blood.

Afterwards, not knowing where to go, he had driven the car aimlessly through the Jungle, until he had found himself passing their old pub, the Bang Bang. He had stopped the car and gotten out. Breaking the seals, he had entered the premises.

It had been strange, walking through the empty pub. He had switched on the lights and entered their private room. He had poured himself a glass of Jim Beam at the bar in the corner. He had put an Otis Redding record on the juke-box and, as "Pain in My Heart" took possession of the room, he had found himself once again staring at the photographs of his boys on the walls.

My family, he thought, lightly touching the images with his trembling hands. I saved them. In the end I did it . . .

"That was Santo's favorite song," came Giorgio Varga's toneless voice.

Biagio turned abruptly and saw Giorgio pouring himself two fingers of bourbon. In his hand he held a pistol.

"What are you doing here?" Biagio asked, taken aback.

"We had the same idea," Giorgio said, sipping his drink.

He came up to him, and together they stood there looking at the photographs.

"I know everything, Biagio."

Biagio turned to him, holding his breath.

"The pact with Piscitelli and the Calabrians, Natale Pugliese, the drugs, the murder of the father. I know everything. She told me."

"How did you get her to talk?"

"What matters is that she talked. Why did you push me away, chief?"

"I didn't want you involved in this shit."

"You wanted to protect us."

Biagio turned back to the images. "That's right."

"And we thought you were betraying us, that you were going to get us all killed."

"That was a risk I had to take. If I'd told you what I was going to do, you would have followed me, and that wasn't right. I got you into this mess, it was only right that I should sort things out. I used you, Giorgio. I used you to force him out into the open. But I would never have killed you. How could I?"

"What about Vito and Carmine?"

"Carmine has nothing to lose, and I couldn't have done it all on my own. As for Vito, well, I was forced to bring Vito in on it. It was the only way to rid him of his guilt over Messina, to give him an aim, a reason for living."

"What happened with Pugliese?"

Biagio's voice dipped to an anguished whisper. "I kidnapped his wife and son. The child . . . I . . . I hit him to make him scream, Giorgio. I hit a child . . . "

Giorgio saw that his friend's hands were shaking. "You had no choice, Biagio."

"I know. Tomorrow he'll give himself up, because I've had a price put on his head by his own men. The separatists will be forgiven by San Luca only if they abandon and isolate him. Right now the only way he has to stay alive is to give himself up to me."

Giorgio nodded, his eyes glued to the snapshots. "Forgive me, my friend," he said, tears streaking his face.

"There's nothing to forgive, handsome," Biagio said, sipping the bourbon. "The family, before anything else."

"Yes."

"You know it isn't over yet, don't you? There's one thing I still have to do. I don't want to but I have to, to protect all of you right to the end."

"I know."

"I have to do it for our families, Giorgio. Believe me, I really don't want to, but—"

"Do what you have to do, Biagio. I'm with you."

"Again?" Biagio said.

"Again."

On the juke-box Otis Redding started singing "Nobody Knows You When You're Down and Out." The two men lost themselves in memories.

"You know something?" Biagio said. "After the death of Santo, after Ste, after Sonja . . . this place means nothing anymore." He took a photograph down from the wall: it showed him and a younger Santo holding Nicky as a child. She was laughing happily at the camera. "This place is full of ghosts."

"Then let's burn it," Giorgio suggested, drying his tears. "That's the only way they'll be free."

Biagio nodded, slipping the photograph in his pocket.

They threw all the bottles from the bar on the floor, smashing them, then Biagio poured the contents of a bottle of whiskey over the photographs and over Santo's jukebox, from which Otis Redding's voice continued to pour out, sweet and passionate.

A few minutes later, they threw a box of matches on the ground.

Giorgio took down a Borsalino hanging on the wall and handed it to his friend. Biagio turned it over in his hands and then threw it into the fire.

"Goodbye, handsome," he said, watching the flames consume the hat.

He left with Giorgio by his side, the two of them once again together, while Otis Redding continued singing through the flames, saying farewell in his own way to Santo Spada.

Better to be a king in hell than a slave in heaven

Natale Pugliese had been forced to come to an agreement with Biagio. Biagio had brought his organization to its knees, had his best men killed, and now, as far as the world of organized crime was concerned, Natale was just a walking corpse. Wherever he ran, the 'Ndrangheta would find him. In addition, Biagio had threatened to hand his son over to the Southerners if he didn't give himself up. With his wife and their child in Biagio's hands, Pugliese had had no other choice.

Biagio arrived at the construction site with Claudia and Carmine, in two different cars. He had brought Claudia because as far as Piscitelli knew she was in Pugliese's hands: she had to appear as the object of the exchange.

The three of them got out of their cars with their pistols in their hands and waited for Pugliese.

He arrived after a few minutes. He got out of his car and came toward Biagio, who was standing waiting for him, framed by Claudia and Carmine.

"Where are my wife and son?" Pugliese asked, his hands up.

With a nod of his head, Biagio indicated the 4x4 in which they were locked.

"Let me say goodbye to them one last time," Pugliese said. "Please."

"Search him," Biagio ordered, icily.

Carmine went up to him and checked him. "He's clean," he said.

Biagio approached and stood three feet from Pugliese.

"You've won," Pugliese said. "Let me say goodbye to my son for the last time, I beg you."

"About Inspector Braga. We're agreed, right?"

"Yes. I'll take the blame for the death of the cop, I'll say I sent my men to kidnap her, and that I've been keeping her hostage until today."

"Congratulations. Try to change your story and your family will die."

"I won't change my story."

"Handcuff him," Biagio ordered Claudia.

She obeyed. Carmine brought out the woman and the child. Both had their faces covered with black hoods. As if it were a scene they had previously rehearsed, Carmine went behind Pugliese and took his throat in an iron grip, while Claudia forced the woman and the child, who couldn't see what was happening, to get down on their knees.

"Santo Spada," Biagio said in a low voice. "He was a father to me. He had a daughter who will never see him again. Santo didn't deserve to die."

"I . . . They don't . . . "

Biagio took a large revolver from his jeans. He opened it up and showed Pugliese the empty cylinder. "Six shots, one bullet," he said, inserting a bullet in the magazine. He shut the revolver and spun the cylinder.

"No! I beg you, don't! You're a cop, for God's sake! No, don't do it!"

Biagio aimed the revolver at the child and pulled the trigger.

Click.

"Nooo!" Pugliese cried, vomiting from the tension.

Biagio aimed the revolver at the back of the woman's neck and fired. *Click.* Empty again.

He continued this perverse game for another three shots that were all empty, while Pugliese writhed as if he was on the electric chair.

When Biagio came to the last shot, the decisive one, the only one with a bullet, it was the woman's turn.

"I'm sorry," Biagio murmured, while his men looked on impassively. Pugliese was struggling like a possessed animal, but Carmine was too strong for him and he couldn't break free.

Biagio aimed the weapon at the woman, who begged for mercy through her tears.

"An eye for an eye, Pugliese."

"No! I beg you! Please no!"

The shot echoed through the construction site.

Pugliese collapsed to the ground, eyes bulging. Carmine had let him go. He was shaking convulsively and was foaming at the mouth as if the victim of an epileptic fit.

"You . . . You . . . "

"It was a blank," Biagio sneered, dragging the woman, deafened by the shot, to her feet. He removed her hood and let her see her husband lying humiliated on the ground, stained with vomit, his pants wet with urine and shit, shaking and in tears.

"Natale!" she called to him, trying to throw herself on him, but Biagio grabbed her by one arm and shoved her toward Carmine. "Put them both back inside," he ordered, "and take them away."

Carmine obeyed, and less than a minute later the SUV with Natale's family on board disappeared into the distance.

"You . . . you . . . a blank . . . you . . . she isn't . . . she's alive," Pugliese continued stammering, in a state of shock.

"I don't kill women, you piece of shit." Biagio said, crouching down and lifting his chin with two fingers. "You were right, earlier. I've won, you son of a bitch." He spat in his face.

Biagio got up again and met Claudia's eyes. He stroked the platinum ring. Ivankov would have been proud of him: he had managed to avenge himself, and at the same time get rich, all the while protecting his family. "Do you want to say something to him before we hand him over?" he asked Claudia.

Claudia nodded, pulled Pugliese to his feet, and also spat in his face. "This is the end of the line, scumbag. Just one thing. Why did you need to kill his girl Sonja? Why did you do that?"

"W-what?" Pugliese said, his head jerking up. "I . . . I didn't have any girl killed."

Claudia laughed. "What's the point of lying now? Just tell me why."

"I swear to you on my son's head I didn't have her killed."

"But—" Claudia said, letting him go and turning to Biagio.

She didn't have time to say anything else.

Biagio shot her in the middle of her forehead.

She fell to the ground.

Biagio stood looking down at her for a few seconds. When he started speaking to Pugliese, his eyes were still fixed on her body.

"You killed her to take revenge on me. There were only the three of us here at this meeting. You'll take the blame for her murder. But if you come against me, I'll tell the Mother House where your family is. My colleague is taking them to a secret place. I'll be the only one to know where they are, do you understand what I'm saying?"

Pugliese nodded, in more of a state of shock than ever.

"I want to hear you say it."

"I'll say I killed her. For revenge."

"Good."

"You said you didn't kill women."

"I lied."

Biagio took out his BlackBerry and dialed Irene Piscitelli's number. He told her where he was and to come immediately with an ambulance. As soon as he hung up he stood in silence looking down at the slender body of Claudia Braga.

Neither he nor Pugliese said a word until the paramedics arrived.

*

Nicky had slept little and badly. All night long, all she had done was think over and over about the letter Santo had written her and those last words: *Keep away from him . . . He's a dangerous man. . .*

Nicky loved Biagio. He had never done her any harm. On the contrary, he had always protected her, he had always run to her aid when she had needed him. Why had Santo written something like that? It was as if he was talking about someone else.

As she re-read the letter for the umpteenth time in the bathroom, she told herself that, much as Santo had loved her, he had been wrong about Biagio, all down the line. She stared at the letter and slowly tore off the final part of it. She crumpled it, threw it down the toilet, and flushed it away with a smile on her lips. She couldn't wait to hug Biagio again.

As Irene Piscitelli officially handed Pugliese over to the men of the task force led by Augusta Barberi and Corrado Tortora, accompanied by Deputy Prosecutor Piero Magri of the Regional Organized Crime Directorate, Biagio told them yet again the story of what had happened.

"I'll take him now," Irene cut in, moving him away. "I need to talk to him."

"Congratulations," he said with a sneer as he got into her BMW. "You did it. You arrested Pugliese and stopped the war, are you pleased?"

"Drop it. I'm sorry about your colleague."

"Right. I want her to be remembered as a policewoman, not as a criminal."

"I'll see what I can do."

"I kept to my side of the agreement, will you do the same?"

She nodded. "You and your men are free and cleared of all charges."

"There's one last thing."

She frowned. "What?"

"You blackmailed me. You knew everything about my affairs, about our secrets. You couldn't have been aware of all these things without someone on the inside. And it could only have been one of my men."

"I don't know what you're talking about."

"Of course you do. Who's the mole?"

"Mazzeo, you got out of this in one piece, do you want to screw up your life again?"

He looked at her. It was clear that she would never tell him. He had to be patient: he would find out for himself.

"I'm very tired. Can I go home?"

"Of course, you're a free man."

Biagio got out of the car and walked to his. Now for the hardest part: facing his men.

General meeting tomorrow night. I have to talk to you, he texted them. Having sent the message, he took from his wallet a photograph showing him with Claudia a few years earlier. They were smiling happily. Biagio folded it in two, neatly separating the two faces. He tore off one of the pieces, screwed it up, set fire to it with his cigarette lighter, and dropped it through the window. He looked at the other half for a few more seconds and then put it back where he had gotten it, knowing that he would never again get rid of it.

Roberto Messina had gotten into the habit of having an early dinner with his mother and sister-in-law. He would sit down at the head of the table, taking the child in his arms and spoon-feed him, as if he were his father, while listening to the two women telling him about their day.

With Carlo's death, everything had changed. His mother had made it clear to him that he would have to take care of Chiara and the child, and he had every intention of doing so.

When the doorbell rang that night, he thought it was strange, given the hour.

"Are you expecting anyone?" he asked his mother.

"No."

"I'll go," he said, passing the child to his sister-in-law. When he opened the door he saw one of the men from Mazzeo's squad standing there.

"Hi," Roberto said, taken aback.

"Hi. Forgive the hour and the intrusion, but I have to speak with you."

"Regarding what?"

"Your brother."

Roberto came outside. "I'm listening," he said, looking the other man in the eyes.

"Biagio Mazzeo lied to you about everything."

"Excuse me?"

"The man you killed wasn't Carlo's real killer."

"What?"

"Biagio used you, I'm sorry."

"Wha— No, that's impossible. It was the Calabrians who—"

"No."

"Who was it, then?"

"I had to kill her. I did it myself because it was the only thing I could do to put an end to the business of the cop who was killed. And now that you know that Claudia betrayed us with Ivankov, well, I hope you understand she couldn't get away with it. Do you think it was easy? Like hell it was. I loved Claudia, just as I love all of you. But I had no choice. Should I have forgiven her about Ivankov? Maybe. But you gave me no choice. That day, you did things your own way and someone got killed. Would you have trusted her in my place? I don't think so, and what's more I didn't want your families involved. If someone had to pay, I was the only one to be involved. Because . . . because it was my fault it all started. I was the one who created the pack. And I had to stop it being destroyed. At any cost. I know it was a risk, but what else could I do?"

Nobody said a word.

"Now you know everything. The pact with Piscitelli and the Calabrians, the arrest of Pugliese, the consignment I handed over as security, how I used the dead cop's brother . . . and Claudia's death. It's for you to judge me."

With this, Biagio took his last sip of Guinness and stood up. His men were speechless, lost in a forlorn silence.

"I'm going outside, so you can decide what to do, I don't want to influence you. Call me when you've finished."

"Why don't we get out of here?" she asked, held tight in his arms on the veranda that looked out on the garden.

"Where would you like to go?" Biagio asked.

"Somewhere a long way away."

"Such as?"

"Oh, just away. I'm not saying forever, for a while."

It doesn't depend on me, sweetheart, Biagio thought, stroking her hair. And anyway, first I have to deal with the traitor, because it's his fault I had to kill Claudia.

"Do you miss Sonja?" Nicky asked, distracting him from his thoughts.

"Yes, a lot."

"I miss her too."

"Nicky?"

"Yes?"

"The man who killed Santo."

"Yes?"

"He'll never hurt anyone again."

"I . . . Thanks."

"Don't thank me, sweetheart."

They were silent for a few minutes, until Giorgio joined them.

"Biagio, we've finished. Are you coming?"

"Of course. I'll be right back," he told Nicky, kissing her on the forehead.

He went down the stairs leading to the basement in silence. As soon as the basement door was closed behind him, they all got to their feet.

Biagio looked at them one after the other, nodding to himself.

When they started beating their fists on the table—short, isolated blows at first that then became a rapid, almost tribal rhythm—it took him by surprise. It was a long, frenzied ovation. Some were crying.

They came to him, hugged him, kissed him on the cheeks, thanked him.

All of them.

Even the one who had betrayed him.

Epilogue

H is biggest mistake hadn't been killing Sergej Ivankov.

But leaving *her* alive.

It didn't matter what state she was in. Or that she had been raped. Or even the wound in her side that burned like crazy. Let alone the fact that she had a black hood over her head, that she was bound hand and foot, with a cloth in her mouth that prevented her from saying a word. Or that she had no idea where the van was going, the van they had put her in when she was still under the effect of the heroin.

None of this mattered, because she was still alive. And every breath she took, every beat of her heart, was dictated by revenge.

She didn't know how long it would take, or what she would have to sacrifice. The only thing she, Vatslava Demidov, knew was that she would get her revenge. Trapped in the hidden compartment of an old van that, like an iron Charon, was transporting her to Hades with other girls destined, like her, for the street, she tried not to think about the man she had loved madly and the little girl he had tried to protect at the cost of his life. Biagio Mazzeo had taken them both from her, condemning her to become a streetwalker. From paradise to hell in one night. That had been her destiny.

Cry now, she told herself. Weep all the tears you have, because you won't be allowed to cry again. You won't have time.

And that was what Vatslava Demidov did. She cried all through that endless journey, until all her tears were gone, while the other girls knocked against her with every bend in the road and a man's voice ordered them in Albanian not to make any noise.

When the van stopped—from the way it turned she realized they were entering a garage—Vatslava, who knew perfectly the methods used to enslave the Albanian "merchandise," said a prayer in her mind: "Irina, Sergej, if you're looking at me right now, just look away."

Acknowledgements

Heartfelt thanks to Cicci Peddio who gave me the impetus and the motivation I needed to write this novel. He is the adviser and the friend everybody would like to have. I have the undeserved gift of being dear to him.

Colomba and Massimo, my vivid constellations in the dark night that is creation.

My father and my mother for having fought together with Mazzeo and the Panthers.

Alessia, for her constant and all-enveloping love.

All my Sabot Brothers, and my traveling companions in the Sabot/age family.

Special thanks to: Luisa Peralta, Silvana Battaglioli, Stelio Secci, and Emiliano Longobardi for their wise advice and encouragement; to Carmen Brancato, Mirko Giacchetti, and Corrado Tortora for putting in an appearance in the novel; to Alessandro Zangrando for his deep injection of trust.

To all the readers and booksellers who have sustained me with great affection and strength, my warmest thanks.

To all the decent law enforcement officers, my deepest respect.

ABOUT THE AUTHOR

Piergiorgio Pulixi was born in Cagliari, Sardinia, in 1982. He is a member of Sabot, an experiment in collective crime fiction writing created by Massimo Carlotto, Italy's preeminent author of crime fiction. He lives in London.